ARTE BLANCHE

INCLUDES THE BONUS SHORT STORY:

THE BLACK RING

ALSO BY DAVID W COONS JR

SHORTS

BY THE HOUR: A HORRIFIC NOVELETTE

CHAPLAIN: A NOVELLA OF EXTREME TERROR

NOVELS

SIXTEEN YEARS AGO (coming soon)

The things a man will do for pussy!" Gabe joked.

"You can say that again," the tinny voice agreed through the phone's earpiece.

"I guess that I can think of a lot worse ways to get laid than going to an art gallery," Gabe mused. "Like that time you had to go to that horrible Britney Spears tribute concert 'cause that girl you were trying to bang was singing. What was her name?"

"Becky," the voice informed. "Becky Thomas."

"Yeah, that's the bitch." Gabe laughed into the phone. "And you didn't even get *any* after." More laughing.

"Hey, fuck you Gabe!" The voice rang loudly through the speaker, followed by matching laughter. "I'm going to be laughing my ass off when you wind up jerking it by yourself tonight."

"Yeah...yeah..." Gabe dismissed. "Don't worry about warming up your laugh box, Ronnie. You ain't gonna need it, cause I'm getting some to-*night*!" Gabe's machismo was damn near palpable as he spoke.

"Whatever, man," Ronnie countered. "Have fun at the art show, loser. Say hello to all the hipsters for me."

"It's an art *gallery*," Gabe corrected, sharply. Then, nonchalantly, "Apparently there's a difference."

"Of course there is." Ronnie's sarcasm practically dripped from the phone's speaker. "Fucking art types, man." Gabe heard a slight rustling from the phone as Ronnie shook his head on the other end. "Anyway, man, I'll catch you later. Give me a call when you get home and start jerking it. I'll bring over some popcorn and my gift of shit-talking."

"You're a sick motherfucker, Ronnie," Gabe related with disgust. "But yeah, I'll call you tomorrow. Let you know how shit went."

"Mmm mmm. All the dirty details?"

"We'll see, pervert." Gabe smiled as he ended the call. "Fucking Ronnie," he mumbled, shaking his head as he stuffed the cell phone into his pant pocket.

"You ready?" The voice came from behind him. A sultry, feminine voice that gave Gabe jubilant shivers down his spine.

"Yeah. Sure thing," he replied, turning to the source of the sexy voice.

Even sexier was the sight of her, all dolled up exactly the way that Gabe loved. Black boots that ran all the way up to contrasting pale knees, quickly giving way back to black in the form of a tight-fitting skirt.

Parts other than his spine shivered when Gabe thought about what she was hiding underneath that skirt.

The raven-dark fabric switched to a snowy white where her blouse took over. The blouse was loose-fitting, looking pillowy as it softly caressed her skin. Buttons ran down the front, though the top couple were left undone, leaving exposed the pleasing lines of her cleavage.

It wasn't the same outfit she had been wearing the other night when he'd first laid eyes on her, but it was a fitting homage. He had been on stage, belting out one of his favorite tunes, when he had spotted her swaying along in the crowd. Her appearance had been the only reason he had stayed to mingle after the show.

"Damn Becca! You look fine as shit, girl."

Rebecca – "What's this Rebecca shit? Call me Becca!" as she had told Gabe when they first met - Larson smiled at Gabe's crude compliment. Her dark crimson lipstick caused the curve of her lips to stand out among her pasty skin. The deep blue of her eyes shined bright, while her midnight hair was done up in a professional-looking bob.

It wouldn't exactly be fair to call her a *Goth*, but one wouldn't be entirely remiss to assume that she had dabbled in that particular culture at one time or another.

Gabe didn't care either way. She was fucking hot and that was all that mattered to him.

"Well don't you just have the golden tongue!?" Becca laughed.

"After the gallery, I'll let you be the judge of how *golden* this tongue is." Gabe winked.

"You are awfully sure of yourself, aren't you?"

"I am," Gabe agreed.

It had been roughly ten years since Gabe had last stepped foot in a high school. However, many people over the years had often criticized him for never having truly left his high school persona behind; often pelting him with words like *immature* and *boorish*. It's not that Gabe didn't necessarily disagree with such sentiment, but his attitude – or his *charm*, as he liked to refer to it – worked for him more often than not. Why give it up?

Besides, high school had been a great time for him and he hadn't physically changed all that much since then. His body still held the curves and bulges that he had as the varsity quarterback. His smile still remained the same unblemished heart-melter that had won him the homecoming crown.

His only real regret, thus far in life, was that he hadn't accepted any of the scholarships that had been offered to him. On graduation day, he had taken his diploma from the ceremony and never looked back. He had been done with school and even football wasn't enough to commit to four more years of classrooms. Now, at twenty-eight, he could be in the pros, making millions.

Surely enough to buy Becca whatever she may fancy at the art gallery. There was no surer way to get laid than to buy a pretty girl something shiny with a lot of zeroes on the price tag. And, to be honest, despite his earlier blustering to Ronnie, Gabe felt a little intimidated by Becca. Sure, he had partaken in more than his fair share of fine ass, but Becca was a league unto her own. There was something about her that captivated him in a way no other woman ever had.

Instead, the measly paychecks he received from his primary employment as a bartender didn't leave him with a lot of extra cash to blow. Even on a lady as downright sexy as Becca. He did have his gig as lead singer of *Blood Urned*. Unfortunately, still unsigned and relegated to playing small shitholes in the local area, the notoriety of a rocker was worth much more to him than the money he received.

"You know," Becca said, leaning in and placing her finger over Gabe's lips, "there's a fine line between confidence and crudeness."

"What?" Gabe feigned a look of shock. "Not I, my lady. I can't help it if my charming demeanor is a little over-exhilarating. That's just my charisma coming out to play."

"If you say so, Mr. Charisma," Becca laughed. "Just tone it down some when we get to the gallery. I don't think the people there will be as inclined to appreciate being over-exhilarated as much as I."

"As much as you, huh?" Gabe winked again. "So you *do* like me!"

That wonderful smile again.

"I'm still deciding," Becca teased as she turned away from him. "We'll have to see how well you play your cards tonight."

"You know," Gabe replied as he followed her, "I play poker almost as well as I play music."

She stopped and turned back to Gabe. "This would be the perfect opportunity for me to say something like 'that bad, huh?', but I'll give you a pass this time."

"Why's that?" Gabe asked.

"Because," Becca explained as she leaned in to fix the top button on Gabe's shirt, "I've already told you how much I loved your playing the other night and I don't want to start off by sounding like a hypocrite." With the button clasped, she smiled up into Gabe's face and gave it a playful pat with her fingers. "Especially that one slower song at the end...what was it called again?"

"*An Ancient Madness*," Gabe answered, turning to grab his keys from the coffee table.

"Yeah...that's the one," Becca confirmed, her eyes sparkling as she turned away and walked towards the door. "Too bad the stage manager cut you off before you could finish."

"Yeah. Fucking California noise curfews," Gabe swore. It had been their last song of the night and the show had run a little long. Instead of letting them finish up, the dickhead venue manager had pulled the plug on them, ending their performance prematurely.

"There's a good story behind that song. I may have to tell you about it some day," Gabe called to her retreating form.

"I can't wait to hear it," Becca called over her shoulder before stepping through the door.

Gabe started following, when Becca's head peeked back through the door for one final suggestion. "Oh, and you may want to roll down your sleeves. We don't want your tattoo scaring the artsy folk."

"Sure thing, Babe!" Gabe rolled his eyes before rolling down his sleeve, covering up the ink on his forearm that read *IRON MAIDEN*.

That done, he followed her out the door, steeling himself for a couple hours of droll hell that would surely result from being stuck at some shitty art gallery.

Holy fucking shit!" Gabe remarked in awe as he slammed his truck's door shut. "You didn't tell me this place was going to be the fucking Smithsonian."

Becca giggled. "It's not the Smithsonian, but it is pretty damn large. By far, the largest gallery on the west coast."

Gabe took in the massive white structure in front of him. He had been expecting some quirky little place tucked away between a Starbucks and a Panera, not this monstrosity before him.

A well-manicured lawn surrounded the white marble structure. The bright green grasses starkly popped against the pure white of the building's walls. Taking in the scene easily brought a sense of wonder as both colors complemented each other nicely.

Wide steps led up to a courtyard containing a massive fountain made of the same unblemished marble the building itself was constructed of. Gabe roughly estimated twenty to thirty of them ran up between the black asphalt of the parking lot and the grandeur of the art gallery. Gabe smiled as he considered ascending the steps like Rocky Balboa; the inspirational theme song playing him up to the top.

A throng of people were milling about up near the fountain, a majority of them bunched up near the left side of the massive glass doors that gave entry into the gallery. The glass doors were heavily tinted, giving the appearance of a black hole amidst the sparkling white surrounding it. Gabe wasn't sure if that was intentional, though he liked the idea. A celestial black hole sucked in light, while this metaphoric one would suck in customers.

Gabe silently congratulated himself. Maybe he had an eye for this art shit after all?

"Well, are you going to stand there and gawk all day, or are you going to lead a lady up?" Becca joked, breaking Gabe from his stare. She was holding her arm out, inviting him to slide his through.

Gabe gladly did, the two walking forward with their arms entwined like something you'd see in one of those olden movies.

"Is that the name?" Gabe asked, indicating the massive letters above the gallery's doors. They were a blood red and looked like they had been hand-painted onto the white marble.

"Yep," Becca confirmed. "The *e*'s are silent, in case you were wondering."

"I knew that!" Gabe lied. He had been working out how to pronounce them, guessing they were French.

Becca gave a knowing laugh. "Sure thing, slugger."

Gabe's face darkened a shade of red. This girl wasn't dumb. He was going to need to step up his game.

As they approached the base of the stairs, they were greeted by a short, balding, fat man donned in a fancy, white tuxedo. A name tag – one of those "My Name Is..." stickers – had been slapped onto the tuxedo's lapel. Black marker had completed the sticker's statement, marking the man as Cliff.

Cliff extended them a pamphlet as they neared. Gabe took the pamphlet as the greeter began to speak.

"Good morning, sir." Cliff nodded to Gabe, before sharply snapping to attention and turning to Becca. "Ma'am." Another nod, this time in her direction. "Welcome to the grand opening of the *Arte Blanche*."

******

They arrived at the top of the massive stairway, albeit without the fanfare of Stallone's iconic boxer.

"Jesus! This place is like fucking Disneyland," Gabe remarked as he scanned through the pamphlet he had received from Cliff. One side was filled with information – which Gabe hadn't bothered reading – while the other was a line diagram of the *Arte Blanche*. Looking at the map reminded him of those he had received upon entering any of the famed amusement parks that littered the greater Los Angeles area.

"I know! Should be fun, right?" Becca's smile beamed as she squeezed his arm a little tighter.

"Yeah. Should be pretty awesome." The large map left Gabe with the impression that this was going to be an all-day event. He had been hoping for a couple quick hours; in and out. Still, Becca's giddiness was rubbing off on him a bit. He just had to keep reminding himself that this journey was for the greater good...or, least, *his* greater good.

Gabe stole a glance at the beaming woman attached to his arm. Yeah...he'd easily do *two* days at this place if it meant that he could win over this beauty.

They were approaching the gathered crowd to the left of the entryway. Dozens of people were gathered around, focusing on something that Gabe couldn't yet see.

"What's going on over there?" Gabe asked, though he knew Becca couldn't see either.

"Good question! Let's find out." Becca broke the clasp of their arms and instead grabbed hold of Gabe's hand. She giddily pulled him towards the crowd.

When they arrived, they began gently pushing their way through the gathered mass, uttering lots of '*Excuse me's* and '*Sorry's*.

Once they had pushed their way to the front, Gabe was surprised to see a semi-circle of children's school desks, each one containing the body of a person penciling in various sketches. Their subjects: five people in medieval garb, posing atop a small stage made to look like a throne room. Each model wore a mask, with flowing robes beneath. Lots of purples and golds ran through the satin-looking fabrics. The masks were porcelain white, with random colors splashed on to form facial features. All were a similar style, but unique in their painted-on expressions.

Gabe swore the one on the end nearest him was the same mask worn by V in the movie *V for Vendetta*.

"What the fuck is this shit?" Gabe asked in a hushed voice.

"Art students, I think." Becca answered. "Lots of galleries will set up little things like this for aspiring artists to sketch."

"Kinda like those classes you can take where some hot naked chick sits in a chair for hours while a bunch of horny old dudes paint her?"

Becca rolled her eyes, but her radiant smile stayed firm on her lips. "Yeah...something like that."

"Hello." A tall woman greeted. She had snuck up on them from behind and wore a similar tuxedo as the parking lot attendant, Cliff. "Fascinating, isn't it?" She was addressing Gabe and Becca, but her eyes were planted on the classically-garbed models.

"Yeah," Gabe agreed, careful to keep the sarcasm out of his voice.

"They're just so mystical, aren't they? Frozen in time, yet wild with meaning." Her voice was quiet, but excited. "Take this one for instance." The woman pointed towards the one Gabe identified as V. "Look at him smiling. Such a big, vibrant smile. I have to keep telling myself that it's just a mask, but he just looks so...so happy! That smile unwavering; it gives me ecstatic chills."

"Yeah...I can totally see that." He couldn't. Gabe wanted to roll his eyes at this quirky woman, but Becca's attention was focused on the exchange and he didn't want to risk offending her.

"I mean, I know that it shouldn't, because it's just cold ceramic. Dead, really. But it's there, just exuding happiness and joy. I wish all people could smile like that; all the time, every day and all day," the woman continued.

Fucking artsy types! Gabe did his best to keep his thoughts from showing in his expression. "Yeah...I know, right?" he clandestinely teased in his most conciliatory tone.

Becca wasn't fooled, however, as made evident by a silent jab of her elbow into his ribs. She was smiling, though; a sparkle still glinting in her eyes.

The woman in the tuxedo remained oblivious, though. Perhaps still too filled with the joys of the creepy mask to notice his sarcasm.

"Anyway," the woman joyously exclaimed, "I'll leave you two be. Enjoy the *Arte Blanche*. It is truly a magical place." With that, she scampered off, making her way over to similarly converse with the next group of onlookers.

"Wow!" Gabe whispered. "Kooky bitch, huh?"

Another jab of Becca's elbow. "Behave yourself!" she laughed.

"Okay...okay..." Gabe rubbed at his ribs, laughing. Becca had a mean jab.

"Come on, pussy" Becca prodded, snatching his hand away from his ribs. Her sudden vulgarity had stunned Gabe into silence as she led him toward the entryway. "Let's go check this place out."

Gabe let her lead him towards the black hole. He couldn't help but wonder if maybe this chick was *the* one.

3

The other end of the black hole ended up opening into an enormous foyer.

Those damn astronomers would be severely disappointed, Gabe silently mused.

Still, while perhaps a rather lackluster result when compared to those celestial planet killers, the grand entryway was quite impressive by Earthly standards.

"I could fit my damn house in here," Gabe stated in awe. His eyes wandered the vast space, taking it all in.

"And still have room to play a game of field hockey out front," Becca added.

A sports reference? Goddamn, this chick gives me a boner, Gabe thought as he watched the mass of people that littered the foyer. A string of velvet ropes were strung up, blocking entry into the exhibits. An enormous stage curtain was draped several yards back from the ropes, hiding something massive. Some of the patrons were pacing, others sat cross-legged on the floor, while still others walked around the perimeter, admiring various paintings that draped the walls.

Everyone was waiting for the velvet ropes to come down.

"So, what's the deal with this place?" Gabe asked after taking in the entryway's grandeur.

"What do you mean?"

"It's not what I was expecting at all. It's *huge*, for one thing. For another, I noticed that the map has all these individual rooms marked with names. Not artist names, but things like *Wanders Never Cease* and *The Nine Lives Of The Frisky Feline*."

Instead of answering, Becca gave a short chuckle.

"What? Why is that funny?" Gabe defended.

"It's not. It's just cute," Becca explained. "This place has been all any of my friends have talked about for the last year or so. It's even been covered by several of the major news outlets. And you have never even heard of it."

Gabe was struggling for a response when he was saved by Becca continuing on.

"Don't worry," she soothed, gently taking his hand in hers, "it's kind of refreshing actually."

"Listen, in case you couldn't tell, I'm not *that* into art." It was weak, but it's what Gabe had.

"No shit!" Becca laughed. "I never would have guessed." The sarcasm in her tone was thick as molasses. After a moment, "But you came with me anyway. That counts for something." Becca leaned in and gave Gabe a reassuring peck on his cheek.

"Nice!" he exclaimed. "Our first kiss?"

"Ha! That shit doesn't count as a first kiss, bucko. Trust me, you'll know it when – and *if* – we share a first kiss." Becca's tone was seductive. Gabe's heartbeat rose a notch.

"Now, to answer your question, this place isn't like other art galleries. Every room is its own exhibit. Blake loves two things: excess and art. So here, he found a way to combine them both," Becca explained. "It's basically an artistic expression of artistic expression."

"Blake?"

"Yeah. Blake Zellers. He's the creator and proprietor of all you see before you." Becca dramatically waved her hand through the vast space, like a conductor leading a symphony.

"Blake Zellers? The son of the billionaire, Thomas Zellers?"

"The very same," Becca replied.

Gabe knew the name. Everybody who had ever watched the news, or seen an internet blog, knew the name. Thomas Zellers had made a vast fortune in the nineties with the rise of the internet. He had been among the first to recognize the need for cyber security and had created a company to fulfill that need. He had started with government contracts, but eventually took his product to the private sector and had made a killing marketing everything from antiviruses to identity fraud protection services. He had been one of the top 100 richest men in the world.

Had been.

Several years back, he had been found by a housekeeper in his mansion. Actually, he had been found by *several* housekeepers; parts of his body having been brutally torn apart and scattered throughout the plethora of rooms on his estate.

No suspect had ever been arrested.

"Didn't the police investigate him in the murder of his father?"

"They did, but they never found anything to connect Blake to his father's death. Blake was here in Los Angeles at the time; nowhere near the estate in Rhode Island."

"Yeah, but a billionaire's son surely would have the means to hire somebody for a hit," Gabe assumed.

"They looked into that, too," Becca continued. "They scrubbed his bank accounts, but couldn't find any irregularities. Hell, he didn't even have *that* much money when his father died. The only money Blake had at the time, he had poured into his first art gallery, the *Magna Arta*. Much smaller than this one. It paid the bills, but didn't exactly leave him wealthy. From what I understand, Thomas Zellers wasn't very generous with his money, even with his own son."

"So this was all built with inheritance money?" Gabe gestured to their magnificent surroundings.

"Yep, with a few billion left over. His mother died giving birth to him and he had no siblings. He had to wait until the investigation into his father's death was complete, but he got the money. All of it."

"Hmm. Sounds like motive to me," Gabe surmised. "And they had no other suspects?"

"Nope. Nobody knows what happened, but Blake was thoroughly investigated and found clean of any wrongdoing. There were rumblings about it for a while, but it happened nearly fifteen years ago, back before Facebook prolonged suspicions." Gabe was about to ask what she meant, when she coughed into her hand. He was pretty sure he heard her say "Birthers" through her cough.

Two white-tuxedoed personnel came into view on the adjacent side of the velvet rope barrier, when a curious thought struck Gabe.

"You sure seem to know a lot about the Zellers family?"

Becca nodded. "Blake has a genius eye for art. It got my attention at an early age." A mysterious glint entered her eye. "Let's just say that I came to know him fairly well."

Gabe was about to prod further when the crowd burst into activity. Gabe looked to the source of the sudden rambunctiousness and saw the tuxedoed men unclasping the velvet ropes from their stanchions. A third gentleman – looking like he had just stepped off a college campus, but wearing a black tuxedo, contrasting with the white of the others – stepped through the new opening in the barrier.

"Ladies and gentleman!" he announced loudly through the hall, his voice echoing off the cavernous ceiling. He was waving his hands downward, attempting to hush the crowd. It took another attempt, but the crowd noise finally diminished.

"Welcome everyone to the grand opening of Mr. Zeller's latest creation, the *Arte Blanche*." The man had the crowd captivated. "I'm sure that you will find this to be the most unique of the world's art palaces and will leave with nothing less than supreme satisfaction at what Mr. Zellers has presented here." The man had a warm smile, which he turned up to full blast as he continued. "But don't take my word for it. Soon, you will be roaming the halls and exhibits of the Arte Blanche yourselves."

The crowd around Gabe was growing restless. It reminded him of the crowds at a football game just prior to kickoff.

"But first," the announcer continued, "a word from the man himself. Ladies and gentleman, Mr. Blake Zellers."

With that, the crowd erupted.

INTERLUDE 1

The boy awoke with a start.

What time is it? He asked himself as he glanced over at the red LED screen atop his nightstand. The numbers read *5:56*. The little red dot could be seen next to the numerals, letting the boy know that the hour displayed was in AM.

Perfect!

On any given school day, the boy would have to be practically dragged out of bed to be up by 7am, giving him enough time to bathe, dress, and make it over to the schoolhouse. However, on this particular day of the week, the boy had an internal alarm clock that seemed infallible.

Saturday. Time for cartoons.

The boy crawled out of bed and made his way down the stairs to the living room. He grabbed the remote control off of the coffee table and hit the power button for the television. He heard the satisfying click the device made as it powered to life; the screen slowly building with brightness. He typed in the desired channel, bringing up a picture of a waving flag and the sounds of "The Star-Spangled Banner". In front of the flag was a message informing viewers that the network was about to resume broadcasting for the new day.

Still clad in his loose pajamas, the boy sat cross-legged on the floor in front of the large screen, awaiting the flag's eventual replacement with the animated programming that he longed for.

First on the docket was *Winnie the Pooh*. It wasn't his favorite show, but he considered it a good warmup for the cartoons that would follow.

Soon, the show's theme song started up while the opening credits played out on the screen. The boy settled in for what he expected to be a long morning that would seem to rush by entirely too quick.

Before the theme song had completed, the screen suddenly changed; replaced by the iconic tones of news programming.

"Hey!" the boy protested. "What's going on!?"

"This is an ABC News Special Report," the serious-faced newscaster unwittingly answered. "We're bringing you coverage on what is now the third day of offensive operations in support of *Operation Desert Storm*."

"Dang it! Nobody cares about that," the boy complained. He switched the channel. He wasn't a fan of the other cartoons airing in that time slot, but it would sure beat the news. He was greeted by another newscaster's face, uttering nearly identical words. Another switch of the channel led to the same thing. It didn't take long for the boy to realize that this story was infiltrating all of the major networks.

"Why can't they wait until Sunday to fight a war?" the boy asked aloud, though nobody was around to hear him. He sat the remote down, leaving the television on in case the special report ended soon and his cartoons started back up.

He stood from the floor and walked towards the kitchen. Normally, he would wait until the end of the second cartoon before pouring himself some cereal to take back to the living room, but today was already shaping up to be a day that countered routine.

The boy opened the pantry and withdrew the box of his preferred Saturday morning cereal: Cocoa Pebbles. The best part was the chocolatey milk left sitting in the bottom of the bowl. He started to take it over to the kitchen counter when a loud thud sounded from the rear of the house.

What was that?

The thud had come from the back of the hallway. It had to have been in his father's study. Another thud reverberated through the hall, followed by the sound of glass breaking.

"Let go!" he heard his father shouting, his voice wispy as if exerted.

Another thud, then rustling noises that made the boy picture Hulk Hogan hashing it out with "Macho Man" Randy Savage.

The boy absentmindedly set the cereal box down on the counter and began inching his way towards the shuffling sound. He had just crossed the threshold from the kitchen to the hallway when he heard his father's voice again.

"Danner, get this asshole off me!"

It was no surprise to the boy that his father and Danner Hackett were up so early in the study. His father had brought Danner to live with them nearly a year prior, explaining that the young MIT graduate needed a place to stay and was in turn helping his father with a new business venture. Since then, the two had spent countless hours locked away in the study, cooking up whatever it was that they were cooking up.

Whoever the "asshole" was that his father wanted off of him, however, the boy had not a clue.

Through the doors to his father's study, the boy heard a strange sound. A sound that the boy could only think of as the ripping of a wet rag. Then the wrestling noises vanished, replaced by the sound of a man screaming.

"What the fuck are you doing!?" the stranger's voice shrieked.

Another ripping sound, followed by the huffing sound of a man moving something heavy. That same heavy something smacked hard against the wall of his father's study. Another shattering of glass followed, that the boy assumed was one of his father's framed pictures being knocked off its spot on the wall.

The boy, tip-toeing, had almost arrived to the door, when the knob suddenly started turning.

"Stop him!" the boy heard his father shout from within.

The door started to swing open, but was quickly withdrawn; a loud crashing sound as it was violently forced back into its jamb. The boy's progress had stopped, leaving him frozen in a stunned terror.

Another ripping sound could be heard coming from beyond the door. This one louder and wetter than the previous two, though it was hard for the boy to hear it over the immense wails of pain that suddenly erupted from the study.

The agonizing wailing didn't last long, disappearing quickly and taking all other sounds from the study with it. For a moment, all was perfectly still. Then, as the boy witnessed with horror, a red stream began flowing from beneath the door.

The silence was broken by his father. "Get this piece of shit down to the basement and wait for me there."

The door opened, revealing the face of a man that the boy had never seen before. The boy would never again be able to *un-see* that face, however. The face was frozen in death by wide-mouthed terror and resting in a large pool of red. The blond hair surrounding the face was stained in the pool's crimson darkness.

Standing over the body, his hand holding the door open, was the shocked face of Danner. Not shocked by the dead corpse at his feet, but shocked by seeing the boy standing there on the other side.

"What are you doing here?" Danner asked.

"What? Who?" the boy heard his father's voice from further in the room. A hand joined Danner's on the edge of the door and forced it fully open. The boy's father appeared from behind it.

"You!" the man spat at seeing his son. "What are you doing awake so damned early?" his father asked, momentarily stunned. "Shit!" his father suddenly cursed. "It's Saturday." The older man rolled his eyes at the realization.

"Sir?" Danner broke in, rousing the father's attention from his startled son. "Should I take care of this?" Danner swiveled his head towards the body splayed out on the floor.

"Yes, Danner. Please get rid of it," the father answered, not letting his eyes wander from his boy. Silently, Danner reached down and grabbed the limp arms of the body and dragged it past the boy, continuing down the hallway until it was out of sight.

His father leaned down and firmly gripped the boy's shoulders. "Son, I know this may be confusing for you, but try your best to put it out of your mind. I'll explain it to you someday, when you're older. I promise."

"Why?" the boy replied in a frozen tone.

"He was going to do something very bad. Trust me on that," the father pleaded. "Like I said, I'll explain it to you better when you are older."

The boy's eyes shifted over the father's shoulder. The father turned to see what had drawn the boy's attention. The older man's pulse shot up a notch when he saw what his boy's eyes had found.

"Don't worry yourself about that. That's nothing that concerns you," the father tried. The boy, despite still being caught in a flood of emotion, could sense that his father was hiding the object's importance.

"What book is it?" the boy asked.

"Like I said, forget about it. It's not important."

The boy knew his father was lying.

Whatever the book was, it was clearly important. For one, his father saw fit to keep it in his personal safe. The safe, its door hanging freely open by virtue of its newly shattered spin dial, had possessed all of his father's most important items. Two stacks of cash, rubber-banded and sitting on the top shelf. Several notebooks containing the research his father and Danner had been working on. Those, and several other miscellaneous items were stored neatly on the safe's shelves. All except the book, which had been formerly stored somewhere within, but now lay on the floor in front of the safe, having been hurriedly dropped there during its extraction. The boy couldn't see enough of the book to know what it was. Only a corner was visible, as the rest was wrapped in an elegant-looking white cloth with gold embroidery running throughout.

The father was still staring into his boy's eyes. He could see that the boy was not convinced.

"Listen, I'll tell you this much," the father started. "That book is going to allow me to take good care of you. It is helping to make us rich so that you'll never have to face a day of worry. At least, not financially. Good enough?"

The boy continued staring at the wrapped tome long enough the his father began wondering if his son may be in a state of serious shock. Eventually, the boy nodded his understanding and the father let out a breath that he had not been aware he was holding.

"Okay, Father. If you say so," the boy conceded.

The father smiled and gave his boy's shoulders a reaffirming squeeze. "Good. Now go back to watching your cartoons and we'll go somewhere fun later."

"I can't. All the channels are showing news stuff this morning."

The father momentarily frowned at the boy's revelation, before a soothing smile retook his features. "Well, then I guess we'll have to go out even sooner. Get a shower and then we'll go get some ice cream."

"Ice cream? The sun's not even up yet," the boy answered.

"Sometimes you have to bend the rules a little," the father finished with a wink.

"Okay, I'll go take a shower now!" The boy ran off toward his room, the earlier horror already seemingly forgotten.

"Oh, Blake," the father shouted after his boy, "don't forget to put your towel in the hamper when you're done."

Thomas Zeller let the smile linger on his lips until the boy had vanished, then turned back to the bloody mess in his office.

lake Zellers wasn't what Gabe would call an imposing man. Surprising, given the larger-than-life status afforded the billionaire class. He was a decent height – around six feet – but he looked as if he hadn't visited a weight room since high school; if even then.

Though, judging by his boyish good looks, Gabe estimated that high school hadn't been *that* long ago for the billionaire. Gabe placed Blake in his early thirties. Just a few years senior to Gabe himself.

Gabe briefly imagined himself somehow accumulating billions in his bank account in the next few years and had to fight down a small twinge of envy.

"Carte Blanche:" Blake began, "complete freedom to act as one wishes." Blake surveyed the room to make sure that he had everyone captivated. "*Arte* Blanche: *my* complete freedom to create and display art as *I* wish." The crowd stared up at the billionaire, hanging on his every word.

"Ladies and gentlemen, welcome to the Arte Blanche." The crowd applauded as the billionaire gave a bow. As the applause died down, he continued. "I can't begin to express my great pleasure at seeing all of you here in support of this great vision. The Arte Blanche has been a dream of mine since I was a little boy. Today, that dream has finally come to fruition."

More applause rang out in the foyer, but it was a calm and controlled applause. *Respectful.* Completely unlike the hooting and hollering from Gabe's days on the football field, or at his current shows with *Blood Urned*.

The applause died down easily as Blake continued.

"Not only is this one of the largest galleries in the world, but it is one the most unique. For starters, every room is its own exhibit. And there are a *lot* of rooms." Blake smiled. A polite laughter seeped through the crowd.

"Additionally, we have a multitude of exhibits the likes of which I guarantee you have never seen before. Including the one behind this marvelous drapery behind me." Blake extended a hand behind him, mimicking one of Barker's Beauties showing off a prize on *The Price Is Right*. "Even that curtain is unique. It was commissioned by me over a year ago with only two demands; that it be crafted from the finest velvet found on Earth and that it be the largest curtain ever fashioned." Blake paused for effect and flashed the crowd a smarmy smile. "For those of you that have read up on me, that shouldn't come as a surprise."

More polite laughter followed.

"Opulence *is* his middle name," Becca whispered sarcastically.

"Is it really?" Gabe asked in a serious tone.

Becca looked over at Gabe in astonishment. Gabe tried, but couldn't keep a straight face. Accompanying Becca's realization of Gabe's jest was her elbow in his ribs. Gabe almost yelped at the surprise assault, but was able to wrangle it in as the foyer was already dwindling back into silence.

"Now," Blake continued, "while that is a marvel unto itself, it's what's behind the curtain that I find exceptionally titillating." He paused, the crowd's breath pausing with him.

Seeing that he had the gathered patrons fully captivated, Blake broke the anticipatory silence. "But we'll get to that in a minute." A large smile creased Blake's lips at his little joke. A polite laughter rumbled through the crowd.

"As many of you know, I've been a stout fan of art for most of my life, having gone as far as to open my own gallery, *Magna Arta*, over a decade ago. It was a modest hit in the community, even garnering a fair bit of notoriety from its most famous exhibit, *Suffering For Art.*

"*Suffering For Art* was actually the jumping off point to build this vast gallery here. That, and my inheritance, of course." Another respectful laugh from the crowd. "That particular piece grows more and more each year, and I could see that the Magna Arta just wasn't going to be large enough to contain it for much longer. I knew that I'd soon need to build a larger gallery to accommodate its expanding majesty. That's when the idea for the Arte Blanche formed in my mind."

Gabe glanced around the foyer. The entirety of the crowd was hanging off of Blake Zeller's every word. Gabe personally felt that Blake was rambling on, but the gathered patrons stared on in complete fascination.

"Now that you are all here to finally witness my vision, let me explain the layout a bit. I know that you all possess brochure maps of the gallery, but, as brochure maps generally are, they're not very helpful."

A soft murmur of agreeance traveled through the crowd.

"You will find that the gallery is separated into two distinct sections. The first, just beyond these ropes, I call *Free Market.* Nothing in there is free, I assure you, but this section contains exhibit rooms where individual pieces within may be purchased.

"Beyond that is *Monarchy*. Those exhibits are all permanent features – i.e. *not* for sale. Those pieces are held subject to my every whim and desire, as I am king of this little world." Another polite rumble of laughter. "Of course, me being me, you'll find a majority of the Arte Blanche's exhibits in *that* part of the gallery." Even more laughter. Gabe didn't appreciate the light humor as much as the crowd, but he managed to not roll his eyes.

"And, with that explained," Blake continued, "the map should suffice for the rest." A shuffling of paper could be heard as the crowd simultaneously unfurled and reviewed their individual brochures.

"Now, who is ready to witness what's behind the curtain?"

The patrons responded, letting their desire be known.

"So, I present to you the first exhibit that will henceforth be seen upon walking through those doors behind you, *Living In A Glass House*!" With that, Blake motioned behind him and stepped off to the side as the curtain dropped. The foyer rang out with the *oohs* and *ahhs* of the crowd.

Gabe found himself *oohing* along with them.

Behind the curtain was a house, set into the middle of the area known as *Free Market*. While that would have been impressive unto itself, even more spectacular was the fact the entire house was made of glass. It was shaped roughly like a standard three-story home found all over the wealthier suburbs of America, but it was completely transparent. The walls and doors. The counters and sinks in the kitchen. Most of the appliances, including the fridge. All were constructed of glass; or, at least, some other see-through material that Gabe couldn't distinguish from glass. The toilets and the shower. Even the beds in the bedrooms were made of mostly-transparent material. Not glass, surely, but some translucent plastic filled with water.

Gabe smirked as he hadn't seen an actual waterbed in many years. He supposed it made sense here, though.

While even Gabe had to admit that the structure was impressive, the house itself was not the most exciting aspect of the extravagant scene. It was what was currently happening inside the glass house that most impressed Gabe.

"Holy shit," Gabe whispered to Becca. "Are my eyes playing tricks on me? Or am I seeing two people fucking each other's brains out in there?"

"Either that, or they're doing one very risqué impression of the *Cirque De Soleil*," she quipped.

On one of the waterbeds set in a third-floor bedroom, two naked bodies were going at it. The woman was riding in the cowgirl position, her stout tits swirling in the air.

"Wow," Gabe awed in a hushed tone. "I wasn't expecting to see live porn on this trip."

Becca laughed. "It's not considered porn if it's art."

"All porn is art if you ask me," Gabe joked, his face set in a smirk.

Gabe surveyed the crowd again, perhaps expecting them to digress into a frat-boy atmosphere at the live display of copulation occurring in front of them. He was stunned to see that most of their eyes were busy scanning the glass surfaces and were hardly drawn at all to the erotic boning happening inside.

"Man, these art-types are no fun at all," Gabe dismissed with a shake of his head. Becca employed what Gabe guessed was quickly becoming her favorite weapon – her elbow - and once again jabbed into his ribs.

Gabe was still rubbing at his side when Blake began readdressing the crowd.

"Astonishing, isn't it?" He asked. A slight murmur from the crowd affirmed Blake's statement and he continued. "This house is available for the public to rent for up to two weeks at a time. Living your life for all to see is one of the ultimate expressions of art."

Gabe wasn't sure if that was the case – seemed more like an embarrassment to him – but the crowd seemed to agree.

"However, tonight it will be the venue for our Grand Opening celebration. I'm sure you will all enjoy that, if only because the alcohol will be provided free of charge."

This time, Gabe found himself chuckling along with the crowd. He always enjoyed some good booze humor.

"Anyway," Blake continued, "I do believe I have eaten up enough of your time. It's time to unveil the remainder of Arte Blanche for you all to enjoy." The applause that followed held more energy than previously, though only slightly. Blake unclipped a segment of velvet rope from its stanchion, holding it as he turned back to the crowd for one last announcement.

"Feel free to peruse at your leisure; though take care not to be *too* leisurely. *Monarchy* will be closing at 10:00 pm for a private party. Invited guests only, I'm afraid. However, *Free Market* will be open until the sun breaks dawn." The crowd murmured their acknowledgment and Blake stepped aside.

The *Arte Blanche* was now officially open for business.

Gabe allowed Becca to lead their way into *Free Market*.

As the first patrons crammed through the opening, the remaining velvet ropes were hustled off to the side by the tuxedo-clad staff, making the entry much less of a cattle call than it had originally been. Still, Gabe's passage through was nearly suffocating.

The individual exhibits ran along the outer edges of *Free Market*, allowing the crowd to disperse in multiple directions. As the crowd surrounding Gabe thinned out, he was able to breathe a bit easier. Becca chose the first exhibit for their journey and led him inside.

"*Rainbow Parfait*," Becca read off the exhibit name as she dragged Gabe in by his hand. He wasn't sure exactly what he had been expecting, but it assuredly wasn't what his eyes took in upon stepping into the room.

"What the hell are these?" Gabe asked as he studied the assortment of paper clinging to the walls. The white squares littering the walls looked like the plain stock that his computer printer was filled with. The only difference being that each page had random lines of color streaked across its bleached façade.

"It looks like someone took a fistful of crayons and beat them against the pages," Gabe observed, his disappointment evident in his voice.

"Maybe," Becca reluctantly agreed. "But that's art."

Gabe's eyes fell on a price tag hanging below one of the pieces.

"Jesus Christ!" he exclaimed. "Two hundred bucks for *that*?" His tone was incredulous. "I could do that blacked-out drunk while pissing in my pants."

"You're paying for the artist's expression. Not the physical piece itself," Becca tried to reason.

"The artist's expression?" Gabe balked. "What is he trying to express? That he's a child caught in a temper tantrum?"

Becca rolled her eyes, but chuckled slightly to show that she wasn't offended. "Maybe this wasn't the best exhibit to pop your cherry with."

"I'm just saying," Gabe continued, "music is an artist expression too – which requires much more work put into it than these do – but you don't see me charging two hundred bucks a song."

"Point taken." Becca flashed a smile. "Let's move on." She re-snagged Gabe's hand and led him out of the underwhelming exhibit, into the next room over. A plaque over the door read *From Rags to Riches*.

"This should be interesting," Gabe muttered.

Inside, the walls were lined with green shapes of differing dimensions. Gabe easily recognized the foresty tones as the color of money. And that's exactly what the walls held.

Random-sized representations of American currency greeted Gabe's mocking stare as he took in the exhibit. The artist responsible for this exhibit had taken everyday household rags – everything from washcloths to beach towels – and dyed them to resemble money. Several smiling faces of Washington were plastered around, though Lincoln, Hamilton, Jackson, Franklin, and even Grant, were all represented equally as well.

Gabe took a sharp intake of breath as his gaze caught the price tag for one of the wash cloths.

"$600! You've got to be fucking kidding me."

"Nope," Becca replied.

"Jesus," Gabe whined. "I think by *Rags to Riches*, the artist isn't saying how he turned cloth into facsimiles of cash, but rather how he is turning simple rags into money lining his pocket." He glanced at Becca and, though she was still smiling, Gabe thought that he was maybe complaining too much. This was her thing and he needed to approach the experience better if he planned on sealing the deal afterwards.

"Though, at least this actually took *some* talent, I'll admit." He amended. "Much better than the last one."

Becca looked over at Gabe with a wide grin. "Look at you trying to impress," she mocked. "You don't have to lie to *hit* it." She followed her twist on the popular expression with a wink.

Gabe mentally rebuked himself. This girl was too damn smart for these kind of games. Still, apparently he hadn't blown his chances yet.

"You caught me," he admitted. "Though I stand by my statement that this exhibit is way better than the last."

"Okay then, Mr. Art Critic," Becca joked, weaving her arm through Gabe's. "Care to join a lady into the next exhibit?"

Gabe cared very much indeed.

******

Like a good puppy dog, Gabe let Becca lead him through several more exhibits in the *Free Market* side of the gallery. Not a single one garnered more than a rolling of the eyes from him.

"I must admit," Becca voiced while staring at a dyed cat's scratching post, "I kind of like these."

"Does it make your cat frisky?" It was the best pussy-related quote Gabe could come up with on such short notice.

"I don't like it *that* much," Becca teased with a gentle prod to his rib cage.

They were currently in the last room on their side of *Free Market*. The plaque above the door read *Cat Scratch Fever*.

Gabe was trying to think up an appropriate retort, when suddenly the powerful wails of Bruce Dickinson erupted from his pocket. Gabe quickly fumbled in his pants to retrieve his cell phone, earning several looks of irritation and repulsion that the arty patrons were throwing his way. After what seemed like forever, he finally got his hands on his phone and hurriedly hit the button to silence his ringer. With Bruce's voice silenced, Gabe shot an embarrassed look over to his date.

Becca was still smiling, but Gabe could tell that she was perturbed by the embarrassment that his phone had wrought.

"I guess somebody missed the sign that said to silence all cell phones." Becca waved her fingers inward, indicating that Gabe should hand his phone over to her.

"I suppose I did," he offered with an embarrassed chuckle.

"Come on," Becca prodded. "Hand it over."

"Seriously?"

"Yes, seriously. I'll keep it safe in my purse until we get back to your place tonight." The seductive look she gave him sealed the deal as far as Gabe was concerned. He slapped the phone down into her hand as if were nothing more than a stick of gum.

"As long as it gets you back to my place, I can live with that," Gabe teased as he released his grip on the phone. Becca quickly slid the device into her purse.

"So we have two options now," Becca stated. "We can go over to the other side of *Free Market* and check out the exhibits over there, or we can skip ahead and go straight into *Monarchy*. What do you think?"

Gabe's preference wouldn't be a surprise to anyone. Skipping as much of the gallery as possible was ideal to him, but he wasn't going to voice his distaste any more than he had to. Instead, "This is your thing. I'm following your lead."

Becca considered it for a moment and then said, "Let's skip the rest of *Free Market* and check out what *Monarchy* has to offer."

Thank God!

"Sounds good to me." Gabe concurred, much less excitedly than he felt.

Becca took Gabe's hand again and led him into the main section of Arte Blanche.

Upon first appearance, *Monarchy* felt like the smaller of *Arte Blanche*'s two halves. The large, courtyard feel of Free Market had provided a perception of openness, while *Monarchy* was much more enclosed. Though, judging by the map, *Monarchy* was, in all actuality, easily twice the size of *Free Market*.

Roughly rectangular in shape, *Monarchy* consisted of an enclosed hallway, surrounded by a large, outer ring of exhibits on the three sides opposite *Free Market*. The wall separating the two sides of Arte Blanche was the southern wall, marked only by a thick, black line on the map, containing no exhibits.

The outer exhibits were numerous, running along the western, eastern, and northern legs of the hallway. After a rough count from the map, Gabe guessed it was going to take all damn day to go through each of the exhibits that lined the outside of *Monarchy* .

The immense inner rectangle of *Monarchy* thankfully appeared to be comprised of only three exhibits, each one incredibly more massive than the smaller exhibits along the outer edge. Gabe saw that the middle of the three larger exhibits was the one that Blake had mentioned in his speech: *Suffering For Art*.

"How do you want to play this? Should we hit up the outer exhibits first? Or do you want to go straight to the big ones in the center?" Gabe asked.

34

Becca momentarily studied the map before replying. "Let's at least do a few of the outer ones first. We'll save the center section for later. *Suffering For Art* is in there and I think you may actually enjoy that one."

Gabe doubted that, but nodded his concurrence anyway.

They turned left after entering, walking through the southern corridor to the west. The hallway was very plain, with white walls and tiled floor that reminded Gabe of an everyday, lame-ass office building. The austerity was broken only by expensive-looking paintings and tapestries that lined the walls.

As they walked hand-in-hand, Gabe made a concerted effort to avoid bumping into any of the artwork, not wanting to accidentally knock something over. He doubted his bank account could cover the damage.

The first door they arrived at was marked "Employees Only. Maintenance & A/C Room." The door was painted industrial gray and otherwise unadorned.

"I'm going to go out on a limb and assume that this isn't some clever name for an exhibit," Gabe joked.

Becca laughed. "Your powers of deductive reasoning are strong," she teased. She pointed to the end of the southern corridor where it intersected with the western leg. Gabe saw a line of people that stretched around the corner into the western corridor. "I'm fairly certain that line leads to the first exhibit," Becca reasoned.

Gabe quickly glanced at the map and saw that they would find the first door as soon as they turned the corner. "Perhaps we should skip that one. It looks pretty damn crowded seeing as how everybody lined up at the first damned exhibit they came to. What do you think?"

"What's the next one after it?" Becca asked.

Gabe checked the map. "*Beauty Through Rage*," he read the name aloud.

"Sounds good enough to me," Becca replied. She took off at a hurried pace, dragging Gabe towards the end of the hallway.

They rounded the corner into the western corridor and passed the line that lead to the first door. The exhibit door appeared to be constructed of oak and had been painted with a golden trim.

Looking past, Gabe saw that the door to *Beauty Through Rage* was free of any line. "Score," Gabe elated, pumping his fist.

The door itself looked nearly identical to the first exhibit, with only a few small variations. He was surprised to see that the doors weren't actually wood, but some sort of metal painted to look like wood.

Better for security, Gabe supposed.

As they neared their desired exhibit, Gabe realized that each door had been hand-painted, explaining the subtle differences between them.

The room was larger than Gabe would have guessed from the dimensions on the brochure map. It was roughly square in shape and Gabe estimated each wall to be about twenty feet long. The walls here were white, like the hallways outside, but stood completely unadorned.

Several patrons were already in the exhibit, largely gathered in three distinct areas within. Gabe glanced around the room and saw what looked like smashed pottery strewn all over the floor. Velvet rope separated the standing area from the broken shards.

"Is this exhibit still under construction?" Gabe asked.

"I don't think so," Becca responded. "What has everybody so enthralled?" She pointed towards the huddled masses of patrons. Gabe studied them closer and realized that their attention was on something other than the scattered shards.

Gabe stepped closer to one of the groups, trying to see what had them captivated.

"Well, damn." He announced when he finally saw what he was looking for. "They're watching an iPad."

"An iPad?" Becca asked, stepping closer.

"Yeah. There's a video playing on it."

"I wanna see," Becca said, grabbing Gabe's hand and pulling him into the crowd until they could clearly see the iPad's screen.

The iPad sat atop a metal pedestal that rose from the floor. The pedestal ended in a box that contained the device around its edges, holding it in place while allowing the screen to stay in view.

The walls and floor in the video made it apparent that it was filmed in the room where they currently stood. Gabe watched as a man set a large vase on the tile floor. He spun the vase a couple times until the artist felt that it was in the perfect position; the specifications of which, Gabe had no idea. When the artist was finally satisfied, he hefted a large sledgehammer and brought it crashing down onto the vase. The vase shattered into thousands of different pieces that scattered across the floor.

Gabe removed his eyes from the iPad's screen to glance towards the corner that the filming took place. The broken shards on the ground looked to be in exactly the same arrangement that they had settled in post-destruction.

The video showed the artist set up another vase next to the one he had just smashed. He again lifted the sledgehammer and brought it down on the new vase. After each vase destroyed, the artist would place another one next to it. He kept doing this until he had completely circled the room.

"It's kind of neat, don't you think?" Becca asked.

"What do you mean?"

"Each vase he smashes settles into a different pattern; no two vases winding up exactly the same," Becca explained.

"I guess that's cool," Gabe non-committally agreed. "I do like how he's using destruction as art, though. I'm always down with smashing shit."

"Men..." Becca rolled her eyes and laughed.

Gabe was thinking of a comeback when Becca suddenly knelt down and snatched up a shard of broken vase. She rose stealthily and shoved the shard into his hand.

Gabe's eyes grew wide. "What are you doing?" He nervously spun his head around the room to discern if anybody had witnessed what had just happened.

A twinkle in Becca's eyes was accompanied by a sly smile across her lips. "A memento of our time together," she answered with a wink.

Gabe hurriedly shoved the shard into his pocket, glancing around once again. "They don't have this shit alarmed?" he asked.

"Guess not," Becca joyfully shrugged. "What's next?" she asked, ready to move on.

Gabe shook his head and laughed. "Jesus! You are something, aren't you?" He held out his arm to let Becca take hold of it. "Let's find out," he answered her question. This time, it was Gabe who led the way to the next exhibit.

******

"*Blood Money*," Gabe read from the plaque hanging over the painted door. "I'm always down to see something bloody."

This was the fifth exhibit they had visited in *Monarchy* and, thus far, Gabe had remained mostly unimpressed.

"What are you waiting for then?" Becca teased, waving her hand towards the doorway. Gabe took the invitation and led the way into the room.

Gabe stepped through the door. Each exhibit room had appeared to be roughly the same size. Some were more cramped than others, with this one being the least so far. The exhibit was mostly empty space except for one piece that sat in the center of the room, surrounded by a velvet barrier. A crowd was gathered around the object, keeping Gabe at distance from the display.

"Is that a guillotine?" Gabe asked, seeing only the top of the object.

Becca studied the piece for a moment and slowly nodded her head. "Yeah. Kind of."

"And, is that…" Gabe squeezed between some of the patrons to peer closer at the top of the contraption. "Well, holy shit…it is! It's a football."

"A football?" Becca asked.

"Yeah," Gabe confirmed. "Where the blade is supposed to be, the guillotine has a football hanging from it."

"Strange," Becca muttered.

A large portion of the crowd withdrew from the display, moving off to another exhibit. Gabe stepped into the opening they left behind and now had a view of the piece in its entirety.

Secured to the bottom of the guillotine was a wax body clad in a football uniform. The figure's head was covered in a football helmet, but the head was not attached to the body. It rested in a basket at the bottom of the device.

"So, I'm guessing that this is some sort of artistic expression on the dangers of footballs?"

"I believe you're right," Becca agreed. "The exhibit is named *Blood Money*, leading me to believe that this is the artist's way of saying he isn't of fan of how the league does business, especially when dealing with concussions."

"Boo!" Gabe protested. "These art-types need to leave *my* sport alone. I doubt the artist behind this has ever even watched a game."

"Probably not," Becca concurred. "You won't find too many sports fans here."

Gabe rolled his eyes. These were definitely *not* his people.

"Should we move on?" he asked.

"Ahh," Becca teased in a baby-coddling tone. "Did the poor jock get his feelings hurt?" She pursed her lips and laughed.

"Nah. It's cool," Gabe contended. "To each his own, I suppose."

"We can move on," Becca relented, patting Gabe's hand in a conciliatory manner.

Hand-in-hand, they turned and left the exhibit behind.

******

After visiting several more exhibits, Gabe and Becca were approaching the end of their western corridor. The exhibit they were currently approaching was set into the corner of the gallery, where their current hallway bisected into the next. Instead of the usual ninety-degree angle at the outside corner, the western wall angled softly into a double-door entrance before another soft turn into the northern corridor.

This exhibit had its own tuxedo-clad employee standing near the double-doors, sharing a few words with the patrons as held the doors open for them to pass through.

"That's a tall, Lurch-looking motherfucker right there," Gabe whispered to Becca as they approached the tall, lanky staff member.

"Lurch?" Becca asked.

"Yeah. From *The Addams Family*," Gabe explained.

"Gotcha," Becca replied with a nod.

Once they arrived at the man, Gabe saw that his nametag read Owen. Gabe knew he wouldn't be able to stop thinking of him as Lurch, though.

"Sir. Ma'am." Lurch greeted Gabe and Becca in turn. Lurch's voice was exactly as Gabe had pictured it would be; deep and creepy. "At the top of the hour, Mr. Zellers will be addressing the crowd in *Suffering for Art*, if you care to attend."

Gabe checked his watch. They had twenty minutes until the indicated time.

Becca smiled up at Gabe. "Let's check this exhibit out and head over to *Suffering for Art*. One, as I said, I'm sure you'll like that one. And two, it might be fun to see what Blake has to say."

"Works for me," Gabe nonchalantly agreed.

"Enjoy the rest of your time here at the *Arte Blanche*," Lurch said before diverting his attention to the next group of arrivals.

"What's the name of this illustrious next piece?" Gabe snidely asked as he glanced up at the plaque. "*Wanders Never Cease*," he read.

"That's a cute play on words," Becca beamed.

They entered the room. Unsurprisingly, it was larger and shaped differently than the previous exhibits due to its corner position. However, it was another exhibit of mostly empty space.

"It seems to me that they waste a lot of space in this place," Gabe griped. "I'd figure that they'd do a lot more with a room this size."

"Art aficionados don't like clutter," Becca shrugged.

An open floor led to the back of the room where it met with ornate marble stairs. Atop the stairs was a marble platform that housed one object; an empty throne. Constructed of gold which was inlaid with a variety of jewels, the throne struck Gabe as very old and very expensive.

"Did somebody make this? Because it looks like it might actually be an old throne from medieval days."

"That, or maybe even older. Either way, I wouldn't be surprised," Becca agreed. "Blake has gathered quite an impressive collection of antiques over the years. This is probably from some old castle somewhere."

"If that were the case, you'd think that he'd have a plaque or something somewhere proudly announcing where it was from."

Becca shrugged. "Missed opportunities, I'd guess."

"And what about the title, *Wanders Never Cease*? I don't get how that applies," Gabe asked.

"The throne is empty," Becca replied, matter-of-factly. "I'm guessing that the title may be about who is supposed to be sitting in that throne. They are constantly wandering and never able to find time to just enjoy being still."

"You thinking that it's a metaphor for the struggles of the rich?"

"That's not a bad theory," Becca rewarded. "It'd sure speak to Blake's self-centric personality. Though I think there's more to it than that."

Gabe saw a hint of sadness creep into Becca's gaze.

"You alright?" he asked.

"Yeah," Becca answered. "It just makes me sad thinking about somebody that'll never be allowed to go home."

Gabe wasn't sure how to respond to that. He knew that there was a story behind that sadness– probably something to do with her childhood – but their relationship was far too new to be prodding into personal affairs of that magnitude.

Gabe was struggling with a proper response, when he was saved by the cheerful spark reigniting in Becca's eyes. She turned towards Gabe with a reformed smile on her face. "Should we head over to *Suffering for Art* now?"

"Let's do this," Gabe announced, winding his arm through Becca's. They walked out of *Wanders Never Cease* and made their way towards the large, central section of *Monarchy*.

"Looking at the map," Becca was explaining, "all three of the central exhibits are linked. So we have two choices. We can go straight into *Suffering for Art*, or we could go through this other exhibit on our way in. Kind of a two-for-the-price-of-one deal."

Gabe checked his watch. "We still have nearly fifteen minutes before Zellers gives his speech. Plenty of time if you want to check out another exhibit on the way. What's its name?"

"*A Morsel's Journey*," Becca read from the map.

"Sounds interesting enough," Gabe said, though there was little sincerity behind his words.

The door stood alone on the inner wall of the western corridor, dead center between the southern and northern passageways. They fought their way through the opposing traffic of the crowd, until they reached the doors into the next exhibit.

Another tuxedo greeted them. This one an average-looking gentleman, probably in his early forties, whose nametag identified him as Grady. As they approached, Grady opened the door for them and waved them through. Gabe nodded his head at the man before stepping through.

Gabe was shocked when he realized that the room the entered was little more than a closet. It was a small box with only the door that he had just stepped through, and another door on the opposite side. The only light found within was coming from two square, translucent panels set into the wall above each of the doors. The light coming through the plastic panels was red.

"Once I close this door, the lights should change to green," Grady explained, holding the door open behind them. "Once they do, the other door will unlock and you will be able to continue through into the exhibit." Gabe nodded his understanding, "I suggest you take a moment on the other side to let your eyes adjust before continuing on. And please, remember to close the inner door behind you when you pass through."

Grady waited for their nods of affirmation, then closed the door behind them, sealing them in near darkness. As promised, the lights above the internal door changed from red to green.

"What's with the theatrics?" Gabe asked as he gripped the handle of the inner door and pulled it open. The light above the doors switched back to red as soon as he had turned the handle.

"I'm guessing it's to keep the hallway light out," Becca answered after she saw what awaited them beyond the door. More darkness; though this dark space seemed to be far more vast, a cavern of unknown depth.

Becca stepped through and scooted to the side to allow Gabe to follow. Another light shone red above the door in the main body of the exhibit. As promised, Gabe closed the door behind them. The light above instantly switched to green.

Gabe strained to see through the darkness, but the only other light he could discern through the darkness was a line of very dim red markers on the floor, forming a path for them to walk along. It took a moment for his eyes to adjust, but eventually more light of a different color filtered through the darkness. A mild, blue aura glowed from somewhere further within the exhibit. As his eyes adjusted further, he was amazed to realize the blue glow seemed to fill the cavernous room.

"Is that..." Gabe began asking when a flash of yellow light shot through the room, lighting it just enough to get a sense of the monstrous room's size. The yellow light vanished just as quickly as it had appeared.

"What the hell was that?" It was too dark to see her, but Gabe sensed Becca shrugging next to him.

They stepped forward, towards the blue glow. As he neared, Gabe finally was able to make out a shape in the dim luminescence. "I'll be damned," Gabe astonished. "It's a man."

The yellow light burst through the room again, providing enough light to confirm Gabe's theory.

With the yellow light having disappeared again, Gabe saw that the blue glow formed an enormous silhouette of a man lying flat on his stomach. The large figure appeared to be made of glass, or some variant thereof. The glass shaped the man's body and was radiating with the diffuse blue light. They arrived first at the figure's enormous head, the eyes seemingly glaring right through them. The giant's chin rested on the floor with its mouth standing wide open.

"Ah! I get it now," Becca exclaimed. "A Morsel's Journey."

Gabe looked at her in confusion. His eyes had adjusted enough that he was now starting to be able to make out her wonderful features in the blue glow. Her eyes must have adjusted equally as well, for she saw the look of confusion he shot her.

"Look," Becca grabbed Gabe's arm and pointed him towards the giant blue man. "The path is leading us into his mouth."

A light bulb went off in Gabe's mind. Funny metaphor, Gabe mused, given the darkness of the room.

"So you're thinking we're about to travel through this guy's digestive system?"

"That's what I'm thinking," Becca confirmed.

The yellow light flashed through the dark hall again. It seemed to stretch in lines that ran haphazardly through the large figure's glass body. The illumination was enough that Gabe could see a few of the patrons gathered in the middle of the large, prone figure. He guessed that they were huddled somewhere near the man's stomach.

"After you," Becca invited, extending her arm along the path. Gabe took her hand and led her towards the blue figure's gaping maw.

The path slanted upwards as they neared the mouth. On the incline, Gabe was amazed to look at his feet and see that they now were standing atop the blue glow. He reached down to feel the material and felt that it was a Plexiglass of some sort. The surface was much rougher than Gabe had expected.

"I think we're standing on this guy's tongue," Gabe informed.

"Yeah. Kinda neat, isn't it?" Becca asked, having apparently come to the same conclusion. Gabe had to agree. The large figure's tongue stretched out his mouth, forming the path leading up into his body.

"It's definitely different," he concluded.

"I'm assuming they roughed the surface up to mimic taste buds," Gabe theorized.

Becca knelt down and rubbed her hand along the surface. "Maybe," she replied. "Though I'd bet it serves a double purpose. Blake wouldn't want people slipping and getting hurt in his gallery." Gabe conceded the point with a nod. "Not that he couldn't afford a lawsuit or two," Becca mused as she continued up the incline.

They stepped fully into the mouth. Through the blue glow, Gabe could make out the textured gums surrounding them.

"This must be the uvula," Gabe pointed out, rubbing his hand along a Plexiglass stalactite hanging from the roof where the passage narrowed down into the man's esophagus. Gabe noted that the uvula's surface was much smoother than the Plexiglass beneath them.

"Past this point, we are officially being deep-throated," Gabe joked.

In the soft glow, Gabe saw Becca rolling her eyes. She laughed as she once again jabbed him with her elbow. "Behave," she jokingly chastised.

As they continued along the esophageal trail, Gabe could make out other organs formed in the sculpted body. They passed a heart, complete with lungs on either side. Soon after, they passed a large, shapeless blob of blue that Gabe assumed was the liver.

The tight passage widened into a domed cavern, indicating that they had arrived at the figure's stomach. The crowd that Gabe had seen previously had moved on, leaving Becca and Gabe alone.

"Look," Becca blurted," there's writing on the glass." She pointed at letters written out in glowing blue along the giant's stomach lining.

"It says 'To witness the path of nourishment, press the button below.'" Gabe glanced below the writing and saw that a button had been placed into the Plexiglass.

Becca gripped Gabe's arm and shook it with excitement. "Push it. See what it does," she instructed.

"Okay." Gabe shrugged then pressed the button. The yellow flash immediately flared to life. Several lines of the yellow light ran through the giant's body, leading to many of the organs; most notably the heart.

"Ah," Becca gawked. "It's mapping the routes of energy that food provides the body. Neat-o."

"Is this art, or a science museum?" Gabe tartly replied.

"Art can be educational," Becca countered.

"I guess," Gabe shrugged. "I'll go as far as to say this is probably the coolest thing we've seen so far, but I wouldn't sell it as educational."

The sounds of chattering and footsteps arrived. It seemed another group had arrived and was nearing the stomach.

"Let's continue on, sourpuss," Becca teased. "Don't wanna be holding anybody up."

"Yeah..." Gabe turned from the writing and waved his arm further down the path. "After you this time, m'lady."

"Oh God. Don't start *that* shit." Becca rolled her eyes and took Gabe's hand.

Past the stomach, the corridor collapsed in size again. The path took them through several twists and turns featuring plenty of cutbacks.

"Almost feels like a maze," Gabe related. "Or maybe one of those long ass lines to get on a ride at Disneyland."

"It's the intestines," Becca responded with a shrug.

Soon, the path straightened out and Becca chuckled.

"What's so funny?" Gabe asked.

"I believe we're now in the rectum," she explained.

"Seriously? I'm in a guy's rectum right now?" Gabe scanned their surroundings with a new sense of wonderment. "I never thought I'd be saying those words," he laughed. "Do you think we'll be walking out his asshole?"

Becca giggled and pointed ahead. Gabe looked in that direction and saw the corridor tighten slightly before opening back out into the vast darkness of the room.

"Does that answer your question?" Becca laughed.

"Wow." Gabe shook his head. "Fucking art-types."

They passed through the tightened opening onto a ramp that angled down to the floor. Gabe spun on the ramp to take in at the large asshole staring him in the face.

"I wonder if the artist had a hidden meaning when he designed this?"

"Like what?" Becca asked.

"Like we're all just pieces of shit," Gabe responded with a chuckle.

Becca joined in his laughter. "Meaning this ramp we're walking down is a literal poop chute?"

"Exactly!" Gabe laughed.

They continued deeper into the dark room. Once again, the path was dimly lit by red diodes in the floor. Off to either side of them, the colossal legs of the sculpted figure stretched out into the darkness.

Finally, the monstrous room ended as they arrived at another door. This one matched the door on the other end of the room, right down to the glowing green light set above. Gabe opened the door, turning the light red, and saw that it led into another small room, the same as when they had entered. Becca stepped past him and then Gabe closed the door behind them both. The light on the adjacent door switched from red to green.

Pausing with her hand on the door handle, Becca turned back towards Gabe. "This is the one I promised you'll like the most."

Becca winked at Gabe then turned the handle, popping the door open. Gabe stepped through and finally got his first look at *Suffering for Art*.

The exhibit room was enormous. More of an exhibition hall than an actual room. The map showed it to be nearly the same size as *A Morsel's Journey*, only this one was well-illuminated; its immense volume not hidden by darkness.

It was roughly square in shape, with a large statue occupying the center. Three of the room's edges were currently bare, but lined with velvet rope barriers and plaques that promised future displays. The fourth – the southern wall of the room – was lined with many individual scenes of grotesquerie.

The first item to garner Gabe's attention was the large statue at the center of the room. It would have been hard *not* to have noticed the towering figure first. It was an imposing effigy. The room was nearly four stories in height and the faded-stone statue easily ascended three of them.

"What the hell is that statue supposed to be?" Gabe asked.

"Some ancient demonic deity that Blake dug up several years back; at least, according to the plaque affixed to its base." Gabe threw Becca a waiting glance, sensing that there was more to the story. Becca shrugged.

The figure was humanoid in shape, with a muscular frame from its feet to its shoulders. Atop the shoulders sat a strange-looking head. It contained all the facial features one would expect – eyes, nose, lips – but the shape of its skull seemed elongated, as if someone had grabbed the crown with one hand, the chin with the other, and then pulled it apart like some particularly thick Play-Doh. Then, of course, there were the horns. Its skull was ringed with horns; forming a strange, devilish crown atop its head.

"That looks like one evil ass motherfucker," Gabe admired. "He would make for one kick ass album cover."

Becca laughed. "His name is Peristopheles, if my memory serves correctly. An ancient demon-God believed to hail from Babylon; though the last I checked, very little had been found regarding his history."

The name tickled something in Gabe's mind, though he couldn't quite get a grasp on it. "Peristopheles? Why does that name ring a bell?"

Becca looked quizzically at Gabe. "I doubt that you've heard of him," she finally said. "He's not well-known. Like I said, I haven't been able to find much mention of him at all."

"Maybe you're looking in the wrong places," Gabe teased. "I'll be sure to Google him later. Put your research skills to shame," he promised with a wink at Becca.

"You go ahead and do that," Becca challenged with a sly grin.

Gabe admired the strange statue for another moment — noting the many cracks that traveled through it, indicating it had been torn into many pieces at some point in the past - and then shifted his attention to the room's main attractions. Several square areas had been constructed along the southern wall, each a stage depicting its own scene. The scenes were each the size of a small room that you'd find in an apartment home. Gabe counted twenty-six individual tableaus. Each one different, but created to invoke the same emotion: Horror.

The first square Gabe arrived at was shrouded in a white sheet. A sign hung on the sheet reading: Under Construction.

Gabe passed up the sealed scene to find himself staring at one that contained a large, iron bull. One side of the bull held a sheet of glass that had replaced the outer lining of iron, revealing to the viewer that the inside of the figure was a hollow chamber. The hollow chamber wasn't empty, however; it held a waxy figure of a man lying on his back. His wrists and ankles were bound and his face was twisted into a look of incredible pain. To complete the scene's meaning, a faux fire consisting of orange ribbons flickering upward in the draft of a fan sat below the stomach of the iron beast. The stomach was scorched over, as if a real fire had been applied to it at some point.

"*The Brazen Bull*," Gabe read from the plaque adjoining the display. "Model: Titus Lichtner."

"It was an old torture technique where a man would be placed inside the bull and slowly cooked alive," Becca explained.

"Gnarly," Gabe huffed in awe.

"In fact, these scenes all depict historical tortures, some awfully morbid. It seems the human mind has no bounds when it comes to horrific ways to kill their fellow man." Becca waved her hand down the line of displays. "Pretty crazy, huh?"

"Yeah," Gabe agreed, nodding his head. "Definitely not what I was expecting to see in an art gallery."

"Even artsy folk are subject to depraved fascinations. Hence this exhibits popularity over the years."

"I'm not gonna go as far as to say I misjudged them, but I'll give credit where credit is due," Gabe spoke as they side-stepped to the next scene.

"Damn! That must have sucked," Gabe said when he took in the next tableau.

This scene was named *The Saw*, and there was a rather large one involved; the kind with a long blade running between two handles at either end. The two handles stuck out beyond the vertical shafts of a gallows. Hanging from the gallows by his ankles, legs splayed wide, was another waxy man-figure. The long saw blade was positioned between the man's legs; the teeth facing downward, digging into the figure's robust abdomen. During the scene's depicted moment in time, the saw blade had already sliced through the man's groin area, well into his torso.

Red fluid poured from the wound and ran to a puddle on the floor. Gabe could hear a bubbling sound escape the pool. He studied the red puddle and saw a thin, clear hose running back up to the saw wound, allowing the fake blood to keep flowing from the figure's split abdomen.

"Legend has it that they would often leave the saw exactly where you see it here – buried in the abdomen. The person being tortured would die slowly, suffering in ways I can't even imagine, until the light finally faded from their eyes," Becca related.

"There were some merciless motherfuckers back in the day," Gabe said, barely managing to keep his jaw from drooping.

"Mercy?" Becca laughed. "Their idea of mercy during this form of torture was to keep sawing until they got all the way through. It was quite popular in medieval Europe."

Gabe winced at the idea. "God bless the U.S.A," he mumbled.

Gabe stared at the waxy figure, trying to picture the incredible amount of pain that the man would have gone through. Recognition slowly dawned on him as he stared into the figure's agonized features.

"Wait a minute," Gabe blurted, leaning forward to read the plaque. "Model: Cliff Tawney." Gabe studied the suspended wax figure. The man depicted was short, balding, and quite fat. "Isn't that the usher we saw out in the parking lot?" he asked Becca.

Becca nodded. "It is. Blake's crew pose as models for the *Suffering for Art* dioramas. It's a requisite for hire."

"So the artist fashions wax figures after Blake's workers and then goes about fucking them up in some pretty shitty ways?" Gabe asked.

"That's the story," Becca confirmed.

"Sounds like a pretty cool job if you ask me." Gabe took one last look at Cliff's scene, then let his eyes wander down the line of tableaus.

"Well, that's some bullshit," Gabe said.

"What's some bullshit?"

"Blake is recreating all of these ancient tortures here, but he's somehow neglected the most awesome one of them all," Gabe informed.

"Which one is that?"

Gabe answered by curling his fist, then extending his pinky and index fingers into the air, forming the symbol recognized by metal-heads the whole world over: the horns.

"The Iron-fucking-Maiden!" Gabe beamed.

Becca laughed. "No, I suppose he hasn't included that one yet. Maybe I'll throw that in his suggestion box."

"Make sure to include a copy of their *Number of the Beast* album. One listen to that would win him over for sure."

Becca rolled her eyes, then dragged Gabe over to the next display.

"Hey...that's Lurch!" Gabe pointed at the wax figure in the next scene.

"Hanged, Drawn, and Quartered. Model: Owen Lansky," Becca read. "Yep. That's him."

The scene showed a wax Lurch stretched over an old, wooden table. His wrists and ankles were tied in a rope which extended off to four harnesses strapped onto wooden horses. By virtue of the tightly stretched ropes, the wax figure slightly hovered over the wooden table, completing the illusion of Lurch being in mid-stretch at the moment the scene captured.

"No wonder the guy is so tall," Gabe joked.

Another rope hung from Lurch's neck, but its other end drooped down to the floor where it lay loosely coiled. A leftover remnant of the "Hanged" part of the sequence of torture, no doubt. In a similar fashion to the neck rope, entrails ran from a gaping hole in Lurch's midsection, also finishing its run coiled on the floor. Fake flames similar to those of the Brazen Bull were positioned near the intestinal coil.

"What's with the flames?" Gabe asked.

"During the draw, the torturer would extract the victim's guts and throw them into a fire, burning them in front of the poor soul that found his way onto their butcher's block."

"Seems like overkill to me," Gabe surmised.

"Probably," Becca agreed. "Blake must have modified this scene since its days in Magna Arta. Owen used to have his limbs separated from his body, which would be the next thing to happen to the poor soul given the timing of this scene. He's stretched to maximum tension here. In its own way, it looks much creepier than it did with the severed limbs. I'll have to compliment Blake on his choice here, if we see get a chance to speak with him."

"I like severed limbs. I think he should have kept it that way, but what do I know?" Gabe shrugged.

They were readying to move on to the next scene, when a voice intruded from behind.

"Fascinating piece, wouldn't you say?"

Gabe turned to see who the newcomer to their conversation was. Before he could say "Holy shit! You're Blake Zellers", Blake introduced himself.

"Blake Zellers. Owner and proprietor of Arte Blanche," Blake greeted, his hand extended towards Gabe.

"Uh..." Blake stammered, in shock at being addressed by a billionaire. "Mr. Zellers?" Gabe finally squeezed out.

"Please, call me Blake."

Gabe, the gaping look of being star struck pasted on his face, finally reached out and took Blake's proffered hand. "Gabe. Gabe Daniels."

"Blake," Becca snidely greeted as the two men finished shaking hands.

"Becca Larson," Blake beamed. "I'm happy to see that you made my grand opening."

"You had to have known that I would never be able to resist the opening of one of the largest art galleries in the world."

"Indeed," Blake replied before turning back to Gabe. "And how do you know this fine gentleman?"

Gabe thought that he detected a bit of jealousy in Blake's tone, but he couldn't be sure. Becca wrapped her arms around Gabe and he instantly knew that – if Blake was indeed jealous – the billionaire was a cool customer.

"He's an artist too," Becca said, giving Gabe a sultry squeeze. Gabe was sure that she was trying to provoke a response from Blake, but the billionaire didn't bite. "A musician," she finished.

"A musician?" Blake's eyebrows rose at the revelation. "How quaint." Gabe was still trying to figure out if he had just been insulted when Blake continued. "Perhaps I could interest you in performing a show in the lobby some day? I plan on including music in my gallery during certain occasions, much like this evening. I have two of the best dueling pianists in the industry on tap to play for my opening night celebration."

Before Gabe could respond, Becca answered for him. "I don't think your patrons would care for his style of music," she retorted. "He sings in a heavy metal band."

Gabe almost felt as if he were suffocating in the now-obvious tension between the two.

"Perhaps you're right," Blake concluded with a defeated sigh. "That's not exactly the tone I'd be going for. No offense, Mr. Daniels."

"None taken," Gabe replied. He silently hoped that this moment would be over soon.

Gabe got his wish.

"Anyway, you'll have to pardon me, but it's time that I addressed this stunning crowd," Blake said, waving his hand at the packed room.

"Of course," Gabe replied before Becca could say anything further. "Pleasure meeting you, Mr. Zellers." Gabe couldn't bring himself to call the billionaire by his first name. It didn't seem right for some reason.

"You as well," Blake responded, shaking Gabe's hand again. The billionaire started to turn away, when he stopped mid-spin and briefly turned back. "Oh, and Becca? You should bring your friend and join me for a private reception tonight. Right here in *Suffering For Art*."

"We'll see," Becca answered, a sly smile painted on her face.

"I'll take that as a yes," Blake beamed. "I'll let my security know. The reception starts in here at ten o'clock sharp."

Becca kept the sly smile on her face, but said nothing further.

Blake held her stare for a moment, nodded, and then finally turned away to address the crowd.

9

Gabe watched as Blake ascended three steps of a makeshift wooden platform that had been erected near the front of the cavernous room. He was joined by two other men draped in the black tuxedos: The college-aged kid from earlier, and another gentleman; older, with thick glasses obscuring a sallow face.

"Ladies and gentlemen," Blake began, "thank you once again for showing up on this most wonderful of days." Blake hefted a champagne glass towards the crowd. Several matching glasses appeared above the congregation as murmurs of appreciation rang out through the room.

Gabe leaned over towards Becca. "Why don't we have any champagne?" he asked in a hushed tone.

"I was just thinking the same thing," she replied. "Our first move after this will be to track down the booze," she promised him with a twinkle in her eye.

Gabe's heart fluttered as he turned his attention back to the scene on stage.

"First off," Blake continued, "I have to apologize for not having completed the new scene here in *Suffering for Art* before the opening today. I had hoped to unveil it with the rest of the gallery today." Blake held a hand out towards the end of the row of grisly displays. Gabe shot a quick glance toward the scene blocked off with the white curtain.

"Second, I must also apologize if it feels a little stuffy in some of the exhibits today. Our A/C installation has also been running a bit behind and is currently only working at about half strength."

If the gallery was running on the warm side, Gabe hadn't noticed it. He certainly wasn't chilled, but he hadn't yet been uncomfortably warm either. He spotted a large A/C vent embedded in the roof of the exhibit, directly above the head of the large statue in the center of the room. Gabe wasn't sure, but as his gaze fell upon Blake, he would have sworn Zellers had been staring directly at him; a coy smile twisted on the billionaire's lips. Either way, the moment was brief. Blake resumed his oscillating gaze over the crowd as he continued his speech.

"With the apologies out of the way, let's get back to the celebration." The crowd rustled with their agreement, more champagne flutes extending into the air. Like earlier, Gabe noted, the crowd seemed awfully restrained in their celebration.

"Some of you may know the man off to my left." Blake nodded towards the older man with the thick glasses. "I'll never be able to thank him enough. His unique vision, understanding of human biology, and exceptional skills in artistry are what propelled my art career into the public eye. He is the mastermind and architect of *Suffering for Art*. Ladies and gentlemen, a toast to my good friend, Dr. Jarvis Holtz."

Polite applause rang out through the exhibit. Those with champagne glasses once again extended them above their heads, before lowering them back to their lips.

"These assholes are all going to be drunk before I even get my first sip," Gabe grumbled. "Not a situation that I'm used to."

"Don't fret. We'll be rectifying the situation shortly," Becca promised with a playful nudge to Gabe's shoulder.

"Anyway," Blake pressed on after the applause faded, "enough of my wind-baggery. Please, go forth and enjoy the rest of the gallery. I'll be out there with you and will be more than happy to stop and address any questions that you may have." Blake walked to the end of the stage, shook a few hands, and then stepped down, disappearing into the crowd. "And don't forget, we're closing Monarchy at ten o' clock for a private affair. All invitations have already been extended, I'm afraid, but you're more than welcome to stay in Free Market for the remainder of the night. Like I said earlier, the booze will be on me."

The crowd cheered again. Gabe felt this applause had a little more gusto behind it than those previously. The affects booze had on people seemed to transcend all social barriers.

"That's it?" Gabe asked in astonishment. "All that fuss about an announcement just for Zellers to speak three sentences and move on?"

"It was more than three sentences," Becca countered. "I think." She made a show of counting them on her fingers.

"It doesn't matter how many sentences it actually was, it just seemed awfully short given all the setup for it."

Becca shrugged the complaint off. "Well, ready to get some booze?" she asked, turning Gabe's mind from his gripe.

"Hell yes, I am!"

"Let's do that and continue making our way through the rest of the gallery. What do you say?"

"Sure thing." Gabe had a feeling the gallery was going to get a lot more interesting with some precious alcohol in hand. "Now we just have to find out where the fuck they're stashing it." Gabe had cursed louder than he had meant to. He quickly glanced around to see if anybody had an offended look about them. Gabe's mouth was hard for him to control when he was excited. Like a snake in bloodlust, Gabe reacted instinctively to the presence of alcohol.

"That shouldn't be hard," Becca said. "Here comes Blake's right-hand man now. I'm sure he'll be able to tell us."

Gabe looked forward and saw the black-tuxedoed, college-aged man approaching.

"Becca Larson! How have you been, my dear?" the man asked as he neared. He reached out and wrapped Gabe's date in a friendly embrace.

"I've been doing well."

"Good to hear. I'm sure Mr. Zellers is pleased that you showed up today."

"Maybe. Though, I doubt he's too pleased that I brought a date with me." Becca reached out and pulled Gabe to her side, then rested her head on his shoulder.

The man gave Gabe a once-over as if he had just noticed that he had been standing there.

"Perhaps not," the man agreed, a look of suspicion in his features.

"Anyway, it is nice to see you, but would be nicer still if you could point us in the direction that all this champagne is flowing from." Becca gestured around the room to the multitude of flute-bearers.

"That's simple," the man replied. "Out in the northern hall, you will find Mr. Zellers has created a bar as its own exhibit. You can find it on the map as *Where Everybody Knows Your Name*."

Gabe silently admonished himself for not catching the *Cheers* reference during his earlier studies of the map. The exhibit name should have been a dead giveaway.

"Thank you, sweetie," Becca said, giving the man another hug. "We're going to go check that out and then continue wandering the gallery. We can talk more later. Blake has invited us to the private reception after closing tonight."

As the two broke from their embrace, Gabe found himself wondering how a man so young — certainly several years younger than Zellers — had found himself in the enviable position as the billionaire's main accomplice.

"Of course he did," the young man replied with a warm smile. "I will be looking forward to further conversation." The man nodded towards Becca and Gabe, then vanished back into the crowd.

Just before he was lost from sight, Gabe caught sight of the man's nametag.

"Kind of a strange name," Gabe remarked.

The nametag had read "Danner".

INTERLUDE 2

Danner Hackett dialed in the vault's combination before twisting the large, four-pronged metal handle. Despite its enormous weight, the hefty steel door easily swung open on its well-oiled hinges. Automatic lights flickered on inside the mammoth vault as the door arced open, illuminating the large space inside.

Danner stepped past the large door leading into the vault, and stopped in front of a glass-faced cabinet. The cabinet face was inset with a darkly tinted pane of glass. A LED screen next to the glass displayed several numbers, indicating the current settings for the cabinet's climate-controlled interior.

Danner typed in a combo on the cabinet's keypad and the glass-embedded door popped open with a hiss as the air inside escaped into the normal atmospheric pressure of the vault.

The man reached inside and withdrew a bottle of wine. Several others were left resting on the internal racks as Danner resealed the cabinet and turned to bring the $10,000 bottle of Port to its intended destination.

"C'mon Danner, leave the vault open...leave it open" Blake wished silently as he watched his father's assistant retrieve the expensive wine. He had known this was coming. His father always broke out one of the severely overpriced libations whenever he closed a major new deal.

"I love all these idiots and their Y2K fears. Their paranoia has just easily made us another billion," his father had announced with a large smile as he walked through the door into the large estate. Blake had smiled too, knowing that this was just the opportunity he had been waiting for. Now he just had to hope that his father hadn't veered from his usual instructions to Danner in these occasions.

Blake had seen this play out many times before. He knew that his father often celebrated these events alone, with only Danner as company. The confidant never joined Thomas in the consumption of the expensive wine, but he always seemed to be present. His father – increasingly a creature of habit since joining the billionaire club – would down the first bottle with exuberance, before sending Danner back for a second. The second, Blake's father would drink in silent contemplation as he already began planning his next move – and next billion dollar payday.

This routine provided Blake his opportunity. His father, whose fortune was made in security – albeit digital security – had made sure his real world compiling's were also as secure as possible.

Overly so, in Blake's opinion.

In so doing, his father's vault - already as physically secure as one could hope for with its foot-thick steel-and-concrete walls, four digital combination keypads, and a fingerprint scanner – also contained an extra feature not found in most home security suites. When the safe door was shut, a time lock was automatically activated, not allowing reentry for another two hours. His father had once explained to him that the feature was necessary in case of a break in. All Thomas Zeller would have to do is close the vault door and the burglars would be stuck waiting two hours to access the safe. More than enough time for police to arrive and rectify the situation.

However, one downside with Thomas Zellers' overzealous security feature, was that two hours was far too long for his father to wait between bottles. Danner had once argued that he could remove both bottles at the same time, but Thomas had refuted the suggestion, stating that he wanted his libation perfect and not having sat out in the only-God-controlled environment for any an amount of time prior to consumption.

Money indeed did make people crazy, Blake had surmised immediately after hearing his father's instructions on the matter.

Blake smiled in his hiding spot behind the large oak desk as he watched Danner pass by the open vault door without so much as glancing at the large, steel structure. Danner stepped through the room and exited out into the long corridor beyond.

Blake listened in silence for a moment more, then stood and confidently strode his way into the unattended vault. He glanced up at one of the video cameras that lined the ceiling, satisfied that they were not currently recording. He had made sure to disable them prior to this venture. As long as everything went to plan, he doubted his father would ever replay the footage or be made aware of the time lapse that footage would contain.

Over eight years had gone by since Blake had first laid eyes on the strange book in his father's study, but he had never forgotten about it. After many long and frightened nights of being unable to sleep, Blake had had plenty of time to contemplate all he had seen that fateful Saturday morning. He had come to several conclusions. One: that the dead man he had seen sprawled out on his father's floor had been a burglar. Two: that the burglar had been intending to steal the cloth-wrapped book. Three: for that fact, and based on his father's reactions to the whole matter, that book contained something valuable – or, at least, something *very* interesting.

Blake glanced around the vault, unsure where to begin his search. He had only seen the book that one time. It would have easy to find if he had ever been able to get into the small safe in his pre-billionaire father's study; but, in the post-billionaire vault – installed immediately after their move into this Rhode Island mansion - the task was made much more daunting. He was reasonably certain that it wasn't stored in the ostentatious wine cabinet, but other than that, Blake had no clue where to look.

He finally decided on the simplest path, start on the left and make his way around clockwise. He skipped the stacks of bearer bonds. He almost skipped the stack of paintings that he came across next, but stopped when the top one caught his eye. On first appearance, it looked like someone had randomly splattered paint onto a canvas; almost as if the artist was just trying to shake the paint off of his brush, but the canvas had gotten in the way. Blake couldn't say why, but, despite its simplicity, the longer he stared at it, the warmer it made him feel inside. He let his gaze linger on it a moment longer, then forced himself to move on.

Next, he came upon several briefcases stacked atop each other. The briefcases spanned several ascending shelves.

"What do we have here?" Blake whispered to himself. He reached out and took one of the black briefcases. He unclasped the latch and opened it. A golden aura lit his face, reflected from the lights in the vault. Blake had to stop himself from whistling in appreciation as he stared at the gold bars set into the case. He let his eyes wander at the rest of the briefcases, and was in awe of the obscene amount of wealth those briefcases must contain.

Blake set the briefcase back where he found it and moved on.

Next, his eyes lit upon something that seemed out of place amongst the other riches of the vault. His first impression was that it was a vase of some kind, though a cap covering the top where the flora should have been poking out, betrayed its true purpose.

It was an urn.

There was no name on it. No etchings promising loving memories, or how the person inside was a gentle soul, who loved to make others laugh. The urn was plain and unadorned; made from brushed aluminum. It couldn't have cost more than a couple hundred bucks. Definitely not worthy of being stored in a secure vault.

Blake took the cap off of the urn, sure his father must have hidden something unexpected inside. Looking in, he only saw gray ash - some poor soul forever locked away in a brushed aluminum canister. Surprised by the find, Blake reverently placed the cap back in its resting spot and continued to the next item on the shelf.

Sacks of gemstones. Artifacts of an ancient time. Ledgers from his father's business. Two ancient stones that had a strange writing etched into their surface.

Blake paused at the two stones. He lifted one and stared at it. "Are these the original ten commandments?" Blake asked himself quietly. He stared a moment longer, then shook his head. "Nah, they couldn't be," he assured himself as he set the stone back down, though his skin inexplicably tingled from where the stones had made contact. The commandments were rumored to be buried in the Ark of the Covenant, and if he were to find *that* in this vault, Blake felt that he would probably forget all about his search for the book. He glanced around to make sure. There was no place in the vault to hide something that large, so Blake shook his head and continued on.

Finally, his eyes fell on their desired target. He almost missed it, as it was tucked away behind a stack of rewritable compact discs that held secrets unknown. A small piece of the white cloth sticking out from behind the stack was the only indication that the bundle was hiding in the back.

Blake carefully moved aside the compact discs, trying to avoid having the stacks fall apart and crashing to the ground. After successfully accomplishing this task, Blake retrieved the wrapped book.

He removed the white cloth and was left staring at the book's cover in its entirety for the first time. The first thing that he realized was that it was quite old. The cover was stiff and dusty — the kind of dust that had sat for so long it had become ingrained in the very fibers of that which it dusted. There was not a title inscribed on the cover. No designs of any kind. Only stitching that held several panels of a leathery substance together.

"Okay book," Blake whispered into the silent void, "what makes you so important that my father would kill for you?"

Blake flipped the leathery cover open. Inside were yellowed, brittle pages hand-scrawled in Old English text. Blake hurriedly read through the first couple pages, though slower than he would have liked. He had to reread several parts, trying to grasp their meaning through the dead form of language. He got the gist of what the pages were saying, however.

"No way," he whispered in amazement. "This can't be real...can it?" Blake pondered on the question for a moment, then slammed the book closed. He knew he didn't have long and he still had some work to do.

He rewrapped the book in the cloth and carried the bundle out of the vault. He slowly opened the door leading into the corridor and peeked his head outside. Satisfied that nobody was approaching, he crept out into the corridor, carefully closing the door behind him.

He slinked through the long hallway, until he reached the other end, where his father's home office was located. He entered quietly, momentarily stopping to ensure that no footsteps could be heard. He shut the door behind him and breathed a sigh of relief as he the door latched.

He turned and jogged over to his father's desk, retrieving the backpack that he had stashed prior to entering the vault room. Inside were his school books and several stacks of notes – a necessary alibi in case anybody walked in unexpectedly. He would just say that he was making copies for school. He was nearing his final high school examinations and wanted to be as prepared as possible. He was sure his father would buy the lie, especially considering the small fortune Thomas Zellers had poured into making sure his son received the absolute best education he could at one of the top private schools in the country.

Blake removed the book from the cloth placed it open-faced onto the copier's scanner. He pressed the button to make a copy, shifted the page, then hit the button again. He continued on until the whole book had been successfully replicated.

Blake took the resulting stack of papers and shoved them in his backpack; careful to keep the pages separate from the other loose-leaf inside. That done, he zipped up the backpack and tip-toed over to the door. He checked his watch and saw that his time was quickly running out. His father should be nearly finished with the first bottle of wine. Blake had to return the book back to the vault and get out unseen before Danner came back for the second bottle.

Blake stuck his ear to the door. Hearing only silence, he cracked the door open and snuck out into the corridor.

He slinked down the passageway's length; quietly, but with a sense of urgency. He made it through the hallway without incident. He quickly snapped the door open and pirouetted into the vault room, carefully closing the door behind him.

Blake returned the bundled book back to where he had found it. He took a moment to arrange the items on the shelf, making sure everything was left exactly as he had found it. Satisfied, Blake exited the vault and light-footedly scampered back to the room's exit.

Before his fingers could clasp around the doorknob, the knob turned on its own. Blake flinched as the door was yanked open from the other side. Standing on the other side was Danner Hackett, a surprised look crossing his face as his eyes fell on Blake.

"What are you doing in here?" Danner asked, his tone suspicious.

It took Blake a brief moment to overcome his initial shock and work out a response in his head. He knew that he had been caught doing *something* he wasn't supposed to be doing, and his best option was at least a half-truth. It wasn't like he could claim that he got lost on the way to the bathroom.

"I saw the vault was open and decided to snoop around a bit," Blake conceded. He hung his head in faux shame. "You're not going to tell Father, are you?"

Danner stared at the young man for a moment – a cold, blank look in his eyes – before answering: "I have no choice. He will need to be informed about this."

Blake wasn't surprised by Danner's response. Not even slightly. Danner had never been anything other than one-hundred percent loyal to Thomas Zellers, and Blake had held no serious expectation that would change now.

What shocked Blake – what really shook him down to his core - was the revelation that revealed itself to Blake as he was caught in the man's gaze.

The strange book. The impossible passages within. Blake knew then that Danner was the proof. He was the key. Danner Hackett gave credence to what Blake had seen scrawled upon the book's pages.

Still, though Danner had caught Blake where he shouldn't be, his father's assistant had no knowledge that Blake had found the book, and –especially now - Blake had no intention of letting it be known that he had.

"I understand, Danner. If you don't mind, I will go and tell Father myself. It'd be better coming from me, don't you think?"

Danner looked curiously at Blake and nodded. "I do believe that would be wise," he agreed. "He'll go easier on you if you approach him with it directly."

Blake studied Danner's face as he responded. Initially, he thought Danner's grimace had softened in sympathy, but there had been something else lurking in the background. Blake briefly thought on it, but couldn't figure out exactly what it was. Maybe a sense of relief? Maybe fear? It was hard to tell through Danner's well-practiced poker face.

"I will go tell him now," Blake assured. "Will you be joining me?"

"No," Danner answered. "I will complete my task first, then join you two in the library."

Blake nodded and walked out into the passageway. As he turned to shut the door behind him, he saw that Danner was already scanning the vault's interior, looking for anything that was out of place. Silently praying that he hadn't missed anything when returning the book to its proper place, Blake shut the door and began walking toward the dreaded confession to his father.

Still, Blake smiled as he walked through the hallway. He knew that he had discovered something profound; something with unlimited potential. Danner was proof enough of that - at least as far as Blake was concerned. It answered so many questions in Blake's mind, including some that he was just realizing that he even had. That, and the big one that had been nagging Blake for the last couple years:

After knowing him for almost a decade, how had Danner Hackett seemingly not aged a single day?

Gabe and Becca watched – hands clasped together - as the doors to *Monarchy* collapsed shut. One of the white tuxedoed staff members typed a code into the adjoining keypad and Gabe could hear the internal lock mechanism kick in.

Gabe quietly sighed in tune with the clicking of the lock. This wasn't exactly what he had signed up for. He'd been planning on losing the sunlit hours of the day, pleasing his date with a romp through the gallery. The night, however, was supposed to have been his.

Only a couple more hours and hopefully we can get the fuck out of here, Gabe thought, determined to play the game through until the end in order to claim his prize. The outside world becoming closed off to him caused him to grow antsy, but one glance at Becca went a long way to strengthening his resolve.

As the door had closed, Gabe noted that the last person through had been Cliff, the parking lot attendant. Cliff had hung behind the man who had shut the doors, watching with the others as the locks engaged.

"I loved your scene in *Suffering for Art*," Gabe told the portly man after getting his attention. "That upside-down saw-thingy seems like some pretty brutal shit."

Cliff recoiled, seemingly stunned that he had just been addressed. Eventually, though, his body relaxed and a polite smile crept across his lips.

"Thank you, sir," Cliff replied. "Assuredly, a most horrible way to meet one's demise."

"How did you make it?" Gabe asked.

"Sir?" Cliff looked unsure of the question. "Dr. Holtz makes all of the..."

Gabe cut Cliff off. "I meant how did you pose for it? Did you actually have to hang upside down for a while?"

Cliff, still looking confused by the line of questioning, "It's always a pleasure to serve at Mr. Zeller's behest."

"So, that's a yes?" Gabe asked with one brow raised. Cliff answered with a half-nod.

"Cool." Gabe dragged the word out, awe in his tone. "How long did you have to hang there?"

Cliff, growing increasingly uncomfortable, was saved by Becca. "Stop interrogating the poor man," she spoke gently to Gabe, resting her chin atop his shoulder.

"Many hours, sir," Cliff answered apprehensively, despite Becca's intervention. "Now, sir, if you don't mind, I have to go and help set up for Mr. Zeller's gala." With that, Cliff was off.

"He talks funny," Gabe commented after Cliff had traipsed out of earshot.

"What was that?" Becca asked, ignoring Gabe's quip. Gabe thought that she looked truly annoyed.

Gabe's answer was delayed as he watched Cliff disappear around the corner at the corridor's end. "Sorry," he apologized when his brain caught up to his ears, "I was just picturing that fat man hanging upside down for a few hours. I imagine that was a funny sight."

Becca didn't laugh; instead glaring at him to answer her inquiry.

"I was curious," Gabe explained defensively. "I was thinking that it'd be cool to pose for one of those scenes – maybe see if I could use my completed tableau as an album cover. I was just wondering how much of a pain-in-the-ass that would be to set up."

"*Suffering For Art* scenes are for employees only," a deep voice answered from behind Gabe. Gabe turned to identify the voice's owner.

"Hey Lur-" Gabe was cut off by a forceful pinch from Becca as she heard him getting ready to use the man's assigned nickname. "Uh...I mean Owen," Gabe corrected, having to read the usher's nametag again.

If Lurch was left wondering about Gabe's slip of the tongue, he didn't let it show; instead he gestured down the hallway in the direction that Cliff had disappeared. "Mr. Zeller's is getting ready to kick off his private celebration and has asked me to gather the remaining guests in *Suffering For Art*."

Gabe wound his arm through Becca's and repeated Lurch's gesture. "Would the lady care to follow the man's lead?"

The radiant smile returned to Becca's face. "The lady cares very much indeed," she joked, glancing up at Lurch.

Lurch, catching the queue, began walking down the hallway. "Please follow me. Mr. Zeller's doesn't like being kept waiting."

"Uh-oh," Gabe whispered to Becca. "We wouldn't want to upset the billionaire. I'm sure he's very scary when he's angry. He'd probably drown us in his pit of money."

"Stop being an ass," Becca instructed, though her grin held firm.

Gabe never noticed her smile, though. His attention was on another smile; one that for some reason, caused a shiver to run down Gabe's spine.

Lurch had smiled as well.

Lurch led them around the long way to *Suffering for Art*, having skipped the entrance to *A Morsel's Journey*. The more direct approach, bending around the corridor, had sounded like the quicker route, but it ended up taking far longer than Gabe had thought it would.

"Jesus...If I had known I was going to be walking around this much, I would have worn my FitBit," Gabe griped.

"I'm sure this is nothing compared to football practice," Becca teased.

"You'd be surprised."

Lurch hefted open a large door and gestured for them to enter. "Right through here," he announced in his baritone pitch.

"Many thanks, good sir," Gabe replied in a mocking tone. Becca placed her hands on Gabe's back and gently pushed him through the door.

Once through the door, Gabe took in the large exhibit space for the second time that day. While earlier, it had been filled with a massive crowd of meandering bodies, the huge room was now mostly empty. Only a few people could be seen gathered inside, huddled against the shadow of the large Peristopheles statue. Every single person Gabe could see was clad in a white tuxedo.

Gabe turned back to Lurch, who was still holding the door open. "Are you sure this is the right place?"

With a sly grin, Lurch answered, "Yes, sir. Mr. Zeller's will be joining you all shortly." With that, Lurch closed the door, sealing the couple inside.

"There only seems to be staff in here," Gabe remarked, turning back to Becca.

Becca, scanning the room, looked as if she shared in Gabe's confusion. "Yeah...I guess Blake didn't let on exactly how exclusive these festivities were."

"Maybe I should get Lurch to bring me a white tuxedo so I don't feel so out of place," Gabe joked, though his humor was laced with apprehension.

"White would be an interesting color on you," Becca teased, a glint in her eye.

Gabe pictured himself donned in white and shrugged the idea away. He couldn't see such a thing working for him. In his view, the darker the attire, the better.

"Well," Becca started, waving her hand over the small cluster of white, "shall we resume our mingling?"

Gabe repressed a sigh of futility and clasped arms with Becca, stepping towards the gathering of the *Arte Blanche* staff.

"Ms. Larson," several of the staff members greeted as they drew close. Several others remained silent, seemingly unsure what to say at the presence of the two non-tuxedoed arrivals.

The lone woman in the group – the kooky one that Gabe had first seen at the art lesson in front of the building - stepped forward and clasped Becca's hand, giving it a firm shake. "Becca! It's a pleasure seeing you again," she announced. "It feels like it's been a long while since you last graced us with your presence."

"I suppose you could say that," Becca agreed. "I'm sure Blake knew that opening a grand gallery such as this would bring me back in."

"You think he built this just for you?" The woman – whose nametag read Ophelia - asked with a wink. Like earlier, her voice was overly-excited, as if she were on the verge of breaking into a fit of hysterical giggling at any moment.

"Who knows?" Becca shrugged. "He seems to have a hard time letting go, as I'm sure you know."

Gabe caught a knowing look pass between the two women and knew that there was something being left unsaid. Ophelia's smile briefly wavered, but she corrected it quickly. Gabe figured the older woman – while undoubtedly a fox for a gal in her fifties – was hardly attractive enough to warrant a billionaire's attentions. Gabe was left pondering what other reason there could be behind the bizarre exchange.

He thought on it for only a couple moments and then let it go. Staring at Ophelia while she conversed with Becca, Gabe decided the mystery may be as simple as it first appeared. Who knew the depth of a billionaire's eccentricities?

"Pardon me," a voice from over Gabe's shoulder roused him from his ponderings. "Champagne," the man finished, grabbing a crystal flute from a tray and hoisting it towards Gabe.

Gabe nodded excitedly. "Now that's what I'm fucking talking about," he said as he snatched the glass from the tuxedoed gentleman. The man gave Gabe a snoddy look, then continued to the next attendee.

"Oh, don't mind Lester," Ophelia announced, having caught the exchange. "He's quite dull." She finished with a giggle. Gabe figured that - had he not spoken English – Ophelia's jovial tone would have been interpreted as meaning this Lester-guy was the life of the party.

"Damn! You are one kooky bitch, aren't you," is what Gabe wanted to say. Instead, "So, which scene is yours?" he asked, waving his champagne flute towards the row of torture dioramas.

"Oh, mine is particularly gruesome," Ophelia declared with zest. She let her hand limp over onto Gabe's wrist. "It's called *The Tub*."

"The Tub?" Gabe asked, the name not sounding as impressive as some of the others that he had seen.

"Yes! It's an exceptionally long form of torture that would take weeks – even months – to kill its victim."

"Oh yeah?" Gabe asked, his interest piquing.

"Yeah. The torturer would strap his victim naked into a tub, where they would stay for an exceptional amount of time."

"So, they just left them in the tub to starve to death? Doesn't sound *that* cool," Gabe noted.

"Nope!' Ophelia cheerfully announced. "Quite the contrary. The victim would be well fed. Three squares a day, from what I read. The problem was that the victim was never allowed to move. They'd be fed continually, but when the food had completed its journey through the digestive system, the victim would be left sitting in the refuse."

"So, in his own shit?"

"A crude way to put it, but yes...in the victim's own shit." Ophelia confirmed, still as giddy as ever. "For weeks this would continue, the tub slowly filling with the victim's own urine and feces. Soon, the constant exposure to the excrement would cause the victim's flesh to break out in a rash, eventually leading to the flesh rotting on their body while they were still alive. To further complicate matters, oftentimes flies would birth maggots in the feces, which would begin consuming the man's flesh, eating their way through him."

Gabe wasn't sure if the description made him want to start penning a song, or barf all over Ophelia's shiny white shoes.

"It's the most horrible death imaginable!" Ophelia finished with an air of certainty in her statement. She finally released the giggle that Gabe had suspected was hiding just underneath the surface during her explanation.

"I'll have to check that out," Gabe responded, unsure if he actually wanted to or not.

"We can go right now!" Ophelia beamed. "It's right over here. If you want to follow me, I'd love to..."

The clinking of crystal saved Gabe from answering. All heads swiveled towards the massive statue of Peristopheles.

Gabe saw that Blake Zellers had finally arrived; now standing directly next to the large statue at the center of the room. The party, it seemed, was about to kick off.

Blake Zellers stood next to the statue, lovingly caressing a patch of its stone. Gabe was pondering the strangeness of Blake's actions, when the billionaire finally turned to address the crowd.

"And, with that, day one is in the books!" Blake proudly announced. "Now to officially begin the first night's celebration." Blake hoisted his glass in the air. The staff did the same.

"Amen!" the staff's voices rang out through the room.

"Amen?" Gabe whispered to Becca. She didn't answer; her eye glued on the curious scene playing out in front of them.

"For those of you who haven't yet met him, we have a special visitor with us in the gallery tonight," Blake proclaimed to the gathering. "A guest of honor, if you would."

Gabe glanced around the exhibit, looking for somebody that he may have missed, but saw only Blake's staff.

"Mr. Daniels?" Blake extended his champagne flute towards Gabe. "Would you like to say a few words?"

Gabe - whose jaw had dropped damn near to the floor - stood shocked, staring at the billionaire.

"Blake? What are you doing?" Becca interrupted.

"Nothing untoward, my dear," Blake replied. "Just recognizing your new boyfriend for having joined us on this most special of evenings."

"He doesn't want this kind of attention," Becca sharply rebuked, letting her eyes flicker nervously toward Gabe.

"Nonsense!" Blake stepped away from the statue and over to the stunned couple. "You said yourself that he is a performance artist. I've never known a performance artist to be shy of the spotlight."

Gabe regained his composure at the billionaire's words — not wanting to seem like a pussy - and clinked his glass against Blake's. "I'll grant you that one, Mr. Zellers. I do generally enjoy the spotlight." Gabe tilted the flute to his lips and downed the remaining contents of the glass. "Since I'm the guest of honor," he held the empty glass high, "refill?" Seemingly out of nowhere, Lester appeared and swapped the empty flute for a full one.

"For the crude gentleman," Lester announced as he slinked off back into the crowd. Gabe got the sense that Lester had nearly choked on the word 'gentleman' as he forced it through his lips.

"*Crude* is my middle name," Gabe toasted the retreating figure.

Blake had watched the exchange with interest. A smile curled at his lips. "I barely know you, Mr. Daniels, but I must confess that you have already garnered my intrigue."

"Thanks! If we're confessing things, I must say that you seem a lot less stuffy than I had imagined, as well." Gabe clinked against Blake's glass again. "A lot less British, too." Gabe took another deep swig of the bubbly brew.

"British?" Blake asked, confused. "I'm not British. In fact, I've only ever been to Britain once, and I did not stay long."

"Yeah...sorry," Gabe said. "It's just what I picture when imagining the billionaire class. I picture you all as being refined and proper as shit. Basically, the same way I picture artists, as well. You kinda fit the bill on both." Gabe shrugged. "And, to finish the comparison, when I think of refined and proper, a British accent naturally pops into my head."

Blake stared on, still confused.

"Don't worry, though. It's a personal problem of mine. I'll get over it someday." Gabe finished by once more emptying the contents of his glass. Lester immediately returned with another glass and swapped the two.

"I can get used to this." Gabe winked at Becca, tilting the fresh flute towards her.

Blake laughed. "Intriguing indeed!" he barked. The billionaire emptied the contents of his own glass and held it out. Lester appeared like a snake and replaced it.

"Now," Blake continued, "besides being liberal with my alcohol supply, is there anything else that I can do to make your evening here more memorable?"

"Besides giving me a billion dollars?"

Blake answered that only with a smile.

"Actually, now that you mention it, I was just telling Becca here about my interest in possibly posing for my very own torture scene. I think that would be badass."

Laughter suddenly sprang from the gathered staff. Blake, looking annoyed for some reason, shot them a warning glance and the staff fell silent. When the billionaire turned back to Gabe, his coy smile had successfully been placed back on his face.

"I'm not sure why that was funny," Gabe remarked, looking over at the pool of white tuxedos. "I was being serious; or, at least, as serious as I ever am. I know that those scenes are reserved for employees, but I was hoping that you would be willing to make an exception."

Blake surprised Gabe by clinking champagne flutes and answering, "I'm sure that I can have that arranged."

"Awesome!" Gabe exclaimed, downing another glass. Lester, ever-vigilant, appeared for the swap. Gabe was blessedly starting to feel a buzz. "I figured you'd shoot me down."

"I think you may find that I am full of surprises," Blake answered.

"What's going on, Blake?" Becca cut in. "Surely this isn't the only thing you had planned for your private after-party?"

Blake tore his eyes from Gabe and turned at Becca. "You arc correct, my dear," he said, before spinning to face his huddled staff. "What do you all say? Shall we commence?"

The white tuxedos all raised their glasses as one. The black tuxedo of Danner Hackett emerged from the sea of white and answered, "Yes, sir. We should begin. The night is growing shorter every minute." Danner's glass joined the others in the air.

"Fantastic!" Blake turned his attention toward the line of torture scenes. Gabe turned with him and found Lurch standing near the shrouded scene at the end of the row. "Owen, if you please."

Lurch grabbed an edge of the white cloth and pulled at it. The cloth came off easily, revealing a barren area with nothing but a single steel table in the middle of the square. A placard pedestal rose from the floor in front of the empty scene, same as the others.

"That's the new scene?" Gabe whispered. "There's nobody being tortured." After a moment, Gabe rolled his eyes, assuming that this was another inane artistic statement.

"Let me guess," Gabe mocked, "*The Torture of Being Alone*." Gabe used his hands to draw a box in the air, framing an imaginary placard.

Laughter crept up behind Gabe. "I assure you, what you see is not the completed piece," Blake explained as he approached.

"Then why unveil it now?" Gabe asked.

"Because we finally have our newest star."

A shiver crept down Gabe's spine at the sinister tone that had crept into Blake's voice.

"Go ahead," Blake invited, gently pushing Gabe toward the barren scene. "Read the plaque."

Gabe reluctantly stepped forward until he was in range to read the placard's text.

"*The Rat*. Model: Gabe Daniels."

Gabe's heart was racing when he spun around to face Blake.

Blake's face was plastered with a perverse grin. "I told you that I would arrange something."

Gabe's racing heart stopped cold when a pair of strong arms seized him from behind and yanked him into the air.

13

abe!" Becca shouted, running up to where he was suspended in the air by the towering Lurch.

Gabe instinctively threw a backwards elbow, feeling a satisfying crunch as it made contact with Lurch's jaw. The strong arms immediately released Gabe and he went crashing to the floor.

"Fuck you, motherfucker!" Gabe shouted as he kicked at Lurch's legs, knocking the lofty man off his feet.

"Gabe!" Becca exclaimed again, grabbing Gabe's hands and pulling him off the floor.

"Stay back!" Gabe instantly commanded, pushing Becca behind him so that his body was between her and the remaining *Arte Blanche* staff.

A flood of white moved forward. The staff was coming at Gabe with something resembling hunger in their eyes.

"Be ready to fight," Gabe instructed, his eyes glued on the approaching horde.

The answer from behind him was a scream. Gabe spun to see what had caused Becca's scream, when something constricted around his ankle. Gabe's dipped his head, looking downward. His eyes revealed that Lurch had once again gotten a hold on Gabe. Before Gabe could react, a black boot crashed into Lurch's nose, causing a loud snapping sound to emanate from the man's face. Blood burst from the broken organ and sloshed down Lurch's face. Lurch's grip loosened as the large man's head crashed to the floor, where he lay still; out cold from the vicious kick.

"Nice punt!" Gabe congratulated.

"Thanks," Becca replied. "Maybe we could start our own team someday."

Gabe smiled despite the threat of the hungry mob bearing down on them. "Good. Looks like we're going to have to start with the defense, though."

Gabe recognized Lester at the head of the rushing mob. When he judged Lester was within striking distance, Gabe leapt into action. He lowered his shoulders and burst forward, driving his shoulder straight into Lester's midsection. The impact forced a large huff through Lester's lips as the skinnier man was plowed backwards. Gabe completed the maneuver by driving Lester down to the hard tile floor. A loud crunch erupted from Lester's head as his skull crashed against the unforgiving ground.

Regaining his feet from the pile-driving he had just administered, Gabe felt a pair of hands grasp his back. He instantly reacted, bringing his fist around and smashing it against the nose of another staff member. The newest attacker fell away, joining Lurch in the smashed nose club.

Two more attackers came in from Gabe's side. The former football player juked to the right, avoiding their outstretched hands. His sidestep brought him crashing into a third attacker. Gabe immediately grabbed at the third man, using the man's own weight against him to send him spiraling into the previous two. All three toppled like bowling pins.

A shrill scream brought Gabe's attention back to the row of grisly displays. Two white-clad assailants had converged on Becca. One paid dearly for the move as Becca swiftly planted the toe of her boot into the man's balls. The other leapt into the air and crashed down onto her back. She collapsed to the ground under the man's weight. Two more staff members had arrived and helped the man pin the wildly-flailing woman down.

"Becca!" Gabe screamed, rushing to her aid. Another assailant took the opportunity to pounce on Gabe from behind. Gabe promptly spun his body and pushed the man away. The attacker immediately recovered and took another charge. Gabe shot his foot out to connect with the man's knee. The assailant screamed as his knee snapped backward in an entirely unnatural way.

The man with the busted knee unsurprisingly fell out from the fight, but was instantly replaced by two more men rushing in at the former football star. They came in fast, trying to get their arms around Gabe. Gabe swatted at the two men, barely managing to avoid being ensnared.

Distracted, Gabe never felt the portly staff member Cliff approaching him from behind. Cliff's thick arms wrapped around Gabe, giving the two men in front of him the split-second opportunity that they needed. They instantly snapped forward, snagging Gabe in their arms. All three men combined their weight to finally wrestle Gabe to the ground.

Still, they didn't have control of him.

Gabe thrashed wildly, his arms and legs continuously smashing into soft flesh. He couldn't tell which blow connected with which assailant, but he was slowly squirming free of his trapped position.

His progress didn't last long, however. Several more of the staff members jumped in to help their struggling compatriots, placing Gabe in the not-entirely-unfamiliar position at the bottom of a pile.

Gabe continued thrashing his limbs, trying to fight his way out, but he quickly gave up the struggle. It was no use; he was tightly pinned.

Gabe soon heard clapping filtering in through the mass of bodies that covered him. The white-clad crotch in his face moved out of the way, giving Gabe a clear view of Blake Zellers, looking on and applauding.

"You got yourself a real fighter here, Becca," Blake congratulated. "Impressive for a musician."

"I was a football player in high school, asshole!" Gabe responded. "A damn good one too, so you had better watch out when I work my way loose from these sissy motherfuckers."

"A musician *and* a football player?" Blake looked amused. Gabe couldn't wait to smash the smug look off the billionaire's face. "Like Shaq?"

"Shaq played basketball, dipshit!" Gabe spat. "And I wouldn't exactly call him a *musician*."

A flash of annoyance crossed Blake's face, but it quickly evaporated back to a malevolent grin.

"Either way, it doesn't much matter to me." Blake turned towards Becca, who Gabe saw was suspended in the air by a recovered Lurch. "So, this is what you meant by finding a 'real man'?"

Becca answered by spitting into Blake's face. She looked incredibly pleased with herself as the wad of saliva dangled from Blake's nose.

Gabe watched the scene apprehensively, afraid that Blake was going to respond by slapping the shit out of her. He breathed a sigh of relief when Blake merely wiped the wad from his face and started laughing.

"Feeling feisty today, I see." Blake said, wiping his hand against the arm of Lurch's blood-stained tuxedo.

Turning to face the pile atop Gabe, Blake instructed, "Get them in position."

With that, the mass holding him down erupted into action. Several of the men – being careful to keep Gabe subdued – lifted him off his feet and carried him over to the empty table.

As he was carried over, Gabe saw Lurch slam Becca to the ground and tie up her wrists and ankles to the feet of the table they were hauling him to. She tried to fight free of her bonds, but it was of no use. Lurch's knot-tying skills proved true. Gabe saw her struggle to at least sit up, but a horizontal beam connecting the table legs kept her binds from sliding up more than an inch or two.

Lester – his tuxedo sharing the crimson splotches of Lurch's – was already waiting at the table to greet him as he arrived. The man had a vile grin plastered across his face as he hoisted a tube of Saran wrap.

The men carrying him threw Gabe down on the tabletop, not concerned in the least about doing it gently. Lester immediately began winding the clingy plastic material over Gabe and under the table, pinning his arms and midsection. The mass of men kept the pressure on Gabe's limbs until Lester had wound through the entire tube.

"What is this...fucking *Dexter*?" Gabe growled as Lester stood back, admiring his handiwork.

Blake answered the taunt from where he stood looking on. "Did this Dexter place a rat under a metal container on your stomach, heat the metal with a torch, and listen to your screams as the rat bites and claws its way through your stomach in order to escape?"

Gabe opened his eyes wide in terror, fixing them on Blake's joyous form. "No," he begrudgingly admitted.

"Then no...it's not Dexter, whoever that is."

Gabe nervously gulped down a wad of saliva that had built in his mouth.

"You wouldn't dare!" Becca warned from where she had been tied to one of the table legs.

Blake's eyebrow rose in her direction. "Oh, dear Becca, wouldn't I?" He let his gaze linger on her for a moment, then faced his gathered staff. "Bring in the doctor!" Blake commanded.

Lester nodded from his place in front of the gathering and marched off towards the door. He swung it inward and motioned for somebody out in the hall to enter. Lester held the door open as Dr. Holtz walked through, pushing a metal cart in front of him, the kind used by hotel staff to deliver over-priced room service to guests too lazy to venture out on their own. Two large aluminum bowls sat atop the cart, along with a myriad of unmarked glass bottles. Most disturbing, however, was the item that sat at the end of the cart's flat surface: a small cage containing a white rat. The rat scurried around the cage, already appearing distressed. Its red eyes stood in stark contrast to its white fur. It was a scary-enough looking creature without Blake's forewarning about its purpose.

Gabe kept his widened eyes glued on the doctor as he strode through the room, only stopping after he had arrived at Gabe's horizontal prison.

"Staff of the Arte Blanche!" Blake yelled out. "In ceremonial position!"

The entirety of the tuxedoed staff spun as one to face the large statue in the middle of the room. In unison, they collapsed down to their knees.

"Don't worry," the doctor whispered to Gabe. "It's just art." His lips twisted with a perverse curl.

Then, Dr. Jarvis Holtz got to work.

INTERLUDE 3

Blake took in a deep breath to steel himself. "Don't be nervous...Don't be nervous," he silently chanted.

"Mr. Zellers?" an old, wispy voice asked from behind him.

Blake tore his attention from the large painting that he had been studying. The painting – a tad heavy on the magenta, Blake thought – showed two demons battling it out in the hellish landscape of a deep, fiery pit. A local artist's homage to Dante's *Inferno,* a favorite of Blake's.

As he turned, Blake saw an old man with sunken cheeks staring back at him. The old man was precariously balanced on a cane and held the look of defeat in his eyes.

"Dr. Holtz," Blake greeted, "I am pleased to see that you accepted my invitation." Seeing the old man's obvious distress at trying to stay on his feet, Blake motioned over to a nearby bench. "Please, let's sit and converse."

Dr. Holtz glanced over at the bench, a look of relief settling in his posture. "Gladly." Holtz more coughed the word than spoke it before hobbling over to the bench.

He's worse off than I imagined, Blake thought, joining the doctor on the bench.

"Why meet in an art museum?" the doctor asked after he was firmly planted on his seat.

Blake splayed out his hands to encompass all the sights before them. "It's art! Who doesn't love art?"

"*I've* never particularly cared for it," Holtz replied, immediately followed by a series of coughs. Holtz withdrew a white rag from his pocket to cover his mouth. When the coughing fit had subsided, Blake saw spots of red on the rag as Holtz withdrew it from his mouth. Holtz looked nonplussed by the whole event; it having become commonplace in his life over the last several months.

"Myself, I've always been drawn to it," Blake continued as if the coughing fit had never happened. "There's just something about art that I can't shake. A feeling that it gives me."

"If you say so," Holtz said dismissively.

"I'm actually thinking of opening my own art gallery soon. I'm not sure what I'm going to call it just yet, though I have been toying with the name Magna Arta."

"Magna Arta?" Holtz asked. "I assume that's a play on the Magna Carta?"

"Why not?" Blake exuberantly replied. "The Magna Carta was the foundation of law. A symbol of freedom from oppression. Sounds like art to me."

Holtz didn't look convinced. "If you say so," the doctor repeated. "Look," Holtz continued, his tone more abrupt, "I hope you didn't drag me here to talk about art. As I've said, I never much cared for it."

"Au contraire," Blake replied, "from what I hear, you are something of an artist yourself."

The doctor sat stone-faced in confusion.

"I have heard that you are a master taxidermist."

"I've been known to dabble, I suppose," Holtz answered carefully, unsure where this was going.

"I was hoping to enlist your services at my new gallery when it opens."

With that, Holtz's stone-faced demeanor evaporated into a laughter coupled with intense coughing. "You can't be serious!" he replied once his respiratory fit had subsided. "I doubt I'll be around even six months from now, let alone whenever you get your gallery off the ground."

"I'm dead serious." The humor vanished from Blake's face as he answered. "As I told you in my invitation, I have found a cure for you."

"A cure?" Holtz scoffed, eliciting another round of coughing. "I'm in the advanced stages of COPD – Chronic Obstructive Pulmonary Disease. There is no cure for that. Even if there were, my lungs are already too badly damaged for me to ever hope for recovery. I just showed up here, curious to see what you *really* wanted."

"Doctor," Blake replied pragmatically, "I am Blake Zellers, the son of Thomas Zellers. He made billions last year from the Y2K bug, and that was on top of the billions that he already possessed. Do you doubt that I would have the resources for such a venture?"

Holtz stared skeptically, but Blake could see a twinkle of hope grow in the old man's eyes. It was what Blake had been wishing to see. Now he just had to nurture it.

"How would you like to wake up tomorrow, freed from this horrible disease?"

The skepticism remained in the doctor's stare, but the hope did indeed brighten.

"Tomorrow?" Holtz asked, unable to hide the growing excitement in his voice. "Are you saying that you could cure me tonight?"

Blake nodded, knowing that he had him. "That's what I'm saying."

Holtz stared on for another moment, then used his cane to wobbly rise to his feet. "Well then, what are we waiting for?" he asked.

Blake joined him on his feet and gently took the old man's arm in his, steering him towards the museum's front entrance. "I've got a car waiting for us out front. It'll take us to my lab."

"I can't believe this is happening," Holtz rejoiced.

"Believe it, Doctor. Tomorrow, you'll feel like a brand new man."

******

The drive lasted about twenty minutes. Blake spent that time talking up his procedure to the old man. He hadn't mentioned much on the details of the procedure itself, but Blake didn't need to. His salesmanship was on point that particular evening. When they finally arrived, Dr. Holtz was firmly beaming with relief and excitement.

"What is this place?" Holtz asked, stepping out of the car. They had arrived at a non-descript building, buried deep in the warehouse district of town.

"I know it doesn't look like much, but I assure you, my lab – with everything we need for the procedure - is inside."

"Wonderful!" Holtz responded, his excitement drowning out any wariness he may have formed from laying eyes on the rundown building.

The car sped off, leaving Blake and Holtz alone. Blake took the doctor's arm and led him inside.

"Seems quiet," the doctor remarked.

"Everything is set up already," Blake explained. "Don't worry, things'll pick up when it's time to get started."

Blake led Holtz through a dingy hallway. He could tell by the slight stiffening of his body that Holtz was starting to have second thoughts. Blake hurried the pace a bit until they walked into a brightly lit room that had been installed with hospital-grade fluorescents. Blake could feel Holtz relax again, having entered the new room.

By all appearances, it was exactly like any operating room one would find at their neighborhood hospital. Had a person been blindfolded on the way through the building, said person would have been completely unaware that we were not actually at a St. Luke's.

"Go ahead and get ready. Take off your shirt and lay down on the table," Blake instructed, pumping two squirts of antibacterial soap into his palm. He rubbed his hands together as his eyes followed Holtz to the operating table.

Blake rinsed his hands off in the nearby sink and approached the table. Holtz had just finished his arduous climb up the steel frame and was lying down, sweat glistening on his skin.

"Let's get you strapped in," Blake said, taking Holtz's left wrist into his hand.

"Strapped in? Why is that necessary? You're going to put me out, right?"

"Just an extra precaution, Doctor," Blake informed smiling down at his patient. "Can't have you moving around during the surgery."

As Blake moved down to the left ankle, Holtz's eyes nervously darted around the room. "Where are all your support staff?"

"Help will be here shortly," Blake assured, now strapping down the doctor's right ankle. The doctor was clearly becoming agitated, clearly discerning that something was wrong.

Blake strapped down the right wrist and then stood back from the table, checking over everything. When satisfied all was as it should be, Blake addressed the doctor again. "Alright, Dr. Holtz, the first step of my procedure is going to be the removal of your lungs. I'll be performing this step myself and if everything goes according to plan, you should be your old, fully-capable self by morning."

Holtz's eyes were fixated on Blake as he turned to grab a backpack from where it had been stuffed into a corner of the room. Blake took the time to flash a reassuring smile at the doctor before he unzipped the backpack and withdrew several sheets of paper from within. Black smudging around the edges led Holtz to believe that Blake was looking at Xeroxed copies of some sort.

"Is that your research?" Holtz asked.

Blake looked up from the sheets and threw another smile at the tied-down doctor. "As a matter of fact, it is." Blake looked back down and read silently from the pages for another moment. Nodding his head, he put the pages down and made his way back to the surgical table.

Blake donned a surgical mask and began inspecting an array of cutting tools on a tray next to the table. "You'll have to excuse me if I'm a little nervous. This is my first time."

Holtz's pulse shot up a notch as he nervously looked around for Blake's support team to show up. *Stop being a paranoid old duck*, Holtz thought to himself. *This is going a great day.*

"Well, in that case," Holtz began speaking, attempting to steady his nerves with humor, "don't do like I did on *my* first surgery and leave a cotton swab behind when you put the lung back in."

Blake gave a short chuckle as he inspected a scalpel in the bright fluorescent light. "You ready to begin?" he asked.

"Begin?" Holtz asked, his voice suddenly shaking. "Not without the anesthesiologist I'm not!"

Blake met Holtz's erratic gaze with a smile. "Anesthesiologist? I don't think so, Doctor. I forgot to mention that pain was one of the most important parts of the cure. Without pain, all this would be for naught."

Holtz's fear had taken him over completely enough that he failed to notice the warmth of the stream that had started pooling between his legs.

"And, for the record, you needn't worry about me leaving anything sewn up inside you. I said that I would be removing your lungs...I never said anything about putting them back in."

Blake gave the doctor a moment to process his words – watching the last vestiges of hope drain from the old man's eyes – then he took the scalpel and slammed it down into Holtz's chest.

If his lungs hadn't already been weakened by the illness, it would undoubtedly have been the loudest scream of Dr. Jarvis Holtz's life.

14

Gabe struggled against the tight plastic wrap as he watched Dr. Holtz pour the contents of the glass bottles into one of the two metal bowls. Gabe felt his testicles scrunch tight, knowing the purpose of the untouched bowl sitting idly on the cart.

"I am mixing an elixir of my own design," Holtz smiled down at Gabe, using a whisk to mix the unidentified ingredients together. "It preserves the flesh and keeps it from rotting. It undoubtedly made my taxidermy hobby much less time-consuming."

"You're a taxidermy doctor?" Gabe asked in reply.

Holtz laughed. "There is no doctorate in taxidermy, young man," he explained after his brief snicker. "It's just something I liked to dabble with. However, I suppose my degree in human anatomy has helped quite a bit in my recent taxidermical ventures."

"That's cool," Gabe replied, looking around. Blake and his cronies were distracted by whatever ceremony they were preparing for. He looked back into the doctor's eyes and said, "I was thinking about maybe getting into that hobby myself."

"Taxidermy?" Holtz asked, surprised.

"Yeah."

Holtz snickered. "I doubt that, Mr. Daniels. It's not an easy skill to learn and you don't have a lot of time left, I'm afraid."

"That's alright. When I'm stuffing Zellers' head up your ass, I won't be looking for perfection."

Holtz stopped stirring for a moment to stare into Gabe's eyes. Gabe saw that the doctor didn't like what he saw in there, and went back to stirring the contents of the bowl. He remained silent thereafter, however.

The staff hovering near the large statue, however, did not. They began chanting something Gabe couldn't understand, bowing to the looming figure of Peristopheles.

"What the fuck?" Gabe asked under his breath, watching the strange ceremony.

"Exciting, isn't it?" Blake's voice reached Gabe. Gabe strained against the plastic wrap to look past his feet and saw Blake slowly sauntering toward him; the billionaire's gaze on his worshipping goons as he approached.

"My father found him shortly before his death, buried in the Carpathian mountains," Blake explained when he was close enough to speak quietly. "He was buried deep and in many pieces." Gabe remembered seeing the cracked seams running through the statue when he had first laid eyes on it. "But now I have resurrected him, allowing us to bask in his great power."

Gabe looked towards the statue's feet, where the tuxedoed mass was still bowing and chanting. "You don't really believe that shit, do you?" Gabe challenged. "I never thought billionaires had much use for God. Any God!"

Blake laughed. "Who do you think was responsible for my being a billionaire? It certainly wasn't my father...the greedy bastard!" Blake turned to stare longingly at the giant idol. "Ultimately, it was his money that fattened my accounts, but it was Peristopheles that made that all possible."

Gabe was about to call "Bullshit!", but Blake continued before he could spit out the word.

"And Peristopheles demands sacrifice in return."

Gabe's tight-squeezed nuts scrunched in even tighter.

"Well, Doctor," Blake said, turning towards Holtz, "let's ask our God to humbly accept our offering."

Blake, followed by Holtz, spun to face the statue. The chanting of the staff ceased as Blake began to speak.

"Oh great Peristopheles, we come before you today to offer up this soul to your grand countenance. Through your many eons, you have witnessed a great many things. War, famine…"

"Gabe! Your pocket," Becca's voice came quietly from Gabe's other side. Gabe turned from Blake as he continued his praises to find Becca's chin planted on the table near his head. Gabe knew she had to be struggling mightily against her bonds to stretch herself that high. "Your pocket," she whispered again.

What the fuck was she talking about?

Gabe was confused at first, but, as he wiggled his fingers as much as he could under the tight wrap, his fingertips brushed across a large lump in his pocket. It took Gabe a moment to realize what it was, but then it hit him.

The broken shard from *Beauty Through Rage*.

And with that realization came its significance.

Gabe quickly worked his fingers into his pocket and managed to withdraw the shard with his fingertips. He maneuvered the shard in his hand until its sharpest edge rested against the plastic wrap. Once set, he jostled it back and forth, attempting to saw away at the thick sheets entrapping him.

"We wish only that your blessings be bestowed upon us. That your might protect us and guide us. Amen."

Blake swiveled his head towards Dr. Holtz. "You may proceed, Doctor," he instructed Holtz, then stepped away to join his congregation with their kneels and chants.

Holtz stepped back over to Gabe. "You about ready to begin?" he asked.

"Fuck you, you fucking freak," was Gabe's response. "You look like you sucked too hard on a dick and your cheeks never recovered!"

Just keep him looking up into my face, Gabe thought as he continued to spout vulgarities at the doctor. Anything to keep him from looking down to where the shard was sawing through the plastic sheeting.

"Probably Zellers' dick! You sucked it until –" Gabe made a popping sound with his lips " – it just popped right off." Gabe laughed. "That's got to be it...Zellers *must* be dick-less to have me tied up like this instead of taking me on like a goddamn man!"

Holtz didn't show any of the irritation that Gabe had been hoping to see, but he did keep his attention planted on Gabe's vulgar mouth. Gabe resisted smiling as he felt several of the plastic layers come apart above the shard's tip.

Holtz turned and methodically retrieved the blow torch off of the cart. He hit a switch and the flame roared to life. Gabe's eyes widened as Holtz inched the sizzling flame toward his face, stopping its advance just prior to the point where its intense beam of heat would make contact with his flesh.

Holtz let the flame linger in front of Gabe's face as his held a stone-faced grimace. After what seemed forever, a smile blossomed across Holtz's lips as he leaned down to whisper in Gabe's ear.

"I can't wait to hear you *really* scream."

Pop. More plastic gave way to the shard.

"You first, cocksucker!" The plastic sheet fell away from Gabe's body as his shard-bearing hand flew up at Holtz's throat. The shard easily tore through the soft flesh, releasing a geyser of blood from Holtz's carotid artery. The sticky fluid splashed onto Gabe's face, covering his head in a sickening warmth. Holtz immediately clutched at his wrecked throat and fell away from the table. A small gurgling sound escaped into the room, Holtz unable to force a scream through the blood flowing down his opened throat. Thankfully, the sound wasn't powerful enough to overcome the loud chanting taking place at Peristopheles' feet.

Gabe rolled off the table to land near Becca. He untied her hands, but held her down behind the table as she tried to stand. "Come on...we have to get the fuck out of here!" Gabe prodded quietly. He peered through the legs of the table to see that the Blake and his staff were still oblivious to the recent happenings, lost in their worship.

"Let's go while they have their backs turned." Gabe took Becca's hand and pulled her towards the exit to A Morsel's Journey. They moved quickly, yet carefully, trying to avoid making any noise.

They were successful in not being heard, but it ended up not being enough.

"Hey!" Lester's voice reverberated through the cavernous room. Gabe turned, knowing the voice was directed at him. Lester stood at the rear of the worshippers, pointing in Gabe's direction. The chanting instantly stopped and the rest of the knelt personnel turned to stare at the escaping couple, seemingly dumbfounded at what they were seeing. "They're getting away!" Lester continued. Something about the way he warned the others bothered Gabe, but he didn't have time to dwell on it.

"Run!" Gabe shouted, tugging Becca into action. The tuxedoed mass had sprung from where they were kneeling and the quickest of them had already closed half the distance.

Gabe and Becca sprinted for the door. Gabe was a bit surprised when Becca outpaced him, throwing the door open with him still having several steps to go. He jumped through - feeling slightly emasculated – but their circumstance didn't allow him time to reflect on that. He grabbed Becca on his way through and pulled her after him, the door slamming shut behind her. The light above the door immediately flashed green.

No sooner had the light turned green, the handle twisted from the other side and the light flashed back to red. Gabe reacted, thrusting his arms to capture the handle. He pulled as somebody tried opening the door from the other side.

"Quick! Open the inner door!" Gabe shouted back to her, pulling against the force on the door.

"I can't!" she screamed back. "The door's not opening!"

In his upper-peripheral vision, Gabe saw the light was still red. Gabe pulled with all his might, and was rewarded by the clicking of the latch and the light switching to green...

...then immediately back to red as the knob twisted under his grip and the door again inched away from him. Gabe tightened his grip, trapping the handle as best he could. It was enough to keep the door from opening further, but not enough to close it again.

"Fuck! I missed it!" Becca cried.

Gabe managed to keep himself from shouting, *No fucking shit*! Instead, "Keep twisting the handle!" he instructed, placing his feet against the walls surrounding the door. "We're only gonna get a split second to get that fucking thing open!"

Gabe's forearms were burning, but he kept pulling. He almost had it! The latch was being compressed against the door jamb, but it hadn't quite clicked into its notch yet.

"Come on, baby! Come on," Gabe pleaded with the door. He could feel his grip slipping and knew he wouldn't be able to hold on much longer.

"Come one, you fucker!" Gabe shouted, ignoring the intense pain in his arms to give one last surge of strength. His limb was strained to such an extent, that he never felt the latch click home. He only saw the light flash from red to green and back again.

This time, though, the door stayed still in its cradle.

I've got it!" Becca shouted excitedly. At first, Gabe was unable to release his fingers from their white-knuckle grip on the door handle. He briefly feared he'd need to pry his hands off the knob, when they finally came loose and dropped to his side.

"Well, that fucking sucked," Gabe griped while flexing his fingers to force the blood back into his hands. "I've always heard billionaires were a bit eccentric, but Jesus-Fucking-Christ...."

"I always knew there was something going on with Blake...something dark," Becca muttered. Gabe had the feeling that it was more to herself than to him. Either way, he wasn't going to let that statement hang.

"Something dark? More like a black hole of fuck!"

Becca found herself laughing, despite the terror still coursing through her veins. "You are an auteur of the English language, she teased.

The banging from the other side of the door ceased. Gabe glanced at it wondering what Blake's next move would be.

"Speaking of black hole, it seems that we have a problem," Becca's said.

Gabe saw in the minute glow of the red light that Becca was looking through the inner door. He followed her gaze and quickly discerned her meaning.

"Well, fuck!" he swore. "They turned off the damn blue lights." The cavernous room that was *A Morsel's Journey* was completely black. The previous blue glow of the large body had been shut off at some point during the evening.

"I guess we're going to have to feel our way through," Becca sighed.

"Give me back my cell phone. I'll use the built-in flashlight."

"Umm..." Becca started. Gabe could barely make out the motion of her head shaking from side to side. "I must have lost it back there." She tossed her head back toward the locked door.

Gabe sighed and joined her in shaking his head. "Shouldn't be too hard," Gabe said after a moment. "I'm pretty sure we just need to walk straight through. There were no turns that I can remember."

"Lead the way, then, Mr. Navigator."

"Yes, ma'am," Gabe mocked, taking Becca's hand. They slowly stepped through the doorway, out of the red light's soft glow and into absolute darkness.

Carefully shuffling their feet, hoping to avoid tripping on any forgotten obstructions, they proceeded through the room.

"If memory serves, the first thing we should encounter will be the...Fuck!" Gabe suddenly shouted as his hand disappeared from Becca's grasp.

"Gabe!?" Becca screeched.

"I'm okay," Gabe assured from the darkness. "As I was saying, the first thing we should encounter is the poop chute. I think I just found it. Tripped right over the fucking thing," Gabe laughed, though there was no humor in the sound.

Becca felt Gabe's hand wrap around her ankle, then start travelling up her body as he felt his way back to his feet in the darkness. "I must say, this isn't all bad," Gabe joked as his hand lightly brushed past the hem of her skirt and over the hump of her ass.

"Now's not the time to get fresh," Becca feigned irritation as she tore his hand off her ass and pulled it up to get him back onto his feet.

"Sure thing, Toots!"

"Call me Toots again and all this darkness will sparkle when I plant my boot right in your balls!" Becca warned, though her tone was playful.

"Yes, ma'am."

"Same goes for ma'am," Becca added.

The two of them resumed inching forward through the darkness, carefully ascending the incline until it flattened out.

"We are now officially going the wrong way down a one-way street," Gabe joked, knowing that they had just entered the large figure's rectum.

"Homophobe," Becca teasingly accused.

"I am not," Gabe defended, still inching forward.

A dull thud reached Gabe's ears from somewhere out in the inky blackness. "Shh!" he hissed, stopping in his tracks. "Did you hear that?"

"Hear what?" Becca asked, confused.

"Footsteps," Gabe ominously warned. "At least, I think they were footsteps." Gabe listened intently, trying to recapture the sound.

The darkness remained silent.

"I don't hear anything," Becca informed, now whispering.

"Maybe I'm just trippin'," Gabe conceded. He placed one foot forward and stopped again to listen. Still nothing.

He stepped forward again. Paused. Nothing. Another step, another nothing.

Finally, Gabe continued on as he had before, except this time he kept his mouth shut as they proceeded forward.

Then the sound came again.

"Alright!" Gabe exclaimed. "I know I heard it that time. It was definitely a footstep."

"I heard it too," Becca whispered.

"Who's there?" Gabe shouted into the darkness. "Speak up now if you don't want my fist rammed down your fucking throat!"

Again, silence.

"I *know* I fucking heard footsteps," Gabe reiterated. "There's somebody in here with us."

"Well, I doubt they can see any better than we can right now."

"Yeah...maybe," Gabe cautiously agreed, not sounding entirely convinced. "Do you think we've made it into this asshole's stomach yet?"

"Uhh...that seems about right from what I can remember," Becca answered, surprised at the sudden change in topic.

"I have an idea. I'm going to let go of your hand. Just stay right here for a moment," Gabe instructed.

"Okay..."

Gabe slipped his hand from Becca's and angled out in the darkness. He slowly stepped towards the side of the path, his hands outstretched before him to avoid walking face-first into the walls of hard Plexiglass. After the first couple steps, the lack of contact betraying the openness of his current space, Gabe knew that he was in the right place. A few more steps forward and his hands finally slapped against the walls of the stomach cavern.

Gabe slid his hand down the wall to where he felt was the approximate height of his target and then ran them horizontally along the smooth wall. "Where is it? Where is it?" Gabe muttered as he searched blindly.

The sound came again, much closer this time.

Gabe hurried his search the best he could in the darkness. He was about to give up and switch directions when his hand collided with a protrusion from the wall.

Suddenly, the silence in the air erupted into a frenzy. There was no mistaking the footsteps now. They were heavy, plodding; the hidden figure now running directly towards Gabe. The sudden outburst told Gabe two things. One, that apparently, whoever was stalking them in the darkness, *could* see. Two, the stalker had figured out Gabe's plan and was hurrying to stop him.

Gabe pressed the large plastic button on the wall.

The dark cavern exploded with yellow light, the button having activated the trail of veins running through the large figure's body.

Gabe didn't even have time to properly thank God that the yellow light hadn't been deactivated with the rest of the body's illumination. The flash of light revealed a large figure looming over Gabe, bringing a knife down toward his skull.

Gabe screamed.

The knife-wielding man screamed.

The room went dark.

Gabe had released the button as he had fallen back to avoid the swinging blade. The attacker's scream ended as something crashed against the floor, accompanied by the sound of shattering glass.

Gabe pounced forward and slapped the button down again.

The light once again shot along the narrow pathways built into the figure's body, illuminating the assailant. He was rubbing at his eyes, a strange looking device at his feet.

Gabe recognized the device as a pair of night-vision goggles. His attacker must have been wearing them when Gabe had smashed the button. The light-sensitive device would have been flooded, delivering a searing flare straight into the man's retinas.

Gabe had narrowly avoided the assailant's last attack. He wasn't inclined to risk another. The assailant was still rubbing at his eyes when Gabe slammed his shoulder into the man's sternum with all the force he could muster. Through his shoulder, Gabe felt a rib – maybe even two – crack under the pressure of his blow. The attacker was initially lifted off the floor and then Gabe drove him straight into the floor. A sickening crunch penetrated the air as the back of the man's skull collided with the hard surface.

"That didn't sound good," Becca observed.

"Yeah...something wet splashed my face. I think his head may have split open."

"Do you think you killed him?"

"I don't know," Gabe admitted. "But, to be honest, I don't give too much of a fuck right now if I did. I'm pretty sure he was trying to kill me."

The darkness stood silent for a moment before Becca spoke up again. "Do you think you could activate the light again? Keep it on and I can use the light to run over and open the inner door before the rest of them can come in that way."

It was Gabe's turn to be silent. "I'm surprised that they haven't tried that already. It'd be the first thing I'd think to do and they've had plenty of time," Gabe said. "Are they that stupid?"

"I don't know, but do you want to wait around to find out?"

"No. I suppose not." Gabe found the button and pressed it in again. He quickly found Becca in the illuminated room and their eyes met. She nodded at him and took off in a jog toward the door.

After a short moment, Becca's voice rang through the space. "Got it! They should be locked out!"

Gabe released the button and was plunged back into darkness. He felt his way along the wall until the Plexiglass fell away into the walkway tunnel. He inched his way forward until the path descended at the figure's tongue. Gabe could now see the faint light from the red indicator above the exit. Target in sight, he picked up his pace until he had rejoined Becca at the inner door.

"All's quiet," she informed Gabe as he arrived, pointing at the outer door.

"I don't get it, but whatever," Gabe replied.

Gabe ushered Becca through the inner door, then placed his ear against the outer. Satisfied that she was correct and nobody waited for them on the other side, Gabe reached behind him and closed the inner door. The light immediately flashed to green.

"Time to find out if these assholes are truly as stupid as we think they are," Gabe warned. He gripped the handle to the outer door and turned it. The door crept open, Gabe holding his breath and praying that they were truly alone.

The corridor was empty!

"Thank God!" Gabe breathed. "Those assholes are probably still back in *Suffering For Art*, trying to paw their way through the door. Fucking idiots!"

Becca murmured something that sounded like non-committal agreement.

"Now, let's get the fuck out of here!" Gabe prompted.

They ran down the corridor, aiming for the turn into the southern corridor that would lead them *Monarchy*'s exit. As they neared, Gabe could hear voices coming from around the corner.

Gabe came to a sudden halt, holding out his arm to stop Becca's progress as well.

"Shit!" Gabe swore in a whisper. "They've got somebody posted at the exit."

"It seems they're not completely inept," Becca commented.

"It seems not," Gabe agreed, straining to listen to the voices around the bend. The voices were too far distant to make out what they were saying. "I need to see how many we're dealing with. I can't tell from here."

"What are you going to do?" Becca asked nervously.

"Peek around the corner, maybe?" Gabe shrugged.

"That doesn't sound like a very good idea," Becca argued. "If any of them happen to be looking this direction, we'll be fucked."

"You have a better idea?"

Becca thought silently for a moment. "Maybe." Her eyes lit up. "Wait here!"

Gabe stood shocked when she suddenly turned and sprinted off toward the northern corridor, away from the exit. She kept running until she vanished around the corner. He wanted to shout "What the fuck are you doing?", but that wouldn't have exactly been the best way to *not* attract attention.

Gabe resumed listening to the dim voices around the corner, making sure that they weren't approaching his hidden position. After a moment, he heard the squelch of a handheld radio and then a raised voice coming from the sentries. "An alarm was just tripped in the northern corridor. Let's go!" The clod of sprinting footsteps began approaching Gabe's corner.

Gabe backed away from the wall and swung his head around, frantically looking for a new place to hide. As he was searching, Becca reappeared from around the corner; sweaty, but smiling.

"What the hell did you do?" Gabe wondered.

"I knocked one of Blake's paintings off the northern wall," Becca hurriedly explained, running straight at Gabe. "Now let's move!" She grabbed his shirt and dragged him towards the nearest door. She flung the door open and shoved Gabe through it, before running through herself, carefully shutting the door behind her.

Gabe quickly examined the room they had entered. It was the exhibit that they had skipped earlier due to the long line for entry. The exhibit consisted of a roped off section in the back of the room with a tall mannequin. Nuggets of gold were strung from its ears, suggesting the gold was pouring from the two orifices. On the ground below the mannequin sat a pile of the golden nuggets. Miniature figurines of people were mixed in, some apparently being crushed by the pile, with a leg or an arm sticking out at random. Others had their tiny heads poking up through the top of the pile, their faces twisted in horror, as if they were drowning in the sea of gold.

Gabe remembered the exhibit being titled *Affluenza*.

"Jesus! Is that real gold?" Gabe asked, eyeing the nuggets in the display.

Becca had her ear pasted to the door, but answered, "Probably!" Becca scoffed. "Have you met Blake Zellers?" she asked sarcastically.

Gabe continued staring in awe at the pile of gold. He considered pocketing some, but had a feeling that the massive wealth was probably alarmed. Even a rich fuck like Blake Zellers wouldn't leave a pile of gold lying around without something to keep it guarded.

"Why do I have a feeling that Zellers meant this exhibit as more of an affront to the other ninety-nine percent, as opposed to sympathy for them?" Gabe shared, refraining from snatching up some of the gold.

"Now you're getting it," Becca teased. She kept her ear to the door for a moment, before turning to Gabe and nodding. "Alright, I think they've passed us," Becca informed. "We need to move...now!"

Becca threw the door open and ran out into the corridor. "Hurry!" she quietly prodded. Gabe followed her out into the hall.

At a sprint, they rounded the corner and shot directly for the door. Gabe almost stopped his advance when he saw that the southern corridor held a lingering sentry near the exit. He recognized the lone man as Cliff, the pudgy parking lot attendant. Gabe's instincts kicked in, keeping him from slowing at the unexpected presence of the staff member. He instead pumped his legs to full speed, as if he had the ball and a straight shot to the end zone.

Fortunately, Cliff was looking in the opposite direction as they came bounding around the corner. That bought Gabe an extra couple seconds for his charge, though he knew the loud clomping of their footsteps were sure to give them away long before he arrived at his target. Cliff turned towards the sound of the stampede and stood frozen for a few precious moments, shocked at the sudden appearance of Becca and Gabe. He recovered and fumbled around trying to extract the radio clipped to his belt, but by the time he had his thumb at the call button, Gabe had arrived, slamming into the pudgy man with his shoulder. Despite the man's hefty weight, Cliff was lifted into the air and went down hard.

"Try the door," Gabe instructed Becca. She ran to the door handle and tried turning it, but to no avail.

"It's still locked," she said, her voice devoid of any surprise.

"What's the combo?" Gabe asked the pinned fat man.

"I don't know," Cliff stammered.

Gabe drove his fist into the man's cheek, a little harder than he meant to. A shattered tooth flew from Cliff's mouth. "Tell me the combo now!"

"I swear, I don't know!" Cliff shouted, tears welling up in his eyes.

Pussy! Gabe thought, before again ramming his fist into the pudgy cheeks. "Bullshit!"

"We don't have time for this!" Becca shouted from the door. "It won't take them long to see through our ruse. They'll be coming back."

Gabe knew she was right. He man-handled Cliff off the floor and pushed him toward the eastern corridor, away from where they had been before. He stopped, though, when he heard footsteps approaching from that direction.

"Shit! They're coming back already!" Gabe glanced around for another escape route. The only thing he could find was the door labeled *Maintenance & A/C Room*. Every instinct Gabe had told him that the room would be locked to the public, but barring another choice, he pushed Cliff towards it and tried the handle.

It turned!

So much for instinct, Gabe thought as he pushed Cliff inside the room. Becca immediately followed and slammed the door behind them, twisting the deadbolt above the knob to lock the door.

"Where did Cliff go!?" Gabe heard somebody shout as the sentries arrived back at the exit door. Cliff's eyes widened as he heard the shouting too. His eyes wildly scanned the room and Gabe was fairly sure he was about to scream out for help. Perhaps he would be smarter than that, but Gabe wasn't in the mood for taking chances. He drove his fist into Cliff's mouth, shattering more of the fat man's teeth.

"Find him!" came an order from the other side of the door. Gabe heard the men's footsteps pound off in different directions, now looking for their lost man as well as the escapees.

The handle on the maintenance room's door turned. Gabe held in a deep breath, fist poised to reign more damage to Cliff's face should he recover enough to try something. The door was pushed inward, but held where the deadbolt hit against its notch. The knob spun back to its original position as whoever was on the other side accepted the door was locked and continued on with his search.

Gabe let out the breath that he had been holding.

"That was a close one," Becca whispered.

"Too close," Gabe replied. He looked down at the stunned Cliff and smiled. "Now that we've got a moment though, it's time to get some answers."

Cliff had recovered enough to recognize the threat in Gabe's tone. He looked up into Gabe's smiling face and gulped in terror.

hy the fuck are you all trying to kill me!?" Gabe asked, his fist positioned for another trip to Cliff-town. "Answer me truthfully and perhaps I'll refrain from pulverizing your face into a human smoothie!"

"Mr. Zellers ordered it, not me!" Cliff cried.

"I don't give a fuck who ordered it. I want to know *why* it was ordered."

"I don't know!"

Gabe faced Becca with an eyebrow cocked. "What do you think? Is he lying?"

Becca studied Cliff for a moment, then shrugged. "Probably."

"Agreed," Gabe said, turning back to Cliff and driving another fist into the cowering man's face.

"Stop!" Cliff whined after the blow. "I don't know! I swear to God, I don't know!"

"Which God might that be?"

"Huh?" Cliff was caught off guard by the question.

Gabe shook his fist menacingly above Cliff's reddened face. "Which God? Peristopheles?"

A light sparked in Cliff's eyes as Gabe's words filtered into his brain. "Uhh…yeah. Peristopheles," Cliff shakily confirmed.

"What's the deal with that fucker anyway?"

"Who?"

Either Cliff was a complete idiot, or he was fucking with Gabe. Either way, Gabe delivered another blow into the man's face. This time the knuckle broke skin and left blood trickling down Cliff's cheeks.

"Don't fuck with me, fat man!" Gabe warned. "Peristopheles! What's the deal with Peristopheles?"

"What do you want to know?"

Gabe considered sending his fist into Cliff's temple again – just for good measure – but he held back.

"Who is he? How did Zellers find him? Why the fuck were you all chanting to his ass while I was tied up to a table?" Gabe asked. "You know, the obvious shit a man in my position would probably want to know." Sarcasm - Gabe's specialty. To emphasize, he shook Cliff violently.

"Okay! Okay!" Cliff exclaimed. "I'll tell you. Just don't hit me again."

"Then start talking," Gabe warned, loosening his grip slightly as a show of good faith.

"Peristopheles was known in ancient Babylonia as the Demon God of art, mischief, water, and some other things. Have you heard of the Hanging Gardens of Babylon?"

"Yeah," Gabe confirmed. "One of the Seven Ancient Wonders. What of it?"

"Mr. Zellers once told us that Peristopheles was credited as being associated with the gardens. He said that King Nebuchadnezzar worked with the demon to design something grand for his gift to Queen Amytis on their wedding night."

"Strange," Gabe said, "why have I never heard any of this?"

"Are you a student of ancient history?" Cliff asked, Gabe detecting a little smarminess in his tone. He decided to let it pass without another shot to the face.

"No," Gabe said instead. "But let's say that I occasionally catch a Discovery Channel special."

"Peristopheles is not well known," Cliff explained. "While the Hanging Gardens are known in their context as one of the Seven Ancient Wonders, not much is known about the Gardens themselves. Where they were? What they actually looked like? It shouldn't be surprising that none of this made it onto Mythbusters."

"I'm more of a Shark Week fan myself," Becca joked from behind Gabe.

Gabe flashed Becca a smile and turned back to Cliff, his face reverting back to his *business* scowl. "Fine. Let's say I believe you and that most historians – after devoting years to their studies - have never discovered any of this shit. How in the fuck did Zellers?"

"I don't know for sure," Cliff answered. "Something about an ancient text that he found. And I only know *that* from whispered rumors among the other staff members." Gabe made a show of looking for the lie in Cliff's statement, his fist still hovering threateningly. "That's all I know about that, I swear!" Cliff blurted quickly to avoid another face-smashing.

"Okay," Gabe continued, "now how about that last question? Why were you all worshipping while I was strapped to a table with Doctor Fuck-nuts trying to kill me?"

"I can't answer that," Cliff replied, looking determined with his answer.

"Oh? You can't, huh?" Gabe wound his fist back for another strike. A hush from Becca was the only thing that stopped Cliff from eating another knuckle sandwich.

Gabe turned around to see Becca's ear hugging the door. All was silent for a moment, then Becca looked towards Gabe. "I heard some voices, but they're gone now," she explained quietly.

Gabe nodded at her and turned back to Cliff...

...just as the white-clad staffer swung a blur of metal at Gabe's head. Gabe flinched back far enough to avoid a more-devastating blow, but the edge of the metallic object still clipped his temple, sending stars flooding into Gabe's vision.

Gabe fell off of the pinned man, who used the opportunity to scurry out from underneath. All Gabe saw was a white blur sprinting towards the exit. That same white blur tumbled to the ground before reaching the door.

Becca had tripped Cliff, delaying his escape. *Way to go!* Gabe silently cheered.

Gabe reached out and scooped up the metal object that had nicked his skull and saw that it was a large wrench. Cliff must have grabbed it from somewhere nearby while Gabe had his back turned.

The fat man recovered from his fall and made another attempt at the door. Gabe shook his head to clear out some of the stars from his vision, and pounced forward.

Gabe managed to get the wrench's handle around Cliff's throat just as the man reached the door. He jerked back on it, cutting off Cliff's momentum and sending him tumbling towards a cluster of pipes that ran up the side of the maintenance room. The hurried reaction, coupled with the wooziness still plaguing his vision, hadn't allowed Gabe to steady himself as he used his weight to pull Cliff backward, causing Gabe to fall to the ground in the opposite direction.

From his limited vantage point on the floor, Gabe couldn't see Cliff as the robust man crashed into the vertical pipes. He did hear it, though. A sound like an egg cracking, followed by something wet dripping down to the floor.

"Oh fuck!" Becca gasped.

Gabe groggily picked himself up from the floor, looking to see what had transpired. He found Cliff sitting against one of the pipes, his rotund ass suspended inches above the floor while his legs flopped against the tile like they were a pair of dying fish.

It took a moment for Gabe to notice the circular edge of a valve wheel sticking out from behind Cliff's head. A glance at a similar valve on a nearby pipe and Gabe had the sickening realization of what had just happened.

"He...he fell backwards...right onto the valve shaft," a stunned Becca confirmed for him. "It went right through his skull."

Gabe studied the nearby valve and could easily imagine the threaded shaft impaling the thin layer of bone that was the human skull.

"Well...fuck..." Gabe breathed, shocked by the recent turn of events. "I didn't mean to kill the fat fuck."

"I imagine this isn't going to help our cause any, if they end up catching us," Becca commented.

"No..." Gabe agreed. "Probably not." He swiveled his head, searching the confined space. "Which is why we should try not to get caught."

"Thanks, Captain Obvious," Becca replied, complete with a rolling of the eyes.

"Well, I'll be flabber-fucked!" Gabe suddenly exclaimed.

"Huh?" Becca asked, seeing that Gabe's eyes had lit up.

"I think I found us a way out of here," he explained.

Becca followed Gabe's gaze to a ventilation shaft that extended down from the ceiling. The shaft's outlet joined with the main vent passage running horizontally along the roof. "Through there?" she tepidly asked.

"Hell yeah! Why not?" Gabe shrugged. "This looks like it runs along the wall between *Monarchy* and *Free Market*. We can crawl through the vent shafts until it branches off over *Free Market* and then use it to get the fuck out of this place."

"Umm...I guess so."

"What?" Gabe asked, seeing Becca's reluctance. "You claustrophobic?"

"No!" Becca snapped. "Maybe a little," she begrudgingly admitted after a moment.

"Ouch!" Gabe teased. "Sore subject?"

"No...not really," Becca said. "I just don't like feeling trapped."

"Well, it's the perfect place to *vent* your frustrations," Gabe joked with his cheesiest smile on his face.

"Weak!" Becca mocked with a laugh.

Gabe removed the grate from the vent shaft and carefully set it against a nearby wall. "Ladies first." He waved for Becca to enter the open shaft.

"Yeah...I don't think so, buddy. You'll go first so I know that you're not using this as an excuse to look up my skirt." Becca was joking, but she still looked reluctant to commit to their prospective journey.

"As you wish, m'lady." Gabe faked a bow and then crawled into the open ventilation shaft.

He heard Becca mutter something profane behind him as he squeezed his way up to the main ducts of *Monarchy*'s ventilation system.

18

"Now I know what a Bruce Willis feels like," Gabe joked as he squirmed through the tight ventilation shaft. So far they hadn't had any luck with the ventilation branching off in their desired direction, but there was still quite a bit of tubing ahead of them.

"What's that supposed to mean?" Becca asked from behind his feet.

"You haven't seen *Die Hard*?"

"No," Becca admitted.

"Damn! I guess the Cliché Spouter's of America are right when they say that nobody is perfect," Gabe teased.

"Ha-ha, asshole," Becca replied. "Just for that, I'll make sure to drop you off at home with your consolation prize when we get out of here."

"What's the consolation prize?" Gabe asked.

"A jar of Vaseline. You just lost out on the grand prize for the evening."

"It's a good thing the game isn't over yet. I've still got the lightning round to win you back," Gabe teased.

"We'll see about that. The lightning round is notorious for being the toughest round of the game," Becca quipped in her sultry, playful tone.

"Thankfully, I'm the Ken Jennings of pussy," Gabe said, the progress through the cramped tube slower than he'd like.

Becca briefly laughed before quietly continuing their crawl. "How much further does this damn thing go on?" she eventually asked, breaking up the silence.

"I can see the turn not too far ahead. That should hopefully be our ticket out of here."

"I hope so," Becca griped. "I think I'm starting to cramp up in some pretty strange places."

Gabe tried his best not to imagine where those places may be. He failed.

"I can hear you smiling up there," Becca accused.

"Nope. Just crawling along. Minding my own business." Gabe couldn't hold back the playful tone in his voice.

It took another minute or two – time did funny things when you were squished into a metal cylinder – before they reached the end of their current ventilation wing.

"You've got to be fucking kidding me!" Gabe swore, looking in the direction that should have taken them over *Free Market*.

"What?" Becca asked concernedly.

"The fucking shaft only runs about two feet and ends at the damn wall. There's another grate here, but that's it."

"It doesn't lead into *Free Market*?"

"No!" Gabe admitted, placing his forehead down on the cool aluminum of the shaft. A gesture of defeat. "That sadistic motherfucker has *Monarchy* completely sealed off."

"What now?" Becca asked.

Gabe considered their options and found they didn't really have any. "I don't know, but being squeezed in like a sardine isn't going to help my train of thought any. Let's go back to the maintenance room and figure out another plan."

"If you say so," Becca sighed.

"Come on. We can at least use this bullshit intersection to turn ourselves around. Beats crawling backward the whole way." Gabe crawled forward into the dead-ended section of the shaft and backed his way past the intersection, allowing Becca to pass. Maneuver complete, the two crawled back towards the maintenance room, this time Becca leading the way.

"So, just to be clear," Becca spoke while crawling, "the plan is to go back to the maintenance room so that way we can make a plan?"

"Yeah," Gabe huffed, "that's the plan. Not exactly Patton-level, I admit."

"Yep," Becca mocked, "I do believe we are royally fucked."

It took a few more moments, but they finally arrived at the vertical shaft that led back into the maintenance room. Becca crawled over the opening, and then backed herself down, feet first, into the vertical shaft. Gabe copied her move and followed her down in the same manner.

When Gabe finally emerged from the cramped tube, he found Becca staring off towards the front of the room, her jaw hanging low.

"What is it?" Gabe asked, following her gaze.

He found that she was staring at the wheel valve that had impaled Cliff's skull. It was as they had left it – blood and brain matter still dripping to the floor – but with one notable exception.

"Where the fuck is the body?" Gabe asked in shock.

Cliff's corpse was no longer there.

19

"Remember how, a moment ago, you said we were royally fucked?" Gabe asked Becca.

"Yeah."

"I think that you may have been understating the level of shit we're in," Gabe said in a matter-of-fact tone.

He was staring at the dripping wheel-valve, now devoid of one fat man. He had already scanned the room and found no sign of the missing body. "We need to get out of here," Gabe said after a moment, heading back towards the vent.

"You think they know we're here?"

"Well, that fat fuck didn't walk out of here by himself," Gabe pointed out. "They may not know we're in here now, but they knew we were. I'm sure they'll be coming back."

Gabe stuck his head back into the vent, readying to climb his way up into the main shaft. That's when the knock came.

Knock knock

Gabe brought his head back out of the vent and stared slack-jawed at the door. "What the fuck?" he asked.

Knock knock

A voice followed through the door.

"Mr. Daniels? Ms. Larson? I know you're in there."

Gabe froze deathly still at the sound of the voice. Not because the voice meant that they had been discovered. No...

...because of the voice itself.

"No fucking way..." Gabe whispered to Becca. Seeing the shock in her eyes, he knew he wasn't the only one who had recognized Cliff's voice.

"No need to worry. I'm alone out here."

"Do you think he's telling the truth?" Becca asked nervously.

"Who gives a fuck?" Gabe shot back. "I'm not answering the door to find out."

"Come on, Mr. Daniels...aren't you curious to know how I'm still alive?"

"Not really, motherfucker!" Gabe shouted through the door.

Then, the doorknob turned. Gabe cursed himself for not checking the damned lock after he discovered the body missing.

The door creaked open. Gabe snatched up the same large wrench that he had used to assault Cliff earlier. He wielded it, ready to smash its bulk into anybody that walked in through the door.

Instead of the army of white tuxedos that Gabe expected, it was only Cliff that appeared through the open doorway. He stuck his head into the room and looked down at the inner knob.

"I apologize, Mr. Daniels," he said. "It appears that I forgot to lock the door on my way out." Cliff looked up into Gabe's eyes and smiled at his own little joke.

Gabe was considering swinging the wrench into the man's smarmy face- if for no other reason than payback for the lame joke - when Cliff stepped fully into the room, taking care to close the door behind him. It was impossible not to notice the lack of a large, gaping hole in the back of Cliff's head as his back was turned while shutting the door.

"How the fuck *are* you still alive?" Gabe asked in awe, despite his denial only moments prior. The large red stain down the back of Cliff's white tuxedo let Gabe know that he hadn't imagined the whole thing, leaving no doubt that the fat man should have been dead.

"Funny you should ask," Cliff said, turning back to face Gabe. "Unfortunately it's a question that cannot be answered."

"Why not?"

"Because the question is unanswerable," Cliff answered in a chummy tone.

"What the fuck are you talking about?" Gabe demanded, losing patience

"It's unanswerable, because I am not."

"Not what?" Gabe asked. The hairs on the back of his neck rose, despite feeling like he had suddenly been transported to some sort of bad British comedy.

"Not alive, of course."

Gabe let that hang in the air for a moment as his brain tried to process the words.

"Bullshit! You..." Gabe stopped midsentence as Cliff reached up and touched his ear. That's when Gabe finally noticed the earpiece Cliff was wearing.

"Yes, Mr. Zellers. Understood."

Two-way communications. It was more than likely that Blake Zellers had heard their entire conversation, also meaning that he knew exactly where they were at.

"We need to go, Becca," Gabe warned. Then, shaking the wrench at Cliff, "If you come after us, I'll bust in your fucking skull." Gabe considered his warning. "Again," he added.

Cliff laughed. "Don't leave just yet. Mr. Zellers has just given us all permission to come out and play."

"Huh?" Gabe asked, increasingly confused by everything that had been came from Cliff's mouth since he had stepped into the room.

Cliff didn't answer. At least not verbally.

He only laughed as a loud sound came from Cliff's crotch area – a ripping sound that reminded Gabe of tearing apart a wet towel. A deluge of crimson followed, completely engulfing the stark white landscape of Cliff's trousers.

"Jesus Fuck!" Gabe gasped as Cliff's hips came apart under the red stain. Something heavy slapped wetly into the tuxedo's crotch, causing it to bulge.

Cliff's legs wobbled, having become useless to hold his weight. The legs slipped off to either side, leaving Cliff to do the splits. The wet crotch of his tuxedo split under Cliff's weight, freeing the large mass that had slapped across the fabric. A mass of coiled intestines emerged through the tear, gravity grabbing hold and unwinding them, until they became a tangled mess on the floor.

Through all this, Cliff continued laughing.

Gabe barely acted in time to clench his cheeks and keep from shitting himself.

Gabe immediately recognized Cliff's new form from *The Saw*; Cliff's scene from *Suffering For Art*. There were no gallows or actual saw, but Gabe would be damned if it wasn't an accurate representation of Cliff's destroyed body in the display.

Gabe stood frozen in horror as Cliff started using his arms to crawl forward, heading directly for Gabe. A heavy smear of blood, along with several lengths of trailing intestine, was left in Cliff's wake as he propelled himself forward.

Becca snapped Gabe out of his stupor. "Come on! We have to go!" she screamed, tugging Gabe's arm towards the vertical vent shaft. Becca entered first, apparently no longer concerned about Gabe looking up her skirt.

Gabe quickly followed, getting himself into the vent just as Cliff neared enough to take a swipe at him with his meaty arms. The grotesque abomination's fingers brushed Gabe's ankle, but Gabe instinctively kicked the hand away and quickly ascended the vent.

"Enjoy your journey, Mr. Daniels," Gabe heard Cliff's voice follow him up the metal tube. "I'd come after you, but my current physical disposition renders that impossible, I'm afraid."

Gabe resisted the urge to yell a particularly colorful string of obscenities in response. He looked forward to see Becca making haste down the tube and started off after her.

Somehow, the tight confines of the ventilation had grown to seem even more suffocating.

INTERLUDE 4

"Dr. Holtz," Blake laughed, "I'll admit, when I first laid eyes on that book in my father's vault, I didn't really believe what I was reading. But now, you can most definitely consider me a believer."

Holtz hadn't been too happy with Blake Zellers after he had awoken from the "surgery". Reporting the psychotic, spoiled brat to the police would have been the doctor's first move. Failing that, Jarvis Holtz wouldn't have minded one bit turning the tables on Blake and providing him a little surgery of his own. Bitching, griping, refusing his compliance, would have been other acceptable – if considerably inferior - outlets for his anger and exasperation.

Of course, none of that was possible any longer. Even those final, inferior options were no longer available to Dr. Holtz, as evidenced by his current endeavor.

One fleshy sack sailed through the air, followed closely by a second. Next, both sailed upward at the same time. Their trajectories crossed, each spongy blob landing in the opposite hand that Jarvis Holtz had used to launch them. It wasn't exactly the first time that Dr. Holtz had attempted juggling – he never had shown any proficiency with the skill. He was reasonably certain, however, that it was the first time *anyone* – even the behemoths of the sport, if there was such a thing - had attempted juggling their own two lungs.

Blake watched the event in giddy amazement. "That is amazing!"

"If you say so, sir," Holtz answered, continuing to toss his lungs back and forth through the air.

"And I still don't understand how you can talk without any lungs." Blake said, scrawling notes on a legal pad sitting on his lap. "Fascinating."

It had been almost a full week since Blake had conducted his experiment with Dr. Holtz, and he was still learning something new every day. It undoubtedly would cause the rising stars of the medical and scientific research communities to drool all over themselves, if given the opportunity to study. Of course, *that* was never going to happen.

"Alright, Doctor, you can go ahead and put those things away now," Blake allowed. Holtz complied, stuffing the left lung back into the corresponding bloody gash in his chest, followed by the right. With the lungs back in their rightful place, the two gaping holes magically repaired themselves, leaving only a normal human chest in their wake. It looked as if the doctor's flesh had never been pierced at all.

"I'm going to enter these notes onto my laptop," Blake informed. "In the meantime, I could sure use a sandwich. You mind, Doctor?"

"Of course not, sir," Holtz huffed. He *did* mind, but knew he had no choice in the matter. His feet carried him into the kitchen of their own accord, with no concern at all for what his brain preferred them to do.

"And make sure to wash your hands first!" Blake called out after him.

Blake began transcribing his notes via his keyboard when a knock rang out from the front door of the house.

"What the hell?" Blake asked the empty room as he rose to answer the knocking.

Swinging the door inward revealed a pimple-faced teen holding up a familiar red-padded bag. "A large pepperoni, bacon, and olive and a two-liter of Mountain Dew. With tax, that'll be $16.87," the kid informed, looking disinterested.

"Huh? I didn't order a pizza," Blake rebutted.

The kid lifted the receipt and read the address aloud. "1681 Belmont Street?"

"Not quite." Blake replied. "This is 1618 Belmont."

The kid rolled his eyes to the side, reading the numbers nailed into the blue-painted wood near the front door. His annoyed façade quickly morphed into red-cheeked embarrassment as his error was revealed.

Barring the numbers, it was easy to mistake one house for another in this part of town. They were all similar, two-story complexes. Sure, it may be somewhat ostentatious for a college kid's dwelling, but being a billionaire's son, Blake wasn't about to be squeezed into a tiny dorm room, void of privacy.

"I apologize, sir. It seems that I have made a mistake."

Blake nearly slammed the door in the kid's face, but stopped himself when an idea popped into his head. "No need for an apology," he said instead. "In fact, why don't you come on inside?"

The kid looked unsure. "I can't, sir. I've got to get this to the right address."

"Nonsense," Blake said. "Pepperoni, bacon, and olive, you said?"

The kid nodded, a nervous glint in his eye. There was no reason — at least no *apparent* reason — that the kid should be nervous. Blake assumed the kid wasn't adept at dealing with fluid situations.

"That *does* sound good. My mind has changed, I will take the pizza after all."

"But...somebody else is waiting for it," the kid stammered. "Once again, I apologize for my mistake. Have a good day, sir." The kid turned from the door and started his retreat toward the company's delivery car.

Blake began to wonder if maybe the kid had a sixth sense.

"Wait!" Blake called out after him. "I'll tip you an extra five hundred dollars if you let me keep it."

Whatever the kid's holdup was, the lofty sum caused him to reconsider. The kid stopped his retreat and turned back towards Blake. "Five hundred bucks?" he asked, not believing what he had just heard.

"Yeah, I'm an impatient sort, and pizza delivery takes forever to deliver around here" Blake offered as explanation.

"Actually, we have a thirty minute delivery policy or your pizza is..."

"You want the five hundred bucks or not?" Blake asked, cutting the kid off.

Blake watched the internal struggle within the kid as he considered the offer. As Blake knew was usually the case, the money won.

"If you insist," the kid relented.

"I just have to get the cash out of my wallet," Blake explained. "Come on in and wait here. I'll be right back with the cash." Blake stepped to the side and waved the kid through the open door. Once through, Blake closed the door and left the kid waiting as he disappeared into the kitchen.

"Who was at the door?" Holtz asked from the kitchen's island where he was using a large knife to cut into a freshly-made sandwich.

"You in the mood for some pizza?" Blake asked.

"It's been a week since you killed me. Have you seen me eat anything at all during that time?"

"No," Blake admitted. It was something that hadn't even crossed his mind.

"I have no appetite," Holtz related. "I'm not even sure if I *can* eat."

Blake mulled it over. "Well, let's find out, Doctor." He reassuringly grabbed Holtz's shoulder. "Make sure to bring the knife." Blake added with a menacing smile.

They walked together into the entry foyer where the kid was waiting with the pizza and two-liter.

"You got the cash?" the kid asked. He still looked nervous, but the promise of money was the ultimate soother for such things.

"My colleague brought up a good point just now," Blake said. "I've never partaken from your particular chain before. Would you not agree that I should sample the product before I shell out such a large amount of money?"

"What? No. That wasn't the agreement," the kid anxiously argued.

"Dr. Holtz, would you please cut me off a slice?" Blake's ominous smile burned into the kid's retinas.

Holtz stepped forward, knife in hand.

The kid flinched backwards against the door. The fear in his eyes made it obvious that the money had quickly been forgotten. The pizza fell to the floor as his hands flailed behind him, hysterically trying to turn the doorknob for his escape.

The unfortunate kid realized too late that the door was locked. Holtz was already on him.

The doctor wrestled the kid to the floor and covered his mouth with one hand, using his other slice into the kid's flesh with the blade. The kid's muffled screams could be heard from through Holtz's hand, but there was no danger of anybody outside the house hearing them.

The knife easily sliced through the kid's skin until Holtz had clipped off a triangular chunk of flesh, roughly the size of a pizza slice. Holtz held it up for Blake to see.

"Very nice, Doctor. Is it worth the money?"

Holtz grimaced against the idea, but was helpless to keep his hand from bringing the slice of flesh up to his lips where his teeth proceeded to gnaw off a bite. After he swallowed, Holtz answered, "I believe you'd approve, sir."

Blake gave a quick chuckle, then approached the still-struggling - and now crying - kid. He pulled the promised amount of money from his wallet and unceremoniously let it fall onto the pizza boy.

Blake smiled inquisitively at Holtz. "How many slices are generally in a pizza?"

"Eight, sir."

"Good. Make sure I get my money's worth." With that, Blake left the two of them alone to go after the sandwich awaiting him in the kitchen.

He never had cared much for pizza.

hat the fuck was that!?" Gabe felt himself losing control after what had just transpired with Cliff. "Did they fucking drug us or something!?"

"I don't think that's the case," Becca tried, calmly.

"What then? A dead man was just up and walking about? Holding a fucking conversation? Hell, even mocking me!? Does that make more sense to you?" Gabe was incredulous.

"No!" Becca retorted. "At least, I think not. I don't know" she finally admitted with a shrug. She was clearly flustered as well.

"The answer is *no*! A big, fat fucking *no*!" Gabe argued. "Shit like that doesn't happen. Period!"

"Calm down," Becca soothed.

"Calm down? *Calm down*!? Fuck your calm..." Gabe's rant was silenced when Becca kicked her boot out behind her, smashing its heel into Gabe's cheek.

Gabe, stunned into silence, shook his head to clear his suddenly woozy vision. As it cleared, his erratic breathing steadied. His heartbeats slowed to a manageable rate.

"You kicked me in the face!" Gabe whined after he was back in control.

"I did," Becca concurred. "Are you calm yet?

Gabe considered it. "You know, when we get a down moment, you're gonna have to kiss that better, right?"

"And...he's back." Becca rolled her eyes and resumed her forward crawl. "Come on, Don Juan, we got to keep moving."

"Where are we moving to? We already know we can't get out this way."

"You never know what we might come across," she informed. "If nothing else, maybe we can find some other place to hide out in."

"Sounds like a plan, minus one key detail that you left out."

"What's that?" Becca asked.

"We're not exactly traipsing through the Amazon here," Gabe chided. "Even with this group's *fuck*tarded search skills, they're bound to find us sooner or later in this limited of a space. We can't hide forever."

"Maybe we won't have to?" Becca theorized. "The Arte Blanche is now officially open. Blake *has* to open Monarchy tomorrow."

"He doesn't *have* to do anything. You ever heard of 'Closed for Maintenance'?"

"Blake would lose face if he couldn't open the biggest part of his gallery the day after the grand opening. If there's one thing Blake loves, it's his face. Both of them; the metaphorical one and the one his mother gave him."

"Zellers has a mother? For some reason, I just kind of assumed he came dripping straight out of the ball sack."

"Colorful," Becca said after a moment. Then, "I'm sure Blake has – or, at least, *had* - a mother, but he never speaks about her. I've just assumed that she died sometime in the past. If she is still alive somewhere, I'm sure she ran as soon as she saw what a prick her son was growing up to be."

"I can see why you two broke up," Gabe joked as Becca reached the turn at the end of the corridor.

"Ha!" Becca replied, starting down the next corridor. "If I would've known about the real shit he was into, I would have stabbed him in the fucking heart before I left."

"Perhaps you'll still get that chance." Gabe shrugged. Not an easy thing to do with his broad shoulders in such a cramped space.

They crawled on in silence for a long while. They crossed into the eastern run of tubing. Their path took them over the many exhibits set into this wing until they finally hit the crossover with the northern corridor. The only other branches of ventilation tubing they had come across led inwards, most likely towards the gallery's central exhibits, including *Suffering For Art*. No promise of any exits, unless you counted one of the numerous grates to the below exhibits that they had simply crawled past.

After the turn, Gabe broke the contemplative silence. "I suppose it'd be too much to hope for a way out at this point."

"Who knows...?" Becca answered. "We should be running along the back part of the building right now. If there is a an outdoor intake built in anywhere, it'll most likely be along here."

"Yeah...if that happens, I'm immediately taking that luck with me to Vegas."

"Shh!" Becca suddenly burst out.

"What?" Gabe whispered.

"Did you hear that?"

"Hear what?"

"I'm not sure," Becca replied. "I thought I heard something at the cross-vent up here."

Gabe tried looking past Becca to see what cross-vent she was talking about. It was no use; he couldn't make out anything beyond her frame. Her lack of excitement told him that it was most likely another inward travelling branch of the ventilation system.

"Did Blake finally pull his head out of his ass and have his goons follow us up here?"

"I don't think so," Becca related. "It didn't sound like a person. It sounded small and scrabbly...perhaps a mouse."

"Thank God," Gabe whispered. "It wouldn't exactly be easy to fight these fuckers off up here."

"Shh!" Becca hissed. "I just heard it again."

Gabe thought he had heard something this time as well, only his ears registered it from the wrong direction. "Are you sure it's coming from up ahead? I thought I just heard something behind us."

"No, it definitely came from around the corner of the cross-section just ahead."

"I'm pretty sure there's another one behind us then," Gabe informed. "Maybe you were right about it being mice – or perhaps even rats. This place is newer than the my last shit and it's already infested with vermin? If nothing else, maybe we can get Zellers on a health code violation when we get out of here."

Another sound suddenly came at them from inside the aluminum tubing. This one was unmistakable; loud and rumbly, like a rolling thunder.

"What the fuck?" Gabe swore. "Wait a fucking minute! That sounds like..."

Gabe was cut off when a continuous blast of freezing air careened over him like an invisible freight train.

"They turned the air conditioner on!" Becca needlessly confirmed, yelling to be heard over the roar of the rushing air.

"Fucking Zellers!" Gabe cursed. "A/C is busted, my ass!" He was already shivering. "Jesus fuck, that shit's cold!"

"Uh, Gabe?" Becca said, her voice sounding fearful. "I think they found us." She suddenly screamed and barreled backward into Gabe. "Back up! Back up!" she yelled as her feet hurriedly pummeled Gabe backward through the tubing.

"What the fuck is going on?" Gabe yelled over the thunder of the freezing wind. He had started backing up on his own, trying to avoid Becca's boot heels as she madly scrambled.

Becca suddenly stopped her retreat, screaming, "Oh my God, Gabe! It's…" then Becca's warning was drowned out by her shrilly shrieking. Gabe could see her thrashing as she attempted to fight someone off in the enclosed space. He couldn't make anything out past the point where her body stuffed up the tube and only got glimpses of some fingers twisting in her hair.

"Let go of her!" Gabe shouted, starting to crawl forward to help in any way he could. He wasn't sure how, but instinct didn't often allow time for reflection.

He didn't get far in his attempt before something seized his ankle. "Fuck!" Gabe screamed, frantically flailing his legs to knock away whatever had grabbed him.

His foot only extended into open space, not connecting with anything. He kicked out again, with the same result. Gabe kicked a third time, now feeling fingers as they crawled up past his ankle. He couldn't twist enough to positively identify who was grabbing him, but what little he could see made it seem like nobody was there at all. Gabe briefly wondered if maybe Zellers had ghosts in his entourage, in addition to whatever Cliff was.

He continued swinging his foot, aiming for where he was sure his attacker's head should have been. When his foot refused to make contact with anything other than empty space, Gabe switched up tactics. He ground his foot into his leg where the fingers were crawling along his calf. Definitely not a ghost, Gabe thought when his foot landed on flesh other than his own. He dug his heel against the soft flesh, causing the hand to loosen its grip. Instead of jerking away from Gabe, as pain would cause most people to do in such a situation, the hand tightened its grip and crawled further along his leg.

Gabe again kicked his leg out towards what should have been somebody's head. Still nothing.

What the fuck! That damn hand is almost to my crotch! Somebody has to be there!

Gabe kicked again and again, swinging his foot in all directions. All to no avail as the hand reached his back and continued crawling upward. Gabe shimmied an arm between his body and the aluminum tube, stretching it around his back as far as he could. Barely having enough room to maneuver his arm into position, Gabe had to wonder how the fuck this guy was squeezing his entire body between Gabe and the aluminum walls of the shaft. The hand being near his shoulders now, Gabe's attacker had to either have the longest arms ever created, or the ability to flatten his body out like a damned ferret.

Gabe felt around until his fingers finally brushed against those of the hand on his back. He seized the fingers, twisted them in his own, and pulled. At first, he was surprised by how easily the hand slid forward, as if there were no resistance at all on the other side of it. Once it was in view, he quickly understood the horrifying truth.

The hand that was attacking him was just that: a hand! In all actuality, it was a whole arm, but close e-fucking-nough. The arm ended in a ragged, bloody stump at the curve of the shoulder. Nobody attached to the other end.

Despite that, the limb kept attacking. No sooner was the severed arm freed from its pinned position between Gabe's bulk and the flat aluminum, it began trying to claw the eyes straight out of Gabe's skull.

Gabe held tightly to the damned thing's wrist as it fought towards him. The arm's length beyond the wrist wriggled like a fish for a moment. Eventually, it seemed to get its bearings and buried its stump against the flat aluminum for leverage. The arm's muscles flexed and the whole fucking thing pushed its way toward Gabe. He fought against it the best he could. Fortunately for Gabe, the arm was wily, but not especially strong.

A Gabe struggled to keep the arm at bay, he heard a loud clanging come from past Becca's bulk. She was smashing something against the walls of their aluminum cage. "I've got it," she shouted back to him. "At least for the moment." Her breathing was rapid as she struggled against her own assailant. "What the fuck is this thing?'

"Is it a body missing an arm?" Gabe asked.

"No!" he heard called back. "Um…just the arm actually." She said it like it was the silliest thing somebody could say. Normally, she'd be right, but there was nothing silly about their current situation.

"In that case, I believe I've got its match back here," Gabe yelled back to her.

"We need to get out of here…now!" Becca shouted, after a brief pause. "We just passed over a vent a little ways back. It should be near you somewhere."

Careful to maintain his grip on the rogue arm, Gabe slowly backed his way through the tunnel. Almost immediately he felt the grate ripple across his knee. "Found it," he informed.

"What!?" Becca shouted.

"I said I found the vent!" Gabe repeated louder, in order to be heard over the roaring of the rushing air.

144

He continued backing over the grate, when he heard a loud sound like twigs snapping. It came from the wayward arm he carried. When Gabe looked up, he found the hand's fingers were twisted at an unnatural angle, the bones broken loose within their fleshy skin sack.

"What the hell happened?" Gabe asked aloud. He didn't have to wait long for the answer.

The loose hanging fingers bunched up and, like four miniature snakes, struck at his hand. The fingernails acted as fangs and pierced through his skin. Gabe yelped as the fingers started twisting, trying to burrow their way deeper into his flesh.

Gabe wailed at the pain, but managed to keep his grip tight. He fought through the agony to smash the arm against the vent grate. His frantic mind hadn't consciously been trying to knock the grate out of its housing – just jar loose the attacking fingers digging their way into him – but that's what happened. The grate broke loose and vanished into the void below.

Seeing an opportunity, Gabe thrust his assailed arm out into the open air of the room below. He used the newly-available space to lower his other arm down to aid the afflicted one. Gabe pried the wormy fingers out one by one as they kept attempting to wriggle their way in deeper. After successfully extracting the last of the fingers, Gabe tossed the arm out into the room.

"Jesus Christ!" Gabe huffed as the arm flew away. He turned his attention back to Becca. "Becca, back up towards me. I've gotten the vent open. And watch out for that fucking thing trying to turn your arm into a finger spa."

"I'm pretty sure it already trying that. It broke its own damn fingers to come after me. I've got them held pretty steady with my other hand, though. They can't get to me."

Gabe shook his head. "Why didn't I think of that?"

Becca began backing up. Gabe moved back as well, allowing Becca room to reverse. "When you reach the vent, back over it and drop that fucking thing down into the room below," Gabe instructed.

Becca complied.

"Okay. Now c-crawl forward again until you can drop your legs through the opening. It's a bit of a d-drop, so you don't want to go head first." Gabe heard his voice beginning to stutter. Now that the immediate threat was over, the intense cold of the frozen air was starting to catch up to him.

"Okay," Becca nodded. She moved forward over the vent until her legs dangled freely.

"I'm g-going to help lower you down," Gabe said as he put his hands around her waist.

"We're not g-going down into the same room with those arms, are w-we?."

"W-we don't have a c-choice. We n-need to get out of these v-vents now, before we f-freeze to death," Gabe explained. His lips were already growing numb.

"F-fine," Becca reluctantly agreed. "just w-watch your hands, buddy," she warned through chattering teeth. "Don't be g-getting fr-fresh with me." Gabe could feel her shivering through his arms as he wrapped them around her lithe form.

"I'll t-try my best. No p-promises for later though."

Becca dropped slowly through the vent. Gabe guided her down – ready to grab her if she fell. She lowered herself until she hung at the end of her arms, gripping the edge of the vent grate's housing. After glancing down to judge the distance to the floor, she released her grip and disappeared.

"Everything okay?" Gabe hollered through the hole.

"Yep," came Becca's reply.

Gabe stuck his legs through the opening to follow her down and lowered himself through the hole. With half his body dangling free, he heard a dark laughter coming from behind him, down the shaft. The kind of laughter that chilled one's soul.

Gabe was balanced on his elbows, which he used to turn himself toward the source of the laughter. The sight of the *thing* laughing was worse than the laughter itself. It was a man's torso lying into the vent. No arms, no legs – at least, no *attached* legs. Gabe could barely make out two legs behind the torso, both ending in torn stumps where they should have been connected to the rest of the body. Polished shoes capped the other end of the legs, planted against the vents corners where the sides of the shaft rose from the bottom panel. The legs' inner thighs ran perpendicular to the torso's ass, slowly pushing against it to scoot the torso forward through the tubing.

There was also a head in Gabe's view – also separated from the torso, only a bloody stump where its neck should have been. The decapitated head was plunked down in front of the torso's mass. It was easy to understand that the chilling laughter had originated from this head, as the head was still chuckling . It was smiling; a smile which Gabe instantly recognized, even under the blood dribbling from its lips.

"Lurch?"

"Good to see you again, Mr. Daniels," the deep, scraggly voice greeted.

Gabe's planted elbows were shaky and weak. And *not* from the freezing air.

Gabe's eyes were glued to the Lurch as his legs continued scooting the rest of him forward. He barely had time to gasp before his shaking arms finally gave out, sending Gabe plunging through the hole, and into the deep recesses of the room below.

Gabe landed on his feet, his knees bending to absorb the impact. He immediately rebounded to a standing position, with his head cocked upwards toward the approaching abomination in the vents.

"Gabe, duck!" Becca shouted.

He twisted to look at her, and, once his brain caught up to Becca's warning, Gabe hurriedly dropped back down into a crouching position. A loud clanging rung out as two swords connected where Gabe's head had just been.

Becca leaned forward and grabbed hold of Gabe's shoulders, then forcefully pulled him over the velvet barrier as the same two swords found their way down to where he had been crouched.

"What the fuck?" Gabe squawked, picking himself up off the floor. Beyond the velvet barrier, he saw two armored knights performing a choreographed sword fight. One's armor was black, the other's white. The white knight had a facsimile of a loosely-clothed maiden hanging onto his side, her lips twisted into a grimace of worry and she watched the battle rage on before her.

"They're animatronic," Becca explained, following Gabe's confused stare.

"Spared no expense," Gabe mumbled, his eyes tearing away to stare back up at the vent opening. Thankfully, there was no sign of the Lurch creature. "I saw the owner of the arms up there, just before I dropped. It was Lurch," Gabe explained.

"Owen's scene was *Hanged, Drawn, and Quartered*," Becca reflected. "Makes sense."

Gabe shot here an incredulous look.

"Well, as much sense as any of this makes," she quickly corrected. "You know, *quartered*. Legs and arms removed."

"Yeah, I know what quartered means," Gabe informed, keeping his eyes glued to the vent opening.

In his peripheral vision, Gabe saw something shooting directly at him. He immediately reacted, snatching the flying limb out of the air. How had he forgotten about the fucking arms!?

The black knight had his sword extended outward, readying to bring it back in for another strike. Gabe took the convenient opportunity and impaled the struggling arm onto the sword's blade, where it was left squirming in a hopeless attempt at escape.

"Where the fuck is the other one?" Gabe scanned the room and quickly found it. It was perched up in the back, almost as if it had been watching its counterpart's attack. Perhaps in seeing the other arm's failure, the second arm curled back, readying a leap towards Gabe.

"I don't fucking think so," Gabe swore, grabbing the exposed part of the white knight's sword handle and wrenching the heavy instrument from his grip. The arm leapt. Gabe stabbed the sword forward, catching the limb in midflight with the blade. Gabe stepped over the velvet barrier, carrying the skewered arm, and thrust the sword's blade into the maiden's soft exterior, pinning the free-range appendage in place.

"We can't stay here," Gabe said, stepping back over the barrier. "Where is *here* anyway?"

"This has to be *A Medieval Knight's Dream*," Becca postulated.

"A play on Shakespeare's *A Midsummer Night's Dream*?" Gabe asked.

"Indeed," Becca confirmed. "Which means we are in the center of the northern corridor."

"We went room-to-room through the entire northern corridor," Gabe said. "Why don't I remember this one?"

"Like I said, it's in the center, right next to the restrooms." Becca was staring at Gabe as if she expected her words to spark some recognition in him. "Remember, we skipped it because you saw the restrooms and *suddenly* had to take a piss," Becca chided.

"Oh yeah," Gabe remembered. "That's right," he admitted, blushing.

Then it hit him. *The restroom!*

"You know what? I may just have an idea," Gabe relayed to Becca, checking the vent opening again. Still no sign of Lurch.

"I'm open to suggestions."

"You know how sometimes buildings like these will have a cabling corridor running underneath the floors? You know, for electrical wiring, sewer pipes, that sort of thing?"

Becca nodded.

"When I was taking that piss, I noticed an unlabeled door back of the room, the kind of door that normally leads to a supply closet of some sort. At best, there could be a hatch or something that leads down to that cabling corridor. Maybe even a way out. At worst, it should have something we can use as a weapon. Perhaps we could break some mop handles or something."

"Why not just use these swords?" Becca asked.

"Those are only replicas; unwieldy and dull as shit. Besides," Gabe looked over at one of the impaled arms still trying to squirm its way free, "they're currently busy, serving a different purpose."

Becca considered Gabe's plan, then shrugged. "It's not like I have a better plan...let's do it." She started turning towards the door when a splotch of red at Gabe's feet caught her eye. "Jesus! You're bleeding."

Gabe looked down at his punctured arm. "Yeah, that fucker got me good."

"Hang on, we've got to take care of that," Becca said, stepping off toward the figurine of the hopeful maiden. "I hate the depictions that modern society has associated with women back in those days. It's like they were all a bunch of defenseless twats," she related, tearing a strip of cloth off the maiden's dress.

"There wasn't exactly a strong women's rights movement back then," Gabe offered. Becca shot him a funny look, as if she was going to argue the point. She shrugged instead, dropping whatever line of thought had been running through her mind.

"So what the fuck is going on around here?" Gabe asked as Becca brought the strip of cloth back over the barrier. "From what I can gather, all these assholes have scenes in *Suffering For Art,* which they are somehow able to mimic in real life, despite the fact that such mimicry involves missing limbs, eviscerated intestines, and who knows what else. In what fucking world is any of that in the least bit possible?"

Becca arrived with the cloth and started wrapping it around Gabe's dripping punctures. "I'm starting to think it's more than that. Remember how, when you were strapped to the table, Dr. Holtz was talking to you about taxidermy and that special concoction that he made?"

"Yeah."

"Well, if he was going to turn you into one of those fucked-up displays, it stands to reason that you probably weren't going to be the first one that he's done that to," Becca theorized.

"Wait...what *exactly* are you saying? That those other scenes contain the actual bodies of Zellers' staff, all stuffed and put on display like some sort of fucking grotesque hunter's den?"

"I don't know," Becca admitted. "I'm just trying to put what few puzzle pieces I have together. We were just attacked by a pair of severed limbs, so it's hard to rule anything out at this point." Becca finished tying off the impromptu tourniquet and moved off towards the room's door.

"Point taken," Gabe relented. "But, even if Zellers has been killing people and somehow bringing them back as some kind of nightmare Mr. Potato Head, why would he risk keeping the bodies around at all? And don't even bother saying it's because of how in love with art he is; I don't buy that shit for a second."

"If we come across Blake again, I'll be sure to ask," Becca replied, hugging her ear to the door. "It sounds clear out there," she informed after a moment.

"We don't have far to go. Just a quick hop to the next door over. You ready for that?" Gabe asked.

Becca nodded and gripped the handle, but held off on twisting it, instead turning back to Gabe. "This whole mess is too impossibly fucked-up for us to have any hopes of figuring it out, so let's just focus on getting the fuck out of here, okay?"

Gabe nodded. "Sorry. I just don't like not knowing what the fuck is trying to kill me, but I guess it's not like there's a book lying around out there with all of the answers, right?"

Becca kept her expression cold, eyes drilling into Gabe.

"Okay, okay," Gabe relented, "purely focused on getting out alive...check!" He gave her a thumbs up to show his sincerity, though they both knew the gesture was false. His mind was already betraying the notion, circling through the circumstances of their predicament. The mention of a book had stirred a memory in Gabe that he had long since tucked away.

It couldn't be, Gabe told himself.

He shook his head to clear the nagging memory as best he could.

Pure focus, he had promised.

Becca twisted the knob and vanished out into the hallway, Gabe right on her tail.

The vague memory followed him the entire way.

INTERLUDE 5

Blake flipped through the Xeroxed pages, trying to find an answer to the question that burning through him.

"Why didn't it work!?" he asked the pages in frustration.

It was the reanimated Dr. Holtz who answered. "You didn't perform the steps of the ritual. Not all of them, anyway"

"What are you talking about?" Blake shot up from his seat. "I most certainly did!" Blake protested. He nearly knocked the mocking pages off the desk, barely managing to stop himself from the foolhardy gesture. Just because he *imagined* the pages laughing at him, didn't mean they actually were. "Did you not bury the pizza boy's body in the basement as I instructed you to do?"

"I did, sir."

"Then we still have control of his remains. He was feeling plenty of pain and fear as you carved those slices out of him...that I guarantee."

"Yes, sir...I agree that you certainly met *those* wickets, but when you performed the ritual on me, I was ecstatic with the idea that you were about to end the years-long battle I had been waging against my ailment."

"I did cure you, didn't I?" Blake rebutted.

"In a manner of speaking, I suppose you did, sir. But you offered no such elation to the boy before he died," Holtz explained.

Blake contemplated Holtz's words. "Perhaps not," he agreed after a moment. Blake sat back down in his chair, placing his head in his hands as he analyzed this most recent information.

"We need to come up with a system for this. Something that'll hit all the wickets," Blake eventually said, looking up from his hands. "Too much is left to chance when we're just winging it." Truth be told, the pizza boy had been entirely unplanned. A casualty of Blake's over-excitement at this new game he was playing. He knew he would need to better control his urges in the future if he didn't want to unnecessarily arouse suspicion.

"While you're figuring that out, sir, if you plan on continuing these rituals, might I suggest you find a better way to hide the bodies," Holtz said. "I doubt you're going to want a basement full of dead bodies if the police ever come sniffing around. And I would wager, at some point they will."

"Excellent point, Doctor," Blake agreed. He leaned back in his chair, racking his brain for a satisfactory solution. As he ran through scenario after scenario, he let his eyes linger on a painting that graced the wall of his study.

It was one of Blake's favorites. An original of Vincent Van Gogh. It was eerily similar to another work of his, *Girl In The Woods*. Other than a slight aspect change, this painting could have been an exact copy. It wasn't officially titled, but the proprietor of the gallery he had acquired it from, had informed him that it was rumored Van Gogh had intended to call it *Deeper In The Woods*. Being unimpressed by the lack of contrast with his earlier work, Van Gogh had ultimately decided against adding it to his repertoire, instead giving it to a private collector whom he had prior dalliances with.

Blake loved it, though. It was dark. It was mysterious. He often tried to imagine the girl's emotions as she stared up at the dark, imposing figure of the tree before her. Did she feel intimidated? Or, did maybe the tree represent some form of hope to her? It was unlikely that Blake would ever know the true answer to that. To himself, the answer changed depending on the mood he found himself in on any particular day.

Today, he imagined the girl feeling a great disappointment as she stared up at the wooden behemoth. A resounding dread that she would never be able to surmount such a steep obstacle and witness the beauty of the world from atop its glorious height.

At the time Blake purchased it, the painting had been his most rewarding expenditure. And quite a hefty expenditure, at that. The art gallery he had bought it from had charged him a fortune for the piece. Of course, any of the serious art galleries always did.

Blake stood from his chair so quickly that it caused Holtz to flinch.

"That's it!" Blake exclaimed. "Doctor, go into my bedroom and bring me back my phone. It should be sitting on the nightstand. I have to call my father."

"Yes, sir," Holtz acknowledged. "Before I go, sir, may I ask what has gotten you so excited."

"I'll explain the details to you later. First, I'm going to have to ask that old codger for another advance from my inheritance."

"Yes, sir." Holtz nodded, turning to complete his assigned task.

"And make it quick, would you?" Blake called out after the doctor. "We have an art gallery to build."

As soon as the door to the restroom opened, Gabe's nostrils were assaulted with the horrid stench.

"Jesus Christ!" Gabe swore. "Do those fucking things still need to take shits?" Gabe waved his hand in front of his nose, as if it would somehow dispel the foulness of the air. "Because somebody just blew up this fucking joint!"

"Oh God," Becca squeaked out through her wretching. Gabe was sure that she was about to barf all over the tiled floor.

"Come on," Gabe prodded when he saw she'd temporarily won her battle with her digestive rebellion, "let's just get this done." He stepped toward the plain door built into the back of the room.

As he passed the open stalls, his peripheral vision caught sight of a large, dark stain. He glanced over to see that the stain coated the entirety of the affected stall. Covering the floor, the walls, and everything in between, the layer of brown muck was enormous. So much so, that, had he not known the toilets were completely white, he would have never been able to guess the color of this particular one.

"It seems that somebody should have avoided the chili dogs," Gabe joked.

"Jesus," Becca swore, seeing the stain herself, "men are disgusting!"

"I hate to dispel your fantasies on the grandeur of the male bowel movement, but that shit's not normal," Gabe informed. "I've taken some ginormous shits in my time, but the beefiest of them wouldn't hold a candle to this."

"So *not* a turn on," Becca replied, pinching her nose hard enough to turn the skin white underneath.

Gabe moved past the gnarly scene and tried the nondescript door's handle. He was pleased when the knob turned freely. "Fucking A!" he expressed. "It's unlocked. Perhaps our luck is changing for the better."

"Don't jinx it," Becca warned. "We're still stuck in this shithole."

Gabe laughed, nodding back towards the defiled stall. "Never have more accurate words been spoken."

Becca punched him in the shoulder in response.

"Let's see," Gabe said, moving a mop bucket out of the way. "Well, fuck me! No trap door."

"Plenty of mops, though." Becca pointed to the back of the tiny room. Four mops hung upside down from a rack built into the wall.

"That'll do nicely," Gabe rejoiced, removing one of the mops from its perch. He used his knee to snap the handle near the base and held up his newly-made, wooden spear. "God help the next poor fucker that tries to fuck with me."

"Don't get too excited," Becca cautioned. "We don't know if that thing will do any good against those freaky, undead fucks."

"I'm pretty sure the term *'undead* fucks' refers to zombies," Gabe jokingly chided. "I don't think that's exactly what we're dealing with here."

"You better watch yourself, mister," Becca advised, snapping another mop handle in two. "I'm pretty fucking sure this thing will work just fine on you." She playfully stabbed the broken handle's jagged edge towards Gabe's heart.

"Alright, Plan B it is then," Gabe announced.

"What's Plan B again?" Becca asked.

"We run like hell for the front door and, this time, we make one of those assholes punch in the code," Gabe explained. Becca shot him a disapproving look. "I won't say that it's a good plan, but what else do we have?" he admitted with a shrug.

"The brute force approach, huh? That *never* goes awry," Becca sarcastically agreed.

Gabe sighed. "Like I said..."

"Yeah, yeah," Becca cut in, "what choice do we have? Got it."

Gabe carried his mop handle with him back into the main part of the restroom. The atrocious smell had been present with them in the supply closet, but hadn't been nearly as powerful. Immediately upon stepping back into the restroom, the smell assailed him with its full potency.

"I suggest breathing through your mouth until we get out of here," Gabe called back to Becca, copying her earlier move by pinching his nostrils together.

Becca followed suit and joined him back in the restroom.

Gabe took one last look at the putrid pile of fecal matter as he stepped past, intending to make his way to the exit. Something in that glance stopped him cold.

"What is it?" Becca asked, seeing Gabe's mid-step halt.

"Something in that shit pile just moved."

"What are you talking about?"

Becca, obviously reluctant to lay eyes on the toxic splatter, slowly turned to see what had Gabe's attention. She gasped when she saw what he was seeing. Gabe wanted to believe that his eyes were playing tricks on him, but seeing how Becca was staring in similar awe at the splattered shit stain, he knew they were not. Several chunks of – well, something! Gabe couldn't say for sure what they were, because the chunks were masked by the brown sludge. Whatever the chunks were, though, they were slowly crawling around in the murky pool.

More motion drew Gabe's attention to the wall at the back of the stall. He looked up to see that the brown stain was receding down the walls. The white of the toilet started to show as the sludge on it also began receding toward the middle of the stall floor. There the chunks the sludge began coalescing upward, the strange chunks ascending with it, becoming a rising pile of pure awfulness. The forming pile rose toward the roof like a miniature, fecal-based, Tower of Babel.

"Umm...maybe we should get out of here," Becca broke through their trance.

Soon, the thick pile split apart into two distinct columns. A slight shifting in the shape of the column revealed what looked like a pair of female legs.

"Uhh...yeah. Let's do that," Gabe agreed. As soon as he turned to flee, a fountain of brown squirted out from the rising much and splashed against the door handle, leaving it coated in cocoa-colored mire.

"Crap," Gabe simply replied.

"I don't think it wants us to leave," Becca pointed out.

"Thanks, Captain Obvious," Gabe mocked, turning back to the rising monstrosity. The strange chunks were melding themselves together in the two different spires as the shit continued piling higher. The two columns eventually spilled together at their tops, and continued their ascent. As the shit pile climbed, Gabe recognized the slight curve of a lady's waist. That's when Gabe realized the previously unidentified chunks were stitching themselves together under the covering of shit. That's when he recognized what the chunks actually were. Slabs of human flesh.

"I'll rock-paper-scissors you to see who has to get their hands dirty so we can get out of here," Gabe offered, tilting his head toward the shit-covered door knob.

"Can we just say that I won?" Becca countered.

Gabe glanced at the door knob and said, "Fuck it!" He sprinted toward the knob, but had to pull back as another stream of shit shot through the air directly in front of him, intentionally cutting him. Most of the foul substance sailed past by him, splashing against a nearby wall. Though, he managed to avoid the bulk of the brown stream, a couple stray drops sprinkled onto his arm.

"Fucking gross!" Gabe protested. Gabe's gut wretched in disgust as he looked down at the feces clinging to his arm. Gabe looked around for something he could use to wipe away the brown spots when his arm began burning underneath the dark slop. "What the fucking hell!?" Gabe yelped, jumping toward the row of nearby sinks. He flipped the water on and ran his infected arm underneath it. The shit easily rinsed off, leaving Gabe's skin a bright red where the offending drops had previously been.

"Umm...Becca?" Gabe called out after seeing the brown stains disappear into the drain. The skin underneath the two red spots pulsed with a burning itch. Gabe fought down a growing urge to scratch at them.

Becca was frozen in place against the wall as her mind took in all that was happening. "Yes?" she managed to respond.

"Remember that loony bitch we met? One of Zellers' staff. What was her name?"

"Ophelia?"

"Yeah, that's her," Gabe confirmed. "Remember how she told us her scene was *The Tub*? And that *The Tub* was designed to have its victim suspended in their own fecal matter for weeks on end, until their flesh was chafed raw and eaten away?"

"I remember," Becca assured.

"I have a feeling she's about to say hello." Gabe pointed toward the stall. Gabe couldn't see inside the stall from where he was standing, but based on the angle of Becca's terror-filled eyes, he guessed that the shit covered chunks of flesh had risen to somewhere near Ophelia's breasts. "Oh, and FYI, her demon shit works a lot faster at chafing the flesh, so fighting back our revulsion is the least of our worries if we want to turn that knob and escape."

Gabe was relieved when he saw Becca break from her horrified trance to swerve her eyes around the room, searching for something as her mind knocked around this new information. "Fuck that!" Becca chimed, her eyes growing bright. She turned and sprinted back into the supply closet.

Gabe inched forward from the sink, hoping to see what Becca was doing. After a moment, she reappeared at the supply closet's door brandishing a pair of latex gloves. "We'll use these," she said.

She made to sprint toward Gabe, but was cut off by a large, brown shape exiting the stalls. It was Ophelia, now fully formed. Becca's sudden halt caused her feet to slip out from under her, sending her crashing backward onto the tile. The hard landing didn't faze her, as she immediately began backpedaling away from the shit-covered woman.

Gabe reacted instantly, spearing his broken mop handle directly through the layers of muck and desiccated flesh covering Ophelia's back. The handle emerged from her chest in the vicinity of where her heart should have been. Rather unsurprisingly, the move didn't amount to much.

Ophelia's back morphed around the wooden rod, quickly becoming Ophelia's front. Gabe's mouth dropped in awe as he recognized the signature move of the T-1000 from *Terminator 2* - only, you know, if the T-1000 had been made out of human feces instead of liquid metal.

"Hello, Mr. Daniels," Ophelia's voice escaped from the putrid, human-shaped turd. Her shit-covered lips curled down to form her patented, kooky smile.

"You are one, loony fucking bitch!" Gabe fired back, his arms burning as he fought to hold the staff at arm's length.

Ophelia's smile faded into a frown. She reached out to grab further down the makeshift stake and used the leverage to scoot the entirety of her slimy body down the shaft, toward Gabe. Gabe was frozen, unsure what to do as she reached down again. The next such move would easily bring her into reaching distance of Gabe. He was about to release his grip on the mop handle to turn and run, when another wooden shaft suddenly broke through the muck.

It was Becca! She had used the distraction to impale her own mop handle through Ophelia's back. She had struck the woman's back at an angle that caused the staff to rise upwards out of her chest. With the two mop handles impaling her in nearly perpendicular positions, Ophelia was unable to easily slide herself in any one direction, effectively pinning her in place.

"Quick! Swing her around. Aim for the supply closet," Gabe instructed, already turning himself to accomplish the feat. Becca turned with him, carefully maintaining her grip on the end of the wooden shaft. Using the stakes, the two carried Ophelia to the supply closet entrance and swung her inside, simultaneously releasing their grips to let the shit-covered woman go flying into the small room.

Ophelia hit the ground and immediately sprung back onto her feet. She charged at the door, prompting Gabe to quickly slam it shut. The last thing he saw was the two unmanned ends of the mop handle hitting against the wall on either side of the door, twisting the rods inside of her and halting her forward progress.

"Give me the gloves," Gabe demanded as soon as the door had slammed shut. "It won't take her long to get out of there."

Becca handed Gabe the pair of latex gloves, which he quickly slid over his hands. They ran to the restroom's exit, where Gabe briefly paused before grabbing onto the soiled handle. "As soon as we're through, we're running straight for the exit to *Free Market*, got it?"

Becca nodded. Satisfied, Gabe used his gloved hands to turn the knob and fling open the door.

Behind them, the door to the supply closet burst open, the Ophelia shit-demon emerging from within.

It was too late, however. Gabe and Becca had already leapt out into the hallway, the restroom door having slammed closed behind them.

INTERLUDE 6

As usual, Blake's father had been stingy with his money, bequeathing him far less than he had hoped for. Of course, Blake considered himself lucky to get any money at all from the old man. As soon a Thomas Zellers had heard what the money was for, he had nearly shit a brick.

"An art gallery?" Blake's father had spat over the phone. "A fucking art gallery? Are you serious? Why would I waste a dime of *my* money on that?"

"What are you talking about, Father?" Blake argued. "Did you forget that I grew up under your roof? I cannot even begin to count the amount of ostentatious pieces that you have hung from your walls since making your billions."

"That's different," Thomas Zellers protested. "High-priced art is for showing off one's money. A mere status symbol. Like a $400,000 watch, or a *second* private jet. It's relatively useless, other than for someone to be able to say, 'See!? Look how rich I am!'.

"You may see a rich person point out a piece that he is particularly proud of to his guests. He may wax poetic about how it evokes some inane emotion, or even impress upon his lesser-statured guests the aesthetic pleasures he may get from certain colors or squiggles. But it's all bullshit!

"Now art *galleries...*" Thomas paused at that point and Blake had almost been able to hear his father wagging his finger at him through the phone. "Art galleries are different. Art galleries are for faggots! Are you a faggot, boy?" His father had asked him.

The conversation had only spiraled downward from there.

Eventually, Blake had been able to convince his father for a small loan. He had just needed to appeal to his father's baser instincts.

"It's about the money, Father," he had explained. "I simply want to make a few bucks of my own while I'm out here. I'm not interested in the art itself, just in how much I can weasel out of other people's pockets."

Thomas Zellers had finally agreed, though still with a fair amount of reluctance. Truth be told, it hadn't been *that* hard to figure out his father's weakness on the matter. Blake had paid careful attention growing up with the man. After all, it hadn't taken Thomas Zellers long, once his company began to grow, to start upselling his products to the most gullible client out there: the United States Government.

"Nothing feels better than some other fool's money in your pocket," Blake's father had once told him during those first years of success.

Having endured all of that - and the months since; ripping apart, redesigning, and reconstructing the empty supermarket that Blake had been able to acquire with the money his father had parted with — Blake was finally able to lay his eyes on the completed fruits of his labor.

Magna Arta, the sign out front read. Situated at the end of a strip mall, it wasn't everything Blake had hoped for, but it'd make do.

"Tomorrow we begin," he promised the looming building. It was the night before his grand opening and he fully intended to celebrate.

The sounds of Beethoven's *Moonlight Sonata* chirped from his pocket, interrupting his self-congratulatory appraisal. Blake grabbed the phone from his pocket and glanced down at the green screen to read the digital, black letters showing the identity of the caller. Irked by the interruption, Blake flipped the earpiece open, arcing it over the green-tinted screen.

"Yes?" Blake asked.

"Mr. Zellers, sir," Jarvis Holtz's voice came through the speaker, "we have a slight problem."

"What is it, Doctor?" Blake asked, his voice betraying his annoyance.

"I think it is best you come to the house, sir," Holtz said.

"I'm kind of busy here," Blake protested.

"Sir, you ordered me to only call you if it was important. Seeing as how I'm incapable of defying your explicit orders, that should let you know that this is indeed important."

"Well, what is it?" Blake spat. "Just tell me."

"Yes, sir. Your..." A loud rustling on the phone cut Holtz off, followed by the phone losing connection to the other end.

Blake stared at the now-silent device. His wariness had risen a notch, but he wasn't yet overly worried.

"This had better be a matter of life and death, Dr. Holtz," Blake threatened the silent phone as he stuffed the device back into his pocket. He casually strode back to his car and took off, headed for home and whatever awaited him there.

23

"Run!" Gabe shouted as soon as they had crossed out into the northern corridor. He had immediately spotted the crowd of bodies gathered at the western end. More importantly, they had immediately spotted *him*. "This way!" he instructed, grabbing Becca's sleeve and pulling her toward the eastern wing.

The white-clad mob leapt into action, chasing after them.

"Gabe?" Becca called out, trailing just behind.

"Stick to the plan!" Gabe yelled over his shoulder.

They ran until they hit the intersection with the eastern wing. Earlier in the evening, Gabe had been ecstatic to have run out of time before they had had a chance to explore the exhibits in this wing. If anybody would have told him then, that – only a few hours later – he'd be running for his life through it, he'd have had a good laugh at them.

They rushed by doors bearing placards that read things such as *Love Is Blind*, *Like Lands Through The Hour Glass*, and *The Miracle Of Birth*. Gabe promised himself that, in the extremely unlikely event he ever walked back into this fucking hellhole of an establishment, he would avoid that last one at all costs.

They had made it nearly halfway down the corridor. Gabe could hear the clomping footsteps of his pursuers round the corner behind them at nearly the same time another group of bodies rounded the corner in *front* of them.

Gabe skidded to a halt. Becca tried to match, but her boots slipped on the tile floor. Gabe caught her mid-tumble and propped her back to her feet.

"We're fucked," she cried as Gabe steadied her.

Gabe's eye caught on a light flaring above a solitary door to his right. A green light.

They were on the opposite end of the gallery from *A Morsel's Journey*, but this exhibit appeared to have the same airlock-type door configuration.

"In here!" Gabe yelled, dragging Becca towards the door with the green light. He pulled the door open and shoved Becca into the darkness within. As he leapt through the door, he caught sight of the exhibit's placard.

It read *Midnight in the Garden of Good and Evil*.

INTERLUDE 7

Blake Zellers slammed the door behind him, making his irritation obvious.

"This had better be good, Doctor," he called out to wherever Holtz's waiting ears happened to be.

"In here, sir," Holtz's voice returned to him from the kitchen at the back of the house.

Blake was in his foyer, near where the pizza boy had been killed. Off to his right were stairs leading up into the second story of the house. To his left was the living room. Straight ahead, past the stairs, was an arched entryway into the kitchen. Blake stepped forward to the archway. Before he could step through, a familiar face appeared, blocking his way.

"Danner?" Blake said in surprise, rolling his eyes. "Where's Father?" He knew that if Danner was here, his father was as well. Thomas Zellers was never without his pet.

"In the dining room, boy," his father's voice carried past Danner.

Blake stepped past Danner, under the archway, to see his father standing off to the left, in the open dining area. "I'm pleased to see that you are making good use of the table that I bought you," Thomas said sarcastically. The dark oak table was part of a kitchen set that his father had purchased for him when Blake had first moved out to the west coast. The seller had promised that it had once belonged to John D. Rockefeller. Upon presenting it to Blake, Thomas Zellers had championed the piece as bearing the marks of greatness and fortune.

Blake glanced at the top of the table, already knowing what he would see. The table top held scattered cartons of Chinese food, several tipped over with their contents spilled out onto the dark oak. Two day old rice could be seen stuck to the lacquered surface in several areas.

Blake may have been tempted to break into a smile if it weren't for the scene directly next to the table. Dr. Holtz was tied into one of the kitchen set's chairs, the handles of two kitchen knives protruding from his chest.

"What are you doing here, Father?" Blake asked coldly.

"Yes, yes," his father said dismissively, "I know you are in a hurry to celebrate the opening of your *art gallery*." Thomas made the final words sound rancid. "But that's not why I am here."

Blake remained silent, inviting his father to continue.

"No. I am here because I have had certain friends of mine in the area keeping tabs on you. These friends have been wagging their tongues about this strange affiliation you have had recently with a man much older than yourself. Mind you, this was about the same time that you approached me with your idea to build an art gallery. So, naturally, I just assumed that you had gone the way of the queer. I figured I'd put a stop to that eventually, but I was in no rush.

"Then I heard this older man's name. A brief search revealed that this man – a Dr. Jarvis Holtz – was suffering from a very serious disease of the lungs. In fact, all of the medical reports I came across showed that he should have died months ago. Now this," Thomas paused, shaking a finger up in the air, "*this* stoked my curiosity. I knew I had to come and check this doctor out for myself."

The hairs stood on the back of Blake's neck. He had a feeling that he knew where this was going.

"Imagine my surprise when I arrive on your doorstep and am greeted by – a not only alive, but, by all appearances, very healthy – Dr. Holtz. So, to make sure I'm not imagining things, I had Danner here stab a knife straight through one of the doctor's supposedly infected lungs." Thomas reached down and jiggled one of the knife handles. Holtz flinched against the pain, but he didn't cry out.

"Yet, even with a knife having pierced his lung, Dr. Holtz kept breathing."

Blake gulped as his father broke from his story to throw him a cold, hard scowl. "So, tell me boy, how in the hell did you get your hands on the book?"

The book didn't need to be named. There was no confusion on either of their parts about which book Thomas Zellers was referring to.

"Did you find the second copy?" Thomas asked, a strange hope in his eye. "I've been trying to find the damned thing for years. How did you manage?"

Second copy? There was a second copy of the book? That little fact caught Blake by surprise.

"No, Father. I have not *found* a second copy of the book. I didn't even know that there was another copy of the book." Blake considered not telling his father about the Xerox copies he made the night he had been caught sneaking into the vault, but decided there was no point in hiding it any longer. He told him everything that had happened that evening.

"You foolish, foolish child," Thomas sneered after Blake had finished recanting his tale. "You don't understand the power that you are playing with."

"It's not like I have done anything that you haven't already," Blake pointed out, gesturing to Danner.

"Yes. I may have trifled once with the dark magic the book holds, but only ever the one time. After Danner, I locked the cursed thing away from the world."

"Why would you do that?" Blake asked.

"Because it's evil!" Thomas Zellers immediately answered. "I have no illusions that I am a good man, but I am not an evil one. The power of the book is far too dark and dangerous for this world. I was young, I was naïve, and I was hungry for wealth. Danner's thousand-pound brain was the key to that wealth, but he refused to join with me, so I performed the resurrection ritual. The entire time I felt sick, sicker than I had ever felt before, or since. I got what I needed and I locked the book away, never daring to let its darkness infect another."

"Good? Evil? Such things don't matter," Blake countered. "The book is power. You yourself have told me many times that power is what really matters in this world."

A look of sadness swept across Thomas' face. It was only there a moment before his father's stern countenance reabsorbed it back into whichever depths it came. Still, it jarred Blake, for he had never seen such a look on the man's face before.

"This is a pointless argument. As soon as I suspected that the book's power had been used again, I destroyed the damn thing. Burned it in my fireplace," Thomas informed.

"You didn't!" Blake exclaimed, stunned.

"I did," Thomas coldly assured.

Blake remained silent, but his blood was screaming in his veins.

"Give me the pages," Thomas demanded.

"And if I refuse?" Blake challenged.

"Then I will cut you off. All my wealth, all my power; none of it will be yours any longer."

Blake stared challengingly at his father for a moment, before finally relenting. With a shrug, he said, "They're upstairs in my safe."

"Danner," Thomas said, "would you please accompany my son to retrieve the pages?"

"Yes, sir," Danner agreed.

Blake dejectedly motioned for Danner to follow him as he walked out of the kitchen area. A few moments later, they returned, Danner carrying a stack of pages in his hand.

"Good," Thomas nodded at his lap dog. Like a good puppy, Danner stuffed the pages into a briefcase and locked them away from sight. "As soon as we return to the manor, these pages will join the originals in the hearth."

"Is that it?" Blake asked mournfully.

"No," Thomas coolly replied. "We'll be taking Dr. Holtz with us, as well."

"Like hell you will!" Blake stepped up to his father, his face only inches from the older man's.

Thomas was unintimidated. "Move out of my way, boy. Dr. Holtz *will* be accompanying us to Rhode Island, so that I may keep an eye on him."

Blake stood resolute for a moment longer, then – seeing no other choice - he backed down.

"Good," Thomas said, straightening out his suit, though Blake had never actually touched him. "Now, where is the good doctor's body so that Danner may retrieve it?"

"In the basement," Blake said, anger burning in his eyes. "Let me get the key." Blake moved around to the other side of the kitchen bar that separated the dining room from the actual kitchen. He opened a drawer beneath the sink and reached inside.

Instead of a key, however, his hand came out clutching a semi-automatic pistol.

"You're not taking *my* doctor," Blake warned. "I need him."

Danner hopped into action, intending to defend his boss, but Thomas waved him off. "No need for that Danner," Thomas said. He stared into Blake's eyes for a moment. Blake knew what he saw in there; his father saw a fire raging in fierce commitment to the current threat.

"Fine," Thomas relented. "We'll leave Dr. Holtz behind as *your* responsibility. Know this, however. From this moment on, you are no longer my son. Don't come to me for money. Don't come to me for my influence. You will never so much as speak to me again. Is that understood, boy?"

Blake wanted to argue – part of him even wanted to beg. What his father had just decreed was no small matter. Blake's pride won out, though. He stayed silent, staring his father down through the sites of the gun. He refused to betray just how much his father's curse had affected him.

"And if you're thinking about using my name to garner your own influence," Thomas continued, "you can drop that idea right now. As soon as I return home, I will be scheduling a press conference to announce to the world all that I have just told you."

Blake gulped back the acid building in his throat. His father never had been one to half-ass something.

"Have a great life, boy," Thomas said, nodding and walking away. "Come Danner," Thomas instructed his servant. Danner's eyes had never once left Blake since the appearance of the gun. As he retreated, Danner kept those eyes drilled into him until the house's infrastructure blocked his line of sight.

Blake held the gun steady on the wall where the two had disappeared, only lowering it when he heard the front door slam shut. Blake let out a deep breath that he hadn't even been aware that he was holding.

"Doctor, pull those knives out of your chest and clean up in here," Blake ordered, attempting to regain a small amount of control over his life.

"Yes, sir." Holtz complied, spurts of blood followed the blades from their fleshy sheaths. "No money and no book. What are you going to do now, sir?" he asked.

Blake smiled. "Get them back," Blake promised. "Get *everything* back."

His father may have taken the book from him, but there were an awful lot of those copied pages. Blake was sure that his father would never notice that one of them was missing.

At least, not until it was too late.

24

The light above the door changed from green to red and Gabe breathed a sigh of relief.

They were standing in the small entryway between the two doors, the inner standing wide open to reveal the darkness beyond.

"Great! Exactly what we needed," Becca griped after the inner door had been hastily flung open, "another pitch black room."

Gabe had instantly recognized that this dark room was a little different than the last. The first indication was the stacked bin of night vision goggles tucked into the alcove of the entryway. A solitary red light shone down on the stack. There was a sign on the wall, just visible at the edge of the red light's reach, which read: This Exhibit Requires Night Vision. Please Take One Pair Of Goggles From Below and Return Before Exiting.

"At least we know where that asshole that attacked us is *A Morsel's Journey* got his NVGs from," Gabe said.

Becca nodded, but otherwise did not respond. She grabbed a pair of goggles off the stack and put them on. "Cool," she said, after strapping them into place. "Wait here," she added, surprising Gabe by sprinting through the darkened doorway.

Gabe could hear Becca's clomping boots as she ran through the exhibit, but his other senses betrayed him in the stark blackness. The sound ceased after a moment. "Becca?" Gabe asked the darkness. The resuming clod of boot-on-tile was his answer.

Soon, Becca reappeared in the faint glow of the red light from above the door. "Door's open on the other end," she explained, only a slight huff in her voice after the run. "Just in time, too. As soon as I had it open, somebody began trying to pull the outer door open from the other side."

"Good call," Gabe praised her quick thinking. "I guess we couldn't expect Blake's morons to make the same mistake twice."

"Here," Becca said, grabbing another pair of goggles and shoving them into Gabe's hands. "Put these on."

Gabe slid the goggle straps over his head and pulled at the bands, tightening the straps against his skull. The blackness immediately morphed into a wonderland of differing green shades.

"Cool," Gabe repeated Becca's earlier appraisal.

Gabe could finally make out the various shapes of his current surroundings. Not that there was much to see just yet. The doorframe and the door itself were readily apparent in the goggles' illuminated screen. All four corners of the small barrier room stood out from their surroundings. The red light above the door flared a bright green in his vision, but supplied the alcove the low-level illumination necessary for the goggles to do their work.

Stepping through the open door, the first thing Gabe noticed was a bright moon suspended in the sky. He was sure the moon hadn't been there before he had donned the goggles.

"I'm guessing it's an infrared bulb hanging from the ceiling," Becca posited, following Gabe's stare. "The goggles need some kind of light source to amplify. Infrared would do the job and still be invisible to the unaided eye."

"Yeah, thanks," Gabe said sarcastically. "I've read Tom Clancy, too."

The faux moon gave life to a wonderland below. A myriad of objects could be seen in the green glow. Gabe couldn't quite make a majority of them out, not without getting closer. What Gabe could clearly see was a path set into the floor, looking as if it was made of cobblestone. The path split directly in front of the entrance where he was standing. One path ran to the left, the other veered off to the right. A sign was planted into the floor where the two paths split. Two words, each accompanied by a drawn arrow, stood out in green, glowing letters scrawled on the sign's front. The arrow pointing down the left path read "GOOD", while the right arrow read "EVIL".

"Which path do you suggest we take?" Becca asked.

Gabe considered his options. "When in Rome..." he finally said, starting down the path to the right. The first item they arrived at was a looming tree; its branches thick and knotted with what looked like a screaming face scraped out in the bark near its base. It was the typical tree you'd see in a horror movie. The kind of tree that said that you should turn around and get the fuck out of there, made even creepier by the fact it stared at him in only dark shades of green.

Gabe wasn't deterred.

When within arm's reach, Gabe rubbed his hand on the tree's bark and smiled. "It's plastic," he shared.

"Makes sense," Becca said. "It's not like real trees would survive long in this darkness."

They passed the first tree and found that they had entered a miniature forest of the plastic giants.

"Is this supposed to be some kind of haunted forest?" Gabe asked.

Becca shrugged.

Gabe startled when he rounded a particularly thick tree and was faced with a hand reaching out for him. He instinctively swatted at the hand, ready to deliver a beat down. His reactive assault was stopped cold when the swatted hand broke off its limb and crashed to the ground.

"It's fucking plastic," Gabe breathed a sigh of relief, studying the jagged stump left on the end of the reaching arm. His eyes followed the arm up to a figure of a smiling imp that clung to the base of the tree. The imp's face was frightening - with a long chin and slit pupils like that of a snake – but the imp was clearly a fake. Just another part of the display.

Gabe heard Becca laughing behind him. "Oh, my hero!" she teased. "We can go back to that restroom if you like. I'm pretty sure I spotted one of those fold-down, diaper-changing stations in there."

"Ha-ha. Very funny," Gabe rebuked. He briefly wondered if the night vision in Becca's goggles could pick up the blush on his cheeks.

They continued on. More trees, more imps. They came across some dangling spiders - thankfully fake as well - and even a cat, whose eyes glowed in the night vision as if Satan himself were glaring through them.

They soon reached a break in the trees. On their left side was a field of crooked grave markers shaped like crosses. From beneath the crosses were decimated hands rising out of the dirt – or, at least, some material that resembled dirt.

To their left was a tall tableau that ran up the wall. The tableau was divided into seven layers. Each layer contained figurines shaped like miniature people. The whole display was expertly crafted to make the best use of the shades and shadows of the night vision goggles, each individual layer shining brightly with its own shade of the green aura.

In the top layer, the figures aimlessly wandered, as if they were forever lost. The second layer showed the figures slanted forward in a struggle to walk against an invisible fierce wind.

As his eyes traveled down the figure, Gabe noted each individual layer held a different sort of struggle for the hopeless miniature people. The bottom layer held only a few of the figurines. Of these, only their upper bodies were visible, their lower hidden in a plastic sheeting that resembled ice. Their arms reached towards the viewer, their faces twisted into a horrified grimace that spoke of great suffering and despair.

Gabe recognized the tableau as a rendition of Dante's *Seven Circles of Hell*. A shiver swept across his body as he stared at the depiction.

"This shit is certifiably creepy," Gabe said. "Makes me wonder what we would have seen had we chosen the 'GOOD' path."

"That's the path I ran through to open the door on the other end," Becca informed. "Lots of floating clouds with angels on them. About halfway through, you went through an arch that resembled the pearly gates."

"Sounds more calming, though significantly *less* cool," Gabe judged, his eyes still glued on the Dante tribute. "Come on," he said after a moment, urging her forward into the next set of trees.

They came upon two trees that straddled opposite sides of the pathway. Intertwining branched between the two formed a dark arch that they crossed under. On the other side was a small clearing, with one solitary tree standing off to the side. This one was different; larger than the previous trees, extending up nearly to the roof of the cavernous room. Also unique were the bulbs that hung from the tree's branches. Gabe took one step off the path to study one of the hanging bulbs.

"I think these are supposed to be apples," he said, clutching one of the spherical objects.

"Apples?"

"Yeah, I do believe…" Gabe stopped when something rubbery tickled his face. He turned to see two more of the glowing serpent's eyes drilling into him from only inches away. Only these eyes weren't shining from the head of an imp, but were instead sunken into a pointy face that ended in a slit mouth. Gabe yelped as a forked tongue jetted from the snake's mouth, slapping against his face again. His feet came out from under him as he frantically scrambled to jump away from the bearing serpent.

"It's a goddamn anaconda!" Gabe screeched.

Becca burst into another fit of laughter. "You are too damn easy," she chuckled. "I bet Halloweens are a real hoot with you."

Gabe didn't find it funny. He stared at the large snake's head as it swayed in front of him. His eyes followed the long, cylindrical body up to a branch on the large tree, where it curled its way around the bulky, plastic appendage.

"That snake – like the imp – isn't real, sissy boy," Becca teased, lightly slapping the side of the anaconda's head.

Gabe enjoyed a brief moment of ironic retribution when Becca flinched away from the snake after her hand made contact. It wasn't the snake itself that made her jump, but the well-timed voice recording that sprung to life as soon as she had touched it.

"Ye shall *not* surely die," the slithery voice said through the hidden speaker. Judging by the direction of the sound, the speaker had to have been planted in the snake's mouth.

"Oh shit!" Gabe exclaimed in the tone most people use to say *aha*! "I get it now." If a light bulb did indeed appear over his head, its light had no effect on the night vision goggles. "It's the Tree of Knowledge of Good and Evil."

"From the bible?" Becca asked.

"Yeah," Gabe confirmed. "From Genesis. 'Ye shall surely not die' is what the serpent told Eve to get her to eat the forbidden fruit. God told Adam and Eve that, should they eat of the fruit of the tree, they should surely die. He neglected to mention that they would die much later, after living a full life, and that eating the fruit would be necessary to procreate and replenish the world. Another command that he had given them." Gabe shrugged. "It was the original catch-22, though the bible follows that up with plenty more of them."

Becca studied Gabe for a moment, a strange smile on her face. "Where were men like you when I was growing up?"

"I'd like to think that I was invading your dreams," Gabe joked, then grew serious. "Why?"

Becca stared for another moment, before shaking off her trance. "Nothing," she answered. "It's just that the men where I grew up were a bunch of religious zealots. I could have used a man like you by my side back then."

"I'm hoping you can *still* use one like me. I can point out biblical fallacies all day. Perhaps while cooking up a mean omelet in the morning, what do you say?" Gabe winked at her, then realized how stupid a move that was, given his eyes were covered by the screen of the NVGs.

"We'll see," Becca promised, then walked away, further down the path.

The path led them through two final trees. As Gabe walked between them, a wintry breeze wafted over him from above. A quick glance upward revealed an air vent planted into the roof near the crest of the left tree. Gabe shuddered at the sight of the vent.

Moving on, the path led them into a clearing past the woods. The wall connecting the exhibit to *Suffering for Art* stood only a few yards away. The path veered left before it reached the wall, but Gabe stopped to take in a large figurine tucked into the corner.

"Well, hello Satan," Gabe greeted the figure. The model was enormous, filling the entire corner of the room from floor to ceiling. The figure was a typical likeness of the prince of darkness; a muscular body with a beastly face. Two curved horns jutted from the top of his skull. In a fun little trick with miniature infrared bulbs, Satan's eyes glowed brightly in the olive screen of the night vision goggles.

"Creepy," Becca said, cuddling up with Gabe's arm.

"Kinda cool, though," Gabe related. A quick glance to the adjoining corner of the room revealed another looming figure. This one familiar to Gabe as the Judeo-Christian God, complete with a full beard and a warm smile. Instead of glowing eyes, this figure had a halo suspended above its head that glowed from its own inlaid bulbs. The God statue hunkered in its corner in much the same manner as the enlarged visage of Satan.

"Come on," Becca said, dragging Gabe away from the towering statue of Hell's dark lord.

Along the eastern wall, halfway between the two massive statues, they came upon an open door with a bright flare above it. The light was bright enough to be damn near white in the NVG screen, with only a shade of the usual green, but Gabe knew if he removed the goggles, the light would be much dimmer and red in color.

The two differing paths met up again in front of the door, with a third path branching off to run straight back into the center of the exhibit. Near the apex, was an old sign post made of cast iron. It rose straight up to a height of just over six feet. An arm extended perpendicularly from the top, anchoring a wooden sign that dangled on a small chain.

"The In-Between," Gabe read off the words etched into the wooden sign.

The sign post was positioned just off the third path. Gabe let his eyes wander down the trail to find what looked like a typical cul-de-sac found in the vast suburbs of America. Gabe let his feet carry him into the middle of cul-de-sac. Instead of houses lining the mostly-circular alcove, the large frames were nothing but wooden house fronts, like those found on a Hollywood stage set. Each faux house had a smiling family waving from the replica of its front yard. The families were all made up the same. Each family was of a different ethnicity, but they all consisted of two parents, two children of separate gender, and a family pet. Cats, dogs; one family even had a parrot stationed on the father's shoulder.

Each yard appeared to be caught in a different season of the year. One family was clad in light shirts and shorts, appearing as if they were enjoying a nice, summer day. Another family was standing in two inches of replica snow, donned in heavy garments, including thick coats and snow boots.

Two of the houses even had vehicles parked in their driveways. One was an SUV, the other a sports car. The family with the sports car was the Caucasian one, clad in the fanciest clothing of the entire group. Gabe shook his head, holding a strong notion that this set up wasn't by accident.

Becca approached the sports car and ran her hand along it. "I shouldn't be surprised," she mumbled.

"What?" Gabe asked.

"These are real vehicles," she informed. "Blake truly spared no expense for this place." Gabe watched as she tried the door handle and was surprised when it swung open freely.

"I don't suppose he left the keys in the ignition?" Gabe asked. Becca leaned around the wheel to check, then brought her head back out, shaking it from side to side. "Nope. Apparently, he's not quite *that* outrageous."

"Know how to hotwire a car?"

Becca shook her head again.

"Damn! That would have made things easier." Gabe suddenly wished he had a little more criminal influence in his upbringing.

At the center of the cul-de-sac, on what should have been empty asphalt, was a thick, stubby obelisk. The pillar was roughly pyramidal in shape, each of its three sides containing a different theme. On one side hung framed photographs. Each photograph featured a smiling family on it, eerily similar to the families in the faux lawns, but these pictures all showed the exact same family. The photos prints were brightly reflecting the infrared light. Gabe briefly wondered what was added to the photo ink that caused such a reflection.

Walking counter-clockwise around the obelisk, the next section of the stone's face showed a vertical line running from the top down. The line was littered with dots accompanied by etched words and dates. It was a timeline. The dot at the top signified the time of prehistoric man. As it traveled down, it highlighted other times of significance in human evolution. Some based on religious myth, some on historical science. The last dot at the very bottom was labeled "Man Destroys Earth". In the time block was just a question mark.

"Blake sure is a cynical son of a bitch, isn't he?" Gabe mumbled before moving around to the third side of the obelisk.

The final side was plastered with various symbols of world religion. The Christian Cross. The Star of David. The Star and Crescent of Islam. The Mormon's Angel Moroni, tooting his own horn. A five-pointed star surrounded by a circle, symbolizing the Wiccans; known as the Pentacle. The pillar even held the inverse of that, the Sigil of Baphomet for the Satanists. It appeared to Gabe that all the various religions of the world were represented. Except for Scientology. Gabe wasn't sure what L. Ron Hubbard had chosen for his religion, but he was sure it wasn't present on the obelisk. "Because *fuck* Scientology, that's why!" Gabe mumbled the popular expression to himself, appreciating Blake's gesture.

Strangely, mixed in with all the religious iconography, were decidedly *non*-religious logos. The bold letters of CNN stood adjacent to the logo for Fox News. A representation of the dollar bill. An analog wall clock that appeared to only have two hands of equal length: one pointed at the 9, the other the 5. The golden arches of McDonald's. Several other easily recognizable company brands.

Gabe scratched his head as he stared at the final wall of the pillar.

"What does all this mean?" Becca asked, letting her gaze travel around the cul-de-sac.

"It's all about man," he answered. "Or humans, if you're inclined *against* gender-exclusive terms."

"You think it's trying to say that humanity is between heaven and hell?"

Gabe considered her question. "No, that's not quite it, I think. The exhibit isn't necessarily about heaven or hell. It's named *Midnight in the Garden of Good and Evil*. Even the sign when we first came in labeled the two directions as 'Good' and

'Evil'," Gabe explained. "I think it's trying to say that humanity is both good and evil. We are the 'In-Between'."

Gabe saw Becca slowly nod in the glow of his screen.

"Well, that's kind of a downer," Becca replied.

"Yeah," Gabe agreed. "Much less of a downer than the rest of this God-forsaken gallery, though."

"God seems cool with it to me," Becca said. Gabe was about to ask her what the fuck she was talking about, when he saw her pointing over at the large statue of God. She was smiling.

"Funny," Gabe remarked dryly. He thought her jokes were sounding more like his as the night went on. That wasn't necessarily a good thing.

A brief silence followed, until Becca asked, "So what's the plan? Hole up here until morning?"

"It's as good a place as any," Gabe shrugged. "Though I'm not entirely convinced Blake will allow us to wait it out that long. I'm sure he doesn't want to damage his new baby here, but eventually he'll get desperate enough to break through those doors. He can't let us leave. Not after everything we've seen."

"So, what do you suggest?"

Gabe scanned the area through the lit screen. After a moment, he smiled.

"I may have an idea."

INTERLUDE 8

Mirrors were among the cruelest of man's creations. Seemingly, not a day would go by where the mirror didn't grow nastier in its reflection of a person. New wrinkles in the skin, growing splotches of grey in the hair; just a couple of the sinister tricks the sheet of glass would play on the human eye.

Thomas Zellers scoffed at his aging façade as his hands worked on autopilot to weave the end of his tie through the final loop, completing the double Windsor knot. One good pull downward tightened the formal noose against his throat. Thomas gave his suit a once-over in the malevolent reflector. Satisfied, he turned to grab his suit jacket from off the nearby chair and called out to Danner. "Have those damn reporters arrived yet?"

Danner popped his head through the open doorway of Thomas' bedroom. "No, sir. As of yet, there is still no sign of them."

"What is taking them so damn long?" Thomas asked. "I scheduled the press conference for 10:00 am. That's in less than thirty minutes. They should already be here, getting set up."

"I couldn't say what's keeping them, sir."

"Well, call the station and find out," Thomas instructed, locking his cufflinks in place.

"Right away, sir," Danner obliged, vanishing from the doorway.

Thomas turned from the door and bent down to retrieve the notes for his speech. It was a short speech, less than a page in its entirety. Necessity barred him from providing details, so the announcement of his son's loss to the rights of the Zellers name hadn't required many words.

Thomas stood straight, his eyes glued to the scrawled notes. Through his peripheral vision, Thomas caught sight of a man's shadow having appeared in his doorway. "Is there something else, Danner?" Thomas asked, not bothering to look up from the page. He was answered by the unmistakable sound of a round being chambered in a pump-action shotgun.

Thomas tore himself away from the paper and turned to the shadow in his doorway.

"There is indeed something else, Father," Blake greeted when he saw that he had gained his father's full attention. "A matter of the utmost urgency, in fact."

"You!" Thomas spat the word as if it were a kernel of dog shit that had found its way into his mouth.

"Yes, me…" Blake returned. "Your spawn! Your bastard child!"

"Not anymore," Thomas refuted, seemingly unconcerned with the shotgun Blake was brandishing. "In less than thirty minutes, I will be announcing to the whole world that you are no longer any kin of mine."

"Yeah, I know. I'm cutting it close," Blake admitted. "I planned on being here much sooner, but it took longer than planned to set up the trip in such a way that nobody would know that I had ever left Los Angeles."

Thomas' stern demeanor momentarily faded as he considered the threat behind the words, his eyes flickering between the shotgun and his son's cold stare.

"Though I find it strange that the press haven't already gathered at your front door for your impending announcement," Blake continued.

Thomas' eyes narrowed in suspicion. "What did you do to call them off?"

"Me?" Blake looked genuinely surprised by the accusation. "Nothing. I swear." Blake crossed his heart. "Honestly, I figured I'd have to sneak around the back to avoid being seen. I'm just as surprised as you that they weren't huddled up on the front lawn. My good fortune, I guess."

Thomas was unsure whether he believed his son about the delay in the press' arrival. "What do you want?" he asked, changing the subject.

"There is *so* much that I want, Father. So very much," Blake informed. "But, first, I *want* into the vault."

Thomas' brow dipped in confusion. "The vault? What would you want in there? I don't keep my money in the vault."

Blake briefly chuckled. "No...just a shit-ton of gold and other priceless artifacts," Blake mocked, before rolling his eyes. "I'm not after your money, Father. At least, not yet."

"Then, what? Like I told you in Los Angeles, I already destroyed the book."

"Yes, well, fortunately for me, you lied about that." Blake smirked.

"What do you mean?"

"Oh, come on Father," Blake spouted, "I'm not an idiot. I checked your flight logs. You made a quick stop over at your estate in Switzerland before flying out to see me. You were only there half a day, so you weren't exactly vacationing. It doesn't take a genius to figure out what you were really doing. You locked the book away in your other vault."

Thomas' face dropped and Blake knew his assumption had been correct. He couldn't help the smile from forming on his lips, but he did manage to hold in his sigh of relief.

"Say that you are correct," Thomas tried, "the book is still not here. What could you possibly want from my vault? Anything you take from there, I will get back soon enough. *That* I promise you." The threat in Thomas' voice was blatant.

"Enough banter, Father. Take me to the vault." Blake waved the shotgun towards the door, ushering his father through. Thomas unwittingly tugged at his lapel, then followed his son's prompt.

They made their way through the various twists and turns of the house towards the long hallway that led to the vault. Thomas led, while Blake followed closely behind, keeping the shotgun barrel planted against his father's back. They walked mostly in silence, except when Thomas asked, "Where is Danner?"

"Don't worry about Danner. He will be joining us in the vault room. He is in good hands, being escorted by Dr. Holtz," Blake answered.

They arrived in the vault room to find Danner and Dr. Holtz already waiting. As soon as Thomas came into view, Danner prepared to come to his master's defense.

"Don't do it, Danner," Blake warned, pressing the barrel deep into his father's flesh. "I'll blow his heart straight out of his chest."

"It's okay, Danner," Thomas assured, flapping his hand to stave off his servant. "My son would never have the balls to pull that trigger."

Blake shook his head. "I've never understood the need for people to taunt someone that has a gun pointed at them. I believe it's a consequence of Hollywood. I understand that there's a stigma of bravado to such a gesture, but I assure you, there's a thin line between bravery and stupidity. Taunting the man who can end your life with the pull of a trigger lies firmly in the latter."

Thomas remained silent.

"Danner," Blake addressed, "be a dear and open the vault, would you?"

Danner looked to his boss for confirmation. Thomas nodded.

The servant stepped towards the vault door, and typed in the code. After hearing the loud sound of the lock engaging, Danner twisted the four-pronged handle and heaved open the mammoth door.

"Wonderful!" Blake proclaimed. "Thank you, Danner. Dr. Holtz?" Blake twisted toward the doctor. "Please retrieve the item and bring it to me."

Blake didn't need to specify which item. The plan had already been discussed in full on their way east.

Holtz stepped past Danner and walked into the large vault. He briefly searched the shelves until he found what he was looking for. He picked up a featureless chrome urn - the same one Blake had stumbled upon those many years prior - and brought it out to set at Blake's feet.

Thomas' brow furrowed when he saw the item that his son had asked for. "What are you going to do with that?" he asked in a wary tone.

"Just saying hello to the real Danner Hackett." Blake grinned at his father and tapped the urn with his foot. Seeing he had his father's undivided attention, he pulled a folded sheet of paper from his pocket. "I regret to inform you, Father, that when you stole the copied pages of the book from me, you missed a page."

For the first time that morning, Thomas Zellers looked afraid.

"You're probably wondering which page it is that you missed," Blake said, playfully waving the sheet in front of his father. "Well, it starts with a warning." Blake straightened the page in front of him and read from the top. "Beware: The acquisition of an enslaved soul must be made in the presence of the soul's earthly body. If the body is not present, the enslaved soul will be set free to roam the Earth at its leisure."

"You damn fool!" Thomas shouted. Blake knew the anger in his father's voice was only there to cover up the intense fear that was overtaking him. "Danner! Stop him!" Thomas ordered, no longer fearing the shotgun's mighty power.

Danner started towards Blake, prompting Blake to hurriedly read the first line of the enchantment scrawled on the page. "Be still all trapped souls that hear these words."

Danner froze in place, his foolish attempt halted. Blake's heart was filled with a dark joy as he saw that the words were already proving their dark magic. He read on.

Blake read through the end of the stanza. Thomas' eyes continuously flickered between Blake and the shotgun he held firmly pointed at the older man's chest. In his mind, Blake gave his father 50/50 odds on whether or not he'd do something stupid to try and stop him from finishing the verse.

Having read off the final words of the passage, Blake folded the page and stuffed it back into his pocket.

"You happy now, boy?" Thomas asked, seeing Blake's smug smile.

Blake nodded with a gleam in his eye. Reading the words had left a sense of power flooding through his veins.

"Danner," Thomas tried, "remove this shotgun from my boy's grip and shove it up his ass."

Danner didn't move.

Blake laughed. "You didn't really think that'd work, did you? Did you doubt the power of the book?"

Thomas shrugged. "No, but I figured I'd try anyway."

"Cute," Blake replied, then turned toward Danner. "Danner, how did you feel when my father took your life and resurrected you as his own personal slave?"

"Not too happy about it, sir."

"Were you angry about it?"

"Yes, sir," Danner answered.

"Angry enough that you could just tear into him? Rip him apart limb by limb?"

"I couldn't deny that the thought had crossed my mind," Danner said, his eyes like piercing daggers into Thomas' flesh.

"Well, then, Danner," Blake said, turning back to his father, his lips curled in a cruel and sinister grin. "Have at it."

"With pleasure, sir," Danner approved. Blake saw a dangerous smirk spread across Danner's face as his body began to disintegrate. Starting at his feet and traveling up the length of his body, Danner's flesh broke apart into thousands – perhaps millions - of grey specks. Resembling a swarm of insects, the man transformed into a whirlwind of ash that flew toward Thomas and enveloped the older man's body.

Blake watched in fascination as the cloud consumed his father. The ash lifted Thomas off his feet and violently spun him around in the air. As his father spun, a mass of the pallid particles spread out from the main body and wrapped around Thomas' arm. The grey tendril seemed to coalesce around the older man's limb, growing thick around his bicep. With a sickening crunch, the ash tentacle twisted Thomas' arm a full one hundred and eighty degrees. Blake couldn't blame his father for the screams of agony that the twisted limb elicited from him. The ash wasn't done with the arm, however. It twisted it further. And further. And further. It spun the arm around until the bicep was nothing more than a tightly-wound coil of skin, like some kind of freakish bread tie. Even then, the thickened ash cloud continued to twist. Eventually, the arm twisted to the point that the skin's limited elasticity could bear no more. The strained flesh came apart, freeing Thomas Zellers' limb to fall lifelessly to the floor.

The ash tentacle reabsorbed into the greater mass of the ash cloud, another tendril forming on the other side to repeat the process with Thomas' other arm.

More howls followed.

Blake had seen enough. He turned from the grisly display and left Danner to finish his bout of vengeance. Surprised by the queasiness that had taken over his stomach, Blake grabbed onto Dr. Holtz's shoulder to steady himself as they walked down the long hallway.

"Doctor," Blake said, trying to keep his mind off the fading screams behind him, "check to see if the media vans have arrived. If not, great. If so, then we'll need to ready the back passage. Either way, we'll be leaving soon."

"Yes, sir," Holtz responded, moving off toward the front of the house. Blake let the door at the end of the long hallway swing shut behind him, further drowning out the wails of agony coming from the vault room. He found he was in the kitchen and walked over to the cabinets to retrieve a drinking glass. He filled it with fresh water from the tap and chugged the entire glass down. He had somehow grown incredibly thirsty. He filled the glass again, this time sipping at the cool contents.

Blake had finished the second glass, still with no sign of Holtz' return. Curious, he set off toward the front of the house. "Dr. Holtz? What's taking so long?" Blake called out as he entered the sprawling front room of the manner. He stepped through the doorway and found Holtz staring at a large television screen mounted on the wall.

"I believe I know why the press never showed, sir," Holtz informed, having heard Blake enter. "They are most likely tied up at the moment."

Blake looked from his servant to the television screen. At first, he wasn't sure what he was seeing. Two columns of dark smoke rising from nearly-identical towers. Some Hollywood production, Blake initially assumed.

"What is this, Doctor?" Blake asked, pointing to the screen.

"Planes have apparently hit the World Trade Center, sir. Both towers."

As Blake watched, one of the smoking towers collapsed into an enormous cloud of dust. Turning his attention to the scroll at the bottom of the screen, Blake saw that it was 9:58am, September 11th, 2001.

A satisfying crunch split the air as Gabe smashed the night-vision goggles against the tiled floor. Through the pair he wore, Gabe saw the shattered shards of the pair he had just smashed join the multitude of others already resting on the floor after their own violent liberation.

"Well, that's the last of them," Gabe informed Becca.

"Good. Now we need to search for the light switch. This will all be for naught if they just stroll in here and flip on the lights," Becca said.

"You sure that there are any in here?"

"Of course there are. It's not like they constructed this whole exhibit wearing night vision goggles," Becca said. "Plus, I'm sure the janitor would appreciate some light in here as well."

"Good point," Gabe conceded. "Any ideas where they would have placed a switch in here?"

"Oh, I don't know," Becca spoke in a sarcastic tone. "Maybe where most people put a light switch...near the door." She brought her hand up to a nondescript box set onto the wall, about a foot beyond where the door frame transitioned into the flat wall. A hinge ran along the side of the box's faceplate, with a small key receptacle set into the opposite side. "Of course, they have it locked in a box, away from the prying hands of a less-mature sort of patron."

"Perfect!" Gabe exclaimed. "I'll be right back." He left Becca waiting by the door as he took off through the exhibit, headed back in the direction of the staged cul-de-sac. When he returned, he was hefting a cross-shaped tire iron.

"I had a feeling I'd find this guy under the back panel of that SUV," Gabe explained. "The spare tire is back there too, but I couldn't think of any good use for that right now." Gabe took the lug wrench up to the lockbox and began mercilessly smashing at it. It only took three swings to knock the box loose. A chunk of plaster fell from the wall as the lockbox dropped away, becoming suspended in the air by wires running out its backside. Gabe - realizing that the switch was still in the lockbox - gripped the aluminum container and tore it away from the wall. The wires easily broke apart, successfully ending the threat of light for the exhibit.

Gabe and Becca ran back to the other side of the room, repeated the process on an identical lockbox, and sat down with their backs against the wall. Gabe felt strangely successful after the endeavor.

"What now?" Becca asked.

"We wait," Gabe answered. "If they manage to break in, at least we'll have an advantage in the darkness." Gabe tapped his goggles, one of only two operable pairs remaining; Becca wearing the other.

They sat back against the wall in silence, each lost in their own thoughts. Gabe stared out at the olive landscape and the green shadows it contained. Fear still coursed through his veins, but sitting silently, looking out at the darkened exhibit, brought him a certain type of calm.

It was Becca who broke the silence. "So why did you never go pro?"

"Huh?" Gabe asked, confused by the question.

"In football," she answered. "You talk about it like you were the next Tom Brady, and I've seen the way you handle yourself, so why become a struggling musician instead?"

"Tom Brady!?" Gabe asked with disdain. "I would never compare myself to Tom Brady. That guy can never seem to figure out what to do with that mop on his head."

"You know what I mean," Becca insisted.

"It's nothing," Gabe said after a silent moment, his tone having grown more serious. "Just some shit went down a while back. I didn't feel like playing the game anymore."

"Wow!" Becca teased. "Sounds like it must have been some *serious* shit. I kinda get the feeling that football was your life's dream once."

"You could say that," Gabe agreed as matter-of-factly as possible.

Becca stared at him a moment longer, challenging him to continue. When she saw that Gabe wasn't going to be baited, she sat back in defeat. "Okay, then. What about that song I liked? 'An Ancient Madness', I think it was. You promised me that there was a story there, as well."

Gabe briefly snickered at her question, but otherwise remained silent.

"What?" she prodded.

"It's just kind of funny you would ask that as a replacement question," Gabe admitted.

"Why is that funny?"

"Because, truth be told, they're kind of the same question," Gabe said.

Becca shook her head, as if trying to clear something plaguing her brain. "Okay," she said, "now I'm confused."

"I have this awesome story baked up about how I wrote that song, but it's bullshit. Or, at least, it's *mostly* bullshit. I stuck some tidbits of the truth in there, but the rest is as made up as a Ted Cruz speech."

"Well, what's the true story?" Becca urged. "I'm beginning to think this will be a good one."

"It's not *that* great," Gabe lazily countered. "In fact, I don't even remember a large portion of it, so it's really not worth telling."

"It's not like we have much else going on," Becca argued. "We are pretty much just stuck here waiting until either they make a move or we figure something else out."

Gabe almost argued further, wanting to refuse the request. Instead: "Ah hell!" Gabe relented, rolling his eyes skyward. "Why the fuck not? We're probably going to die tonight anyway, right?"

"No!" Becca blurted staunchly, "we are not going to die! We'll figure something out."

"I was joking," Gabe reacted to Becca's sudden outburst. Then, mumbled under his breath, "Maybe."

"*However*," Becca said smartly, probably having caught Gabe's mumble, "in the meantime, I'd appreciate a little story."

Gabe sighed in an effort to steel himself for his story. "Okay...here goes nothing..." And Gabe started in on his story.

It was the summer between our junior and senior years. I always loved summer. The beaches, the babes; the big "fuck you" to the schoolhouses that kept us as prisoners for the other nine months of the year.

Oh...and the start of football season just around the corner. During those high school summers, I would often hang out with members of my team, working on chemistry and camaraderie. And drinking...lots and lots of drinking.

You know...jock stuff.

That particular summer, two of my teammates had gotten together with me and we had planned a trip up to New England. Boston, mostly. They were two of my larger teammates. Some real giant motherfuckers; offensive linemen for the team. Running backs are cool, and there's no doubt that quarterbacks should spend a lot of time with their wide receivers to build chemistry, but linemen are the ones that protect your ass on every play. I always made a point to get in real tight with my linemen, so they'd have that little extra motivation to keep me from getting creamed.

Besides, these motherfuckers were cool-ass dudes. Geoff Bagson, my right guard, could easily match you drink-for-drink *until your ass was planted on the ground. My left tackle was Danny Bagson - yes, they were twins. I can only imagine the look on their mother's face after she pushed the first of those two mammoths out of her vagina, only to realize that a whole 'nother freight train was already chugging down the tracks.*

Anyway, everyone called Danny by the nickname D-Bag. I know...not the most original of nicknames, but he was cool with it. I always took it a step further and just straight-up called him Douche. It caught on with others after a while. When somebody would ask him if the name bothered him, he would simply reply, "Why would it? Like the douche, God put me on this Earth to reside in pussy!"

Douche was definitely my kind of people.

Now, Douche wasn't quite the drinker that Geoff was, but he would put you on your ass quicker in other ways. He was stronger than Geoff, and much faster. He was also way smarter. He loved football for sure, but he also loved school. History, science, even art – he'd probably have loved this fucking gallery, to be honest. At least, before acidic shit demons started trolling around.

So, in Boston, we ended up being invited to a party at a creepy old mansion. This place had to have already been collecting dust back when George Washington was removing his wooden teeth to eat out his wife's pussy. It didn't look inviting from the outside, but that shit was hopping on the inside.

The mansion was owned by some guy named Joseph Curwen. It was outside of town, tucked away at the edge of the wilderness. Surrounded by woods and a large iron fence, the mansion spoke of a reclusive personality. Now, from what I gathered during our time there, the Curwen family had owned the place for quite a long time. I never did figure out exactly what their business was, but, despite the reclusive appearance of their estate, they had apparently been pretty popular in the Boston social circles for a long fucking time. Or, in the words of the young lady who had invited us to this party, "For, like, forever." And yes, she was twirling her blonde hair around her finger as she said it.

Her name was Henrietta, but she wanted us to call her Hetty. We had met her while watching the Sox play in Fenway. Let's just say that she took an instant shine to Douche. A fact made evident by how they disappeared near the seventh-inning stretch and, after returning, Douche asked me if I wanted to smell his fingers. That's the kind of shit he always played at, after living up to his nickname.

Hetty was the daughter of some famous socialite. If you ask me, she was a spoiled bitch, and ditzy as all hell, but Douche had neglected to ask and had no interest in my opinion anyway. So, when she told us about the party that evening and practically begged us to go - "Please come! These things are always so droll, but my father loves showing off his precious daughter," she had whined - Douche was all about enlisting the team to her aid.

Hetty turned out to be a pretty popular gal among the old socialites, though. Even though we were only in our late teens, the old fogeys that doted over her had no problem letting us attack the bar. They were trying to impress her, after all.

Not everybody there was of the inner circle, though. Nor were they all perverted old men. Some were simply invited as we were, though because they were rich, famous, and just happened to be in town. I had figured I was going to absolutely dread every moment of that damn party, but I was pleasantly surprised when I spotted some celebrities I recognized. In fact, I was frozen in total fanboy mode when I spotted Iron Maiden's Bruce Dickinson at the bar- The Dick himself.

******

"Wait," Becca interrupted the story, "did you just refer to Bruce Dickinson as 'The Dick'?"

Gabe shrugged. "Yeah. Just consider it a term of endearment. Besides, I doubt he'd give a fuck what a nobody like me calls him anyway, so why not?"

Becca shook her head and twirled her hand in the air, urging him to continue on.

"Anyway, as I was saying..."

******

Bruce looked as if he was as bored by the party as I was. Or, as I was before the party took a decidedly upward turn when The Dick was thrust in front of my face.

Okay...that sounded bad. But, still, the point stands.

I was star-struck, mouth gaping like a damned fucktard. Probably why I didn't notice Douche sneaking off with Hetty to find some private place in the mansion.

I'm not sure how long I was standing there, looking like some kind of creeper. Eventually Geoff snuck up behind me and slapped my back entirely harder than necessary. Just something we did to each other.

"Seeing your dumb face from across the room, I would have sworn you were bird-dogging the perfect pair of fuckable titties," Geoff said, looking unimpressed by the focus of my attentions.

"Dude!" I protested, "That's fucking Bruce Dickinson!"

"Bruce Dick-in-what?" Geoff joked. I almost punched him in the face for his irreverence. Before I could, though, he slapped me on the back again and said, "By the way, it's two minutes to midnight."

"What?" I glanced at my watch. Sure enough, it was. I was sure it had to be a sign. A sign of what, I'm not sure. Either way, at that moment, you could have fired a bullet through my skull and it wouldn't have driven the chorus from the classic Iron Maiden song out of my head. Two Minutes to Midnight!

"Anyway, when you're done mentally jerking off, meet me at the bar for a shot," Geoff interrupted my internal shred-fest.

"Fuck you," I replied, not entirely sure what I was rebuking him for.

"Nope," he said. "I must decline, leaving only one Bagson brother getting fucked tonight."

That was the first time that I noticed Douche was missing. "Where's your bro?" I asked.

"He snuck off with Hetty for some primetime boning," Geoff answered. "Which is why I need your punk ass to stop gawking at random dudes and come join me for some shots."

"Okay," I begrudgingly agreed, tearing myself away from my idol. Besides, I think he had finally noticed my staring and I figured I should retreat before he called security. Yes, this place had security. It was that upper-class.

I followed Geoff over to the bar where he went straight to the Bacardi 151 and poured us each a shot. I wanted to protest that you should never start with the 1-5-1, but he thrust the shot glass into my hand, clanked it against his own, and upended the contents down his throat. To not be thought of as a pussy, I followed suit. I immediately felt like I was getting throat-fucked sans lube as the fiery liquid raced down my gullet.

I erupted into a fit of coughing, hacking, and maybe even a little drooling.

Geoff erupted into a fit of laughter.

Good times.

Anyway, Geoff started pouring another shot, but this time I called him off. "Hold off on that for now, you sadistic fuck," I begged him. "Let's just grab a beer."

Geoff downed another shot anyway, but thank-the-baby-Jesus, he didn't make me join him for it.

Turns out, there is a God after all!

Anyway, beer in hand, we unsuccessfully tried to mingle. As it turned out, we didn't have much in common with socialites.

I'm not sure how much time passed – probably about an hour – but I started growing worried about Douche. There had been no sign of him since he had disappeared with Hetty.

"Not to diss on the Bagson name," I started, fully expecting him to punch me for what I was about to say, "but your bro isn't exactly known for his longevity in the sack." I glanced at my watch for effect. "What's keeping him, you think?"

"He's not a cuddler either, so probably not that," Geoff subtlety agreed. "But you never really know with Douche."

Like I said earlier, the nickname caught on.

"You think we should go find him?" I asked.

Geoff shrugged. "Why the fuck not?" He chugged the remaining contents of his bottle and slammed it down onto the counter. I remember being surprised that the fucking thing hadn't shattered. One random party-goer threw him a disapproving look at not properly disposing of the bottle, but - their eyes travelling up Geoff's tall, bulky frame – wisely thought better of going so far as to actually rebuke him.

Geoff led me to the door that Douche and Hetty had disappeared through and waved me inside. The noise of the party quickly vanished as the door swung closed behind us, leaving us in a large, empty hallway.

"This place is pretty fucking creepy," Geoff said in the disturbingly silent wing of the house.

The only word I could think to describe the hallway was ornate. *Gold molding ran along the creases at the top and bottoms of the walls. The walls themselves were covered with a silky wallpaper that was inlaid with vertical lines of differing brown and golden hues. The carpet that ran along the length of the hallway was mostly red with a golden pattern sprinkled throughout, reminding me of some form of Ming Dynasty bullshit.*

Mirrors and paintings aplenty lined the walls, as well as various tables from a bygone Victorian era. Many of the tables held vases. Most of the vases held flowers. About half the flowers were dead; limp, dark, and withering on their stems.

Lastly, several doors could be seen spaced along the wall. They were painted gold as well, completing the hallway's ornate, old-money motif.

"Did we just fucking warp into Dracula's castle?" I said after taking it all in. "You'd think Douche would have been a bit intimidated coming through here."

"He was running on boner vision," Geoff pointed out. "Probably didn't even notice."

"Well, I'm guessing they went through one of these doors," I said, trying the first one we came to. Inside was a restroom, though much fancier than any I had ever had the pleasure of dropping a turd in. Lots of floor space, covered in the same dreadful carpeting as the hallway. I don't think I'll ever understand carpeting in a bathroom – seems like the mold alone would be hell to manage.

Golden sinks and a golden tub stood atop the carpet. The old style of tub; bowl-shaped and sitting on top of feet that looked like they were designed by Da Vinci. No shower head, just the tub with a built-in faucet.

Even the shitter was formed out of gold. A literal golden throne.

What the bathroom didn't contain was one bare-naked Douche plugging up various Hetty holes. I say various, because – while I didn't actively seek out information on Douche's sexual proclivities – I had heard some things. Things I wished I could unhear.

We moved on to the next door, and then the next. Bedrooms of similar gaudiness as what we had already seen. It was when we arrived at the second-to-last door of the hallway that I heard it. The unmistakable sounds of ecstasy.

We followed the moans to the last doorway at the end of the hall. It was an enlarged entrance, containing two doors that connected in the middle. The doors radiated an ominous feel about them, which Geoff and I would have maybe wondered about if we hadn't started giggling like little girls when we put our ears to the door.

"Oh Douche! Oh Douche!" came the moans through the door.

Apparently Hetty had adopted the nickname as well. She had just taken a decidedly upward turn in my book.

Geoff and I stood in the hallway, snickering outside the double-doors. "You do realize the fucked-up opportunities that have just been presented to us, right?" Geoff asked with a mischievous grin.

"He's your brother. Lead the way." I waved my hand at the door to suggest he open it and walk through.

He took the invitation and slowly swung the door inward. He crept through quietly and waved for me to follow.

And...

"And what?" Becca asked, after realizing that Gabe had stopped speaking.

"And…that's it," Gabe answered. "That's all that I remember. Next thing I know, I am lying in the woods somewhere outside the mansion, head bleeding, and no idea how I got there."

"Really?" Becca - who, by all appearances, had been enthralled in his story - protested. "That's it?"

"That's it." Gabe threw his hands in the air in a gesture of hopelessness.

"What happened after you woke up? What happened to Geoff and Douche?"

"That's just it. I'm not sure," Gabe explained. "After waking up in the woods, I made my way back to Curwen's manor. It's not like it was the first time I woke up bleeding - complete with a loss of memory - after a night of drinking, so I wasn't overly concerned. When I got there, I was basically told to go fuck myself. Mr. Curwen's staff used more cordial terms than that, but the meaning was clear.

"When I asked about Douche and Geoff, they told me that they had wandered off with me during the night and they had all assumed we had just up and left. I didn't like their tone, so I accused them of letting minors get shit-faced and then leave unsupervised, and that the cops might be interested to hear what I had to say in the matter. That got the man himself's attention. Joseph Curwen came out to meet me. I tell you what, that was one chill motherfucker. He smiled at me the entire time and seemed as if he didn't have a care in the world. Even when I threatened him with the police, he just waved it off. Eventually, he asked me to leave and I got the feeling that it wasn't a request he was going to let me disagree with. At that point – with a splitting headache and my nerves growing increasingly frantic – I walked away. I promised him I'd be back - more of a threat really – but I walked away.

"I went back to the hotel we were staying at and waited. I never made good on my threat to involve the police. I had never been serious about that threat anyway. I was just grumpy and pissed off. I *should* have gone to them, though. I realized that too late.

"Two days went by and still no sign of Douche and Geoff. Needless to say, I was worried. Very worried. I was finally ready to go to the cops with my story when they came to me. The police had found Douche and Geoff. Dead. Tucked into some dark corner, miles away from Curwen's mansion."

"Oh my God," Becca blurted, her hand going to her mouth in a sign of shock.

"Of course," Gabe continued, "me being their travel buddy, I was under suspicion. They hauled me into the precinct and questioned me for hours. I told them everything that I could remember. Including, and especially, the party at Joseph Curwen's. Strangely, I thought, they seemed disinterested in Curwen's providing to minors. They promised to have a word with him about it, but that was it. At that point, I wanted them to throw the book at him. Send him to the fucking chair. Silly, I know, but I didn't give a fuck right then. I wasn't thinking rationally. Two of my best friends had just been found dead.

"Anyway, the police kept me around up there in Boston for a couple of weeks. They told me I was not to leave the state while they investigated my friends' deaths. I guess they questioned Mr. Curwen about it, but I wasn't invited to that interrogation. I wish I would have been. I would have loved to have seen his face when he recounted what had happened. To be honest, I wasn't sure if Mr. Curwen had anything to do with what had happened – hell, he could have been telling the truth about us simply walking out on our own for all I knew – but something in me told me that he was complicit in some form or another. In fact, for some reason I've never been able to figure out, I would get chills down my spine when I even thought of Joseph Curwen. Still do, in fact.

"Jeez...I 'm sorry. That's a horrible story," Becca sympathized in a gentle tone.

"Yeah, it's horrible," Gabe agreed. "But that's not all of it. Something else strange happened during those weeks that I was stuck waiting.

"During those weeks, I searched for Hetty, hoping she could shed some light on what-the-fuck had happened. I knew who her family was, so I went for a little visit. I found her father – drunk; his eyes soaked with tears and red, as if they'd been that way for days. He cursed me out and *literally* told me to go fuck myself. And that's before I had even said hello.

"I did manage to eventually get one actionable piece of information from him, though. Apparently, Hetty had found herself a job. A 'no-good, fucking piece-of-shit, evil cunt-bagging, fucking might-as-well shove razorblades up my asshole' job, as Hetty's father explained it. I had a hard time imagining what job she may have gotten based on his description – maybe a lawyer?

– but, before he slammed the door in my face, he let it slip that she had started working for Mr. Curwen. He leaned heavily on the word *working,* as if the word were a mockery of her actual purpose there. That left me to believe that she had become Curwen's personal whore, or something similarly degrading."

"So, I fought through my inexplicable fear of the place and made my way back to Curwen's. You could say I was surprised when Hetty answered my rapping at the door, though that wouldn't do it justice. After my initial shock, I laid into her with a barrage of questions. Speedy questions. To-the-point questions. 'What the fuck happened to my friends?' questions.

"After who-knows-how-long of my being lost in the verbal assault, I began noticing that there was something off about Hetty. She had been standing there, taking my abuse without any reaction. No smart-ass remarks, no twirling her blond hair while rolling her eyes - nothing! She looked stoned. She looked dead to the world. I asked her what was wrong with her and she replied, 'Nothing, sir. I am splendid. How may I assist you today?' That was so *not* the Hetty we had partied with a couple nights before.

"I laid into her again. This time I was more colorful and instead of just asking questions, I started throwing out accusations amid other less-than-pleasant innuendos. When my tirade had finally tapered off, she responded 'I apologize, sir, but I am going to have to ask you to leave now.'

"I considered punching her in her inanimate face, but that's when the cops showed up and removed me from the house. They took me back to the station and informed me that I was no longer a suspect. They had officially ruled the whole thing as a murder-suicide, saying Douche had killed Geoff and then himself. I never did find out what led them to that conclusion. Something about the way they found the bodies. To this day, however, I haven't bought into that explanation. There is no way – no *fucking* way –

that Douche would kill his brother and then himself. It just doesn't make any sense.

"But what could I do?" Gabe threw his hands up in defeat. "Nothing! There was absolutely nothing I could do about any of it. So I packed my bags and came back home."

"After the summer ended, I went back to school for my senior year. I even resumed my place on the football team. I played for a while, but about halfway through the season, I pulled myself out. For one, I had taken a lot more sacks than I ever had before. As much as I would like to blame that on the diminished talent of my offensive line - Geoff and Douche's replacements weren't anywhere near as talented as those two – I knew deep down that it was mostly because I was slower in my scramble. I felt haunted whenever I would line up for a play. There were physical bodies in the places where Douche and Geoff were supposed to be, but in my vision, it seemed as if there were black holes haunting those positions instead. Sometimes I would call out one of those two's names when I was running an audible. I'll tell you what, my replacement Left Tackle sure didn't appreciate being called a douche." Gabe rolled his eyes while shaking his head.

"Anyway, after that whole thing, I just wasn't feeling the sport anymore. I didn't want to play...no...I *couldn't* play anymore. I was done. I hung up my cleats and picked up a guitar. Music had always been my other passion and I delved into it. Hard! Like a junkie with a needle. That and alcohol. For a while there, there was just me, the guitar, and enough alcohol to bring Amy Winehouse back to life."

"Jesus," Becca said. "You poor baby." She didn't say it in a condescending way. Her tone was caring and sympathetic. She wrapped Gabe in her arms and held him in a conciliatory embrace. She held him that way for a long moment, then backed away and released him.

"When you started your story, you mentioned that the story was the answer to both: why you left football behind *and* the story behind 'An Ancient Madness'. Where does your song play into all of that?" Becca asked.

"Remember the part about where I had awoken in the woods after the blackout?"

"Yeah," Becca confirmed.

"Well, before my eyes had even opened, those words were ringing in my skull. Even so long after that, whenever I think back to that night at Joseph Curwen's manor, those words play back like a recording in my head. I don't know if they're a fragment of memory, or what...but they're the only thing my mind settles on whenever I have attempted to peer through the darkness."

"Wow," Becca awed. "That song hits even harder now that I know its story."

"And you didn't even get to hear the whole thing. We barely got past the intro before that fuck-head venue manager cut us off."

"Intro? You guys were playing for nearly five minutes before you even started singing."

"It's mostly an instrumental," Gabe explained. "It's fucking awesome, though. The guitars get to the point where they really start booming and then I come in to sweep you in the rest of the way. I have always felt it was the most powerful way I could get those words out to everybody. The closest I could come to haunting others with the words that have haunted me for so long."

"Well it worked on me," Becca informed. "I can't wait to hear the rest of it."

"I can sing it for you now. No awesome lead-in unfortunately, but at least you'll get to hear it if...you know...if we don't..."

"Don't even say it," Becca cut him off. "We'll make it out of here." Becca was silent a moment as she considered the offer of him crooning to her. "Save it for after we escape," she finally decided. "It'll be our little celebration."

"I can think of better ways to celebrate, but..." Gabe stopped when Becca reintroduced him to her shoulder punching technique. "Ow!" Gabe protested, rubbing his shoulder. "I was going to say that we could do that, as well."

Becca shot him that cute little smile of hers. "Song first, and then we'll see where that leaves us."

Gabe nodded in agreement.

That's when the light above the door went out.

INTERLUDE 9

It had taken over a year for the investigation into Thomas Zellers' death to finally conclude. Hell, with all the craziness that had gone down at the time, it had taken nearly two weeks before anybody had even realized he was missing. Blake Zellers didn't envy that first poor sap who had wondered into the Zellers estate to find several rotting limbs parsed out among the many rooms of the massive house. That had to have been a foul and merciless experience.

Blake had managed to make it out of Rhode Island and back to the west coast without being noticed. The Presidential grounding of all US flights had surely made things inconvenient, but a fake driver's license and an unknown face like Dr. Holtz's, made getting a rental car while remaining incognito a relatively easy task.

As expected, remaining unseen had been vitally important for Blake. As soon as his father's body had been found, the investigation roared to life like an unstoppable supernova. The feds got involved. The media went crazy. And, of course, the spotlight quickly came to rest upon Blake's faux-horrified face. It wasn't a stretch to suspect Blake in Thomas Zellers' murder. As far as motives go, the number of ways Blake would benefit from his father's death numbered in the billions.

Unfortunately, during the investigation, Blake only had limited access to his father's funds. Now that the investigation had finally concluded, with his father never having had the chance to amend his will, Blake's accounts had usurped all that was his father's.

With everything now his, Blake stepped into his father's Rhode Island estate for the first time since that fateful day that the nation had forever changed. He took a moment to soak in the view of the foyer in a way that he had never done before. It seemed different somehow, now that he owned it.

"Have you decided what you are going to do with the place, sir?" a voice asked from behind him.

Blake slowly nodded, then cocked his head to answer Danner over his shoulder. "Burning it would have been my first choice, but selling it off seems like the more practical decision."

"Very good, sir," Danner cheerily replied.

"I'm sure you won't be crushed knowing you'll never see this place again," Blake mused.

"Is it too late to convince you to go with your first choice, sir?" Danner joked. Blake smirked.

"Let's get what I need out of here, and then follow suit ourselves," Blake instructed. "I'm ready to be rid of this place."

"Yes, sir." Danner signaled to Dr. Holtz and the two made their way towards the back of the house to retrieve the requested items from the vault.

Blake took a moment to himself, walking around the mansion and reminiscing about the days gone by that he had spent in this place. He was surprised that he felt a mild sadness at saying goodbye. A *very* mild sadness, to be sure, but a sadness nonetheless.

"Maybe it'd be better if I actually did burn this place," Blake mumbled to himself, rebelling against the unexpected emotion.

Blake's waltz through the mansion's halls eventually took him to the vault room, where Danner and Holtz were still busy boxing up the random artwork and artifacts of his late father.

"How's it coming?" Blake asked.

"Fine, sir. Just finishing up," Danner answered, carefully placing the original manuscript of Capote's *In Cold Blood* into a box.

"Very well," Blake replied. He stood silently for a moment, staring into the vault. He took himself back to the night that he had snuck inside and discovered the book. A small grin twisted his lips at the memory. Oh, how that night had sent his life careening down a greater path.

With the last of the boxes sealed, Danner approached Blake, breaking him from his reverie. "Sir, if I might make a suggestion?"

"Go right ahead."

"Sir, in your father's study are some materials that you may find interesting," Danner said. "I know that you instructed us to retrieve only a few items from the vault, but I think you should see what it was that Thomas Zellers was working on when he met his end."

"Why?"

"I believe the object your father was seeking could be beneficial to your quest for more acolytes."

"Really?" Blake's eyebrow raised. Since opening the Magna Arta, he had thrice attempted to create new slaves such as Danner and Holtz, but had only managed one success out of the three. He was positive that it was a consequence of failure of the first of the crucial parts of the formula for reincarnation. Instead of having a personal slave, Blake kept winding up with nothing but grotesquely dead bodies. "Lead the way."

Danner did just that, leading Blake to his father's study. Once there, Danner walked around Thomas Zellers' desk and rifled through one of the drawers. He came out with a stack of papers that had been clipped together. Blake quickly rummaged through the sheets. They were mostly requisition forms, journal entries, news articles, and various other documents.

Blake delved deeper into the documents, raising an eyebrow at what he saw. "Is this real?" he asked.

Danner nodded. "You're father seemed to think so. He spent several years trying to find it. He was obsessed. He was certain enough of its existence that he dropped millions of dollars setting everything up for its retrieval."

"Where did he leave off? I see here that he had already hired a crew to excavate the item. Did they ever actually get it?"

"No, sir." Danner answered. "You're father hadn't yet given the green light before we made our trip out west to visit you. It was the very next day that his life was brought to an end."

"So where's the crew now?"

"Well, they were a local crew up there in the Carpathian Mountains, so I would assume that they are still somewhere nearby. I could look into it, if you like."

Blake nodded. "I would like that, yes. See to it, Danner. This is not anything I would have ever come up with on my own, but now that the idea has been planted, I do believe I am in love with it. Do what you have to do to make it happen."

"Yes, sir." Danner acknowledged. "According to the timeline your father had constructed, once I have greenlit the excavating team, we should expect delivery of the item within two months."

"That works for me," Blake agreed. He stared at the documents for a moment longer, then added, "This is exciting. Thank you, Danner."

"Of course, sir."

Blake handed the stack of documents off to Danner and glanced around the manor one last time. "I wonder how difficult it would be to sell you off, *then* burn you to the ground?" Blake asked the silent beige walls.

They didn't answer.

Gabe stared in awe at the dark spot that had previously stood out as a bright beacon in the viewfinder of his night vision goggles.

"I think we may be fucked," Gabe suggested.

"Blake must have cut the power to the electronic door locks," Becca postulated.

"Alright, this is what we planned for," Gabe assured both Becca and himself. He faced the nearest door – the one that led into *Suffering For Art* - and raised the tire iron in his hand, readying its use as a bludgeoning tool.

"I'm thinking that I'm not a fan of this plan anymore," Becca breathed. "Any plan Bs in mind?"

From behind them, they could hear the door on the opposite side of the exhibit crash open, followed by a rush of footsteps pounding through. Gabe didn't risk looking back. He kept his eyes frozen on the door nearest them, tire iron at the ready, intent on fucking up any poor soul that decided to walk through it. As of yet, the door hadn't moved.

"They destroyed all of the NVGs," one voice carried through the darkness. "Mr. Zellers is not going to be pleased by that."

Good...Fuck Zellers! Gabe thought as a narrow smile crept over his lips.

"The light switches, too," another voice called out.

Another sound carried across the room to Gabe. A whooshing sound that Gabe couldn't place. Something similar to somebody flapping leather sheets in the air.

"Anybody have a flashlight?" the original voice asked.

"I don't," a voice answered. This one Gabe recognized. It was Lester, the champagne butler/total asshole. Gabe figured that Lester was the one man in this place – or *thing*, perhaps – that Gabe despised more than Blake. Alarmingly, Lester's voice was coming from the same area that Gabe heard the flapping sound. "It'd be nice to have a cell phone right about now," Lester continued. "Somebody needs to bring that up with Mr. Zellers for the next time."

"You're not going to get a cell phone. It's not even worth asking," the original voice definitively said. Gabe began thinking that he may have recognized this voice too. He was increasingly sure it was that quack, Dr. Holtz.

Gabe had his suspicions confirmed when Holtz yelled out through the blackness. "Mr. Daniels? Ms. Larson? We know you are both in here," Holtz called out. "Save us all a lot of trouble and come out of hiding. We *will* find you."

As much as Gabe wanted to send a resounding 'Fuck you' back to Holtz, he wisely kept his mouth shut as he scanned around for other options.

"That's it!" Becca's sudden outburst caused Gabe to flinch. "Cell phones." She kept her volume low, but it was easy to hear the excitement in her voice.

Gabe wasn't sure what she was getting at. He declined to respond as he kept searching for another way out. His eyes stopped on the cul-de-sac family that were huddled together in the snow.

"We're so close," Becca persisted, pulling at Gabe's sleeve. "They are right on the other side of that door." Becca gripped his chin and twisted his head around until he was facing the door to *Suffering For Art*. "Nobody has come through there yet. Maybe they're all coming in from the other side."

Before Gabe could stop her, Becca ran towards the door. Gabe jumped after her and barely managed to reach her in time, tackling her off the path to the side before she could cross the threshold of the first door. No sooner had he dragged her off to the side, a beam of light burst through the doorway as somebody opened the second door.

Becca initially struggled against Gabe's grip, but soon saw the light as well. It was hard to miss. Their entire view screens were nearly saturated in a blindingly bright green flare. Gabe instinctively knocked his goggles upward and onto his forehead. Becca did the same next to him.

They crawled behind a faux bush and examined the figure in the sudden influx of light. It was one of Blake's stooges that Gabe didn't recognized. He was standing at the door, peeking through. He scanned to search what little he could in the spill of light. Gabe and Becca stayed perfectly still behind the bush, peeking through its branches as the thug searched. After a moment, he stepped back into the light and closed the door behind him, the light immediately turning green, then red.

Gabe felt his heart pound faster in his chest as he realized the door that Blake's staffer had closed was the one on their side of the entry room. He heard the screech of a handheld radio somewhere off in the distance.

"Shit," Gabe swore under his breath. "They're trapping us in here until the search team combs through the entire room."

"We still have an advantage. They're going to need light to do a thorough search. Maybe we can hide somewhere," Becca suggested.

As if on cue, Holtz' deep tenor broke through the darkness again. "Ah, good. Joel, you're here." Gabe heard a murmured reply, but couldn't make out the words. "Go ahead. Do your thing," Holtz instructed.

Suddenly, without aid of the goggles that still hugged his forehead, Gabe could see. A golden glow ate through the darkness from the other end of the room. Gabe couldn't see the source of the glow, but he could easily see the orange light as it flickered against the exhibit's lengthy walls.

"Did they just light a torch or something?" Gabe asked.

"Umm..." Becca started, suddenly sounding very worried, "I don't think that's a torch."

"What the fuck is it then? It's not a lighter. No way a little Bic would cause that much glow."

"I think it's one of *them*," Becca said, leaning on the final word. Gabe didn't need to ask to know that she was referring to one of Blake's undead, demon fucks. You couldn't create an exhibit about torture without *somebody* being burned alive.

"Fuck it!" Gabe dismissed. "Even if it is one of them, there is only *one* of them. They'll have to choose a path to go down. They'll probably leave some kind of guard at the end of whatever path they don't choose, but that won't matter. I have an idea I've been working on. Now, let's just hope they go down the Good path."

"Well, *that* may be a problem," Becca warned.

"What do you mean?" Gabe asked, watching the reflected light carefully, trying to follow the glow's intensity to determine which path they were choosing.

"I think I know which of Blake's servants that is, and – if I'm right – they could light up *both* paths."

"How so?"

"Early on, Blake wasn't building models of historically-based tortures," she began explaining. "He was creating his own. At the time he explained it, I figured it was just him releasing a hidden sadistic side."

"Can anybody say *understatement*?" Gabe teased.

"Anyway," Becca dismissed the tease, "there is only one scene in his collection that features a man on fire."

"Which one's that?" Gabe asked, dreading the answer.

"*Split Kindling*," was Becca's dour answer. Gabe didn't like the sound of that one bit. Even less so when she explained what it meant. "At the time, Blake was just combining popular tortures. In this case, he set a man on fire, while simultaneously using a table saw to split him in half. Slowly, I might add."

"So, basically just Cliff, only with fire."

"Cliff wasn't split through all the way, but yeah...close enough I guess," Becca replied.

Watching the flickering golden light, Gabe knew that she was correct. The intensity of the glow was equal along both walls, but had moved up further than it could have without traversing the paths. There were now two sources of light, one on both the Good and Evil paths. Gabe glanced back to the cul-de-sac, knowing they only had a moment to act before it would be too late.

"Come on," Gabe ordered, assisting Becca to her feet. "We've got to move."

"Move where?"

"Just move!" Gabe persisted. He led her to the winter house in the cul-de-sac and started to strip the obnoxiously-happy family of their winter clothes. "Put this on," Gabe instructed, holding the woman's fur coat out to Becca. She took it and slipped herself inside.

"I don't understand," she said, buttoning the coat.

"We're going back in the vents," Gabe informed, slipping into the father's thick jacket.

"Uhh…" Becca got out before Gabe grabbed her arm and dragged her to the trees along the Evil path.

"Climb," he ordered boosting her up onto the lower branches of the tree. She didn't question it, she just climbed.

Gabe followed after her, having to carefully balance his hold on the tree branches while maintaining his grip on the tire iron. He would have killed for a gun – or even a machete – but he wasn't going any further without some sort of weapon.

Nearly halfway up the tree, he stopped and chanced a glance down the path. From his new vantage point, the source of the orange glow was easy to discern against the dark backdrop. It was as Becca explained. There was a man alight with fire; or, half a man, to be more accurate. The half-man slowly slid his foot along the path as several other bodies swarmed around him, using the golden glow to search under and through the trees. They had already neared the clearing with the mechanical snake. The branches of the tree were enough to keep Gabe hidden in shadow for the moment, but he knew that wouldn't be the case for much longer. They needed to climb quickly.

Gabe quickly scrambled up several more branches until he caught up with Becca. He was pleased to see that she had already made it to the top, fumbling with the vent grate to get it open. He was about to offer his assistance when the vent grate popped loose from its housing. Becca slowly lowered the grate, careful not to drop it, and tucked it between two branches of the tree. Becca smiled down at him, pinching a dime between her thumb and forefinger. "Makes a great screwdriver," she informed with a smile.

Gabe wanted to kiss her, but he shoved her upward instead. The orange glow was starting to penetrate the shadows of the tree branches. "Go!" he quietly urged. Becca climbed up, disappearing into the vent.

Gabe slid the tire iron through the opening, leaving it lying on the aluminum sheeting. He gripped the edges of the vent opening to haul himself up. He briefly thought he heard the strange flapping again, but ignored it to pull himself into the opening. The freezing air chilled him instantly, despite now wearing the thick coat. "Brrr," he enunciated before squeezing his upper body into the vent, his legs left dangling in open space. He looked forward through the vent and saw only an empty corridor travelling away from him. His heart skipped a beat.

Where the fuck was Becca?

His hairs barely had time to stand on end, when somebody grabbed him from behind. If he hadn't been supporting his weight with his arms, his fist would have instinctively turned and smashed into his attacker's face. When he heard Becca giggling, he was glad that he hadn't had that chance.

"Are you fucking kidding me!?" Gabe furiously whispered.

Becca was looking at him with a gleam in her eye. "I know, not funny," she said. "But I couldn't resist. I crawled back here, figured you could take lead this time."

Gabe nodded, briefly wondering just how psychotic this woman was. If so, she was his kind of psychotic, though, so he let it go.

He inched his way forward to bring his body fully into the vent. He could feel the edge of the grate housing digging into his knee when something began tugging at his pant leg.

"Ha ha, Becca," Gabe said sarcastically. "You done fucking with me yet?"

She hadn't even had time to answer when Gabe was violently wrenched backward. Gabe frantically tried to latch onto something – anything –to stop his rearward slide. Unfortunately, there was nothing in the smooth recesses of the ventilation system to grab onto.

Gabe plummeted back into the dark void of *Midnight In The Garden Of Good An Evil.*

29

Gabe's fingers snagged the edges of the vent opening, stopping his freefall into the vast, open space. He didn't take the time to celebrate his last-second save. Instead, he instantly recoiled and began trying to climb back up into the vent shaft.

A pair of strong arms held him fast, wrapped around him from behind. "Where you going, lover?" a voice whispered in his ear, before something wet and slimy travelled up his neck to his ear. Gabe shivered – in disgust as much as in fear - as he realized that the voice belonged to Lester and that the fucker had just teasingly licked him.

How the fuck did Lester climb the tree so fucking fast?

Was he some kind of Olympic climber?

Did they even have climbing in the Olympics?

These thoughts travelled through Gabe's mind as he instinctively threw his fist over his shoulder, connecting with Lester's face. Lester's grip slipped loose and Gabe used the opportunity to shoot upward. Lester may have been tough, but he was thankfully light. Gabe was able to pull both himself and Lester up into vent shaft where Gabe could use more than just his fingertips to hold himself up.

It didn't take long for Lester to recover from the blow. "You're going to fucking pay for that," he threatened before digging his teeth into Gabe's ear. Gabe screamed at the piercing pain in his earlobe and tried to swat Lester away. Maintaining his balance on his elbows severely limited Gabe's reach, though, and he was unable to connect with his clinging assailant.

Lester made growling sounds, much like a feral dog, as he gnawed on Gabe's ear. Gabe tried his best, but couldn't shake the wily fucker off.

"Mmm mmm. You taste good, boy. Like pork rinds," Lester teased after rearing back, a hefty piece of Gabe's earlobe clenched between his teeth. Gabe more heard than saw as Lester swallowed the chunk of skin and cartilage.

Gabe's arms were pulled out from under him as Lester changed tactics and pulled at Gabe, dropping him back into the exhibit. Gabe managed to get a hold on the housing's sharp edge again. He successfully saved himself from the long drop to the dark forest's floor, but his forearms already burned and his fingers were growing numb. He knew he wouldn't be able to hold on much longer, but there was nothing he could do to free himself from Lester's grasp.

Gabe grunted in horror as his fingers began slipping toward the edge.

He braced himself for the fall to come.

"What the fuck are you doing!?" Becca's voice suddenly screamed from above. "Let him go!" Becca reached over the opening's edge and started scratching at Lester's face. Gabe felt the bastard's pull weaken as Lester had to change focus to avoid Becca's slashing claws.

"Fuck you, you psycho bitch!" Lester yelled up to Becca as he freed one hand to try to swat both of hers away.

Becca stopped her pawing, seeming shocked by Lester's taunt. Then a fire grew in her eyes, a fire of pure rage. "You contemptuous little fucker," she snarled before swatting down at him again. This time, instead of merely swatting, she tightly clutched Lester's brow, viciously driving two of her fingers into his eyeballs. Dark fluid instantly burst from where her fingers dug into his skull.

Lester screamed as the tips of Becca's fingers disappeared into his eye sockets. Then the first knuckle. Then the second. All the way until the last stretch of her fingers had vanished into the bloody muck, leaving only her knuckles exposed. It had all taken maybe a second, but Gabe had watched the grisly scene over his shoulder, it seeming as if it had been a slowed recording.

Gabe made a mental note to *never* call Becca a psycho bitch.

Becca's fiery attack worked. Lester released Gabe and fell away into the darkness, screaming in agony as he dropped into the deep space. Gabe guessed that the thirty foot drop was far better than having a pair of fingers lodged through your eye sockets.

Gabe looked beneath him, hoping to see Lester splat. He didn't see that, but what he did see was the rest of the gathered acolytes staring up at him. They weren't making a move to climb the tree. They were just staring. Gabe felt a chill sweep across his flesh. He was sure he'd have been less creeped out if they had actually been pursuing.

Becca grabbed onto the back of Gabe's new coat and helped him lift himself back up into the vent. He situated himself, took a couple deep breaths, then turned to look toward Becca. "Now why did you go and do that?" he asked.

Becca was stunned. "Do what? Save your ass?"

"No," Gabe answered with a mischievous smile. "Thanks for that, by the way. I meant why did you have to go and get my fresh, new coat all bloody?" Gabe had seen the smear left behind on the vent after his back had rubbed up against it. It had to have come from where Becca had grabbed his coat after being knuckle deep in Lester's eye holes.

"Fucking ingrate," Becca said, rolling her eyes. "I'm glad to see you've maintained your sense of humor despite losing half an ear."

"Yeah," Gabe said, gingerly tapping his wound. "Hurts like a bitch. I'll probably need a fucking rabies shot after this."

"I wouldn't doubt it," Becca joked. "Tell you what, I'll call you a veterinarian as soon as the police are on their way. Now, should we go get the cell phones?"

"Cell phones?" Gabe chuckled. "You still think we're going for the cell phones? Those assholes probably have *Suffering For Art* swarmed by now."

"Maybe not," Becca said. "It seems most of them are standing down there, just staring up at us for some damned reason."

Gabe pictured the eerie scene and felt a shiver that had nothing to do with the freezing air. "Even so, we don't know how many were already in there. We know there's at least one - that asshole that peeked through the door at us - but I'd be willing to bet he has friends."

"Well, what then? Do you have a better idea? Something to get us out of these vents? The coat helps, but I'm already freezing in here."

No," Gabe relented. "I guess there's no harm in checking it out. If there are too many of them, we can crawl right past and figure where else to go from there."

"That's the spirit," Becca said, before grabbing his foot and giving it a reassuring shake.

"Women and their damn cell phones," Gabe muttered as he started forward.

"What was that?"

"Nothing, dear!" Gabe mocked. "Just saying that I was thinking about sex."

"Nice alibi. Totally believable," Becca quipped.

Gabe smirked and led their way toward *Suffering For Art*.

30

Well, fuck me sideways with a nine iron," Gabe breathed, looking down into *Suffering For Art* through the slats in the vent grate.

"What?" Becca asked.

"The door to *Midnight*. It's still open on this side," Gabe informed.

Becca caught the suspicious tone in Gabe's voice. "That's a good thing, right? Means they haven't flooded in here yet."

"I don't know," Gabe said, shaking his head. "Why the fuck wouldn't one these assholes on this side close the door so the assholes on the other side can get through? I count two of them down there, though there may be more. I can't see the whole exhibit through here."

"What's that saying about looking a gift horse in the mouth?" Becca challenged.

"What's that saying about not walking into a trap lest your balls get cut off?" Gabe countered.

"Is that an actual saying?"

"It is now," Gabe said, still staring through the slats.

"Do you see my purse down there anywhere?"

Gabe searched through the slats, trying to peer in the area where he had been pinned down to the table. His eyes searched for a moment until they fell upon a black strap sticking out from behind the table.

"Bingo," he announced. "It's there."

"Thank God," Becca said. Then, "Say we decide to chance the trap and go down there, that's a thirty foot drop. How do we get down without breaking our legs?"

"That's easy," Gabe said. "We're going to use that fuck-head Peristopheles' statue. It's directly under the vent. It's only about a five foot drop to his head. Easy enough. Then we can climb down from there."

"Yeah," Becca said in such a way that Gabe knew she had rolled her eyes while saying it. "Easy peasy."

"It'll be fine," he assured her, though he wasn't able to assure himself. He watched the room through the slats for a moment longer. "Well," he eventually said, not seeing any sign of additional guards, "if we're going to do this, there's no way we're going to be able to simply sneak in, so we may as well just go for it, balls blazing."

Becca hesitated, obviously ill at ease with the whole plan.

"Or we could just stay up here all night and freeze to death. Your choice," Gabe offered.

"No," Becca huffed. "Let's do it."

"FYI," Gabe said, using the Twitter-friendly acronym for 'For Your Information', "as I said, we've got *two* fuck-heads down there. The one we saw in the doorway earlier, and one other. Our doorway friend appears normal. Either he's actually human or he's not currently in dead-fuck mode. The other one is definitely dead. He looks like some charred beef brisket I had at a barbecue joint the other day. I'm think it's the guy from that scene with the bull-shaped oven."

"*The Brazen Bull*," Becca corrected.

"Yeah, that's it. I think his name was Titus something," Gabe recalled.

"*Lichtner*. Titus Lichtner," Becca finished for him.

"Yeah, that's it," Gabe agreed. "Not that I give a fuck."

Gabe let his eyes wander around the space below, picturing what their next moves would be. After a moment, he felt ready.

"Alright, let me fill you in on my plan," Gabe said. "Step one: I'm going to smash this fucker in," he explained, patting the vent grate, "then I'm going to jump down. Let me get clear of the statue before you follow. Cool?"

"Cool."

"Step two: I'll distract these two assholes while you run over and get your purse. I don't know how long I'll have. I'm guessing not long, so, once you have the purse, run like your ass is on fire, got it?"

"Got it," Becca confirmed. "Now, where exactly do I run to?"

"That's step three. The light is green above *A Morsel's Journey*. They must have gotten in there at some point. We'll use the door trick again. Now that they've figured out how to kill the power to the doors, we won't have long, but hopefully it'll be long enough to call the police. Which takes us to step four."

"What's step four?"

"Wait for them to cut power to the doors, hope like hell their idiocy holds up and they don't block us at both ends, then run like hell into the western corridor. We'll duck into one of the smaller exhibits and hole up until the police get here," Gabe finished. "I know…I know," he said, seeing Becca's disapproving stare. "Not the most well-crafted plan, I admit, but this isn't exactly Ocean's Eleven, is it?"

"Just do me a favor and try not to die," Becca said warmly, giving Gabe's calf a little squeeze.

"Trust me, I'll try my best," Gabe promised. "You ready?"

"Ready as I'll ever be," Becca confirmed.

Gabe raised the tire iron over the vent grate. "Fuck it, then," Gabe swore. "Let's do this!"

"One..." Gabe said, giving the tire iron a practice tap against the corner of the grate. He didn't have a lot of room to gather momentum for his swing, and that worried him. "Two..." Another tap. "Three!" Gabe smashed the tire iron against the grate with as much power as he could summon, despite the limited swinging room. The result was a loud clanging and some minor damage to the vent grate, but it didn't pop loose. Hurried, Gabe smashed the grate again, this time the corner broke free of its housing. One more swing and the vent bent enough that Gabe was able to wrench the rest of it free and let it drop. It ricocheted off the statue head, then went crashing to the floor. The entire event had been quite raucous and Gabe wasn't surprised to see the two acolytes staring up at him from below.

"How are you gentlemen doing today?" Gabe greeted them as he slipped through the vent opening and landed feet-first on the elongated head of Peristopheles. He noticed some writing etched at the figure's crown as his feet hit the carved stone. They were words, but not of any language that Gabe recognized. He didn't have time to ponder it, though. He had an audience to engage. "Would either of you two happen to be janitors?" he asked the undead men. "Cause I see a couple shit stains that need mopping up, real bad."

Neither man laughed.

"Tough crowd," Gabe said, climbing down Peristopheles' arm. They surprisingly hadn't moved to attack him yet, just staring at him as he made his way down to the floor. His foot landed in the crook of the statue's elbow. He looked down and judged the remaining distance to be about ten feet. Gabe leapt the remaining feet to the ground and stood straight, seeing the normal looking man start to beckon him in with his a wave of his fingers. The classic gesture for 'come and get some'.

"Well, at least I know who I'm going to fuck up first," Gabe said, facing the beckoning man. He took a step forward, keeping his eyes locked with him...before swinging the tire iron to his side, smashing one of its ends into Titus "The Brazen Bull" Lichtner's face. "And that would be you," Gabe said to the half-charred, half-broiled man. Gabe ran up to the prone body and repeatedly swung the tire iron into the charcoal demons head. The skull – like any normal human skull – easily gave way to the brute force attack, crushing inward until the man's head was morphed into a mixed pulp of gristle and blood.

"Come back from that, fucker!" Gabe hollered at the charred body now lying on the ground. Movement caught Gabe's attention from the corner of his eye. He turned and saw two things at once. One, that Becca had already jumped down to the statue's head, following Gabe's path down to his shoulder. Two, the other one of Zellers' slave fucks had started charging him. The first Gabe was happy about, but otherwise dismissed. The second, Gabe met with another swing of the tire iron.

The tire iron crashed into the rushing man's gut, folding him over at the waist. His momentum continued carrying his body forward, causing him to somersault over the extended tire iron.

The man hit the ground and immediately tried regaining his feet. Gabe pirouetted and sent the tire iron crashing against the back of the man's skull.

"Stings, don't it?" Gabe taunted as the man crashed back to the ground. The man started shaking his head, clearly dazed by the blow.

Gabe hit him again. And again. And a third time. Until he was lying still on the floor, back barely rising with inflated breath.

Movement caught Gabe's attention. He looked up and saw Becca running towards her purse. She stopped when she saw Gabe smiling at her. "Turns out these assholes aren't that hard to take down after all," Gabe bragged. He lifted the tire iron for one more good strike, mostly to show off for Becca.

Becca looked down at the sprawled body. Recognition hit her eyes and she screamed, "Gabe! Stop!"

But it was too late. Gabe was already mid-swing.

In the split second it took for the tire iron to crash into the prone man's body, *it* happened. Something Gabe never imagined he would see. Something he never even imagined he *could* have imagined.

The sound of ripping flesh tore through the air as the man's asshole widened and collapsed deep into his abdomen, forming a large cavern in the space that his ass cheeks had recently occupied. The entire arm of the tire iron disappeared into the newly-opened cavity. The slimy flesh snapped closed around the metal tool, gripping it tight. The man swung his ass to the side, wrenching the tool from Gabe's grasp. Another swing sent the tire iron crashing against Gabe's skull.

Dazed by the blow, Gabe fell backwards onto his own ass, thankfully still its original size. The man charged backwards, still on all fours. He was inexplicably trying to bludgeon Gabe to death with the ass-brandished tool. Gabe was in utter disbelief. Out of all the horrid and unbelievable things he had witnessed that evening, this was by far the most bizarre. If he had been watching it in a movie, he'd have laughed it off as some of the cheesiest shit imaginable. But, somehow, it was much less funny when it was actually happening.

Gabe used his hands and feet to hurriedly scramble backwards, unable to regain his feet in his urgency to escape the approaching abomination. The gaping-ass demon – as Gabe's mind had started referring to the strange creature - was moving incredibly fast, the speed unnatural for a man moving at a backward crawl. Gabe's back hit against the exhibit's wall with the tire iron fast approaching. He rolled to the side just as the tire iron crashed into the wall where his head had just been, the tool's momentum enough to pierce the painted concrete blocks.

Gabe recovered quickly and saw that the tire iron had become lodged into the wall. The gaping-ass demon was stuck in a battle to free the tool. Gabe took action, making the most of the momentary distraction. He slid between the man's spacious asshole and the wall. Grabbing hold of the tire iron, Gabe kicked his leg out at the gaping-ass demon's body, trying to tear it away from the tool.

It worked...though not the way Gabe expected.

When Gabe's foot collided against the man, the tire iron *was* freed, released by the cavernous asshole as the puckered flesh opened wide, moving over to where Gabe intended his foot to make contact. Gabe's foot disappeared into the foul crater as the extended orifice's lips crashed inward to constrict around his ankle.

"Fuck me!" Gabe cried, as the gaping-ass demon charged forward, dragged Gabe with him. Gabe got ahold of the tire iron as held on for dear life. The forward momentum was briefly halted, until, finally, the tire iron broke free from the wall.

If the gaping-ass demon had travelled backward fast, it travelled forward even faster. Too fast. Gabe tried swinging the tire iron at the galloping entities legs, but the momentum was too much to fight against. He couldn't swing far enough forward to connect.

Goddamn, I'm going to have to do more core workouts if I survive this shit, Gabe silently promised himself.

As they neared the looming statue, the gaping-ass demon suddenly veered to the left, using Gabe's asshole-ensnared leg to swing him towards the statue's base. Gabe managed to get his hands up in time to avoid his head crashing into the hard stone, but his body still bowled into the rigid sculpture. The air was forced from his lungs and his muscles protested against by the harsh blow, but Gabe somehow managed to hold onto the tire iron.

He hadn't had time to consider any damage that may have been done, before the creature was off and running again. Gabe huffed as he tried catching his breath. He had barely managed to force some breath back into his lungs when the gaping-ass demon reached the end of the room, reared up, and performed another spin move. Gabe barreled hard into the wall. Though the impact was less severe than the previous, his battered muscles still endured a surge of agony. This time, he lost hold of the tire iron and it went crashing into the wall. Gabe quickly reached out to regain hold of the tire iron as the monster resumed its four-legged rush. As Gabe was pulled away, his fingers managed to brush on the tip of one arm of the tire iron. It was just enough to regain his grasp on the tool.

Gabe resumed his fight against the momentum, once more trying to reach the monster's legs with the tire iron. Falling short again, Gabe knew he had to try a new tactic. He steeled himself for one more attempt, sat up the best he could, and threw the tire iron at the gaping-ass demon's legs. His timing ended up being great, as the same time that the tire iron became entangled in the creature's legs, Becca appeared in the thing's path, swinging her purse directly into its face. The combined events caused the gaping-ass demon to trip up and go tumbling across the floor, eventually skidding to a stop near the motionless body of the charred man.

Gabe safely watched from a few feet away. In the creature's confusion, the puckered hole's grip had slipped, allowing Gabe to forcibly remove his foot from the fleshy confines. His boot came out covered in brown muck and, as he watched the gaping-ass demon roll to a stop, Gabe had to fight back a surge of vomit.

What was it with Blake's creatures and their affinity for human feces?

Gabe quickly got his stomach's rebellion under control and knelt for the tire iron. As the gaping-ass demon picked himself up from the floor, Gabe swung the tire iron down into its skull. He was very careful this time to avoid aiming anywhere near the creature's backside. The tire iron hit with a sickening crunch as the stiff metal cracked the skull open as if it were nothing more than an egg shell. The gaping-ass demon collapsed to the ground and ceased moving.

"What the fuck was that thing!?" Gabe shouted, pointing the crimson-dripping spoke of the tire iron at the lifeless form below him. "Was that another one of Blake's made up tortures...the thousand-cock ass rape!?"

Gabe was clearly perturbed.

"No," Becca answered. "I'm pretty sure it's that." Becca pointed over at one of the *Suffering For Art* dioramas. "The Judas Cradle," she revealed. "Grady Fenton I believe is his actual name."

Sure enough, the figure in the scene was the man lying at Gabe's feet. His modeled replica was hoisted in the air, sitting atop an lengthy wooden stool. By all appearances, he was *not* sitting comfortably, however. The man-figure had a grimace of agony forever etched on his face. The figure's ankles were shackled with chains running down towards large iron blocks that Gabe assumed were old-school weights. The weights floated a couple feet above the ground, having the effect of weighing the man down onto his stool.

At first, Gabe wasn't exactly sure what constituted the *torture* aspect of the scene. It took him a moment to realize that – other than being significantly taller than a normal stool – the seat of the stool wasn't flat. It was square shaped at the base, but the four corners rose from upward, travelling at an inward angle. The wooden seat appeared to be melded in with the buttocks of the man in chains, losing the distinction between where the wood ended and the man's flesh began.

"The seat is shaped like a wooden pyramid," Becca explained, following Gabe's gaze. "The torturers would place the victim up onto the seat with the tip of the pyramid placed inside their anus. They would slowly add weight to the chains, weighing the victim down deeper onto the pyramidal seat. As the seat widened, the victim's anus was forced further and further open, until it eventually began to split. The torturers would keep adding weight until the victim finally died from impalement. Though, I'm guessing Blake may have gone a bit further than that," she finished, looking at the display with disgust.

"I'm going to plant my fist so deep into Zellers' face when I see that demented fuck," Gabe said, catching the acrid smell of shit drifting up from his foot. "Nah, fuck that!" Gabe amended. "First, I'm going to make him lick the shit off my shoe, *then* let him chase it down with my fucking fist." Gabe shook his foot to try to expel some of the brown gunk. Brown splatter rained off it, but most of the vile sludge remained. "Anyway, you get ahold of the police?" Gabe asked.

"Oh shit!" Becca swore, stuffing her hand into her purse.

"You haven't called yet?" Gabe asked with incredulity.

"Sorry! I was busy saving your ass," she snapped, rifling through the front pocket of her purse. "Again!" she added, pulling out her phone.

"Fuck!" Becca swore, seeing the cracked screen on her phone. "It must have shattered when I hit that guy with my purse." She let the busted phone fall to the floor and began digging through her purse again.

"What about my phone?" Gabe asked.

"Getting it now," she answered, sounding annoyed. "A-ha!" She withdrew Gabe's phone, the screen thankfully still intact. "Thank God!"

Becca activated the phone's screen and swiped the bottom to unlock it. Gabe had never been a fan of passwords. "In case you were wondering, you have seven missed calls from somebody named Cocksucker," Becca informed, pushing the icon for the phone app.

"That's my boy, Ronnie," Gabe explained. "I was supposed to call him and let him know if I got lucky tonight."

Becca rolled her eyes. "How's that working out for you?" she playfully asked while dialing on the phone's virtual keypad. "Alright, it's ringing," she relayed, placing the phone to her ear.

Gabe heard a tinny, far-off voice answer, then "Yes, hey! We need the police now. We're trapped inside..." Becca was cut off by her own screams as a charred and smoking arm shot up from below and snagged her hand with the phone inside. It was the hand of Titus Lichtner, his skull having reformed from the bloody pulp that Gabe had left it as. A gray smoke rose from where Titus Lichtner's hand gripped Becca's. A light sizzling and the acrid smell of melting flesh and plastic soon accompanied the smoke.

Gabe snapped into action, raising the tire iron and sending it crashing down into Titus' skull. The thin layer of bone cracked beautifully. The smoking hand fell away from Becca's as Titus' body slumped back to the ground. Gabe applied a few more whacks from the tire iron, leaving the creature's skull looking like a strawberry-kiwi puree.

Gabe left the smoldering body alone to come to Becca's aid. After being released, she had collapsed onto her ass, where she sat frozen, staring at her affected hand. One glance and Gabe knew that it wasn't good. Her hand had turned a very dark red in spots, and those were the spots that looked the most normal, the spots that had only been *near* the charbroiled monster's flesh. Where Lichtner's hand had actually made contact, her skin had been left much the same as the monster's: blackened and still smoking.

"Oh my God! Hang on, Becca," Gabe said, reaching up to his shoulder and tearing off his sleeve. While Becca wept, he took the sleeve and wrapped it around her smoldering hand. The worst part was her palm. His phone was still there, but had now become a misshapen lump of plastic and glass that had fused with the flesh of her palm. A visit to the emergency room was definitely going to be necessary, but barring that, or any other options, Gabe bundled it all together, phone and all.

As Gabe tied off his wrap, he briefly wondered what the hell good the temporary tourniquet was going to do. Why did people always seem to do that? It wasn't going to keep out infection. To pad the infected area, maybe? He shook the thought away and used Becca's other arm to help her to her feet.

"Hey, if nothing else, at least you've cut your nail polishing time in half," Gabe sheepishly tried consoling. He'd never been very good at such things.

Amazingly, Becca broke from her sobs and gave a little laugh. "You really are an asshole, you know that?" she joked through her tears.

"Yeah. Sorry. I know I can say some stupid shit sometimes," he admitted. "Do you think you can go on? We still need to find a way out of here."

"Yeah, I'm good," Becca said, sounding unconvinced. "Maybe we could avoid crawling around in the vents for a while, though." She waved her injured and in front of him, making clear the reason for her statement.

"Yeah, sure," Gabe agreed, glancing up at the vent opening. "It'd be a pain in the dick to get back up there anyway."

A wry smile twisted Becca's lips as she added, "Oh, and if you were expecting a hand job later, that's probably out of the question now."

If Gabe had been drinking a beer at that moment, a sudsy geyser would have assuredly erupted from his mouth. After a stunned moment, "Jesus! I think I've ruined you," he joked.

Becca shot Gabe a look of longing, complete with a twinkle in her eye. Gabe would have been embarrassed to admit that the look started a stirring in his nether regions. The moment didn't last long, though. Becca's smile morphed into a wince and her arm flew up to clutch her ruined hand with the healthy one.

Gabe's smile faded as well, the stirrings below quickly forgotten. "We need to get moving. You need to see a doctor and you need to see him soon," he said.

"Well, it's a good thing there's a doctor on staff," a voice broke in, causing both Becca and Gabe to flinch. Gabe turned to see Dr. Holtz standing just inside the unlocked doorway that led out to the northern corridor. Behind him was a majority of Blake's reanimated staff, and they looked ready to fuck somebody up.

Holtz locked eyes with Gabe and smiled. "Well...it appears the doctor is in," he warned.

We're so fucked!" Gabe whispered to Becca, staring at the mob of living phantasms.

Most of Blake's acolytes were in their *Suffering* forms. There was Split-crotch Cliff and the Five-piece Chicken Mc-Fuck-ett known to Gabe as Lurch. Several other of the creatures lurked their too; all in various states of disarray and grotesqueness. Holtz looked to be in his normal human form, as well as a few of the others. Noticeably missing from the party were the walking shit-stain herself, Ophelia, and Lester.

Fucking Lester! Gabe didn't know what Lester's torture had been yet, but he hoped it had been something truly awful. Fuck that guy!

"Well," Becca spoke up, "if we're going to die anyway…fuck it!" Then Becca surprised Gabe in a way that he didn't realize he still had the capacity for. She leaned over and mashed her lips against his. Their first kiss. In front of a murderous mob. A murderous mob of the undead. Not exactly the way Gabe had been picturing it.

Still, as Becca ground her lips against Gabe's in a kiss of fiery passion, Gabe momentarily forgot all about that group of monsters looking on. He let his lips follow the motion of hers. A little tongue may have even gotten involved. Gabe's heart was beating like a turbo-charged engine. His whole world exploded with the light of a thousand angels, though the only angel that mattered was the one directly in front of him.

Yeah...Gabe was completely smitten. His man card be damned - Gabe was in love.

When Becca finally broke off the kiss, Gabe had a newfound determination coursing through his veins. "Fuck this!" Gabe proclaimed loudly. "We are not fucking dying tonight!" Was it pure bravado? Yeah. Was it also just a matter-of-fact in Gabe's mind? Also, yes. Gabe was sure – no; absolutely, mother-fucking, one-hundred percent *positive* – that this horde of ass scum threateningly staring him down, were all about to be fucking decimated. None of these assholes were going to lay a finger on either him or Becca. Gabe was ready to rumble, ready for war. He was ready to tear the fucking roof off the heavens and shove it up Satan's asshole while whistling "*Ode to Joy*".

"Let's do this motherfuckers!" he yelled at the mob while banging the tire iron against his chest like some kind of tire-changing, battle ape.

The crowd didn't advance. They didn't move. Holtz' smile may have grew a bit, but other than that, the deadly mob stood still, staring.

Gabe stood a bit dumbfounded. He had expected one of two things. One: that they'd back away in horror from his intense warrior-like presence. Yeah...Gabe may have been a little delusional in the moment. Or two: they'd rush him, inviting themselves to their own funerals.

Instead, they basically did nothing.

"What are you bitches waiting for!?" Gabe taunted, beating his chest again, though this time with slightly less conviction.

Then the strange flapping sound came again, from behind and overhead. The same flapping sound that Gabe had heard in the darkness of *Midnight In The Garden Of Good And Evil*.

What the fuck was that sound!?

Gabe turned to look over his shoulder and felt his bravado sink like dirty bathwater into a drain. "Holy fuck," Gabe moaned, his jaw dropping.

Floating above Gabe and Becca was Lester, the flapping sound coming from his wings. That's right...Lester had wings! Two utterly gnarly wings. The skin of his back had been peeled from the muscle and sinew, stretched, then splayed outward on spokes of bone that had previously been Lester's ribcage. The ribs had been broken apart at the sternum and folded back along the spine to create the bony support for the fleshy wings. The fluorescent light from the room's roof shone through the thin layer of flesh, allowing Gabe to see an intricate web of red and blue veins running throughout the macabre canvas.

Two pulsating sacks Gabe recognized as lungs, blackened by years of smoking, sat stop Lester's shoulders - completing the foul façade of Lester's undead form. Gabe didn't need this particular method of torture explained to him. It was a myth of common knowledge among the Heavy Metal community. An old form of torture devised by the Vikings, though Gabe imagined if the Vikings had ever seen this particular result, the fierce warriors would have started running fast and far, with only a trail of piss and shit left behind to indicate that they had ever been there at all.

It was the much-lamented *Blood Eagle*...

...and it was currently hovering over Gabe, throwing a devilish grin down upon him. A devilish grin completed by two healthy-looking eyes that had apparently recovered well from their turn as Becca's finger paint receptacles.

"Shitting your pants yet?" Lester goaded, then swept straight down toward Gabe. Gabe instinctively ducked and threw his arm up to block his face from Lester's attack. Nothing happened. At least, nothing happened to Gabe. Instead, Becca suddenly started screaming.

Gabe twisted and looked over to where Becca had been standing, realizing Lester's swoop hadn't been aimed at him. It had been aimed at Becca.

Lester was on Becca's back, his arms wrapped through her armpits in a foul embrace as he flapped his wings and carried her with him off the ground. Gabe leapt at the rising duo, barely managing to get his hand around Lester's foot before it had ascended out of reach. Lester's upward trajectory stalled as Gabe's weight was added to the mix.

"Get off me, asshole!" Lester cried, smashing his foot into Gabe's face. Gabe managed to hold on after the first kick, but he couldn't get his other hand up in time to firm his grip. With only the one hand for support, Gabe never had a chance. A second kick sent him falling free, back down to the floor.

Gabe hit the ground, rolled to his back, then lay looking up helplessly as Lester flew off with Becca. He carried her over the horde of creatures and out the door to the northern hallway.

"Fuck!" Gabe erupted, his voice filled with despair. He punched the hard, tiled surface out of frustration.

"Mr. Zellers had a change of heart," Holtz calmly explained. Gabe looked up into the mad doctor's eyes. They looked on him with pity. "He has decided that Ms. Larson will hold a very special place on his staff." The doctor said that seriously, not seeming to notice the hidden innuendo. Gabe did, but found no humor whatsoever in the statement. "As a consequence, he no longer desires your services."

Gabe was too dismayed to immediately recognize the threat in the words.

"Kill him," Holtz instructed the small army, clearing it up for him.

The horde rushed forward.

His earlier bluster now defunct, Gabe was filled with sheer terror. The courage to stay and fight had fled. Gabe took his courage's cue and fled as well. He didn't have time to strategize. He didn't have time to even think. He just fled. There was only way available to him and he took it instinctively.

Gabe ran to the open door that led back into *Midnight In The Garden Of Good And Evil*. He pounced through and slammed the door behind him, immediately opening the opposite door to engage the lock. He threw open the second door with such force that a lesser door would have been torn straight off its hinges.

Even then, in the temporary safety of the pitch-black exhibit, Gabe continued to run. Despite being completely unable to see, he sprinted forward into the darkness. His ability to think hadn't yet caught up with him. He just followed his feet. He followed them until his chest slapped against a floppy board. He heard the rattle of a chain at the very same time his head collided into something hard and cold.

The black room exploded into a bright whiteness; then, there was nothing.

INTERLUDE

10

As he took the offered seat, Blake stared into the eyes of the man across the desk. His eyes shone with joviality, tempered only by intelligence. This was definitely a man who took life one day at a time. A man who was able to shrug off life's challenges with a shrug and a jest.

A man who gave easily to hope, which was going to make Blake's job much easier.

"It's a pleasure to meet you," Blake greeted. "All my research points to you as *the* man to approach in matters of world history."

"Oh," the man waved off, "please stop. I'm afraid I am easily embarrassed by such compliments." The man did indeed appear to blush.

"Still," Blake continued, "you are an expert on European and Middle Eastern history, are you not?"

"Oh, assuredly I am," the man admitted. "Though, I can name many others that are easily my equal."

"I'm not searching for many experts. I only need one."

"Well, then, I suppose I very well may do," the man said. "What exactly is it that you are looking for?"

"First, tell me a bit about yourself." Blake slouched back in his chair, prepared to listen carefully to what the man had to say. "I know what a quick Google search told me, but I want to hear from you what your qualifications are."

"Oh fun," the man damn near whinnied. "First, can I interest you in a vanilla wafer?" He pushed a bowl of small, crescent-shaped yellow cookies across the desk toward Blake. "They're actually called Vanillekipferl, a most divine cookie from Austria. They're not exactly vanilla wafers, but most people feel uncomfortable being offered things they have cannot pronounce."

Blake shook his head, declining the offer.

"Oh well," the man said, clearly disappointed at Blake's refusal. "Perhaps you should have stopped by last week. I had the distinct pleasure of receiving a fresh batch of panellet from the mountain region of Spain. They're little cookies made from ground almond and covered in powdered cocoa, candied cherries, and flakes of coconut. Never have my taste buds been so blessed." Blake was worried the man was going to have an orgasm as he recounted the cookies. Unsurprising, given the man's portly physique.

"Maybe next time," Blake conceded to appease the man. "So, it's obvious that you are familiar with the regional culinary delights of Europe. What else are you familiar with from those parts?"

"So many things, Mr. Zellers," the man said, getting visibly excited. "The Greeks, the Romans; the Celts and Gauls. Slavs, Thracians, Illyrians, Etruscans; I can recite all their histories in great length. Do you need something translated? I can do that. I'm admittedly weak in the hieroglyphs of Egypt, but studies of the pyramids and pharaohs have always bored me as common and cliché."

"Hungarian?" Blake asked.

"Of course, Hungarian!" the man beamed. "Finnish, Estonian; I am well-versed in all of the Uralic languages."

"What about the Macedonian period?" Blake asked, with a special gleam in his eye. "Babylon, especially. How familiar are you with the history there?

"I absolutely adore Macedonia!" The man reached a hand up to his chest and patted it against his heart. "The story of Daniel and the Lion's Den was always my favorite in the bible. Granted, that particular book is wildly inaccurate in a historical sense, but I am very much fascinated by its splendid tales."

Blake smiled at the man's admission. It was time for him to drop the bomb. "Have you heard the name Peristopheles?"

The man's beaming smile faded at the question. It was replaced by a look of cautious curiosity. "I have heard rumors concerning such a name," the man admitted.

"Really?" Blake leaned forward in his chair. "What rumors?"

"Nothing I have ever been able to confirm." The man was much less exuberant now that the topic of conversation had been directed down this path. "A supposed God of Babylon. A demon God whose name was forbidden to be spoken sometime shortly after the death of Nebuchadnezzar II."

"What would you say if I told you I have proof that such a God existed?" Blake had just placed the carrot. He smiled, knowing this bulky man was going to bite.

"I would say that you have certainly piqued my curiosity, Mr. Zellers."

"Have you heard of my art gallery, Magna Arta?"

"I have," the man replied, a bit of his former joviality returning to his tone. "Art fascinates me to a degree only rivaled by the knowledge of the ancient world."

"Perfect!" It was Blake's turn to beam. "How you would like your own private tour of the place?"

"I would take great delight in such a venture," the man agreed. "But, I must ask, what does this have to with Peristopheles? And why have I been chosen to receive such generosity from a man of your stature?"

"It's not purely out of generosity," Blake admitted. "The gallery tour is to familiarize you with the place. I have a shipment arriving in a couple weeks from the Carpathian Mountains that I will be adding to my gallery. A shipment of great historical significance. I will need a man of your unique talents to aid me with it. During such time, I will be happy to share with you my knowledge of Peristopheles."

"What exactly is it that you'd like me to aid with?"

Blake shook his hand in dismissal of the question. "That'll come later. Are you interested?"

"Oh, most certainly! My skin tingles with intrigue."

"Wondeful!" Blake stood from the chair. "Magna Arta closes at 10:00pm. Can I expect you there when it does?" Blake extended his hand, which the man shook.

"Have the stars ever failed to shine in the heavens?" the man asked rhetorically. "Of course I shall be there."

"I'll see you then," Blake wrapped up. "Thank you for your time." Their hands released and Blake stepped through the man's office door. As he closed it behind him, he glanced at the opaque glass in the door and the name inscribed there.

"I look forward to welcoming you to my staff, Professor Tawney," Blake mumbled under his breath as he made his way through Cliff's reception suite and out to the parking lot.

33

Gabe opened his eyes to a lighted room. Not a brightly lit room, necessarily, but a room with any light at all came as a shock to him.

"Where the fuck am I?" Gabe mumbled to himself.

Only he didn't. At least, not verbally. No sound escaped his mouth, though he was sure that he just spoken.

Somebody was speaking though. No...that wasn't exactly right. Somebody was moaning.

"Oh Douche! Oh Douche!" the voice moaned from somewhere nearby. It sounded muffled, as if it were coming through a wall.

Or a door.

Gabe tried turning his head to find the source of the moans, but found that he could not. His neck refused to relent to his command. Instead, he was stuck staring forward at...at...

No. That couldn't be right. It was a face Gabe recognized well, but had not seen in years. A face he never expected to see again.

What the fuck was Geoff doing here?

Geoff had a shit-eating grin plastered across his face. "You do realize the fucked-up opportunities that have just been presented to us, right?" the former offensive lineman asked through that grin.

This all seemed familiar. Too familiar. The hideous red and gold carpet. The walls lined with mirrors and paintings. The Victorian Era tables; some with flower-bearing vases, some without. The thick, oaken double-doors directly next to where Gabe was standing.

Gabe was back in Joseph Curwen's manor.

"He's your brother. Lead the way," Gabe spoke out loud. He never willed the words to exit his mouth, but they flew from between his lips just the same.

"What the fuck is going on!?" Gabe shouted, though the only things the sound reached were the inner goblins of Gabe's own mind. "Did I just travel back through time? Am I dreaming?" That last one felt the most correct to him.

Gabe's hand – under no control of Gabe's own – waved Geoff through the door. Gabe turned and followed. Both men were crouched as they walked past the large oaken frame. Their steps were soft, but quick, trying not to gain the notice of their prey.

They found themselves in a library, bookshelves lining the walls. Books filled the bookshelves, spilling over in many locations. Some looked newer, many looked damn near ancient. Gabe was sure he had spotted an original copy of Bram Stoker's Dracula as his eyes scanned across the bookshelves.

Several books were lying haphazardly on the floor, near the base of the bookshelves, from where the shelves had no longer had the capacity to hold them. Gabe's foot accidentally kicked a thin one that was sent skidding along the floor. It was named By The Hour, from some other that Gabe had never heard of.

In the middle of the room were two intertwined bodies on a desk that was similarly littered with books. The features of the two tabletop bodies were mostly hard to discern through their entanglement, but one prominent feature that was impossible to miss was the large, stark white ass – its pale brightness only broken by tufts of black hair - that was bobbing up into the air.

"Fuck me, Douche! Fuck me hard!" a voice from the mingled bodies commanded. The bobbing of the ass increased pace until it reminded Gabe of a road worker's jackhammer.

Gabe's independent body was trying to stifle his giggles as he continued duck-walking towards Douche and Hetty. A quick glance at Geoff revealed he was doing the same.

Geoff's trajectory took him near a set of fireplace tools hanging on a stand, though Gabe didn't see a fireplace anywhere nearby. Geoff's eye lit anew as he turned a new plan over in his mind regarding the wrought iron tools. Geoff quietly slipped the fireplace poker from its hook on the stand and held his finger to his lips. A reminder to remain quiet until their quest was complete.

Gabe was unsure what Geoff was going to do with the fire poker, watching as the older brother neared the large, thrusting ass of the younger. "Harder! Fucking harder!" Hetty screamed as Geoff closed the distance. When he arrived within arm's reach, he turned to Gabe and winked.

Gabe again wondered what the fuck Geoff was up to, when the older brother made his move. Geoff deftly extended the fire poker toward his brother's thrusting ass, giving the sharp tip a gentle poke between the massive, hairy cheeks.

Douche jumped. "What the fuck!?" he yelled, looking back to find his assailant. He found them easily enough. They were hard to miss, both hunched over in a fit of laughter. Even Gabe, who – internally, at least - was too concerned with what the fuck was going on to find any humor at all in the deed.

"You assholes!" yelled Hetty, attempting to cover herself with her shirt which she had retrieved from its rumpled ball on the desk. The shirt fell short of covering *all* of the areas that mattered. "I was just about to cum!" Her statement only served to increase the intensity of Geoff's guffawing. Her face made it abundantly clear that she did not share his sense of humor about the subject.

"What about you bro?" Geoff asked through his laughter. "Were you about to, as well?" To exemplify his point, he punched Douche in the shoulder.

Douche's face darkened to a beet red. Not from anger, but from embarrassment. "Actually, I already came."

Hetty's look of scorn turned to a look of worry. "You what!?" She looked past the edge of the shirt at her exposed genitilia to confirm Douche's admission.

"Sorry," Douche squeaked. "I lost control when my ass was poked."

Geoff must have found this to be at the apex of hilarity, his laughter rising out of control.

"It's not funny, asshole!" Hetty protested. "I could get pregnant from this shit." She dabbed at her nether region with a pair of fingers and brought them up for inspection. The look of disgust that crossed her features betrayed that she wasn't happy about what she found.

"That's the problem with unprotected sex," Gabe's mouth spoke without permission, "you never know when it's going to fuck you."

Hetty burned into Gabe with a terrifying scowl. She held it for a moment, making Gabe wonder if he was going to need an ambulance to get out of this place, but eventually she let it go as she scanned around to find her pants.

"Just know that I'm going to be fucking you both up when we get out of here," Douche jokingly warned, slipping on his shirt.

With the two fuck-birds getting dressed, the desk's top was now empty, save for a large book lying open in the center. The book looked old, but not ancient. It was thick, with yellowing pages and a dark cover that appeared leathery. An illustration on the page to the left of the binding caught Gabe's attention. He walked over to the desk to get a closer look.

"What do we have here?" Gabe asked with excitement as he arrived at the desk. He examined the drawing in the book. It took up the whole page, save for a small border around its circumference.

The illustration showed two men. One was holding a chain, the other a rope that had been fashioned similar to a lasso. One half of the chain ran from the man's hand to a broken link. The rope was whole, running from the other man's hand to wrap around a third man kneeling in the middle of the illustration. The third man was on his knees. His clothes were tattered, as was his skin. Bone peeked through several areas of the man's flesh, including half of his skull. Brightly colored red streaks ran down the third man's form, coalescing into a puddle under his knees. The other half of the broken chain hung limply from the third man's throat, its snapped link having come to rest in the puddle of blood.

The third man – the *dead* man, as Gabe was already beginning to think of him – was reaching for the man with the broken chain. He wasn't trying to attack. It appeared that he was reaching for the chain-bearing man with longing, but the man with the rope was holding him back. More than that, it seemed as if the rope man was pulling him further away from the man with the chain.

"Guys," Gabe's mouth spoke, "check this out." There were words scrawled across the adjacent page, but Gabe ignored those for now. He lifted the front half of the book, careful to keep his thumb on the illustration so the page wouldn't be lost. He flipped to the book's cover ad found it blank, just bare leather of some sort. He let the front cover fall to the table as he looked at the first page within. Scrawled on the page was what Gabe assumed was the book's title. "The Book of Peristopheles, the Great God of Babylon."

Peristopheles? Holy shit! That damn name had been bothering Gabe since he'd first heard it earlier in the night. He had been sure that he'd heard it somewhere before.

"Peristopheles?" Douche asked, buckling his belt and stepping over to see what had aroused Gabe's interest. "Never heard of him." Douche shrugged, the name obviously bearing little import to him.

Gabe let the front pages of the book join the cover on the desktop, once again holding open the page with the macabre illustration. Geoff stepped closer, peering over Gabe's shoulder. Even Hetty stepped closer. She still wore a deep scowl, but her eyes betrayed her interest.

"Cool picture. Is that some Cannibal Corpse shit?" Geoff asked, referring to the metal band known for their graphic album covers. Gabe thought the picture was rather tame compared to that band's discography.

"What's that say on the other page?" Hetty asked.

Gabe turned to read the the adjacent page. "That's pretty cool," Gabe muttered, his eyes previewing the content. The Gabe of the past was little impressed by the words, but the Gabe of the present was wholeheartedly intrigued. There they were, written in black and white. The words that had been haunting Gabe since that – *this* – dire night all those years ago.

"It's a poem of some kind," Gabe-of-the-past related. "It even starts off with a warning. *Beware*," he started reading aloud.

"Beware?" Douche asked, interrupting. "What? Is this some kind of pirate treasure map? Please tell me the rest of the line says 'All Ye Who Enter Here'. Or maybe 'Here Be Dragons'."

"Nope," Gabe informed. "Nothing that cliché." He continued reading. "Beware," he repeated, "the acquisition of an enslaved soul must be made in the presence of the soul's earthly body. If the body is not present, the enslaved soul will be set free to roam the Earth at its leisure."

"Oh yeah," Douche said, "even creepier. I like it!"

"Be still, all trapped souls that hear these words," Gabe-of-the-past began. Gabe-of-the-present couldn't help but hear the words in the musical voice that he had since transcribed them to.

"Death has not given you your desired end.

Instead, only another master."

As Gabe read the words, the hairs began rising on the back of his neck. As to why, neither of the two Gabes had the faintest of notions.

"Yet, even another master now beckons.

Come unto me.

Serve me; your new God.

Let loose the shackles that bind you.

With these final words soon spoken, you will be mine.

I claim your body, your soul, your mind.

Now, and forever until your bonds be broken, be obedient unto me."

One final word remained. Before Gabe could choke it out, a voice interrupted, startling everybody around the table.

"Stop reading that!" The voice was stern and insistent, though Gabe thought he could detect a hint of fear behind the words.

Gabe-of-the-past obeyed, his tongue frozen around the final word. He stared into the face of the man who had appeared in the doorway of the library.

"What are you doing in here?" the man asked angrily. Nobody answered. "Well, say something," the man ordered.

"Sorry, sir, we were just…" Douche started to answer.

"Not you!" the man barked. "I want him to answer." Gabe's eyes widened as he realized the man was pointing at him.

"I…We…" Gabe started, unsure what to say.

The man held up a hand to stop Gabe from further explanation. Gabe thought he saw a look of relief flash across the man's face. He stuck his head out the door and used his other hand to wave some as yet unseen person to step through. Two large men – larger than even Geoff and Douche - followed the beckoning hand, blocking the large double-door entrance with their bulk.

"You were saying?" the man prompted, lowering his hands for Gabe to continue.

"Well, sir, we just wandered from the party, was all."

"Yeah. That party was lame," Geoff cut in, earning a scalding glance from the man at the door. Both Gabes silently rebuked Geoff before continuing.

"We just thought we'd check out the rest of the place. You have a nice house," Gabe tried, playing on the assumption that the man they were addressing was the owner of the house.

The man clearly wasn't buying it.

"Why were you reading from that book?"

"It was already open," Gabe hurriedly tried defending. "I saw the picture there and thought it was cool."

The man didn't look entirely convinced. He let his eyes flicker between Gabe and the book. His eyes eventually settled on Hetty. "You are Frederick Knowles' daughter, are you not?"

Hetty nodded.

"Then your father received my invitation tonight?"

"Yes," Hetty meekly acknowledged.

"Strange that I have not yet seen him tonight then. His daughter showed, but where is he?"

"I apologize, Mr. Curwen," Hetty said, confirming Gabe's suspicion. "My father decided against coming. I found the invitation and decided it might be fun to attend anyway, so I showed instead."

"So he has decided not to grace us with his presence tonight?"

Hetty shook her head. "No."

"I can't say that is entirely surprising. Him and I are in a bit of a disagreement right now. In fact, you're showing up may very well prove beneficial to resolving our impasse."

"How so?" Hetty's brow furrowed in confusion.

Instead of answering, Curwen turned towards the three male teens. His shoulders sagged and he sighed.

"I really hate being put in situations like this, gentlemen, but you leave me no choice." Curwen turned to his two brutes. "Take the girl to the ceremony chamber. Kill the others."

Douche reacted first. "Hey! Wait a goddamn minute here! What the fuck are you talking about, 'kill the others'?"

Douche never received his answer, at least not from Curwen himself. The two body guards looked as if they were going to be more than happy to answer Douche's question, though. They were already moving toward the group before Douche had even finished his protest, their faces stone cold.

Douche moved his 6'4" frame to block the bodyguard that approached Hetty. "Don't even think about it, asshole!" he warned.

The stiff sentry didn't appear to give two shits about Douche's threat. A dark smoke began rising from his body, quickly filling the air in the enclosed room. Gabe-of-the-past wanted to shout "spontaneous combustion", but his mouth was sealed by the craziness that occurred next. The henchman's skin blackened to a char right in front of Gabe's eyes, then a majority of it fell away into a cloud of ash, leaving behind a smoldering skeleton with patches of raw flesh sporadically attached. The ash, however, didn't simply float to the floor. It coalesced into a pallid cloud and rushed Douche like a flock of miniature, angry birds.

Douche, having no idea what the fuck was happening, stood frozen in terror as the ash cloud charged. Gabe wasn't sure what he was expecting to happen when the cloud reached Douche - *clueless* was the understatement of the year for the teenaged occupants of the room. What actually did happen wasn't anything that would have made Gabe's list had he had years to consider it.

The ash cloud separated into three tendrils which penetrated Douche's mouth and nostrils, disappearing inside the orifices. Gabe could see bulges rolling just underneath Douche's skin as the ash parsed itself throughout his body. Once the entirety of the ash cloud had vanished inside of him, Douche was left standing still with a shine of pure horror left in his eyes.

Gabe's mind was still racing to figure out what exactly had just occurred when Douche's body turned around and his meaty hand shot up to seize Hetty by the throat.

"Douche!? What are you doing?" she squeaked out through his tight grip. Douche lifted her off the ground, her feet flailing in the air. Gabe's large friend carried her over to the other sentry – the one who was still whole. Hetty's eyes were bulging, and Gabe was sure she was about to pass out, when Douche released his grip on her throat, leaving her in the bulky arms of the other sentry. Hetty was helpless to do more than gasp short, rapid breaths as she desperately attempted refilling her lungs. The sentry easily carried the fightless teen away, out into the hallway.

"What the fuck, Danny!?" Geoff asked, reverting back to Douche's real name. Geoff grabbed his brother's shoulder and turned him around so the two were facing each other. Tears were running down Douche's face, his eyes wild with terror.

"I don't know what's happening," Douche cried. 'This shit is in my skin. It's in my muscle. It's controlling me." He sounded as if his mind was losing a battle against madness. After seeing the ash cloud, coupled with his knowledge of everything he'd seen at the Arte Blanche, Gabe-of-the-present couldn't blame him.

"Snap out of it, bro! That shit's not possible!" It was obvious Geoff had never visited the Arte Blanche.

As if in answer to Geoff's doubts, Douche's arm snapped up and his hand engulfed his brother's throat, much like it had just done with Hetty. Geoff's hands flew up to clutch at his brother's arm, trying to pry loose the iron grip. While the two brothers weren't normally too far apart on strength, Geoff's attempts at removing his brother's hold on his windpipe were about as effective as a small child trying to wrestle with an anaconda.

Douche's other hand reached down and picked up the discarded fire poker that Geoff had used to poke him in the ass. "I'm sorry," Douche said, his cheeks soaked with tears, as the fire poker hovered near Geoff's head.

"Don't!" Geoff begged, seeing what was about to happen. "Fight it, Danny! Fight it!"

"I can't!" The deluge of Douche's tears were great enough that they now dripped from his chin, landing evenly between his shirt and the floor. In a flash of a second, Douche's poker-bearing arm struck, impaling the fire poker through Geoff's head. The poker slipped in so easily, it seemed as if Geoff's skull was made of nothing more than construction paper. It happened quickly enough that Gabe hadn't even realized what was happening until the poker's point burst out the opposite side of Geoff's skull, forcing a geyser of blood and brain matter exploding out with it. Geoff's body immediately stopped all resistance, his arms limply dropping to his side.

"No!" both Gabes shouted in unison. Past-Gabe retrieved the shovel tool from the fireplace kit and swung it towards Douche. Douche easily parried and swatted the shovel away. Douche pulled the fire poker from Geoff's head, causing what remained of the skull to completely disintegrate into loose flesh and peppermint muck. He swung the gore-encrusted tool into Gabe's stomach. Gabe curled forward from the force of the blow and collapsed to his knees.

"Run, Gabe. Run!" Douche begged. Gabe was still hunched over, trying to regain his breath from the vicious blow. Douche's body raised the fire poker, readying it to bash into Gabe's skull. He swung. Gabe managed to get the shovel up in time to deflect the swing, but he could feel the disturbance in the air as the sharp point of the poker barely passed by his face.

Gabe's body then acted on instinct to take Douche down in the most assured way to take down any man, no matter their size. He swung the shovel directly into Douche's balls. Douche's mouth screamed in agony, but his body gave no indication that anything had happened at all.

"Fuck this!" Past-Gabe said, seeing the futility of his situation. He stood and ran for the door.

The skeletal remains of the ash man moved to block Gabe. Without breaking step, he batted the man's smoldering husk with the shovel, knocking him away from the door. Gabe jumped past the tumbling body, grabbing for the door handle. He jerked the door open and ran.

Gabe charged through the gaudy hallway and back into the party. He continued fleeing through the gathered crowd, earning many disapproving glances and leaving a trail of murmurs. He didn't stop when he hit the front door nor did he stop when he hit the estate's gate. He just ran on, all the way to the surrounding forest's edge. Once in the relative safety of the trees, Gabe finally stopped.

He took a moment to catch his breath, looking back at Curwen's estate to see if he was being followed. He was relieved to not see anybody giving chase. He didn't see anybody at all until, a moment later, he saw a large man appear from the back of the mansion. Gabe drew a sharp breath when he recognized the man as Douche, and he was carrying the body of his brother over his shoulder. Even from that distance, Gabe could see the fear and hopelessness still flooding Douche's eye. He was obviously still operating under the ash man's control.

Gabe-of-the-present realized with a horrific certainty where Douche was headed. He would wind up in a dark corner with his dead brother's body, where the police would find them both in two days.

Gabe watched Douche for a moment, wondering if there was anything he could do. About half a minute after Douche had appeared, another person stepped into view from the same area of the house. It was the other guard that had been with Curwen. Before Gabe could figure out a good course of action regarding the newcomer, Gabe-of-the-past freaked out. Gabe-of-the-present watched helplessly as his body fell back onto its ass, immediately scrambling backwards. The body got its feet under it and darted deeper into the trees, far away from the second sentry and whatever crazy dead guy talent that he had.

Gabe wasn't sure how long he sat by helplessly as his body ran on. It seemed like miles. His head kept turning, looking for any sign that the second sentry had given chase. Even after the more collected Gabe was sure that he wasn't being followed, the controlling Gabe kept running and looking back.

After repeating the process for what seemed like the thousandth time, when Gabe's head twisted to resume looking forward, he barely had time to notice the tree branch sticking out over his path. The tree branch was at the same height as Gabe's head. He never had a chance to stop himself before his forehead plowed directly into the thick branch.

The world exploded into whiteness, then faded into black.

Gabe felt his eyelids flutter open, not that their opening made any difference to his vision. He couldn't tell the difference between his eyelids being open or shut, the darkness was absolute. He sighed as he knew that he was back in *Midnight In The Garden Of Good And Evil.*

He was back in Arte Blanche.

"What the fuck?" Gabe asked groggily. He sat up, his head spinning. He could feel a wet stickiness coating his forehead. He reached up to touch the sticky liquid and winced as his fingers brushed against a large gash on his forehead. It was a sensation that reminded him much of the day he awoke in the woods of Massachusetts, with no memory of how he had gotten there. Though, this time he remembered. Not only how he had happened upon such a circumstance here in the present, but also how he had happened upon such a circumstance the first time this had occurred.

"Jesus Christ," Gabe swore, recalling all he had seen in his flashback. "I'm sorry," Gabe whispered to his departed friends, wondering if they could hear him in the afterlife. There is no way he could have known any of this back on that day, but that didn't help assuage the guilt that ran through him.

Gabe glanced up at the door. The light above still shone red. How long had he been out? Apparently not long, but how much time did Gabe have before that light extinguished and Zellers' horde came charging through the door.

He felt blindly around in the dark until his hand hit the tire iron. He reclaimed it, the tool's heft making him feel a bit more secure.

Gabe knew he had to move, and move quickly, but he couldn't see a damn thing in the darkness of the room. Where had he and Becca left their working NVGs? Then Gabe remembered. Up in the damn vents! That did him no good in his current situation. Gabe suddenly reconsidered their earlier decision to destroy all of the other NVGs. Maybe they should have left a pair or two in case they had to return to this damned exhibit.

I'll stay low and follow the path with my hands, Gabe thought. He knew the tree that ascended to the vents was only a few feet after the turn in the path. Even in the dark, how hard could it be to find it again?

Gabe swept his arm through the darkness. It didn't take him long to find the cast-iron "In-Between" sign that he had rammed his skull into. He remembered that the sign hung just off the path. Gabe knelt forward and ran his hand along the ground until he felt the cobblestone path under his palm.

Gabe stayed low, following the path in the direction of the giant Satan statue. He crawled along for what seemed like hours, though it had probably only been a few minutes. When he finally felt the path veer right, he breathed a sigh of relief.

He was nearly halfway through the path's long curve when the scent of rotting methane hit him. "Damn! It smells like somebody took a massive shit in here," Gabe griped, before his

274

mind caught up to the smell's significance and the hairs shot straight up on the back of his neck.

Smelled like shit? Ophelia!

The acrid smell was coming from somewhere in front of him. Gabe stopped his forward crawl and immediately reversed his path. So much for getting to the tree. Gabe knew somewhere up ahead was the acidic shit demon, waiting for him in the dark.

Fuck! Gabe considered his options and found that he didn't have many. He kept crawling backward, trying to put distance between himself and the tell-tale smell of malfeasance. Now that the scent had hit him, it was all that his nostrils could detect.

Through the dark, his ears picked up on the sounds of footsteps. It sounded like somebody was slogging through a muddy puddle. A thud accompanied by a squishing sound. Gabe swallowed the bile that had accumulated in his throat as he realized he was hearing the sound of Ophelia approaching him in the dark.

He amped up his rearward speed as much as he could. The wet footsteps followed. Soon he caught a glimpse of the red door light and knew that he was approaching the intersection of the path and the cul-de-sac.

The cul-de-sac. *What did that offer him for protection?* Gabe pondered as he veered his backward crawl toward the circle of the In-Betweens.

If Gabe could find one of the cars, perhaps he could hide out in it for protection. Would Ophelia know that he was in there? Could these fucks see in the dark? Gabe had no clue, but he also had no better options.

Thud/Squish. Thud/Squish.

Gabe turned around so he was crawling forward. He picked up his pace, carefully feeling along the ground with one hand, while holding the other in front of this face to protect his skull from another crushing blow. His searching hand hit a concrete curb. He stepped over the rise and felt around until his hand brushed through grass.

Thud/Squish. Thud/Squish.

The sound was getting closer, the smell intensifying. Gabe's senses screamed at him that Ophelia had turned into the cul-de-sac, following his trail through the darkness.

Gabe's hand found where the grass gave way to the concrete driveway. He swept his hand outward, his fingertips barely brushing against rubber. The car tires! He'd found one of the vehicles. He ran his hands along the length of the car, feeling for the door handle.

Thud/Squish. Thud/Squish.

Gabe's eyes started watering as the smell of shit had grown strong enough to start robbing his lungs of precious oxygen. He quickened his pace in rubbing down the car. His pinky smacked hard against the door's mirror, jamming in place. It stung, but at least Gabe had found the door. He slid his hand along the door until his fingers bumped into the door handle.

Thud/Squish. Thud/Squish.

The sound was way too fucking close now. Gabe pulled at the door handle, releasing the lock, and ripped the door open. He pounced inside the car's protective body and slammed the door shut behind him. Gabe immediately dropped the tire iron into the passenger seat and slapped at the door's arm rest, smiling as he heard the electronic lock engage.

For the moment, in the relative safety of the car, Gabe let his body fall across the seats, taking in a deep breath. Thankfully, the overpowering stench of shit had mercifully faded once the door had closed it off.

Gabe's relief was cut short as something wet and heavy slapped against the windshield of the car. Gabe reached up and flicked on the internal light switch built into the vehicle's roof. The interior of the car lit up, blessedly allowing Gabe's eyes to serve a purpose again.

Maybe it wasn't such a blessing after all, Gabe thought as his eyes saw what lurked outside the windshield. The thickened glass was completely covered in a coating of brown muck that he knew to be human feces. Or maybe *demon* feces would be more accurate.

"Fuck you, Ophelia!" Gabe swore toward the windshield. "Unless you can eat through glass, you can go fuck yourself." Gabe was all bluster on the outside, but inside he was scared to death that she could do just that.

As he carefully watched, there was no sign of the glass being eaten away by Ophelia's acidic shit. Gabe sighed in relief at the joyous realization. He even laughed a little. It was partly out of the relief he felt and partly the result of his mind coming to grips with the insanity of his situation. He was still trapped, a normal, everyday vehicle being the only thing that stood between him and a mass of man-eating bowel expulsion.

Gabe took a few deep breaths to calm himself, keeping his hysteria at bay. Adding to the checklist of promises Gabe was making himself, he vowed to learn how to hotwire cars should he ever make it out of Arte Blanche alive. Short of that, he had to come up with another plan and he had to come up with it soon. Ophelia may be temporarily stopped, but Blake's other demons – ones who would have no problem breaking through the safety glass – would soon come a-calling.

All this ran through Gabe's mind as he stared at the layer of shit on the windshield. At first, he thought his eyes were playing tricks on him as the top of windshield became translucent again. Then, he realized with continued study, that the fecal ooze was slowly receding down the thick pane of glass.

"What the fuck are you up to, you nasty bitch?" Gabe asked the empty interior.

His eyes focused on the bottom of the windshield. The liquid shit was slowly percolating through the slit where the windshield met the car's hood. Ophelia was dripping herself into the engine compartment.

Why the fuck was she doing that? Gabe wondered.

His nose provided the answer. The smell of feces started invading the vehicle's interior. "Oh fuck," Gabe softly swore. Where was it coming from? Gabe sniffed the air, tracing the source of the smell. He had to work to keep his gut from erupting at the wholly unpleasant scent that he was forcing through his nostrils.

He quickly found the source. The A/C vents in the dash.

"Oh fuck!" Gabe said again, much sharper than before. That bitch was going to force her way through the vents!

The smell had grown suffocatingly strong – Gabe's eyes once again watering up – as he slapped at the vents, rolling them closed. Being made of cheap plastic, Gabe knew they wouldn't keep her out for long. He had barely managed to close off the last one when something thumped against the plastic on the opposite side. The vent briefly bulged, before flattening back into place.

"Shit! Shit!" Gabe scrambled the only direction he could. Up and over the seats. He heard another thump behind him, followed by the crack of cheap plastic. "Shit!" he swore again.

Gabe had the bulk of his torso squeezed between the top of the driver's seat and the vehicle's ceiling. It was tight squeeze. Gabe kicked his feet out against the bottom of the center console to propel him forward. Something in the console gave way and clicked as Gabe's heel collided against it. Gabe didn't have the time to worry about what it was as he hurriedly slid forward over the seat back. As his balls passed over the seat back, Gabe prepared himself for the headfirst tumble into the backseat.

The tumble never happened.

Something ensnared his foot, immediately stopping his forward momentum. Gabe barely had the time to say "Fuck me!" before he was jerked backward, his body collapsing into the front seat.

Gabe turned around and was met with the sight of runny feces dribbling out of the vents. The left-most vent in particular had thin streams of the brown sludge running through the slats, eventually coalescing into a mucky, brown limb that ended in the fist that gripped his shoe. The fist uncurled from the foot, shot up, and slammed against Gabe's chest, the coat he still wore the only thing between him and the acidic goo. The fecal arm pushed him with a surprising amount of strength, pinning him tight against the seat.

The stream of brown muck dribbling from the center vent began to morph, curdling up into a ball. The sphere lifted on the end of a long stream of muck until it hovered directly in front of Gabe's face. Gabe watched in horror as the round circumference of the sphere sank inward, forming Ophelia's shit-covered, smiling face. The curled, fecal lips moved in speech, Ophelia's high-pitched, jubilant voice seeming out of place coming from the monstrous shit demon in front of him.

"Hello again, Mr. Daniels. Isn't this turning out to be a fabulous evening?"

The amount of human shit in the car increased, as Gabe felt his bowels loosen, filling up the inside of his underwear.

35

Pop!

The mechanical noise came from the bottom of the car's central console, where Gabe's heel had hit earlier in his desperate attempt to flee into the backseat. A quick glance from Ophelia's shit-constructed face to the console revealed to Gabe that he had inadvertently activated the car's cigarette lighter.

Gabe started laughing.

"What's so amusing, Mr. Daniels?" Ophelia asked, her shit-covered brow furrowed in confusion.

Gabe continued laughing. "I was just remembering back to my high school days. My buddies would sometimes call me the blue bomber. You want to know why?"

One of the shit demon's eyebrows cocked as she asked, "Why?"

"Because I was a master of lighting my farts on fire. I could turn my ass into a fucking flamethrower."

Ophelia's brows stayed furrowed, obviously not understanding what Gabe was getting at.

"You see, human shit produces methane. Methane is flammable as fuck."

Ophelia's eyes widened and Gabe knew that she now understood. It was time to make his move. Gabe, who had covertly slid his hand over to the tire iron resting on the passenger seat, lifted the heavy tool and swung it into Ophelia's face. The hardened tool literally wiped the smile off her face, morphing the sunken features into brown rain that splashed against the driver's side window.

The arm's strong hold loosened against Gabe's chest and he threw his body down to the side, reaching out to grab the car lighter from its console housing.

Ophelia's facial features quickly reformed, her eyes slanted down at Gabe, who was wielding the red-glowing end of the lighter at her.

"Pee-yew!" Gabe said waving his free hand in front of his nose. "Anybody got a match?" The joke didn't work, but it also didn't keep Gabe from jamming the lighter directly into Ophelia's newly-reformed face.

A sizzle, and the even-worse smell of *burning* feces, were the only things that the move accomplished. Ophelia did not erupt into a fiery ball of shit as Gabe had hoped.

Gabe's heart dropped as he realized that his attempt hadn't worked. That was it. His final plan. As he watched Ophelia laughing in his face, Gabe knew that he was fucked.

He closed his eyes, awaiting death.

Instead, he received only a loud shriek.

Gabe opened his eyes to see Ophelia's mouth wide open, locked in screaming anguish. A golden glow shone through the windshield. Before Gabe could rise up enough to look through the windshield, the same glow roared out of the vents, quickly consuming the muck covering Ophelia's body. The inside of the car quickly heated up, loud with the roar of screams and flame.

Gabe's eyebrows singed, and his lungs started to burn. He was terrified he was going to cook inside the tight confines of the car.

All of this happened in mere seconds, before Ophelia's flaming body rushed back into the vents, almost as if she was being sucked through them by some great gravitational force.

The air quickly cooled to a more tolerable temperature and Gabe sat up to stare out the windshield. For a brief moment, all he saw were a few flames atop the hood of the car as the small amount of shit that had yet to dribble down into the engine compartment burned.

Then, Gabe's whole world exploded into brightness.

The entire vehicle spasmed as if caught in a magnificent earthquake; or, more appropriately, the cusp of an exploding volcano. The hood exploded upward from the front of the vehicle, flying out into the vast darkness of the exhibit. Following it was a huge molten ball of flame. Gabe heard Ophelia's scream coming from the fireball as it flew upward with incredible force. The fireball ascended all the way to the ceiling, where it flattened and clung like a glob of napalm. A shower of yellow sparks rained across the exhibit as the new sun hung in the sky.

Gabe took a moment to wonder what the fuck had just happened. Had there been a delayed reaction to his attack with the car lighter? He doubted it. That theory didn't sit right. Besides, the flame had roared to life from the outside of the car, not from Ophelia's face.

Still in minor shock, Gabe looked out at the exhibit through the car's windows. He could now see the cul-de-sac and the tops of the nearby trees silhouetted against the flickering light.

Gabe shot up to an erect position. The exhibit still stood mostly in shadow, but he could see just well enough to navigate through the maze of the room without need of the goggles. He threw open the door and leaped from the vehicle. He didn't have a minute to waste.

Gabe ran around the front of the car. As he passed what was left of the hood, his peripheral vision caught sight of a small flame flickering against the ground. He nearly passed it by, assuming it was just a lingering speck of Ophelia. A gleam of chrome stopped him. Gabe bent to examine the flame and was surprised to find that it came from a lighter. A Zippo-style lighter, its lid lying open against the ground.

"Where the fuck did this come from?" Gabe asked himself. He picked the lighter up, snapped the lid shut, and stuffed it in his pocket, saving the mystery for a later time. Using the overhead stain of light, Gabe ran out of the cul-de-sac and navigated through the forest of *Evil*.

He arrived at the inner doorway that led to the east corridor and was pleased to see that it was still open on his side, the light above still glowing red. He stepped through the doorway and placed his ear against the closed, outer door. Hearing nothing, he closed the inner door behind him and inched open the outer one.

He peeked into the hallway and saw that it was empty. "Thank-fucking-God," he breathed, then stepped through the door. He dashed down the hallway, careful to keep his footsteps as quiet as possible. He aimed for the turn that would lead him to the door for Free Market. He knew his plan for when he got there didn't amount to much, which at the moment, didn't extend past trying to beat the door in with the tire iron.

Before he reached the corner, unseen voices from the southern hallway reached his ears. A lot of voices. Easily too many to fight his way through. "Motherfucker!" Gabe swore under his breath as he stopped to listen.

"He just opened the door to the eastern wing," he heard a staticky voice yell over a radio. "Get over there now!"

Fuck! Well, that hadn't worked. They knew where he was. Gabe knew that he was fucked. Nothing left but to fight and pray, and Gabe wasn't much into prayer. He backed several feet away from the corner and crossed the hallway, placing his back against a door labeled *The Hanging Gardens Of Babylon*. It was as good a vantage point as he was going to get for when the attacking horde came rushing around the corner.

The sound of clomping footsteps – similar to the thunder of a Wild West buffalo stampede – came from around the corner. They were coming. Gabe lifted the tire iron, readying it for attack. He knew he didn't have a chance in hell, but he was determined to go out like a man.

He was so focused on the loud sounds of approaching death, that he almost missed the noise of the door swinging open behind him.

Almost.

He turned around and saw something that forced his testicles higher into his gut than they already were. It turned out to be the one thing Gabe feared worse than the crowd of demons approaching in haste. A thick cloud of ash hung in the air, a gray tendril snaking off from the main body, still clutching the doorknob.

How the fuck had Curwen's goons found him!? Gabe thought in horror.

That was the last thought that went through his head before the cloud of ash shot at him, completely engulfing Gabe in its dusty, cold embrace.

36

Gabe couldn't see a thing through the tornado of ash swirling around him. He was lost in a drab world of gray. External sound was muffled by the roar of air traveling around him, making matters worse.

Why is this shit not streaming into my body, like it had with Douche? Gabe thought. Not that he was complaining.

A voice broke through the cloud; weak, but Gabe could just make out the words. "Danner, have you seen Mr. Daniels come through here?"

Danner? What did Danner have to do with this?

"No, Dr. Holtz, I'm afraid I have not." Gabe heard this latest voice with great volume and clarity. The voice sounded as if it was coming from the cloud of ash itself.

"Keep an eye out, or whatever it is that you see through in that state," Holtz's voice spoke through the cloud.

"Of course, Dr. Holtz. As Mr. Zellers wishes."

Gabe realized the ash cloud wasn't one of Curwen's goons after all. He was surrounded by Blake's right-hand butt-boy – Danner - instead. Gabe remained silent in the gray cloud, somehow sensing he was safer with Danner than with the rest of Blake's goon squad.

Gabe's world jolted and he could tell that Danner was carrying him off to another location from where he had been ensnared in the hallway. It was a brief journey. Gabe heard the slamming of a door through the cloud, then the overwhelming gray pallet began to dissipate, details of his new locale slowly revealing themselves in his vision.

"Where the fuck am I?" Gabe asked as the last flakes of the ash cloud left his orbit and gathered into a man-shaped form off to Gabe's side. The pallid cloud suddenly bloomed with color as the smiling form of Danner Hackett emerged.

Beyond Danner, Gabe beheld a landscape of beauty and terror. A strange exhibit that was undeniably art, but also discomforting to the senses.

The exhibit's room was easily twice the size of the other rooms on the outer circumference of exhibits. Its length nearly three times that of its counterparts. Gabe vaguely recalled the map possessing an enlarged rectangular shape in this area of the gallery.

Extending out about two-thirds the width of the room from the rear wall and running from end to end in length, were grassy hillocks rising from the floor. The green lumps rolled three times before they reached the back wall, each hill slightly higher than the one before it. Littered atop the hills were seemingly thousands of structures that appeared to be constructed from marble of various colors. Each one consisted of a pole that rose vertically from the grass, with an arm extending perpendicularly from the top of the vertical pole. Miniature figurines shaped like the human body hung from the structure's arms by way of a noose, completing the image of fancily-fashioned gallows.

The multitude of gallows were so numerous, they nearly blocked out the green of the hillocks, the green hills appearing merely as an emerald background among the rolling fields of an earthly rainbow landscape.

The illusion continued far beyond where the sod met the wall. A hue of brightly-colored intensity was painted on the rear wall, extending the scene far beyond what the floor space allowed. The mural traveled up the wall's length. Near the bottom, the hills and their gallows were crafted in a larger aspect, while further up they shrunk smaller and smaller in size. The image made one feel as if they were at the foot of a great mountain of the rolling hillocks that ran far into the distance.

Atop the painted peak was an enormous statue, much larger than all the hills and gallows that ran before it. The statue showed a man and a woman, both draped in multi-colored robes with similarly-colored crowns. The statues gazed down upon the lower hills, their faces twisted in such a way that they appeared to be pleased – perhaps even inspired – by the endless death that was displayed before them.

"This exhibit, Mr. Daniels, is Mr. Zellers' depiction of the Hanging Gardens of Babylon," Danner said, answering Gabe's question.

"The Hanging Gardens of Babylon?" Gabe questioned, astounded. "That fat fuck Cliff mentioned something about the Hanging Gardens of Babylon earlier," Gabe remembered. "But what does this have to do with the hanging..." Gabe stopped speaking as his mind hit upon something in the name. "Oh wait. Like, *hanging*? As in all these motherfuckers *hanging* from their nooses?" Gabe waved a hand over the multitude of gallows. "Wicked interpretation," Gabe commented, actually pleased by the display.

"Not an interpretation, Mr. Daniels," Danner corrected. "Just a rendition of the actual garden as it stood in its time."

"Bullshit!" Gabe snapped. "The Hanging Gardens of Babylon were…" Gabe paused as he searched his memory for the brief clips he had seen on Discovery Channel specials.

"I understand your confusion," Danner stepped in, saving Gabe the trouble of sifting further through his recollections. "Most historians would have you believe the Hanging Gardens were some kind of miracle in botanical engineering. Plants hanging from the sky, or some such nonsense. Indeed, the gardens constructed by King Nebuchadnezzar II were of the *hanging* variety you see before you. Praised worldwide for their beauty, but equally feared."

"Let me reiterate," Gabe said, then mimicked clearing his throat. "Bullshit!"

Danner looked ready to argue the point further, but Gabe started in again before he could.

"Truth be told, I really don't give a fuck why the gardens were called *Hanging*. It could be because they featured a bunch of well-hung men with their dicks swaying in the breeze, for all that I care. I only want to know three things. One: Why the fuck did you just help me escape the rest of Zeller's goons back there in the hallway? Two: What the fuck is going on around here? i.e. How the fuck are you turning into a cloud of fucking ash? Or how is that nutjob Ophelia able to become the flesh-eating shit version of Swamp Thing. Three - and this is the most important one - how the fuck do I get out of here!?"

"Well, Mr. Daniels, I agree that those are some very pertinent questions. To answer them…" Danner began.

"On second thought," Gabe interrupted, "let's just skip to number three and you tell me how the fuck I get out of this God-forsaken place."

"In due time, Mr. Daniels."

"*Fuck* in due time!" Gabe snapped. "Get me the fuck out of here *now!*"

"Aren't you at all interested in saving Ms. Larson?"

The question stopped Gabe in his tracks.

"I can help you save her," Danner promised.

Gabe struggled with Danner's proposal. Why should he further risk his life to save a woman he barely knew? Yet, with her name now hanging in the air, Gabe felt unsure of himself. Not much time had passed since she had been taken. Blake surely hadn't had time to have killed her already, could he? Not with his sucking of Peristopheles' dick, or whatever else went into that ritual. But, once again, why should Gabe care enough to risk life and limb for her?

The more Gabe turned it over in his mind, the more he realized that he *did* care enough. Sure, he had only known her a short time, but damned if she hadn't already made an impression on him. And it was more than just the lust he felt picturing her ass in her tight skirt. He thought back to that kiss they had shared right before that foul fuck Lester had swooped in and whisked her away. The feelings the memory stirred in him – in his heart of all places – ensured that trying to save her had to be the right move.

"I'm listening," Gabe relented, his voice much calmer than before.

"Good," Danner said, relieved. "You are both safe for the moment. It will take Mr. Zellers some time to set her up for the ritual."

"Yeah. What's the deal with that ritual?" Gabe asked, now intently listening to what Danner had to say.

"It is but one of many found in the Book of Peristopheles."

Gabe pictured the book that he had recently recalled from his time at Curwen's house, but he didn't mention it to Danner.

Something told him that he should keep that a secret. For now, at least.

"The Book of Peristopheles?" he asked instead, pretending to have never heard of it.

"I am sure you are unfamiliar with it," Danner incorrectly stated. "This will be easier if I answer your three questions. Most notably, the second one."

"Fuck it," Gabe huffed. "I don't see that I have much of a choice but to hear you out. Proceed."

Danner smiled. "Very well, sir. To understand all that you have witnessed tonight at the Arte Blanche, we must start here." Danner waved his hand behind him, towards the emerald hills of the exhibit. "Over twenty-five hundred years ago, in the Hanging Gardens of Babylon."

BABYLON

610 B.C.

Uh, Great King, I urge you not to proceed with your marriage this day," Ahimelek begged. "Not to *this* woman!"

What an old fool this priest was being, Makru thought, watching Ahimelek's pleas. It wasn't wise to question King Nebuchadnezzar. At least, not of late. Nebuchadnezzar had recently fallen into sporadic moods. Often times, *deadly* moods. Not that Makru thought Ahimelek was mistaken in his assessment which prompted such pleas. The foul moods had only come upon his king since the woman Amytis – soon to be *Queen* Amytis – had arrived in Nebuchadnezzar's life.

Delivered as a gift of peace from her father - Cyaxeres, king of Media – Amytis had brought with her everything *except* peace. Death? Probably. Despair? Most certainly.

"What is it about Amytis that you find so disagreeable?" Nebuchadnezzar asked.

"Sire," Ahimelek continued, "I apologize, but she is a most vile woman. Word has followed all the way from Media of her deeds. Most agree that she is a witch, plaguing the land with black magic."

"Those are bold accusations," Nebuchadnezzar warned his high priest.

"Even now, she has you moving toward Jerusalem's capture" Ahimelek tried. "After your raids against Egypt, you vowed to leave the Israelites be. Reward for aiding your army as our brave men traversed through their lands."

"Preposterous!" Nebuchadnezzar dismissed. "Those traitorous Israelites have been plotting against me ever since my army returned through Babylon's gates."

"I have seen no proof of such plotting. Only the words of Amytis herself has led your mind down such a nefarious path."

"Are you accusing my future queen of telling untruths?" Nebuchadnezzar asked the high priest, his tone crossing the line to cautionary.

Makru saw the hesitation flood through Ahimelek's posture. The old priest approached his next words carefully. "Not at all, Great King. I merely share words to stoke memory of the Gods' distaste for betrayal. Perhaps a little more study into the Israelite mind would be warranted."

Makru looked into Nebuchadnezzar's eyes and saw them overcome with a flicker of doubt. He briefly wondered if Ahimelek's words had actually managed to reach their king's heart, when the doubt in those orbs clouded over with a glazed blankness that Makru knew all too well. It was the same blankness that seemed to appear whenever his king would dive into one of his recent moods, usually prompting some action that was out of character for the usually-fair and jubilant man.

"Perhaps you are correct, Ahimelek," Nebuchadnezzar said, surprising Makru with his concession. "I will consider your words on the matter." Nebuchadnezzar kept his face still, as if it were set in stone. "In the meantime, send the Gods my regards."

Nebuchadnezzar finished with a nod toward Ahimelek, or that was Makru's initial interpretation. It was not Ahimelek who responded to the nod, though. It was the king's guard standing directly behind the high priest. In one smooth move, the guard unsheathed his sword, heaved it forward, and drove its polished length through the back of Ahimelek's skull. The tip of the sword emerged through Ahimelek's mouth, glistening red in the fading light pouring through the windows.

Sharp intakes of breath could be heard throughout the room, followed by an eruption of murmuring. "Silence!" Nebuchadnezzar screamed. The sudden cacophony vanished as the king leapt to his feet. "Ahimelek's mouth shed words against my betrothed, now they shed only blood and the tip of the sword. Let this be a warning to all that feel that Amytis is not worthy of her king."

The room remained silent, no one caring to offer further argument.

"Now," Nebuchadnezzar continued, stepping down from his throne, "with no further debate rising, let us head forth into the gardens to meet up with my new wife. It is time we bind Babylon and Media together in matrimony."

******

609 B.C.

"I must confess, I have already grown bored here in Babylon," the woman said. She rolled on the silken sheets, regrettably concealing the firm bubble of her ass. As a welcome replacement, her milky-white breasts were exposed to Nebuchadnezzar's gaze. The king took a moment to admire the length of her pale, slender body, broken only by a raven-dark tuft of hair set between her legs.

"Tell me, my queen, in what way do you find our great city lacking?" Nebuchadnezzar asked. "Which thirsts are left unquenched in our mighty city? Babylon is renowned world-wide for our offerings of art, wine, games, and culture."

Amytis huffed as she considered the question. "I cannot deny the abundance of joys to be found here. No, Babylon is certainly not lacking in the joys of life." Nebuchadnezzar nodded at his wife's concurrence. "It is other, darker passions that I find severely lacking."

"Of which darker passions do you speak?"

"Death,' Amytis said simply. "In death, I find the perfect balance of intrigue and power. A king beloved is a king held in high regard, but a king *feared*..." she said, leaning on the word. "A king feared is a king whose power will never be questioned."

Nebuchadnezzar felt his skin grow cold and clammy at her words. "And how do you propose a king attains such a stigma?"

Amytis stood from the bed and walked over to a bowl of grapes set into the large room's corner. She plucked a grape from its vine and popped it into her mouth. Her lips seductively rolled as she chewed on the succulent fruit. "Cyaxeres holds your answer," she answered after swallowing the juicy morsel. "My father keeps a field in Media. This field is littered with the bodies of those he has chosen for the purpose of such a statement. The bodies are piled as high as a mountain. Not a seemly sight, to be sure. A flaw that I would see rectified here in a city renowned for its greatness in the arts."

"You want me to make death beautiful?" Nebuchadnezzar asked, considering the suggestion an absurdity.

"I would have it so," she agreed.

"Impossible," the king argued. "Death does not play well on the eyes."

"Surely such a great mind as yours can figure out a way." Amytis walked over to where Nebuchadnezzar was standing, each step a slow and conscious effort, taking advantage of her body's subtle movements to appeal to the king's focused eyes. When within reach, she extended her hand to his face, gently rubbing her fingers along his cheek.

"And who do you suggest fill this construction of death? Do you not think that I'd be averse to killing my people for mere purposes of aesthetics?"

"Citizens of Babylon? Surely not." Amytis laughed. Such a sweet and innocent sound, contrasting darkly with its intent. "Though, do your citizens not possess an abundance of slaves that could be set to such an endeavor?"

"Slaves!" Nebuchadnezzar huffed. "Even a slave's life has more meaning than to be placed to death for purposes of regalia."

"Oh, stop being so trite. Your kingdom already has more slaves that it can manage and, even as we speak, thousands upon thousands more march from Jerusalem to serve your glory."

"Even yet, I still find myself averse to such actions."

Amytis countered only with a narrowing of her eyes and a half-smile upon her lips. It was *the* look. Nebuchadnezzar had come to find that he was powerless against her will when that look came upon her face. Even now, his mind betrayed his reluctance as a multitude of options for giving her desires physical form flooded throughout his mind.

"I shall see it done," Nebuchadnezzar promised, his heart sinking with every syllable uttered.

******

601 B.C

Nebuchadnezzar watched as the body swayed from the marble structure. Thousands more just like it were at his back, though this one was the most recent addition. Two cross-connected columns of marble, the stone stained orange after construction. Soon more would be erected along this line, all matching orange in color. Then the next line would come, much the same as this, but stained a different color.

Perhaps violet, Nebuchadnezzar thought. The last row of violet lay a long way behind him.

He was alone now, save two of his closest bodyguards hovering nearby. He stared up at the swaying man with the same emotions he had felt for all the other thousands that he had condemned over the past years. Joy and despair, both in equal measure. The despair he understood in full. The joy was alien to him, of an uncertain source, though it was always felt whenever he added to his grand creation.

His hanging gardens were already famous throughout the known world. He had heard word that tongues could be heard speaking of it from Egypt to Greece, and even as far east as China. They spoke of the grand spectacle with awe and reverence, though always questioning its purpose. Questioning its nature. Some even questioned its very existence, as most who had not laid eyes upon it could scarcely believe such a thing existed in the world.

Nebuchadnezzar was enjoying the rare moment of peace when the sound of skittering footsteps broke the silence of the hill. Nebuchadnezzar sprung to his feet and called out toward the sound. "Who is there? Show yourself!" His two guards snapped into action upon hearing their leader's call, ready to defend their king.

Nebuchadnezzar spied a shadow extending from behind a nearby gallows. "You there!" he shouted in the shadow's direction. "I see you cowering at column's rear. Come out and make yourself known."

From behind the column, a head leaned into view. It was a man's head; unnaturally white skin forming his face, with the exception of cheeks stained the color of rose petals. His lips were puffy and curved into a beaming smile. His hair was a curly mop of woven gold. A strange looking man for these parts. His visage was more like those that hailed from Athens. The kind whose image spoke of a rich lineage and an affinity for lying with boys.

"You must be speaking to me," the man said. "All pardons, but I did not wish to intrude on such a somber moment."

"Who are you and what purpose seizes you to risk your life, sneaking upon a man of power such as I?" Nebuchadnezzar asked.

"Me?" the man asked, his hands rising to his chest. "I am merely an admirer. An admirer who wishes nothing more than to share words with the creator of such beauty as this." He opened his arms and spun on his feet, encompassing the whole of the hanging gardens with his gesture. His tone belied a boyish jubilance which Nebuchadnezzar was not inclined to share.

"And what leads you to believe that I would be possessive of a mind toward speaking with commoners?"

"A commoner? No, I did not claim that," the man refuted with a sly grin.

"Then you are of royal lineage?" Nebuchadnezzar found himself lost in confusion.

"No. Not that either."

Nebuchadnezzar looked to his guards. "I do not have time for double talk. Seize this man and see that he adds to the *beauty* he so enjoys." The guards instantly stepped to their task.

"Oh joy!" the strange man beamed. "Brutes are setting upon me with a sole mind to forge me forever splendorous."

Nebuchadnezzar stood confounded by the man's reaction. This visitor was obviously not of sound mind.

The first of the guards reached the man and savagely gripped him by the collar of his shirt. "Apologies, sir, but I find my time too lacking to indulge in pleasures such as death." The strange man said as the guard struggled to pull him off his feet. Nebuchadnezzar's guard was easily twice the size of the man, but his efforts yielded no result. The curly-haired man extended a hand to the struggling guard and placed his palm against the guard's forehead.

Instantly, the guard began to scream. A blackness radiated outward on the guard's forehead from beneath the strange man's palm, leaving behind desiccated flesh where it passed. The screams were blissfully short as the blackness did not take long to reach the guard's mouth. Once the mouth was stained, the screams fell silent. As the blackness descended down the guard's throat, the top of the guard's skull disintegrated into black flakes, to be carried off by the breeze. His temples followed, then his cheeks. The spreading blackness, followed by the flaky vaporization, continued all the way down until there was nothing left of the guard but armor crumpled upon the ground.

The second guard wisely stopped short of touching the man.

Nebuchadnezzar, after a brief bout with stunned uncertainty, dropped to his knees and began worshipping the stranger. "Oh Nabu, God of Wisdom, do not strike me, your humble servant."

It was the stranger's turn to appear confused. "Nabu? You take me for that pompous ass? *The God of Wisdom*, as he likes to be called. Now I know you name bears his mark, oh great Nebuchadnezzar, but I assure you that silly old goat is not the kind of God that will travel down to visit with mortals. He's far too snobbish for that."

Nebuchadnezzar looked up into the stranger's smiling face, feeling true fear. "Accept my apologies. Nabu is my God and I am his beloved. I could not fathom any other God arriving hither to converse with me. I ask again, who are you? I'm only asking so that I do not offend further."

"Guessing games are the best of games, but I see that you are not of a mind to play," the man said, curling his bottom lip like a spoiled child refused. "If you must know, I have, of late, been called Peristopheles."

"Peristopheles?" Nebuchadnezzar's eyes glowed with recognition. "The God of Art, Mischief, Water, and…"

"Yes, yes…" Peristopheles rolled his hand, wishing to rush through his elongated title. "…of Intelligence, and so on and so forth. Titles bestowed upon me by man, absent of true meaning. Art? I do love art and suppose I could be called a God of such. Mischief?" A knowing gleam sparked in his eye. "Most certainly well attributed. Though water, I never understood. I have no fondness - nor interest - in lording over such a drab element." Peristopheles reached a hand behind his back. When he again brought it forward, it contained a chalice of red liquid. Nebuchadnezzar was certain that this God had just summoned the cup out of thin air.

"Now wine?" Peristopheles swirled the chalice's contents while deeply inhaling its aroma. "Wine I can surely get behind." He upended the cup and swallowed the whole of the cup's contents.

"I apologize yet again. You are not how I envisioned a God."

"Apology accepted," Peristopheles joyfully announced. "And consider your ignorance forgiven, as it is completely understandable. This is but one of many forms that I assume to lessen my impact on the limited mind of man. Were I to show you my true form, your heart would explode in terror."

"What has brought you - a great God of Babylon – to walk among men on this day?" Nebuchadnezzar asked, wishing to steer the conversation back on course.

"All of this." Peristopheles once again spun in a circle and waved his hands around the hanging gardens. "In all my millennia of prowling various lands and cultures, I have never seen anything quite so remarkable as your hanging gardens. I knew that I absolutely had to meet the mind behind it."

"In that case, I stand before you, most blessed among men," Nebuchadnezzar performed another bow before this strange God.

"It's just so damn beautiful," Peristopheles continued. "Rivaled only by the beauty of your queen."

Nebuchadnezzar's eyes shot up from his penitent position. "Amytis? You know of my bride?"

"How could I not?" Peristopheles jubilated. "Her beauty is praised, even among the Gods. And I speak not only of the mold of her flesh, but also the immaculate blackness of her heart."

"Her heart is indeed dark," Nebuchadnezzar admitted, a kind of sorrow creeping into his tone.

"Oh, don't be so dour. She may have robbed you of choice, but it was your mind – and your mind alone – that dreamt up such a place as this."

Nebuchadnezzar's heart dropped further, knowing this impish God spoke truth.

"Now, in full honesty, I have descended to the mortal realm for more purpose than aesthetic pleasure. For such a pairing as you and your bride, I wish to bestow a gift," Peristopheles added.

"What gift?" Nebuchadnezzar asked.

Peristopheles reached behind his back again, this time bringing forth a tome bound by darkened flesh. Nebuchadnezzar felt a cold breeze fall upon him as the book came into sight.

"This is my book," Peristopheles explained. "My guide, if you will. In it, I have scribed much of my history, as well as words that mortals can utter to share in my powers."

"Which powers?"

"Many powers!" Peristopheles practically giggled the words. "Powers over life, death, will, and riches. Allow me to provide an example." Peristopheles turned to the remaining guard and placed his hand on his shoulder. The guard flinched, looking ready to soil himself as the hand fell upon him. Nebuchadnezzar promised himself that this guard would be greatly rewarded for standing brave and not running far from his king and this deadly, unusual God. To the king's and the guard's shared relief, the guard did not disintegrate into black ash as his partner had.

"I have chosen to let you live," Peristopheles assured the guard. "Not only that, but I will bestow upon you great riches and great honor in continued service to your king. How does that sound?"

The guard actually smiled at Peristopheles' words. "I thank you greatly for your generosity," the guard graced.

"Of course," Peristopheles matched the guard's smile, "the honor lie in that you will be elevated to the highest post in your master's stable. All the other guards will follow your every command. The riches...well, the riches shall be paid in fear."

The guard's smile twisted into uncertainty.

Peristopheles leaned forward and connected his lips with the guard's. Peristopheles ground his lips against the guard, giving the illusion of two men lost in a lustful embrace. There was nothing lustful shining in the guard's eyes, however. His eyes shone with terror.

Nebuchadnezzar's eyes were drawn from the bizarre kiss by a movement lower on the guard's body. The guard's torso began pulsating as something squirmed beneath the flesh. Whatever it was, it began travelling upward, towards the guard's throat. Upon reaching the narrowed channel, the bulge of flesh continued ascending.

Peristopheles removed himself from the guard's lips as the aberrant protrusion worked its way through the guard's neck. The guard tried screaming, but whatever sounds managed to make it through his blocked esophagus were diminished to only low huffs. His eyes now bulged from their sockets, looking as if they would soon explode.

The guard belched up a mist of blood as the protrusion neared his mouth. The red mist stuck to the impish face of Peristopheles. The God proceeded to lick off the few drops that his tongue could reach, though much of his face remained stained in crimson.

The slithering protrusion reached the guard's mouth, then tumbled out through the orifice, exposing its form to the sun's light. Nebuchadnezzar recognized the long, slimy form that emerged as the guard's intestines, having uncoiled to travel up the man's body and out through his mouth. Despite the impossible circumstances of the intestinal unraveling, Nebuchadnezzar could see through the guard's eyes and that he had felt every ounce of pain such an occurrence would cause.

The guard fell to his knees, clearly nearing loss of consciousness. Peristopheles smiled down at the guard, gave him a kiss on the forehead and flicked his hand at him, as if shooing away an unwanted guest. In response to Peristopheles' gesture, the guard – untouched – shot backward through the air. His ascent took him near the nearest empty gallows. The exposed end of his intestines snapped upward into the air like a whip, wrapping around the horizontal arm of the gallows. It constricted around the marble arm and stopped the guard's body from flying further. The guard was left swaying on the post, his intestines acting as a gore-drenched noose.

As the guard's life finally expired, Peristopheles sang a well-practiced verse. "You don't have to repeat the words in song,"

Peristopheles clarified, after completing the phrase. "Merely speak them. I just happen to enjoy uttering a good melody."

Nebuchadnezzar stood in stunned silence, watching as the God proceeded to hop around the columns holding his former guard. "You can come out now," he stopped and sang loudly into the air.

From behind a nearby column, a man stepped into sight. Nebuchadnezzar's heart skipped a beat – likely several beats – when he recognized the man as that of his guard, whose body still swung from the columns.

"Read these words here," Peristopheles instructed, holding his book out to Nebuchadnezzar.

Nebuchadnezzar, his manner plagued with uncertainty, carefully took the book from the God and stared down at the words printed on the exposed page. He glanced up at Peristopheles, who nodded and said, "Read them through in their entirety and be sure not to speak any other words until you have completed the verse."

Nebuchadnezzar nodded and read from the page until the final words were spoken.

"He is yours now," Peristopheles explained, his tone having grown soft. "Forever, and without fear of betrayal."

Nebuchadnezzar's eyes filled with tears and his throat constricted, preventing him from replying. He had never felt terror quite like he felt at that moment.

"Don't be besieged by fear," Peristopheles soothed, reading Nebuchadnezzar's posture. "He is yours to control. My gift to you." After another moment of silence, Peristopheles continued. "If you are not yet appreciative, then bring my gift to your wife. I have no doubt that she'll be fully enticed by its virtues."

Nebuchadnezzar had no doubt of that, either.

"Anyway," Peristopheles continued, "now that I have fulfilled my purpose here, I shall take my leave. May the remainder of your days be spectacular, oh great king." Nebuchadnezzar's title sounded as mockery coming from Peristopheles' tongue.

Peristopheles performed a mock bow, then his body crumbled into thousands of black chunks that fell to the ground. Looking closer, Nebuchadnezzar saw that the black chunks were actually a shelled insect the like of which Nebuchadnezzar had never seen. The insects quickly burrowed into the dirt of the hill and disappeared from sight.

Nebuchadnezzar knelt upon the grass of his great masterpiece, the book held aloft in his extended arms. He stayed like that – not moving nor speaking – until well past the sun's disappearance over the western horizon.

******

Amytis laughed as she once again lay naked upon the bed. "Is this not wonderful?" she asked her brooding husband. A slave girl – her nude front lacking the beauty of Amytis, but not entirely unpleasant to look upon - extended a vine of grapes to Amytis, allowing the queen to pluck off a purple orb and place it into her mouth.

"Wonderful is not the word I would use to describe this. Abominable, I feel, serves closer to intent," Nebuchadnezzar answered.

"Oh?" Amytis replied. "I fear your man, the Jew Daniel, has turned you into such a yawn." Amytis plucked the last grape from the vine. She let the fruit linger in her mouth as she sucked on its juices before swallowing its withered flesh. The servant girl let the empty vine drop and reached behind her. Nebuchadnezzar watched as a red seam appeared along her spine, traveling up from her ample cheeks to the base of her neck. The flesh along the seam parted, revealing an empty cavern where the woman's innards should have been. Empty, save another vine of the delectable fruit, stick with the girl's blood. The servant girl removed the vine and held it out to her queen. Amytis plucked a grape from the new vine and placed it, complete with its slimy red coating, into her mouth. She sucked on it, her eyes rolling upward in delight.

"You have come to know of Daniel?" Nebuchadnezzar asked, surprised to hear the Jew's name part her lips.

Amytis laughed. "Of course, my king! Have you not yet realized that I know all that you know?"

Nebuchadnezzar stood uncomfortably, fearing Amytis' response to the man who had tried often to steer him away from Amytis' influence.

"Oh, don't fret," Amytis soothed. "I will surely take him from you someday, but not today. I do so enjoy when you mistakenly believe that you have power. Besides, I confess to bearing respect for the man's influence. It is nearly as strong as my own."

The king feared for his friend and trusted advisor. Having come to him as a result of his raids on Jerusalem, Daniel had proven himself to be trusted above all. Nebuchadnezzar had always known, given Daniel's powers of influence much the same as Amytis' own, that Amytis would view the slave as a threat, so he had tried to keep him from her. Apparently, all to no avail.

"Anyway, I no longer desire to discuss the Jew. My mind leans to other matters." Amytis plucked another grape from the vine, then shooed the slave girl away, sitting up on the silken sheets. "Slaves are already such pliant creatures. I desire to introduce more upstanding citizenry to the blessings of the mischief God."

Nebuchadnezzar's eyes widened. "You would sacrifice *my* citizen's for your own pleasure?" He asked, appalled, but not surprised.

"It's not really sacrifice," Amytis dismissed. "Nobody can even tell when another has been bitten with the gift of Peristopheles. Take this slave girl, for instance." Amytis pointed towards the grape-bearing girl. "She walks and talks among us even now, and it was days ago that I put her under the knife."

Nebuchadnezzar remembered the event with much horror. Amytis had lured the slave girl with promises of great wealth and the seed of her husband, the king. Once she had started in on her, the girl had screamed for what seemed half a day. Even as Amytis began ripping out the girl's vital organs one-by-one, Nebuchadnezzar had seen the life struggling to remain in her eyes.

"When it comes to the great citizens of Babylon, I must put my foot down," Nebuchadnezzar challenged. "I will not see your suggested deeds come to pass."

Amytis' willful gaze fell upon him, and Nebuchadnezzar knew that he had lost.

"I invite you to stop me then, dear husband. That I would very much like to see." Amytis held her gaze on Nebuchadnezzar as she plopped the grape she had been holding into her mouth and sucked at its red sweetness.

******

"I'm sorry my friend," Nebuchadnezzar apologized. "I should have heeded your words years ago. Amytis must be stopped."

Nebuchadnezzar watched as the shadows were broken by a golden light that licked at his friend's face. Night had fallen, leaving the throne room in darkness save for the fire burning hotly in the hearth.

"Fortunately it is not yet too late," Daniel replied. "She can still be stopped, but it will now require a more cautious touch."

"So you will help me?" the king asked, hope having returned to his eyes.

"Yes, Great King. Myself, and my friends that stand present, will assist. The four of us are unique in that we are immune from Amytis' persuasions."

Nebuchadnezzar let his eyes wander to Daniel's three associates who stood silently nearby. Their face looked familiar to him, but his battered mind found their prior acquaintance hard to recall.

"You know them, Great One. Shadrach, Meshach, and Abednego." The three men nodded in turn.

"You were with Daniel in the great fire," Nebuchadnezzar said, remembering them now.

"We were, Your Highness," Shadrach answered for the three of them. "And we stand the same, unscathed by the fierce flames."

"As we also stand unscathed by Amytis' black desires," Daniel added. "Together we will protect you from her influence and see that you have the strength to remove her from this world."

Loud footsteps against the stone floors of the palace could be heard approaching from the outer chambers of the throne room. "She comes," Meshach warned.

"Damn the Gods! My queen makes haste. We must do this now," Nebuchadnezzar said.

"We are not prepared," Meshach cried.

"We'll make do," Daniel promised, placing a soothing hand on Meshach's shoulder.

"I fear that she brings her unholy beasts with her," Nebuchadnezzar groaned.

Daniel didn't speak and Nebuchadnezzar could tell that he feared the foul creations of Peristopheles. Still, he prepared himself for the coming conflict.

The large, oak doors loudly split open, swinging on their iron hinges. Through the opening, Amytis emerged, accompanied by four men that Nebuchadnezzar recognized as the recently dead. The five of them marched through the shadowy room until they arrived near the gathering of the king and his consorts.

"I thought our love was firmly bound, but here I find you, plotting treachery with your Jews," Amytis scorned.

"You have gone too far, Amytis. I can no longer allow you to murder innocents as if they were nothing more than beasts in the field," Nebuchadnezzar challenged.

Amytis laughed. "And who will stop me? You, oh Great One?" Amytis' amused gaze made clear exactly how much she *respected* Nebuchadnezzar's power – or not, as was the case. "Maybe your Jews here?" Her eyes studied the men around Nebuchadnezzar. She laughed further, clearly unimpressed. "I think not."

"You hold no power here, witch!" Abednego spoke for the first time.

Amytis continued laughing. "Is that so?" She flicked a finger toward Abednego, cueing one of her undead slaves. Nebuchadnezzar recognized him as the guard that had been transformed by Peristopheles himself. After perusing the damned book that had been bestowed by the Mischief God, she had stolen the man's allegiance right out from under the king.

The king's former guard stepped up and opened his mouth wide. Like a striking cobra, the guard's intestines snapped out through his mouth and struck at Abednego. Flying through the air, the intestines coiled around Abednego's throat. Abednego's hands flew up to grab at the length of intestine. He clawed at it, trying to remove himself from its grasp. The intestines responded by coiling tighter and tighter. Abednego's eyes began to bulge. Loud gasps sounded from his mouth as he made failed attempts at drawing breath. The intestines coiled even tighter, until Nebuchadnezzar heard a cracking sound that he knew to be from Abednego's spine. After the cracking sound, Abednego's hands fell free from their struggles to hang limply at his side. Once Abednego's life finally expired, the intestines uncoiled from around the man's formless throat to let the body drop to the floor. Abednego's body rested with the man's neck unnaturally cocked, the back of his skull lying flat against his spine.

Daniel and his partners sprang into action. Shadrach charged, as did Meshach. Daniel grabbed hold of Nebuchadnezzar's shoulder and turned him toward an exit that lay in shadow at their rear. "Come, Your Highness. We must flee to save your kingdom in the coming day."

Meshach dove into another of Amytis' undead guards. They rolled on the floor for a moment, with Meshach ending up on top of the guard. His hands were tight around the guard's throat, squeezing with fervor.

Shadrach took on the remaining two of Amytis' guard. In one smooth motion, he withdrew a knife from his sleeve and brought it along the first guard's throat, opening up a large gash that instantly gushed dark blood. The guard clutched at his newly-opened throat and collapsed to his knees. Bringing the blade around to his other side, Shadrach plunged the knife upward, into the next guard's chin. The blade easily punched through the man's jaw, its length extending up into the brain. This second guard joined the first, dropping to his knees on the rough stone floor.

Seeing that Daniel's associates had this battle well in hand, Nebuchadnezzar turned to follow his trusted advisor toward the throne room's rear exit. He had only managed a few steps when something muscular and slithery snapped around his waist, halting his forward momentum.

"Great One!" Daniel shouted, rushing back to aid his king. Nebuchadnezzar looked down to his waist and saw the length of intestine coiled around him. The intestine spun him around, forcing Nebuchadnezzar to face the horrors he thought were left behind.

Meshach remained atop his charge, still trying to choke the life out of the undead guard. A seam opened around the choking guard's wrists, much like the one that had earlier formed across the slave girl's back. Small rivers of blood dribbled from the freshly-formed wounds.

The guard slammed his hands down on the stone floor, digging his opened wrists into the rough, cold surface. He dragged his arms backwards, using the stone to peel the opened skin from his hands. The layers of flesh bunched up on the floor, revealing the skeletal remains of the guard's paws. Even those soon broke apart at the wrist, the loose bone falling to the floor. All that remained were two stumps of bone that used to be the guard's wrists, sharpened like tips from a spear.

Nebuchadnezzar shivered as he recalled this guard's screams as Amytis had peeled the flesh from his hand, layer by layer. Using an iron file, she then sharpened the remaining bone until they stood the same as the two grotesque objects he once again found before him. "I'm sure he will find these most useful in the afterlife," she had joked while shavings of bone collected near her feet.

The downed guard brought up his two pointed wrists and slammed them into opposite sides of Meshach's head, impaling the skull with ease. Meshach's struggles immediately ceased, his lifeless body tumbling off the guard and lying still on the floor.

Shadrach fared no better. He turned and witnessed Nebuchadnezzar's distress, removing his eyes from the two guards that he had downed with the blade. The guard with the slit throat recovered quickest. He rose from his knees, the large gash already sealing on his neck's flesh.

Nebuchadnezzar remembered this man, as well. Truth be told, he could picture the screams of all Amytis' pets as they succumbed to their horrific deaths at her malevolent hands. This one also fell victim to her blade. Amytis was deeply enamored with the sharp instrument. She had opened his skin from feet to neck and peeled the flesh away from the meat and sinew beneath. She had strangely left the skin attached to the skull, having lost interest in completing her project after the man's life had faded.

Envisioning all this, Nebuchadnezzar was not surprised when the tell-tale seam parted along the guard's legs and backside. Nor was he confused when the skin peeled away from the muscle, seemingly on its own. The skin shot out toward the fleeing Shadrach, flapping and twisting as if it were nothing more than drapes caught in a vicious wind. The loose flesh found its target and ensnared Shadrach, halting his forward progress. Shadrach cursed as he struggled against the web of loose flesh.

The other guard stood recovered and rose to his feet. He stood tall for a moment, until his body collapsed into a puddle of blood filled with smeared flesh and hundreds of white fragments that were all that was left of his bones. Some fragments were as large as coins, while others were as small as dust mites, ground into a fine powder.

Nebuchadnezzar imagined the grisly puddle was an exact impression of how the man's earthly body would lie forever, after Amytis had placed him between two gigantic slabs of marble. She had slaves slowly lower the upper slab until it rested on the lower. The man had screamed heartily as he had been squished flatly in between. A glow of lust had shone in Amytis' eyes throughout the entire proceeding.

The chunks of flesh and the glistening lake of blood remained still. However, the hundreds of bone shards rose into the air, defiant of the laws governing both nature and gravity. The shards clustered up and flew at the ensnared Shadrach like a swarm of white insects. Shadrach screamed as they came upon him. The shards used the opportunity to fly through the wide-open orifice, invading Shadrach's body.

Shadrach's screams instantly ceased as the cloud of shards disappeared into the wide open orifice of his mouth. The terrified man's gut clenched and he heaved. A second heave and Nebuchadnezzar wondered if the man was about to vomit. With a third heave, Shadrach expelled a red mist from his mouth, leaving red droplets sitting on his lips. A fourth heave came, this time accompanied by a geyser of blood erupting from Shadrach's mouth.

Splotches of darkness began to spread across Shadrach's skin as the blood was freed from its controlled pathways inside his body. Nebuchadnezzar knew that the jagged shards were darting around inside Shadrach's body, tearing up all the vital parts that stood in their way.

The whole ghastly scene finally crescendoed into its finale. The shards desired release and they found it, exploding through

Shadrach's skin all at once, shredding him into nothing. His entire body exploded into a rain of blood and viscera.

The bone shards flew back to the bloody puddle where the white cloud hoisted the flesh chunks and the puddle itself into the air, mixed itself in, then reformed the body of the crushed guard. All of the undead guards set their sights upon Daniel, with exception of the one whose intestines held Nebuchadnezzar. Daniel was too busy trying to free the king from the coiled intestines to notice.

"Daniel," Nebuchadnezzar spoke. "Run!"

Daniel looked up from the intestinal coil and saw the three undead soldiers staring at him. "My king, I cannot leave you."

"Amytis won't kill me. She needs my crown. Run!" Nebuchadnezzar urged.

Amytis' creatures sprang into action and Daniel finally ran. "I will come back for you. I swear!" Daniel promised as he ran toward the rear exit, leaving Nebuchadnezzar in the grasp of the intestinal coil.

The three guards chased Daniel out of the throne room. Nebuchadnezzar silently prayed that his advisor – his friend – would make it safely away.

"Now what should we do with you?" Amytis teased, approaching the tied-up king. She looked giddy at the sight of all the carnage left as she carefully stepped around the tattered remains of Shadrach, Meshach, and Abednego. "Daniel has proven as troublesome as you have defiant. Well, he is no longer here to defend you. To hold your mind firm against my warm embrace."

Nebuchadnezzar looked at the bloody remains of Daniel's three friends. He found that he could contain himself no further and broke down into tears. "Why, Amytis? Why do you revel in death so? These men had proven themselves to be loved by their God, surviving the greatest flames man has ever stoked."

"If you believe that, you are a fool, my king," the queen rebuked. "Daniel and his men possess powers of persuasion matched only by my own. They planted the sight of the fire in your eyes. The feel of it on your skin. All of it. The entire thing was a ruse. A trick of your mind, much the same as the tricks I play to bow you to my will."

Nebuchadnezzar considered her words for a moment. "Even so, like I shared with Daniel just now, you cannot kill me. You do not yet bear my child and will have no claim to the throne. Even you cannot control the whole of Babylon."

"You are correct, oh wise one." She let the sarcasm drip from her tongue as she spoke his title. "I do indeed need your body," she said, circling him as she let an extended finger travel along his shoulders. "However, I do not need your mind."

Nebuchadnezzar wondered at her meaning.

He didn't have to wonder for long.

******

594 B.C.

He took the blades of grass into his mouth and chewed. The feel of the blades gnashing between his teeth was blissful, their taste delectable. The sublime warmth of the sun graced his back. There was no more which he desired.

A shadow fell over him, robbing his back of the sun's bliss. Why was this strange creature bothering him? Awkward noises escaped the creature like a rolling thunder of pops and squeals.

Nhoadhifhafs. Dsfjfaj. Diejdfh.

The sounds meant nothing to him, other than being a minor annoyance. Only the grass mattered. And the sun.

Ki-nfd. Dagsdag-chadnezzar.

Wait! What was that last part? It was a familiar sound, the random noise starting to metamorphosize into coherency. His ears perked as his mind started to piece the sounds together into something of recognition.

"My king. Can you hear me? Do you understand my words?"

The odd creature's dimensions clarified into a familiar figure. One he realized he knew.

"Daniel," Nebuchadnezzar mumbled through lips that had had grown out of such use.

"My king? Has your mind returned?" Daniel asked, hope in his utterance.

Nebuchadnezzar nodded. He forcibly expelled green mush from his mouth, the taste of the grass having grown acrid to his tongue. "Where am I?" he muttered.

"The witch Amytis has stolen your mind, turning you into a beast of the field," Daniel explained. "For seven years you have stood as such. I am deeply ashamed that it took me so long to return to your side, but I had to find others immune to her gifts."

"Amytis?" Nebuchadnezzar's mind flooded with the ghastly images of all that had happened since his marriage. Such memories had been blissfully absent for so long, they now stabbed his heart as they resumed their place in his mind. "Is she in my mind even now?"

"She is fast asleep, my king. Her hold on you is tenuous for the time being. A fact which I have worked to my – and *your* - advantage. When she awakens, she will know nothing of this conversation."

"Good," Nebuchadnezzar said. "And she cannot intrude into your thoughts?"

"That is correct, my king. My thoughts are hidden from her."

"Then, the grapes."

"Pardon me, my king," Daniel replied in confusion. "What is your meaning?"

"Amytis is in love with the fruit of the vine," Nebuchadnezzar explained. "See to it that they are tainted and Amytis will fall forever silent." Nebuchadnezzar coughed up more grass, then continued. "And see to the matter yourself!" he warned. "She can peer into the thoughts of mortal man."

"I *am* a mortal, sire," Daniel corrected. "As is she, but I understand your meaning all too well. I will personally see that it is done."

"Good. Now place me back into the mindset of a beast. Quickly! Before she wakes and takes notice."

"Yes, my king," Daniel said.

The world around Nebuchadnezzar quickly dulled into the simplicity of grass and sun. The memory of his trusted friend dulled with it, lost to the void.

******

The grass. The sun. The perplexing creature emitting its awkward sounds.

Daniel!

"My king, it is done!" Daniel spoke to the clearing mind of Nebuchadnezzar.

"Amytis has fallen?" Nebuchadnezzar asked, after coughing up another glob of emerald mush.

"Never to rise again," Daniel assured.

The king plopped backwards onto his bare ass, seeing the green stains on his hands and knees from years upon them in the field. "It was the grapes? All went as planned?"

"Not exactly," Daniel admitted. "She awoke after the grapes were afflicted, but before I had time to escape her chambers unnoticed. She was ready to call for her unholy guards to order my death, so I had to act quickly. I told her I was there to join her. I had spent the last seven years playing everything over in my mind and I came to realize that, with her and my powers combined, we could rule the world entire. Her eyes blossomed with hope and I knew that I played the right move. I appealed to her vanity and thirst for power. She spoke of great conquests and I could feel the fire that my offer had stoked in her breast. That's when she ate of the vine and the poison took hold. A most deadly and painful venom that I had procured from deep beyond the borders of Ethiopia. A servant soon approached and I made my escape before he could gaze upon me."

Nebuchadnezzar considered Daniel's story and began to weep. Not due to any fondness for the woman that had departed this Earth, but due to all that she had done under his watch. The atrocities committed while his hand had been stayed. "I should have acted sooner," he cried. "I should have trusted in you and your God. Your God gives life. Mine only gives death. Had I been more powerful of mind, perhaps all of this could have been avoided."

Daniel laid a comforting hand on his king's shoulder.

After a moment more, Nebuchadnezzar's eyes cleared to purpose. "Take her body and destroy it. Burn it until nothing at all remains and then take the ashes and hide them from sight. I don't care where, just make sure they never again see the light of the sun."

"Yes, my king."

"Place a slave girl in Amytis' bed chambers. Dress her in fine linens, but let no man look upon her face. I would not have the kingdom know of their queen's death nor of her corrosive nature in life. I believe it would be too great a betrayal for my people to accept."

Daniel's heart swelled at the sight of his friend already regaining his composure as a king.

"And on this very day, start tearing down that cursed mountain of death. My hanging gardens shall be no more. Issue a decree that, henceforth, no tongue in my kingdom shall speak of the hanging gardens, nor of the atrocities committed there. I would see the infernal structure forever torn from memory."

"Yes, my king."

"While we are restricting items from tongue, so be the name Peristopheles. Let his name and visage be stricken from all mouths, tapestries, and histories. To be replaced with the name of a false deity."

"Which name would you prefer?" Daniel asked.

"The name does not matter." Nebuchadnezzar dismissed. An image of his loyal guard, the first one that had perished at the hands of Peristopheles, entered the king's mind. "Make the name Ekri. That should suffice," Nebuchadnezzar instructed, sure the name of a defeated foe usurping his legacy would upset the vile God.

Daniel took the name to memory as the king continued.

"And lastly, find that blasphemous book of Peristopheles. I would see it forever removed from this Earth."

Daniel hesitated at that last command.

"What is it?" Nebuchadnezzar asked, noticing the stillness of Daniel's tongue.

"Effort has already been made to find that affront to God. It seems to have vanished from the palace," Daniel explained, his tone sorrowful.

"Tear the palace apart!" the kind ordered. "It must be found and destroyed."

"Yes, my king."

The search went on for many days, but the book was never found.

******

Makru wept at the memory of his queen. After the wedding, and Ahimelek's untimely demise, Amytis had promoted him as her own personal advisor. At first sight of the alluring woman from Media, Makru had fallen in love. He knew Amytis would be forever forbidden to him, but man is helpless to suppress such a desire once it is known.

Amytis instantly knew of his infatuation. He never uttered thoughts on it, but she had known just the same. Immediately after her wedding to King Nebuchadnezzar, she had promoted him to her side and had kept him close. She never had laid with him – despite his strong desires for such a thing – but she had a way of reaching into his mind and giving him pleasures greater than that of which the flesh was capable.

Makru loved her. Greater than any love that he had ever known.

Which is why, when he had come upon her in her bedchambers - face deathly pale, lips dribbling blood - his heart had torn into a million pieces.

Her dying act had been to fumble for the book on her nightstand. The one Makru had seen her use to gain advantage over the dead. He knew the book contained great power and could not blame her for seeking it as life faded from her eyes.

As he now wept, Makru looked down at the book in his hands. Its heft was agreeable, yet severely underwhelming for the great power he knew it contained. Its binding was leathery, though the source of its flesh remained a mystery to him. It held a different glimmer than that of the bovine.

Upon hearing Amytis' final breath, he had taken the book from its resting place upon her mantle, seizing the brief opportunity presented to whisk it away from the palace. With his queen dead – and his heart with her – Makru knew he was henceforth to be on his own.

His lips curled into a cold smile as he felt the power radiate from the tome in his arms. The power to control the dead.

What better way to start a new life.

"So, let me get this straight," Gabe said, wrapping his mind around the connotations of the story he had just heard, "you're saying that this Amytis bitch was able to control minds, right?"

"There are rumors of a race of people that have such powers," Danner confirmed.

"What? The Medians?"

"No. Something else," Danner said with a far-away look in his eyes. "But that's not important. What is important is the Book of Peristopheles."

Ah, yes. Gabe was familiar with that book. "I take it that is the very same book that has allowed Zellers his little army of fuck-wads?" Gabe postulated, choosing to remain quiet about his encounter at Joseph Curwen's manor.

"The very same," Danner confirmed.

"How do you even know that the book exists?"

Danner spread his hands in front of him. "Am I not proof enough of the book's existence? Even if doubt still lingered, I cannot refute my own eyes and hands. I have held the book many times. I have even read from it; though, as a slave, my mouth is forbidden to speak any of the words."

"So, do you speak Babylonian? Does Zellers? How was he able to read the spells from the book?" Gabe carefully crafted his words. There was one thing that troubled him about the whole affair. The book he had seen at Curwen's had been written in English.

"No. What Mr. Zellers has is a translation of the original book. It is the words that have meaning, coupled with the power given to them by Peristopheles. The language they are spoken has no bearing on their potency. An early American scholar is reputed to have come upon the book and twice translated it into the Colonial tongue."

"Why would he translate it twice?" Gabe asked.

"That is not known with any certainty, but it is rumored that he had two buyers lined up, each willing to pay handsomely for a copy of the book," Danner explained.

"Who were the buyers?" Gabe was genuinely curious for *this* answer.

"I know of one. It is how Thomas Zellers acquired his copy. After his fortune was secured, he spent vast amounts of money trying to locate the second copy, but his life ended with his quest unfulfilled."

Gabe had a pretty good idea of where to find that second copy.

"So, it's the book that has caused all of this," Gabe assured himself. "Would it be safe to assume that, if I find that fucked-up book and destroy it, that this whole nightmare will end?"

"I believe so," Danner agreed. "Though I don't think that'll be possible for you. At least not tonight. Mr. Zellers does not keep the book here in the Arte Blanche."

"Where, then?"

"At his house. He has taken after his father and installed a rather impressive vault in his home."

"So I'm fucked!?" Gabe rubbed his temples in frustration.

"Not necessarily, Mr. Daniels," Danner alluded, with a curious gleam in his eye. "If I did not believe that there was a way out of this for you, I would not have put myself in such a position to help. I prefer not to consider the depth of Mr. Zellers' reprisal should he come to learn of my betrayal."

The first spark of hope ignited in Gabe's breast.

"Well, what do you suggest then? I'll entertain any ideas as long as they increase the likelihood that, by the end of the night, my foot will be so far up Zellers' ass that his teeth will be scraping off my toe fungus." Danner's cheek twitched at the picture that Gabe had painted. "It's already been up one ass tonight," Gabe added in a mumble, shivering at the memory.

"Early on, Mr. Zellers had some troubles...um...*recruiting* soldiers to his cause," Danner explained. "It was an issue that his father had explored when he was still alive. The book – and more importantly the words within – are very old. We came to believe that Peristopheles' power in the words may have faded, leaving them needing a charge."

"What? Like a battery-powered dildo?" Gabe interrupted.

Danner paused at the crude comparison. "In a manner of speaking, I suppose," he answered after recovering.

"So how do you charge some ancient-ass words?"

"With something *less* ancient, also containing the blessings of Peristopheles."

"What the fuck would that be?" Gabe asked. Before Danner could answer, Gabe found that he already knew. "Wait a minute..." he said. "It's that fucking statue, isn't it?"

Danner nodded.

"In that story you told, you mentioned that Peristopheles looked like some kind of fruity Greek? I mean, I'm totally down with the LGBTQ community, just paraphrasing the story there."

Danner ignored the disclaimer, and answered Gabe's concern. "If you remember, Peristopheles also mentioned having many forms and that his true form would cause Nebuchadnezzar's heart to explode. Well, the statue is of his true form, crafted by the Mischief God himself, as a gift to somebody I am sure that you have heard tale of."

"Who?" Gabe asked.

"Vlad III, Prince of Wallachia. Though most refer to him as Vlad the Impaler."

Gabe took in a sharp breath. "Vlad the Impaler? As in Count Dracula?"

"Mythology has often rumored him as such. He certainly was the inspiration for those tales. He was from the House of Drăculeşti, hence the name Dracula."

"Wow," Gabe shook his head. "Now Dracula is involved!? What the fuck is going on around here?"

"Don't be too impressed, Mr. Daniels," Danner dismissed. "He was just a man, not the fanged blood-drinker from Bram Stoker's twisted tale."

"Still, a mind-reading bitch of a Queen...Vlad the motherfucking Impaler...this is some deep shit right here."

"Anyway," Danner pushed on, "Peristopheles – much like with Nebuchadnezzar's Hanging Gardens – was impressed by the work of Vlad. The Impaler took great pleasure in the torture of his people. Besides the famed rumors that he enjoyed drinking blood, he committed many atrocities. He would cut limbs off some, disembowel others. For sport, he would smash people's heads into walls, just to see how many whacks it would take to turn them to mush. He would take babies and burn them alive, then watch as the parents were forced to eat their cooked bodies. He was even reputed to have slain his own wife, removing her sex organs and keeping them in his bedchambers until they had grown too foul."

"Gnarly," Gabe awed.

"And, of course, there was his favorite form of torture - what he got his name for - *Impalements*. Historians estimate roughly that he had impaled over sixty-thousand people by the time he was finally captured and put to death."

"I can see why that sick fuck Peristopheles was fond of the man," Gabe commented.

"Enough so that, at some point, the God visited him, gifting him the very statue that Mr. Zellers has unearthed and placed in *Suffering For Art*."

"A fitting piece for *that* exhibit," Gabe mumbled. "Why not give him another copy of the book, though?"

"Thomas Zellers never was able to discern why Peristopheles hadn't given Vlad a copy of his book. The top of the statue is etched with the instructions to resurrect the dead into slaves, but that falls far short of the wonders the book contains."

Gabe remembered the strange writing underneath his feet as he had landed on the statue. Those words must have been in whatever language it was that Vlad had spoken. Carpathian? Was that a language?

"I remember seeing those etchings," Gabe shared. "I just figured they were the lyrics to the latest Rammstein song."

Danner resumed his recurring blank stare.

"So, that statue has somehow refreshed the powers of the book?" Gabe asked, steering the conversation back to what mattered – getting him and Becca the fuck out of Blake's gallery of death. "What the fuck am I supposed to do with that tidbit of knowledge?"

"Destroy the statue," Danner answered. "I can't be sure, but I believe that destroying the statue will destroy Peristopheles' curse."

"What makes you believe that?" Gabe asked. Something didn't sit right with him about the whole idea. "Maybe it'll just keep him from making more of you undead fucks. Besides, didn't Thomas Zellers resurrect you long before Lil' Blakey ever found that damn statue?"

"He had a couple small successes, yes," Danner admitted. "But I believe that destroying the statue is an act that will dispel the curse completely. Both from some entries in the book that I believe may apply, and from my own personal experience."

"What experience?" Gabe asked.

"When Mr. Zellers first received the statue and started rebuilding it, an accident occurred halfway through that sent the rebuilt half crumbling. My alternate form was triggered out of my control and I collapsed into nothing but a simple pile of ash on the floor. I still possessed my thoughts, but those too were weak and fading. I humbly believe that was the closest to true death that I have ever come. And this is coming from a man who was burned alive in a mortuary by somebody claiming to be his friend."

"Well, I have no further argument," Gabe relented, "except why would you want me to destroy the statue if it's also going to destroy you?"

"I've been dead for quite some time now, Mr. Daniels," Danner sighed. "I'm ready to be released. I'm ready for this all to end." A sadness crossed Danner's features as he spoke.

"Gotcha," Gabe said solemnly. He allowed the man a little sympathy. He may be an undead fuck, but Gabe supposed he hadn't chosen to be. "Just one problem. I'm sure you're fucked-up brothers-in-arms are combing this place pretty solidly right now. How the fuck am I supposed to get back to the statue?"

"That's easy, Mr. Daniels." The color drained from Danner's body and his flesh disintegrated back into the swirling cloud of ash. Danner's voice rolled from the cloud like a movie's portrayal of God speaking from Heaven. "I'll give you a ride."

Gabe didn't even have the time to moan "Fucking hell!" before he was swallowed up by the cloud of ash and returned to a world of gray.

INTERLUDE

11

A thunderous clap erupted – similar to the report of hunting rifle - from where the large wooden crate hit the concrete ground of the loading dock.

"Jesus Christ!" Blake yelled. "Are these idiots trying to destroy my shipment!?"

"I'm...I'm sorry, Mr. Zellers," a nearby man apologized, donned in an orange vest and construction hat. He was the foreman for this crew, though Blake hadn't cared enough to remember the man's name. "It may have slipped a little as my man was lowering it. These things happen."

"There doesn't appear to be any damage, sir," Danner assured from Blake's side, eyeing the crate. "It sounded worse than it probably was."

"How would you know!?" Blake snapped. "Did you work construction before you..." Blake stopped himself. They were not in trusted company. "Nevermind," he said, annoyed, but no longer angry. "This is an important package. I'll be very disappointed if it were damaged." The words were spoken as a threat.

"Were there any other problems with the shipment?" Danner asked, giving Blake further time to calm himself.

"No," the foreman said. "I can't speak for its trip down from the mountains, but I personally oversaw the on-load in Constanta. There were no issues there, nor on the trip over the Atlantic."

"Good," Blake said, annoyance still dripping from his voice.

"The Carpathian crew didn't mention any issues?" Danner asked.

"No, sir. They were a rough bunch, seemed in a hurry to get to the bars and brothels," the foreman answered.

"The rather generous amount of money I paid them must have been burning holes in their pockets," Blake griped.

"No small sum, I'm sure," the foreman commented, knowing how *generous* Mr. Zellers had been with his money to the shipping crew. He knew he was being vastly overpaid for a simple shipment overseas, but neither the foreman, nor his crew, were about to complain.

"Open the crate," Blake instructed. "I would see what my money has bought me."

"Yes, sir." The foreman turned to a couple of similarly dressed workers. He stuck his fingers in his mouth and whistled shrilly. After ensuring he had their attention, he rolled a hand in the air, a silent order for them to open the crate.

The workers grabbed up a couple crowbars and got to work on the front of the crate. A couple large heaves from each man did the trick. The nearest wood panel broke free from the adjoining panels. With a loud crash the heavy panel fell to the ground, revealing the intimidating object contained within the crate.

When Blake's eyes fell upon his prize, all thoughts of annoyance and anger melted away like butter in a pot of boiling water.

"My God," Blake praised. "It's so beautiful!"

The slate world of the ash tornado disappeared around Gabe, leaving him staring up into the ghastly stone face of Peristopheles.

"You are one ugly, mudda-fucka," Gabe told the statue in a strange accent.

Danner stood silent at Gabe's observation.

"What? You've never seen the movie *Predator*?" Gabe asked the mute demon. Danner remained silent. "Greatest fucking movie ever! If this plan of yours doesn't work out and you're still around tomorrow, you should check it out."

"I very much doubt I will do that," Danner said dryly.

"What is it with you guys?" Gabe asked. "Does being dead rob you of your personality? You all speak like fucking robots."

"By Mr. Zellers' instruction. He wishes us all to be proper gentlemen."

"Then what's that slimy fuck Lester's deal then? He doesn't exactly come off as gentlemanly," Gabe refuted.

"Lester is a special convert, one I'm surprised the enchantment worked on at all." Danner informed.

"Yeah...he's special alright," Gabe mocked. He nodded, looking around the mammoth exhibit. It was empty, but only because, when they first arrived in *Suffering For Art*, Danner's booming voice had given the remaining demons reason to believe that their assistance was needed out in the corridors to corner their prey.

Gabe let his gaze wander around the exhibit. "Hey...where is Becca? Zellers doesn't have her set up in here?"

"No. He has her in *Wanders Never Cease*," Danner informed. "You can find her there when you have finished in here."

"Why there?" Gabe asked.

"I do not know," Danner said. Gabe saw one of Danner's eyes twitch at the statement and had the feeling that the man was holding something back. Gabe let it go, eager to get on with the plan.

"So, you gonna help me destroy this fucking statue or what? I imagine those fucks won't be fooled for long."

"Regrettably, I cannot assist you," Danner replied. "Mr. Zellers' hold on me may be weak, but I must still obey the specifics of his instruction. One of those was that none of us shall damage the statue in any way."

"That sucks," Gabe shrugged. "I guess I'll have all the fun to myself."

"I recommend aiming for the seams where the statue has been pieced back together. I imagine it will easier to destroy that way."

"Thanks for the advice." Gabe meant it, too. He let the tire iron bounce in his hand, appreciating its heft.

"I will take my leave now and attempt to distract Mr. Zellers further, give you more time."

"I appreciate it," Gabe responded. "No offense, but hopefully I won't be seeing you again."

"No offense taken," Danner assured. "Good luck, Mr. Daniels."

"To you, too," Gabe said.

With that, Danner morphed back into the ashy whirlwind and floated out through the door into the northern corridor, leaving Gabe alone in the large space.

"Alright, now I just have to destroy a giant statue with a crowbar. Great!" Gabe said to himself, sizing up the beastly form of Peristopheles. "Why-oh-why didn't I just stay at home and watch Netflix tonight?"

Gabe often talked to himself. He was just that kind of guy.

"Aim for the seams, the demon said." Gabe swiveled his eyes from the seams of the large statue to the suddenly tiny tire iron in his hand. "Fuck it!" Gabe said after a moment, attempting to overcome his doubt.

He lifted the tire iron over his head, aiming his swing for one of the seams at the Mischief God's legs. If he could break it low, perhaps the whole thing would come crumbling down, gravity doing a majority of the work for him. Gabe gave the tire iron some practice swings, as if he were a batter in the ninth inning.

One swing, two swing, three swings, and...

Gabe put all his power into the fourth swing – the real swing – as if he were aiming for the bleachers. Only, when his hand came forward, the tire iron was no longer there. Something had snagged the tool at the apex of his swing, causing Gabe's hands to slip from its metal surface as he swung forward with mighty intent.

Gabe instantly pirouetted to see what the tire iron had snagged on, and came face-to-face with the insect grin of Lester, his grotesque wings spread to their full length. "Hello, pretty!" Lester said, his breath reeking like hot shit.

Fuck!

Lester was still smiling when Gabe's fist flew up, planting an uppercut into the asshole's chin. Lester flew backwards, caught off guard. The tire iron flew even further, Lester having released it with stunned abandonment.

Gabe propelled himself with several running steps and leapt after the tire iron, lunging his body through the air. He crested and dove towards where the tool had clanked along the tiled surface. He had nearly landed directly on top of the tool, when his descent was suddenly stopped, his body tugged backward into the air. Ignoring the sudden shift in momentum, Gabe swung his arm out to try to grab onto the four-limbed wrench, but it was just beyond his reach. It had been his one chance to grasp it, the gap growing even further as Lester carried him higher into the air.

Gabe kicked and screamed against Lester's grasp, but couldn't get a good angle to beat on the fucker. Lester carried him all the way up to the roof, thirty feet up from the floor. "Let's see if thirty feet is high enough to break any bones, shall we?" Lester teased, then let Gabe go. Gabe plummeted toward the hard tile floor.

This is going to fucking suck! Gabe had time to think as the floor grew near. He braced himself for impact as best he could.

It turned out to be unnecessary. Gabe's downward momentum was suddenly arrested as, just prior to Gabe's rough date with the floor, Lester's arms again snatched him out of mid-air. "Just kidding," Lester said, lifting Gabe back toward the ceiling. Once having re-ascended the thirty foot span, Lester unleashed Gabe again. "Or not!" the acolyte said with a laugh as gravity again took charge.

Another brace for collision, and another save by Lester. Gabe thought, if nothing else, he was sure going to have one hellish case of whiplash when this was all over.

Another thirty foot climb, followed by another twenty-eight foot drop. Gabe realized this asshole was playing with him like a cat played with a mouse before finally snuffing the poor fucker's life out.

Lester swooped down to stop Gabe's fall again, but this time Gabe was ready for him. As soon as he felt Lester's dirty mitts wrap around him, Gabe threw his head back with force. He felt a satisfying crunch as the back of his skull met Lester's nose. Lester's grip loosened and Gabe fell from his arms, crashing to the floor below. The momentary halt to his descent had caused the impact to be softened, having fallen only a few feet as opposed to the full thirty.

As soon as Gabe hit the floor, he rolled. Just in time, too. Lester had recovered quickly and the jagged, broken rib tips of his wings clanked loudly against the tile where Gabe's head had just been. Gabe knew that those sharp wing tips were more than deadly enough to have gone straight through his skull.

Gabe hit his back and raised his legs as Lester re-angled and dove for him. His feet hit Lester in the chest and Gabe used them as a fulcrum to fling Lester up and over him, sending the abominable vulture tumbling through the air. Hearing – more than seeing – Lester crash against the floor, Gabe rolled over to his front and shot off toward the dioramas.

The nearest scene was *The Judas Cradle. Model: Grady Fenton*. Gabe jumped over the velvet rope and continued into the display. He pushed at Grady's model, attempting to dislodge the figure from the pyramidal stool. With his hand on the model's exterior, Gabe realized that the figure wasn't a dummy at all. The figure's skin was an equal mixture of leathery and waxy. A chill ran down Gabe's back as he thought back to when he had been trapped on the table, Dr. Holtz standing over him. "It's an elixir of my own design. It preserves the flesh and keeps it from rotting. It undoubtedly made my taxidermy hobby much less time-consuming." the doctor had said.

Gabe felt his bowels loosen as he realized the replicas in these scenes weren't actually *replicas* at all. They were genuine human bodies, preserved by Dr. Holtz' special elixir.

Gabe had to admit that he appreciated the idea. It was smart. Instead of burying bodies somewhere they could be found – prompting a lot of uncomfortable questions – why not hide them in plain sight and call them art? The matching person, walking and talking nearby, would easily sell the illusion that nothing nefarious was afoot.

There wasn't any time to dwell on the positives of Blake's maneuverings, though.

Gabe pushed at Grady's preserved body, trying to remove him from the stool. It took a couple good jabs to get the body to come loose. Each push scooted the body further up the stool's seat, revealing more and more of the pyramid. The body finally came free, crumpling lifelessly to the floor. A surprising amount of stool had been concealed in the man's expanded asshole.

"I'm going to turn you into my own personal sex doll," Gabe heard behind him. Lester had apparently recovered and Gabe was sure he was already darting through the air toward him. Gabe hauled the heavier-than-anticipated stool off the ground and swung it around just as Lester arrived.

Gabe brought the sharp, pyramid-shaped seat bashing against Lester's side, jolting the flying abomination out of his planned flight path. Lester's momentum was too quick to stop on a dime and his momentum carried him darting past Gabe. On his way by, he tried extending his arms to grab onto Gabe, but he was too far out of the way and his hands couldn't quite reach.

The same thing couldn't be said for his deadly wings of skin and bone. The jagged tips of Lester's torqued ribs caught Gabe across his side, tearing three long gashes into his firm love handles.

"Fuck!" Gabe screamed, his arms instantly clutching at his lacerated flesh. He kept his eyes on Lester as the bat-like fucker crashed into the wall behind the dioramas. The way Lester's neck twisted when he hit the concrete wall let Gabe know that the impact had to have hurt like a bitch.

Good!

Unfortunately, Gabe's side sang in similar agony. He looked down to see his shirt soaked in blood. He lifted a hand to gingerly feel along the wounds. There was a lot of blood, but Gabe didn't think that the wounds were too deep. Still, they stung like a bitch and he knew they'd be bothering him like crazy for the next while. He'd live though...assuming he ever got out of *this* place.

"Mmm..." Gabe heard Lester say as he got up from where he had fallen. Lester was staring at him with hungry eyes. "Those will be the first of many new holes I'm going to put in you. Then I'm going to fuck every one of them."

Gabe was starting to think Lester liked him.

Lester leapt. Gabe swung. The stool hit Lester again, but the demon was ready. He swatted the pyramidal seat aside. Gabe managed to keep his hold on the wooden legs, but the effort cost him his balance and he tumbled sideways.

Lester dove in at where Gabe had fallen. Gabe got his feet under him and propelled himself backward as Lester clapped his wings together in front of him, his ribs acting like jagged teeth snapping together. The wingtips came within inches of tearing off Gabe's face.

Lester flew further forward and tried the move again. Gabe's only option was to drop straight down to the floor. The wingtips crashed together above him.

Without having any time to think, Gabe swung the stool upward, where it crashed into Lester's side and sent him flying.

"I'm getting sick and fucking tired of that damn thing!" Lester cursed, recoiling and flying in for another run.

This time, the undead bird of prey was aiming for the stool. Before Gabe realized what was happening, Lester had wrenched the stool from his grasp, and sent it flying off across the room.

Gabe didn't have time to worry about suddenly being unarmed. He rolled his body away from Lester, springing up to his feet, and sprinting toward the dioramas. He scanned ahead for anything else he could use as a weapon.

Gabe heard a whooshing sound behind him as Lester swooped around and flew in for another run. Keeping his eyes forward, Gabe used his ears to keep track of Lester's progress. Timing his move as Lester neared, Gabe ducked. Lester, quick to react, managed to get a handful of Gabe's shirt and hoisted him off the ground. Gabe twisted and sent a flurry of punches into his assailant's body. Lester hadn't gotten a good grip on Gabe to begin with, and it didn't take much for Gabe to slip out of his grip. Having quickly ascended several feet, Gabe's momentum kept him flying forward into one of the dioramas. An aluminum tub - the kind used to hold water for livestock – sat alone, with a woman's upper body visible from over its rim. The scene made it look like the woman was sitting in a bath – a particularly unpleasant one based on the figure's twisted expression.

Ophelia!

Gabe's trajectory sent him flying over the tub, directly into the woman's exposed figure. He spied a sheet of glass built into the tub, sealing off a pool of brown sludge. Gabe knew what that sludge was, and his stomach turned at the thought. He braced himself for the crash against Ophelia's upper half, expecting...well, he wasn't entirely sure what he was expecting, but it wasn't the easy impact that ended up occurring. He smacked right into the woman's shoulders, but there was very little resistance to his momentum. The mannequin easily came away from the tub, having apparently been set atop the glass boundary. He became entangled with the dummy's arms as he carried it rolling along the floor with him. He had a brief moment to realize that Ophelia's likeness was indeed only a mannequin as he shoved its plastic frame away from him.

Using a mannequin for Ophelia's display made sense, Gabe supposed. He doubted Dr. Holtz elixir would have done much with Ophelia's shit-dissolved flesh.

Gabe used the rear wall to help him back to his feet, his battered muscles protesting against the normally simple task. He scanned around for Lester and found him hovering overhead.

"Mr. Zellers isn't going to be pleased to see you fucking up his little creations," Lester taunted with a smile on his face. Gabe got the feeling Lester was fine with any annoyance Blake was caused. "I'm sure he wasn't expecting that outcome from his little game."

Gabe didn't bother with a retort. Instead, he ran.

Gabe leapt over Ophelia's tub and ducked behind it, just as Lester swooped down to grab at him again. The tub provided the expected protection and Lester missed. Gabe hopped up, jumped the velvet rope, and ran some more. He sprinted to his side. He needed another weapon. His eyes fell on Cliff's saw.

That would do.

Gabe picked up his pace, but Lester had already gotten too close. Gabe slid forward like a baseball player reaching for home. Lester missed again, flying past. Gabe got up as Lester looped around like a Styrofoam toy-plane kit. Gabe barely had time to regain his feet, before having employ another move to avoid Lester's grasp. He threw himself backwards, correctly guessing that Lester would expect him to dive forward again. It almost worked. Almost.

Gabe managed to avoid being ensnared again, but one of the bony wingtips caught the back of Gabe's hand as he flew backwards, spearing its jagged edge right through Gabe's soft flesh. A flash of white hot pain shot through Gabe's arm, eliciting a sharp yelp.

The bone spear was hooked into Gabe's hand, jerking Gabe off his feet. His added weight kept Lester's wing from properly being able to flap and the winged fucker was no longer able to stay afloat. Lester tumbled to the ground with a loud thump, accompanied by something in his body loudly snapping. His bony protrusion tore free from Gabe's palm as his body rolled lifelessly across the room.

Gabe tucked his bloody hand against his chest, pinning it there with his opposite wrist. The pain caused bright flashes in Gabe's vision. A sharp thumping rose up Gabe's arm from the tattered wound as he held it tight. After a moment the thumping dulled and the white flashes faded. The pain was still there, but Gabe was able to start thinking past it.

And those thoughts told him to run.

Lester, who had taken one hell of a tumble, uncurled from the rumpled ball that he had landed in. He rolled over, propping himself up on all fours. His head hung at a weird angle and Gabe saw that his neck had become twisted into a thick, limp noodle. A large bulge rose from under the back skin of the neck which Gabe knew was Lester's broken spinal column.

"You motherfucker!" Lester's angry voice shouted from his drooping head. The neck muscles tightened, propping the neck straight again. The bulge sunk with a sickly snap. A crackle and a pop followed as the broken vertebrae straightened and fused back together. The sounds brought to mind those old Rick Krispies commercials, though in this instance, they didn't stoke Gabe's appetite.

With his neck having finished repairing itself, Lester's head swung up, leaving his irate eyes burning into Gabe. "You're fucking dead!" Lester hopped up and took flight.

Before Lester had even gotten off the ground, Gabe had already turned and ran. He knew he'd never make it to Cliff's saw in time, so he looked to see which diorama was nearest to him.

You've got to be fucking kidding me!? Gabe thought at first, but then an idea struck him. He made a beeline for the roped-off scene, jumping over the barrier while hearing the speedy flapping of leather sheets behind him. Lester was coming and he was coming fast.

With every step, the flapping of Lester's wings was close...closer...closer still. Lester had to be right at Gabe's ass.

Gabe dived the rest of the way to the scene's preserved body, his arms wrapping around its waist. The figure was on his knees, kneeling over with his hands across his lap, palms up and fingers curled into a cup, as if praying to someone – *anyone* – to end his immense pain. The figure's upper body was help up by a length of string that extended from two hooped bolts secured to the floor on one end to the dead man's exposed spinal column on the other. Gabe twisted the body to the side, silently thankful that its stringed setup made such a task possible.

Lester's eyes widened as he saw what suddenly awaited him on his rush forward, but it was far too late to stop himself. His skull hit first, easily pierced by the fractured rib from his own Earthly remains. His momentum continued driving his body forward, his chest getting impaled next, then stomach, as his phantom body folded around the bony wings of his preserved one.

The impact forced Lester's preserved body to be jerked out of Gabe's hand. The two Lesters harmlessly flew by, bouncing off the floor and sent crashing into the rear wall of the exhibit.

"That's right!" Gabe mocked. "Go fuck yourself!" Gabe shouted at the two identical, unmoving bodies. He figured the insult worked well, being close enough to what had actually just occurred.

Gabe let his sight linger on the entwined bodies for a moment, making sure neither was moving. He turned and stepped toward the large statue in the middle of the room. Time to finish this shit up.

On his way, Gabe found the tire iron and snatched it up from the floor. He strode over to the statue, a mad confidence in his step. When he arrived, he curled his hands around the tire iron in a batter's grip. He had to force the fingers on his injured left hand to curl, as they didn't want to bend. Even after managing to wrap them around the tool's shaft, his grip with that hand was weak. Refusing to be dissuaded, Gabe lifted the tire iron over his shoulder and swung at the seam that ran around the giant's left knee. The tire iron bit into the statue, causing a small chunk to fly off and a crack to appear along the seam, spreading out from the point of impact. A disturbingly small crack. Most of the force from the impact traveled back through the tire iron, causing it to violently reverberate. Gabe's injured hand protested against the action causing him to drop the tire iron.

"Fuck!" Gabe swore. He held his hand for a moment until the throbbing faded back into an achy dullness. He looked at where the tire iron had landed and wondered if he'd be able to continue on one-handed.

A rustling sound reached Gabe's ears from where the two Lesters lie. He glanced over and saw the undead Lester starting to rouse.

Gabe bent to retrieve the tire iron, needing to make haste with his mission, one-handed or not. He picked it up, balanced it in his healthy right hand, and swung. The tool hit the plaster of the seam, causing the small crack to spread further around the statue's limb, though not nearly enough. At least, one-handed, Gabe's injured hand was spared the searing pain of the previous swing.

More stirring from the Lesters. "Fu-Fuck…My Head…" came a wavy voice from the entangled bodies.

Gabe swung again, aiming for the left side of the knee where the crack had ceased. Another chunk flew off, the crack spreading further to the back of the knee.

"Mother-fucker!" the undead Lester screamed. A glance revealed Lester pulling his head free from his dead body's spearing rib. Gabe needed to pick up the pace.

Swing. The crack spread.

Another swing. The crack spread further.

Even Gabe's healthy hand was starting to grow tender from the reverberation of the tire iron as it rebelled against the force of Gabe's strikes.

Another swing. The crack had spread fully around the knee of the mammoth idol.

"You are *sooooo* fucking dead!" Lester said, pulling the final rib from his abdomen.

Another swing. This time the cracked seam belched a fine powder. Gabe could hear a creaking sound coming from the damaged limb.

Lester turned with a cold, hard stare at Gabe. Gabe swung the tire iron again. More powder belched from the statue's wound, the statue subtly shifted to lean toward the breached leg. The groaning increased.

Lester's eyes widened when he saw what was about to happen.

Gabe swung again, though he didn't need to. The statue was already starting its slow tumble to the side. Lester jumped and began flapping his wing as fast as he possibly could. The fire in his eyes Let Gabe know that Lester was racing the clock, his murderous rage propelling him.

"Fall faster you fuck!" Gabe yelled at the statue, steadily chopping at the busted limb.

Finally, at about a forty-five degree angle, gravity seemed to be done fucking with the statue's weight and increased its haste. Lester had covered nearly three-quarters of the distance to Gabe by the time the statue hit the ground, instantly crumbling into thousands of little pieces.

Lester stopped in mid-air, as if he had just activated the world's most effective air brakes. "Goddamn you, Zellers!" Lester cursed as he dropped from the air to land on his knees.

Gabe briefly wondered why Lester's final curse had been toward Blake, and not himself – maybe his grudge against the man who had originally killed him outweighed his anger at Gabe - but quickly dismissed his curiosity as blood began streaming from Lester's nose. The hobbled demon started coughing a red mist from his lungs and hunched over as if something was eating his insides.

"This isn't over yet, asshole!" Lester cursed – this time most assuredly directed at Gabe – as he coughed up one final mist of red and collapsed to the ground. He stopped moving, lying still on the tile floor.

Gabe breathed a sigh of relief.

Danner's plan had worked after all.

ARTE BLANCHE

Thank fucking God!" Gabe shouted triumphantly into the air. An excitement flowed in his blood the likes of which he had never felt before. He could feel his heart beating heavily in his chest, a deep thrum of exaltation.

Gabe ran over to Lester and sent a flying kick into the man's stomach. The body flipped over, but didn't move. Gabe could see residual hatred burning in the prick's eyes, but was sure it would dim quickly enough. He was surprised – given Danner's tale – that the body hadn't just disappeared, but he dismissed the concern in favor of celebration.

"Fuck you, Lester!" Gabe shouted. "Fuck you too, Zellers; you fucked-up, little pussy!" Gabe extended both middle fingers in the air, hoping the gesture was somehow transmitted to the billionaire, wherever he happened to be holed up. With a smile, Gabe imagined the little twat cowering in a dark corner somewhere after seeing his creations all drop into nothingness. Gabe would be severely pleased if he could find the fucker shivering in a puddle of his own piss.

Or maybe he could save that piss for the tub, Gabe thought, glancing back at Ophelia's aluminum sepulcher. Gabe would love nothing more than to leave Blake wallowing in such agony, a taste of his own medicine. He took a moment to revel in the image, then shook his head. *Better to let him rot in a cell*, Gabe conceded. Perhaps after a little fun between his fist and Blake's face, that is.

Gabe ripped off the bottom of his shirt and wrapped the freed strip of cloth around his injured hand. A hospital trip was in short order, but first he had to find Becca and get the hell out of the Arte Blanche.

Gabe let his gaze float around the room for a second, eventually having it fall on the door out to the northern corridor. Time to swoop up Becca and get her out of this hellhole.

"Motherfucking-fuck-yeah!" Gabe sang on his way to the door. He even did a little two-step dance as he headed out to save the woman who had blossomed unique feelings in him. Not just the urge to get laid, though Gabe was sure that the deal *had* to be sealed on that front. He was a hero – a veritable Prince Charming – and there was no way in hell Prince Charming hadn't gotten some of that sweet Sleeping Beauty pussy after all that he had gone through to save her ass.

Wait...*was* that Prince Charming? Or some other generic Disney prince? Gabe couldn't quite remember.

Truthfully, he didn't give a fuck.

Gabe cracked the door open and peeked through into the corridor. Seeing the only thing awaiting him on the other side were more lifeless undead bodies, Gabe threw the door open the rest of the way and exited into the hallway.

Cliff was the nearest body to the door - lying still with his lower body in split-open mode. Gabe looked down at the fat man's body and began belting out the chorus to "Bad", even attempting a shitty version of the Moonwalk. He hated Michael Jackson, but goddamn if the song didn't feel right at that moment.

Where the hell was Blake? The thought crept into Gabe's mind. That billionaire cunt hair had to still be around somewhere. Maybe he was still with Becca?

Maybe he was reacting poorly to his minions having dropped dead around him? *Fuck!* Gabe had to hurry.

Gabe remembered Danner telling him that she was being held in *Wanders Never Cease*. Gabe stopped his triumphant fucking-around and ran toward the corner exhibit.

Gabe hoped he wasn't too late. How the fuck could he have been so stupid? He had wasted several precious moments that Blake could have been using to drive a knife through Becca's throat. Or maybe shove a stool up her ass. The possibilities were endless when it came to whatever Zellers' sick mind could conjure up.

He arrived at the double-doors to *Wanders Never Cease* and threw them open. "Becca!" he yelled into the large corner exhibit.

"Gabe!" he heard her voice returned to him.

Thank God!

He looked toward the lone item in the exhibit – the large, ornate throne atop a raised platform – and saw Becca sitting there, bound by rope to the royal chair. Two of Zellers' acolytes were lying prone at her feet, not moving. Other than perhaps a little rattled, Becca looked unharmed.

"Thank the fucking Heavens!" Gabe cried out in relief, running up to her. "Are you alright?" he asked, unwrapping her wrists from their binds.

"I'm fine," she said as Gabe bent to untie her ankles. "Blake has been too busy trying to find you to perform his fucked-up ritual on me. He seems pretty pissed about you escaping his little trap."

"Good!" Blake exclaimed, loosening the final rope. He stood and was surprised when Becca pounced and wrapped her arms around him. She pressed her lips up against his in a deep, sensual kiss. When she abruptly broke it off, Gabe couldn't help but feel a bit of disappointment that the kiss had ended.

"Didn't I tell you, before this all started, that I was a champion poker player?" Gabe asked with a smug smile on his face.

At first, Becca looked confused, but recognition dawned in her eyes. She looked down at the unmoving bodies at her feet and nodded. "I'd say that you have indeed played your cards well, young man," Becca agreed.

"Well, let's get the fuck out here then so I can collect my winnings." Gabe winked at her and extended a hand to help Becca step over one of the prone bodies. They made their way off the platform, toward the door. "Next move: We're going to find Zellers and beat the fucking code to the front door out of him," Gabe informed, his tone having grown serious.

As if summoned by his name, Blake Zellers appeared in the doorway. Not scared shitless, as Gabe had hoped to find him, but smiling, with a chuckle escaping through his windpipe.

"Bravo, Mr. Daniels. Bravo." Blake was clapping his hands in applause. Gabe was confused, but wasn't going to let that stop him from pummeling the fucking twerp. Gabe jumped in front of Becca and made to charge Blake, but stopped when another figure appeared behind him.

Danner Hackett, alive and well – or, *well*, at least.

"What the fuck?" Gabe awed, his jaw dropping.

"What an excellent showing, wouldn't you agree, Mr. Giles?"

From around the corner, Lester stepped into view in the doorway. "I suppose so, Zell...*Mr.* Zellers" Lester said. The smug smile was back on his face, though his eyes still burned with fires of hatred as he stared at Gabe.

Lester's last name was Giles? *What a stupid, fucking name,* Gabe thought.

"Yes, Arte Blanche is a most magnificent place indeed. We're going to have a lot of fun here, I think." Blake looked very proud of his creation.

Gabe reared his arms back in a symbolic gesture of protection toward Becca. "Stay behind me," he ordered. "I won't let these fuckers hurt you."

Becca's hands wound under Gabe's armpits, her arms gently wrapping around him from behind. "I'm afraid not, but if you trust me, I'll make the same promise to you," she whispered seductively into his ear.

That's when Gabe looked down at his chest and the hands that rested there. Becca's two beautiful and healthy hands.

The right one completely healed from the charred and mangled form that Gabe had last seen it in.

INTERLUDE

12

Blake watched as the object that had recently been unearthed in the Carpathians settled into its resting spot. He marveled at how beautifully it fit into his gallery.

"A sublime addition to the treats that await at Magna Arta, wouldn't you say?" Blake said to the man behind him.

"Indeed it is, sir," Danner answered, eyeing the object with curiosity.

"Have you been able to confirm the presence of our friend?"

"Yes, sir," Danner informed. "The scanner shows that there is a hollow chamber inside containing some sort of fine powder. We haven't been able to verify the powder's substance, but I think it's safe to say that results will show it once was human."

"Wonderful," Blake elated. "I want to start the ritual right away. Why waste time?" Blake already held Peristopheles' book in his hands. "Do you believe it will work?" he asked Danner as a kind of afterthought.

"It's already worked once, sir. Obviously the death satisfied the criteria."

"Good." Blake smiled and nodded at Danner's diagnosis, then turned to a robust man standing nearby.

"What about you, Professor? Are you ready to guide our wayward soul to understand our modern world? To speak a tongue we can all understand?"

"Yes, sir," Cliff answered, still looking defeated, having only joined Blake's flock days prior.

Blake nodded and took a moment to gather himself. He was downright giddy.

"Then let's begin," Blake proclaimed.

Blake glanced once more at the object sitting upon its crafted platform. The ornate throne that had only recently been unearthed from the Carpathian Mountains looked beautiful in the fluorescent light.

"Amytis! My Beauty! Your prowess at the game has yet again exceeded all expectations, my dear," Blake said, holding his arms open as Becca walked around Gabe and entered his embrace.

"Amytis!?" Gabe gawked. "As in Queen Amytis?" Gabe had never stood as dumbfounded in his life. And that was saying a lot given what he had already been through that night.

"Blake knows I hate that name," she said, turning her head around to Gabe after giving Blake a kiss on his cheek, "yet he insists on using it to frustrate me."

"I'll never understand why you hate it so much," Blake protested. "It's such a beautiful name."

"It was my mortal name," she dismissed. "I'm much more than that now."

"How in the fuck...?" Gabe left it at that, currently too in shock to form complete sentences.

"Ahh, yes," Blake said to Gabe, as if just noticing that he was in the room. "You must be confused."

Gabe silently nodded, unable to even utter a crude insult; a rarity in Gabe's world.

"You see, she came to us as a dying gift from my father; her body burned and her ashes placed inside that very throne behind you." Gabe glanced back at the lone object in the exhibit. "My father had spent vast amounts of money and years of research to find her, buried deep in the Carpathian Mountains."

"The Carpathian Mountains?" Gabe asked, still trying to process everything. "Didn't you find the Peristopheles statue in the Carpathians?"

Blake burst out in laughter. "No, Mr. Daniels, not at all," Blake said when his laughter finally died down. "I know Danner spins quite a fancy story about our old friend Vlad. Vlad may very well have been visited by Peristopheles and given a gift of some sort, but I assure you it is not the statue that lay in ruins in *Suffering For Art*. That statue was just some sculpture I had commissioned a while back. This is the third time it has been broken up by somebody in a similar situation as yourself. I'm afraid you did too good a job, though. I'll have to replace the whole damn thing this time instead of repairing it like I have before."

Gabe thought back to the seams of the statue where it had been repaired before. Gabe had bought every word of Zellers' story about having discovered it in pieces. He shook his head at how easily he had been fooled.

"Don't worry, Mr. Daniels," Blake said, seeing Gabe's defeat. "Danner is quite convincing. I would have fallen for his story too, if he and I hadn't devised it together. Besides, *most* of what he told you was true, it's only the parts concerning Vlad and the statue that we made up as part of the game."

That was the third time Zellers had called it "the game". Gabe ignored it for the moment as more questions filtered into his mind. "If not Vlad, then why the Carpathians? Last time I checked an atlas, the Carpathians weren't anywhere near Babylon."

"Because I'm not the first one to discover Amytis' final resting place. Another man back in the sixteenth century also found it. He had a copy of the book and brought her back to serve him all those years ago. He just so happened to also be from the Carpathians. I'm afraid those mountains are notorious for breeding twisted minds."

"Who found her?" Gabe asked, though he wasn't sure he wanted to hear the answer.

"Instead of hearing *his* name, how about I let her tell you her name as it was back in those years?" Blake looked to Becca and waved his hand for her to proceed.

"You may be familiar with it," she informed. "My name was Báthory Erzsébet," she said in a Hungarian tongue, "though you'd know me better as the Countess Elizabeth Bathory."

Gabe gulped. If there was one person in those boring history books that fascinated him more than Vlad the Impaler, it was Elizabeth Bathory, dubbed the most prolific female serial killer the world had ever known.

This was single-handedly the coolest – and most horrifying – proclamation that Gabe could have dared hope to hear.

"The man who resurrected her was a nobleman of the region named Stephen Bathory. He claimed her as his daughter, though he never let another man's eyes fall upon her. He knew that her advanced age would be quite a shock to anybody who happened to come across her.

"It was eleven years later that a man named Ferenc Nádasdy came around to be the first man *not* named Bathory to lay eyes on her. Ferenc was a beast of a man, large and from a wealthy family. He was a great soldier and had even earned the nickname of The Black Knight of Hungary due to his military accomplishments during the Hungarian war with the Ottoman Empire.

"Ferenc was visiting the Bathory castle when he expressed his interest in seeing Stephen's mysterious daughter, Elizabeth. It was widely talked about that she had never been seen outside the castle. Many people left wondering whether she was born freakish, or even if she existed at all. Ferenc was a curious man who felt himself above all others, and he wasn't going to leave with his curiosity unsated. His standing, his army, and his size, all prevented Stephen from being able to refuse the Black Knight's request.

"So Stephen presented Elizabeth to Ferenc, which obviously prompted a lot more questions than answers. Stephen refused at first, but after much torture and the murder of his wife, Stephen confessed all. He showed Ferenc where he kept Peristopheles' book, which Ferenc promptly read through. Finding the incantation to transfer ownership of a soul, Ferenc all too happily obliged to read it. I mean, who wouldn't? If owning your own personal undead slave wasn't tempting enough, you see yourself exactly how beautiful she is." Blake finished by kissing her again on the cheek.

Becca/Elizabeth/Amytis *was* beautiful, Gabe had to admit, though that was about the only compliment he would grant her.

"Ferenc soon announced that he had married Stephen Bathory's daughter, though he kept her hidden much like Stephen had, provoking further rumors through the countryside. The obvious reason for the deception was that Elizabeth was only supposed to be eleven years old at the time; though, as is common with men who hate having secrets kept from them, Ferenc also loved having secrets of his own. It's all part of feeling powerful.

"Anyway, some years later, Ferenc died on the battlefield from some mysterious illness. Though Becca assures me that she had nothing to do with it, I still hold my doubts. With her master dead, however, her soul was freed and she was a slave no more. The history books will happily tell you what kind of deeds she performed with her newfound freedom." Blake said this last bit with adoration, not scorn, in his voice.

"From what I remember," Gabe challenged, "Elizabeth Bathory was tried for her crimes and locked away in her castle, where she died years later. How was that possible if she was undead at the time? Do your little resurrected fuck-heads age and die off?"

"No," Blake answered promptly. "They'll live forever if not stopped. Fortunately, the book has an incantation for that, as well." Blake snapped his fingers and Dr. Holtz walked in from the hallway. In his hands was a book bound in dried flesh. Gabe gulped as he recognized the twin of the book he had seen at Joseph Curwen's manor.

"After Ferenc had taken his prize, Stephen Bathory spilled his story to a Hungarian minister named István Magyari. After Ferenc's death, Magyari began publicly seeking Elizabeth's downfall, eventually finding a man named György Thurzó. Thurzó was a direct representative of the monarchy, titled the Palatine of Hungary. He was a man of great power in those times. He was made aware of the book and used his power to arrest Elizabeth, while claiming the copy for himself. He had to make a show of arresting her to quell the rumors of her atrocities that had spread through the kingdom, but his sentence was that she be placed on house arrest. People were confounded by the sentence, but Thurzó knew that she could not be trusted to a prison cell."

"Why not?" Gabe asked.

"Because," this time Elizabeth answered. "He knew that no prison of man would be able to hold me. When I was Amytis, I held power of men. I never had much need to lord it over the dead, though I did enjoy such things. After freed from Ferenc, my influence began to come back to me."

Gabe thought back to Danner's story of Amytis and her control over Nebuchadnezzar. Such a thing scared Gabe more than any undead uprising.

"György Thurzó could hold me, because he was like me. Very few other men in the world would have any hope at all of holding me against my will, so he kept me in my castle and used the book to send me back to the dead."

Gabe saw anger flash through her eyes as she recalled her death as Elizabeth Bathory.

"And I have brought her back again," Blake took the conversation back. "Such beauty shouldn't be kept from this world." Blake gave her a look of longing.

Turning back to Gabe, Blake continued. "She would prefer I still call her by her Hungarian name – she is enamored of it - but I couldn't exactly introduce her as the Countess Elizabeth Bathory, could I? So, upon her resurrection, I gave her the name Becca Larson.

"Of course, her name just recently changed again. Didn't it, darling?" Blake asked her as he leaned in and rubbed his nose against hers in what Gabe knew as an Eskimo Kiss. Gabe's stomach turned at the repugnant display of affection.

"What's her name changed to now?" Gabe spitefully asked. "I fear if it's anything short of Traitorous Cunt, the name will fail to do her justice."

Blake briefly looked annoyed by Gabe's barb, but Becca seemed amused.

"Her new name is Becca Zellers," Blake proudly announced. "We were just married a couple weeks ago, in honor of the completion of the Arte Blanche."

"Jesus Christ, you fucking married her?" Gabe asked incredulously. "You do realize the laundry list of dead husbands that this woman carries, right?"

"Nonsense," Blake dismissed, turning away from the nose kiss to look back at Gabe. "She loves me and I love her." He smiled. "Besides, she is my undead slave and is helpless but to serve my every whim. If only every man could have a wife so devoted." Blake winked at Gabe.

"Yeah...good luck with that, dickhead." Gabe warned.

"So, should we kill him now, dear?" Blake asked Becca.

Becca leaned her head on Blake's shoulder and eyed Gabe as if he were a mouse and she the cat. "No. You've already got the table set up in *Suffering For Art*, let's move this party in there."

"Very well," Blake agreed.

Gabe clenched his fists, ready to beat down the first motherfucker that tried to lay a hand on him. Unfortunately, *hands* weren't going to be a part of the equation. From behind Blake, Danner dissolved into his cloud of ash and rushed Gabe.

Gabe uncoiled his fists and brought his hands up to defense against the incoming form of the gray cloud. There was no point in using his fists. How the fuck was he supposed to beat the shit out of a cloud?

Gabe screamed as he once again entered into a world of gray.

When Gabe was finally able to see something other than gray again, his eyes beheld what had quickly become his least favorite place in the world: *Suffering For Art.*

"I fucking hate this exhibit," Gabe quietly griped as the last of Danner flew off from around him.

Gabe first saw Blake and Becca — he couldn't stop thinking of her by that name — before seeing that Zellers' entire undead crew had also gathered with them in the exhibit. The horde blocked the door to the corridor.

A quick glance over to the side doors revealed they were closed, the dreaded red lights shining brightly above each door. Gabe wasn't going to escape that way.

"Any last remarks while your tongue is still yours?" Blake asked.

Gabe resisted the urge to send some very nasty insults Zellers' direction. Instead, "Yeah. Why me?"

"Just unlucky, I guess," Blake answered, though Gabe noticed Becca shift uncomfortably at his question. "One of the many benefits of having the most beautiful of all women at my side. I can send her out into the world to recruit for me. Men respond well to her summons, but you know that all too well, don't you Mr. Daniels?"

Gabe managed to keep his middle finger tucked away, though just barely.

"She has been very helpful in that regard. And I can use her to guide my new recruits through the game. Everything is so much more effective that way."

There it was again, Zellers' "game". "What the fuck is this game you keep mentioning?" Gabe asked, needing to know.

"It's what you've been playing all night," Blake answered, rather unhelpfully. "It satisfies the trickiest of the three steps for resurrection."

"The three steps?" Gabe wondered. "You don't just say some words and – poof! – undead fuck-wads appears? "

"I wish it was that simple," Blake said morosely. "No. There is a process. A formula, if you will. The second two are the easiest parts for me. Inflict great pain upon your victim, causing suffering that feels eternal. The third step being to read the incantation provided in the book. The first step, though, that has ended up being - by far - the hardest.

"Swell your victim's heart with great hope, then strip that hope away, to be replaced by dreary futility," Blake recited the first step from memory. "*That's* what I use the game for. And with Becca's added assistance of late, the game works like a charm."

Gabe remembered how he had felt after destroying the statue. He had never felt so alive. So filled with *hope*, as the ritual demanded. But...

"Seems like a stupid game to me," Gabe countered. "I don't think it'd have worked if one of your assholes here would have killed me before I destroyed the statue."

Blake laughed. "I assure you, Mr. Daniels, your life was never in any real danger. At least, not until now. Becca had you set up for success from the beginning. Who was it that gave you the pottery shard that allowed your escape from the table here the first time?"

Gabe thought back to when Becca and he had been in *Beauty Through Rage*. He clearly remembered her brazenness as she reached under the barrier to fetch the shard and hand it off to him. She had even been the one to remind him that it was in his pocket when he was trapped on the table.

"Time after time, she continued to save you when all hope was lost in your feeble mind."

It had been Becca that had triggered the alarm and dragged him into *Affluenza*. She had been the one to suggest traveling through the vents. Stabbing Ophelia with the mop handle and shoving her into the bathroom stall, saving Gabe from her clutches? That had also been Becca.

Gabe flipped through his memory book of the entire night and realized Becca had orchestrated nearly every escape from the clutches of certain death. She had been his guide. She had even planted a perfectly-timed kiss to ensure that'd he'd be motivated enough to come back and save her ass after she was kidnapped by Lester.

More than just Becca, Gabe pictured other instances that had troubled him throughout the night. They were all starting to make sense given Zellers' explanation. Lester's seemingly unenthused warning about Gabe getting away during his initial escape from *Suffering For Art*. The relative ease of their escape, in general. "*Are they that stupid?*" Gabe had asked when Blake's goons hadn't gone with the obvious move to run around to the unlocked door while Becca and he had slowly traversed through the lightless *A Morsel's Journey*.

Apparently, Zellers' goons weren't *that* stupid, after all.

Oh…and the fact that Becca had never seen *Die Hard*. *Who the fuck had never seen* Die Hard!?

Gabe felt like an idiot as he realized that Becca and Blake had duped him every step of the way. Blake's revelations put the whole night in perspective, except…

"Bullshit! This fuck here was for sure trying to kill me," Gabe accused, pointing at Lester.

"Yes," Blake agreed, his eyes narrowing in disappointment. "Mr. Giles here has proven himself hard to control. He skirts my orders in every way that he can. I find that I have to be one-hundred percent specific in my instructions to him, and even then it's hit-or-miss. I'm not sure why he is different that way. Perhaps because his brain was wired completely wrong even before he died."

"Wait?" Gabe said. "That dipshit has a brain?"

Lester didn't look enthused by the joke.

"And let's not forget about your shit demon, Ophelia, over there." Gabe pointed at the dripping brown humanoid near the door. Ophelia actually gave a little bow at mention of her name. "She damn near killed me in your *Midnight* cul-de-sac. *After* Becca was taken."

"But did she?" Blake refuted. "Weren't you miraculously saved by a little Bic lighter?"

Gabe's hand subconsciously traveled to his pocket where he felt the hard nub of the lighter still lingering there. He had almost forgotten about finding the Bic mysteriously lying in the cul-de-sac, its flame flickering in the darkness.

"You can thank Danner for that," Blake informed. Danner simply nodded. "Marvelous play with the car lighter, by the way. That would have been a real hoot if it would have worked."

"Wait a minute? How did you know about the car lighter?" Gabe asked, aghast. "Were you watching me somehow?

Zellers burst out in another fit of laughter. "Of course! I'm not going to let you wander around my gallery without keeping tabs on you the entire time. I have miniature cameras set up all over this building. You won't see them, of course. Nothing takes away from the beauty of a place more than an ugly, plastic box hanging in a corner. I can afford stealth, so why the hell not?

"I'll admit," Blake continued, "watching you did make me cringe a few times. You're like a damn bull in a china shop. You caused a lot of damage that I'll have to repair. Nothing money and a few 'Under Construction' signs won't fix, though. You're my first here in Arte Blanche, so at least you showed me a few things to tighten up for the next contestant in my little game 'The Price Is Death'." Blake's laughter increased, as if the prick's joke had actually been funny.

Gabe didn't agree.

"You really are a childish, sadistic fuck-tard, aren't you?" Gabe accused.

The smile vanished from Blake's face. Gabe imagined planting his fist in its place.

"I do love show-and-tell," Blake replied, "but I do believe this session has ended." Zellers snapped his fingers and Danner sprang into action, breaking down into his ash form and swirling around to Gabe's backside. Two arms of ash seized his wrists and twisted them behind his back, while multiple other appendages grew to surround the rest of his body. After Danner had him suspended, Blake casually walked up to Gabe until his face was close enough to smell his breath. It smelled like a fruity blend of potpourri. Gabe briefly wondered what other hidden advantages there were to being rich that he had never thought of.

"I look forward to hearing you speak in a courteous tongue. I have a feeling *that* alone will be enough to drive you crazy," Blake threatened.

"And I look forward to hearing you speak with my cock in your mouth," Gabe retorted.

Anger seethed on Blake's face. "Strap him to the damn table," Blake ordered in ire.

The ash cloud tightened around Gabe and he was dragged backward to his date with destiny.

"**W**ait!" Becca yipped as Gabe was dragged off his feet by Danner's ash cloud. The ash cloud stopped its progress, buzzing with confusion.

Becca stepped over to Blake and placed a hand gently on his chest. "It occurs to me that you never got me a wedding gift, my love," she reminded in a sultry, teasing voice.

"Of course I did," Blake protested. "You're standing in it." He waved his hand around to indicate the whole of Arte Blanche.

"A girl couldn't ask for a more ornate gift," Becca mollified. Watching on, Gabe was surprised she wasn't twirling her hair with a finger, the way that she was acting. "Still, the Arte Blanche is a gift for both you *and* I. I would like a little something just for myself. Something small, I promise." With this, Becca flashed puppy dog eyes at Blake.

Gabe rolled his.

"What is it, my dear," Blake asked softly, obviously completely smitten.

Hello, Amytis, Gabe thought.

"Remember how I told you that I met this one in a bar, performing in his own band?" She said 'this one' as if she were speaking of a cockroach. Exactly the tone a love-struck fool would want to hear from the woman he claimed as his prize when discussing other men.

"I remember."

"He never got to finish his last song," she said with a tone of regret. "I was really enjoying it, too. I wish to hear him sing it for me, before he regales us with his screams of agony."

"Can't it wait until he's turned? Then you can have him sing to your heart's desire."

Becca just deepened her puppy dog stare and begged, "Pretty please."

Gabe couldn't decide if he wanted to laugh, or throw up, as he saw the fight in Zellers fade. "Anything for my moon," Blake relented, planting a kiss on her lips.

Jesus Christ! Even when dark magic put a man in complete, undisputed control of a woman, she apparently could still find a way to wear the pants in the family.

"Release him," Blake ordered Danner. Gabe felt the pressure of the ash cloud's grip loosen around his body.

"How about it, Gabe?" Becca asked, strolling up to him in a tawdry gait. "Will you finish that last song for me?"

"*An Ancient Madness*?"

"Yes," Becca confirmed.

Gabe was about to tell her to go fuck herself, when she leaned in and whispered, "Trust me." It was the second time she had made such a plea. "Sing the verse that has been haunting you. No matter what happens, don't say another word until the verse is complete."

Despite himself, Gabe nodded.

"Get on with it," Blake ordered. He was clearly perturbed by Becca's proximity to Gabe, her luscious lips less than an inch from his earlobe. She even gave it a lick to further entice him into acquiescing.

Why the fuck not? Gabe thought.

"Be still, all trapped souls that hear these words," Gabe began singing. To his surprise, all of Blake's minions – including Becca - suddenly stopped whatever they were doing, their bodies snapping stiff and straight, approximating a military stance of attention. At first, Blake seemed disinterested in Gabe's song, but as the lyrics caught up to him, his eyes widened.

"Death has not given you your desired end.

Instead, only another master."

"Stop singing!" Blake demanded, fear evident in his eyes.

Gabe was satisfied to see the change in the billionaire's posture. He thought about stopping the song to offer a taunt to Zellers, but remembered Becca's warning about not saying another word until the verse was complete. Seeing all that had happened around him since he started, he thought maybe there was something to her request. Maybe he should trust her.

"Yet, even another master now beckons." Gabe continued the song.

"I said stop!" Blake broke from his stance and sped toward Gabe.

"Come unto me."

Blake arrived within arm's reach of Gabe. Careful to remember Becca's warning about not breaking from the song, Gabe sang the next line – "Serve me; your new God" – while driving the fist of his uninjured hand straight into the billionaire's face.

Damn...that felt good!

Blake stumbled backward and crashed onto his ass as a geyser of red gushed from his nose.

"Let loose the shackles that bind you."

Blake tried to rise to his feet, but Gabe picked up the light-bodied billionaire and threw him back to the floor.

"With these final words spoken, you will be mine."

Gabe sent his foot plunging into Blake's abdomen. The billionaire's body constricted into a ball on the floor.

"I claim your body, your soul, your mind."

Blake weakly attempted to rise up on his knees and elbows, but another kick to his side sent him tumbling back to the ground.

"Now, and forever, until your bonds be broken…"

"Stop!" Blake shouted, desperation in his scream.

"Be obedient unto me."

Gabe arrived at the final word that had remained unspoken at Curwen's manor.

Blake stretched out a hand to Gabe, one last desperate plea. "Stop, you fool!" Gabe kicked the hand away and followed it up with a steel-toed crack against the billionaire's already bloody nose.

"Amen."

The gathering of undead around the room broke from their statuesque stillness, looking around in confusion. Except Becca, she wasn't confused at all. She stood and faced Gabe with a smile that traveled far beyond the corners of her lips.

"Holy shit!" Gabe exclaimed, realizing what had just happened. "Did I just steal Zellers' undead arm…"

Becca's fist to his windpipe cut off Gabe's words and sent him collapsing to his knees, clutching at his throat. Loud gasps were the only sounds that escaped his battered throat as he struggled to take in precious air. That bitch knew exactly where to hit!

Before Gabe's knees had even hit the ground, Becca started reciting the verse Gabe had just sung. "Be still, all trapped souls that hear these words."

As she spoke the lines, Blake started laughing from his crumpled position on the floor. "I tried to get you to stop," he laughed, his eyes focused on Gabe. "You had no idea what you were doing." Blake coughed, a red mist flying from his lips.

Gabe couldn't reply, still fighting to suck air through his bruised windpipe.

Becca finished reciting the incantation and Gabe could see that the assortment of undead had once again switched masters. She bent to kiss Gabe on the forehead. "Thanks, hon," she said. She turned to Blake, who had stopped laughing and was staring up at her in horror. "Oh, my loving husband," she mocked, "did I forget to tell you that I found that second copy of the book that your father spent so much of his life searching for? That *you* have been searching for?"

Blake narrowed his eyes.

"Or, should I say, Gabe here found the book. The whole time, it was only a couple hundred miles away from your father's estate in Rhode Island. So close, but yet, so far," she laughed.

"So, you and this peasant were playing a game against *me*," Blake sighed, after visibly struggling with the newly-presented information. It must have pained him to be searching for something for so long, to find out it had been only a state away the entire time. "Nice play," he commended in defeat.

"No, not at all," Becca answered. "Gabe had no idea what was happening. I found him through a quick search on Google. Just because, as an owned soul, I am forbidden to speak the words of the incantation, doesn't mean I am forbidden to type them."

"How did you perform a Google search? I have forbidden all cell phones and computers."

"Lucky for me then that you didn't bother to check the iPads that you had installed in *Beauty Through Rage*," Becca said.

"The ones you had installed are 4G capable. Just a little late night snooping and I was able to use them to find Gabe's band playing a song called 'An Ancient Madness'. And wouldn't you know...the lyrics were an exact match to the transfer spell found in Peristopheles' book. A further search revealed that they had a show coming up at some local dirt bar, so I figured why not. I knew you'd be sending me out after a new recruit soon, so I picked my target and commenced the hunt."

The bitch sure did look proud of herself.

"Of course, it wasn't hard after that. I had this poor boy hanging on my every word. Didn't I, sweet cheeks?" Becca pinched one of Gabe's facial cheeks and gave it a little shake. He wanted nothing more than to launch a verbal assault at her, but he couldn't squeeze any words out through his bruised windpipe.

"Unfortunately, Gabe doesn't remember actually seeing the book, or maybe he'd remember the warning before the transfer enchantment."

Gabe hadn't had the chance to tell her about his memories rushing back to him in *Midnight In The Garden Of Good And Evil*. He thought back, trying to picture the warning she spoke of.

"Beware," Becca began reciting the warning from memory, "the acquisition of an enslaved soul must be made in the presence of the soul's earthly body. If the body is not present, the enslaved soul will be set free to roam the Earth at its leisure." Becca hunched down so she was face-to-face with the choking Gabe. "You see, honey, my earthly remains are *not* present. They're down the hallway, sealed inside the throne of *Wanders Never Cease*," Becca smugly said. "My wanders, indeed, never have," she added as an afterthought.

Gabe tore his eyes away from her to look at Zellers as he spoke again. "I tried to warn you," the hobbled billionaire said with a shrug.

Becca looked back at Blake. She stood and walked over to his crumpled form. "As for you, dear husband, what shall I do with you? I'm thinking *Crucifixion*." She shaped the word with her hands, as if framing a marquee. "That's surprisingly not part of your demented collection yet."

"If I may make a request, ma'am?" All heads turned to Danner, who had spoken. "I was hoping to have Mr. Zellers for myself."

Becca looked confused.

"I believe you may have forgotten that my remains are also not present," Danner clarified, picturing his unadorned, silver urn resting in Blake Zellers personal vault, far from Arte Blanche. "I am free. A thing I have been wishing for over thirty years. The Zellers family have not only taken my life, they have kept me enslaved for longer than I had ever lived. Thomas Zellers made billions off of my brain and his son...well, his son has made me do some truly repugnant things that have left a dark stain on my soul. I assure you that there is nobody that deserves this man's soul more than I."

Becca considered Danner's request. "I still have need of him, I'm afraid. This man – no, this *insect* posing as a man – mean nothing to me, but his money – his power – both mean a great deal."

"And you shall have both," Danner promised. "I have no desire for such things. Leave me his cyber security company – the one my brain created - and you take all his current wealth. You would have a hard time running such a company without me, anyhow."

"And what of the Arte Blanche? This place is pure genius and I very much desire to keep it for my own uses."

"The Arte Blanche as well," Danner confirmed. "This place sickens me and I would live happily never laying eyes on it again."

Becca stared daggers into Danner's soul, judging the man's intent. "If I agree, how would we make this work?"

"Easy," Danner relied. "You two are already married. Once I perform the ritual, I will have him divorce you, leaving all his money and assets to you. He – and by proxy, myself – will keep the company only. Billionaire's have a reputation for being eccentric and doing strange, incomprehensible things, so I doubt it'd cause to much speculation among the masses. Especially not with the man himself around to confirm his intentions."

Becca stared at him a moment longer. "Fine," she eventually ceded, "he's yours. Truthfully, I'd prefer not to have to look at him any longer than necessary. I find him repugnant."

Despite all that had preceded the condemnation, Blake actually looked disappointed by her insult. The billionaire really had fallen in love with the undead wench, Gabe realized.

Danner nodded at Becca, then surprised Gabe by turning and taking steps toward him. When he arrived, Danner extended a hand toward Gabe. Gabe – in a mild state of shock - took the proffered hand. Danner then did something even more surprising and drew Gabe in for an embrace. "Should you get a chance, the door code is 0-5-2-8," Danner whispered into Gabe's ear.

Danner released his embrace and withdrew Gabe to arm's length. "Good luck to you, Mr. Daniels."

Gabe was too stunned to offer any words of reply. That, and Gabe doubted his battered throat would allow much in the way of words to pass through, anyway.

"How are you going to get Blake out of here?" Becca asked. "You can't simply stroll through the crowd out front with him being bruised and bloodied like this."

"No need to worry," Danner promised, then dissolved into his ash cloud form. The millions of ash specks swarmed over the billionaire, blocking him from sight. "I'll give them another sight to marvel at," Danner's voice boomed from the gray tornado. "They'll just think me another of Mr. Zellers' fancy tricks of art."

Before Becca could protest, Danner's cloud flew past the gathered horde and out the door into the northern corridor. Becca let her gaze linger at the spot they had disappeared, then turned back to Gabe.

"Now that that's taken care of," she spoke in a teasing tone, "what shall we do with you?"

Gabe feared he wasn't going to like the answer.

43

How in the holy fuck am I going to get out of this one!

Gabe searched around the exhibit for anything he could use to aid in his escape. He had the goddamn door combo, now he just had to get back to the fucking door itself.

"You want to know something, Gabe?" Becca asked, strolling over to where Gabe knelt. Gabe wanted to tell her that he didn't give a fuck about whatever it was she was about to say, but only a squeak emerged, his throat still unable to pass enough breath for words. "I really do like you," she confessed. "Let's just say that you made an impression on me in our short time together."

Gabe wanted nothing more than to make an impression on her face right then. He had never hit a woman before, but Amytis/Elizabeth/Becca was no fucking woman.

"I believe I will have you serve as my right-hand man," Becca continued. "Or – how does you generation put it? – *bottom bitch*? Yes, that's it. I'm going to make you my bottom bitch." Becca looked pleased with herself. "You live in a time with such colorful phrases. I've grown to enjoy this world immensely."

"C-Cunt," Gabe squeaked. The word managed to climb through his throat and emerge from his lips, but it was so soft, he doubted Becca had even heard it.

The vile woman smiled. "Ah, yes. *Cunt.*" She played with the word as if seeing how it felt on her tongue. "As I understand it, a reprehensible term for vagina; or pussy, as it's more commonly referred to these days. So many different names for such a simple orifice. It pleases me to see that the power of female genitalia has not faded over the centuries."

Gabe rose wobbly to his feet to meet Becca's gaze. She surprised him by immediately leaning in and smashing her lips against his in a repeat of the kiss they had shared earlier. She ground her lips against his and Gabe almost lost himself in the passion.

Almost.

Gabe shot his good hand up and clutched it around her throat. He squeezed.

The undead army immediately started to move in, but Becca held up a hand to stay them. She gurgled, her eyes beginning to bulge as Gabe increased the pressure. He squeezed as hard as he could. If he could choke the life out of her, great. He doubted he could kill her in such a way, but he squeezed anyway. At the very least, he had been hoping to get her acolytes to attack and kill him, perhaps fucking up their ritual and at least offering him a peaceful death. Not an eternity as a slave puppet.

Her holding back the horde caused those hopes to vanish, as did the smile on her face. Through her restricted throat, she managed to push out moans of ecstasy. She was leaning into his grip, encouraging him to squeeze even harder.

The bitch was enjoying this.

Gabe increased the pressure until his forearm burned. He felt something give way and snap under his fingers. Becca's eyes were nearly popping out of her skull and her throat now felt like a bag of jelly in his palm.

Still, she was smiling.

A sense of futility filled Gabe's soul and he finally let her go. She fell hard to her knees and didn't – *couldn't* - speak for a moment. Gabe heard eerie sounds coming from underneath her skin as her throat re-inflated itself back to its normal form.

Becca rose to her feet. "Oh Gabe," she said seductively, "that was fantastic." She wrapped him in an embrace and once again planted her lips against his. He could feel a hot passion boiling off of her as she once again ground her lips against his. "I don't know if I've ever been so wet in my life – any of my lives," she damn-near whinnied as she pulled her lips away from his.

Jesus! This bitch was straight-up psychotic.

"Anyway," she said, stepping away from him with a delighted shiver, "I'll hold that thought until you're officially part of my stable. Dr. Holtz?"

Holtz stepped out of the crowd. "Yes, ma'am?"

"Prepare for the ritual," Becca instructed.

"Yes, ma'am." Holtz stepped over to where his cart still stood near the stark, metal table.

"Any last words?" Becca asked Gabe.

Gabe didn't answer. Instead, he was staring at the flat surface that would be his final resting place while his heart ached with a dull thud in his chest.

"Gabe! There you are! What the fuck, man?"

All eyes in the room turned toward the door that led to *A Morsel's Journey*, where an unknown man stood with his cell phone in his hand. The diode attached to the camera was ablaze from the phone's flashlight app.

"Why the fuck was it so dark in there?" The strange man asked with a glance behind him.

"Ronnie?" Gabe asked in a squeak, dumbstruck at the sight of his friend.

The sound was too soft for Ronnie to hear. Instead, he investigated the gathering of undead demons. "Whoa...wicked fucking costume party, bro."

The rest of the room stood still, obviously as in shock as Gabe was to see Ronnie standing at the door.

"Who in the hell are you?" Becca asked.

Ronnie looked over to her, seemingly noticing her for the first time. "Damn! You must be Becca. Gabe wasn't lying when he said you were hot as fuck." Ronnie strode over to a befuddled Becca and began forcefully shaking her hand. "I'm Gabe's friend. Ronnie. Ronnie Childress."

"Ronnie, what the fuck are you doing here?" Gabe's voice was still raspy as hell, but it was slowly coming back to him. It was enough for Ronnie to hear him this time, though.

"Jesus, Gabe! You sound like shit. Deep throat too much dick at this party?" Ronnie laughed, though his laughter died down after he realized nobody else was joining him.

"Anyway, man," he continued, "I'm here looking for you. I tried calling a few times and you never answered. I wasn't sure if you were having another one of *those* nights again, so I used my GPS Phone Tracker app and saw that you were still here."

Ronnie paused and turned to Becca. "You see, our boy here sometimes gets a little *too* fucked up and I'll have to go stop whatever – or whoever – I'm doing to go and find him passed out in a gutter somewhere so I can drag his ass home. The app comes in handy as fuck in that way."

Another pause, and back to Gabe. "I would have been here sooner, but I was stuck in that lame-ass party outside, since they had the damn door locked to get back here. Let me tell you, bro, those hipsters out there are some fucking boring-ass bitches.

Anyway, some weird fucking tornado thing came through the door a moment ago and I was able to sneak in." Ronnie stopped, a confused look passing over his features. "What was that tornado thing anyway? Some kind of artsy special effect?" The confused expression was replaced by a bored shrug. "I don't think I'll ever understand art," he concluded.

Gabe missed the last part of Ronnie's soliloquy. His attention was grabbed by the door that Ronnie had come through. The door to *A Morsel's Journey*.

He had left it standing wide open.

Becca – apparently recovered from flabbergasted state - snapped her fingers at the horde. "Kill this douchebag," she ordered.

Gabe burst into action. "Ronnie, run!" he yelled, jumping forward and dragging Ronnie by the arm toward *A Morsel's Journey*.

Becca's army quickly jumped after the two fleeing men. Fortunately, Gabe and Ronnie were closer to the doors. Gabe pushed Ronnie through the dark doorway – snatching the lit cell phone out of his hand – and slammed the door shut behind them. He immediately turned and got the other door open just as something heavy thudded into the first door from the other side.

"Go around!" Gabe heard Becca shouting through the door. He knew the horde weren't going to be fucking around this time.

"Keep running, Ronnie!" Gabe shouted, though it came out as a grizzled whisper. He tugged at his friend's arm to get him going again. They ran through the darkened exhibit, using the cell phone to light the way. They sprinted into the large figure's asshole and didn't stop until they had exited its mouth and arrived at the opposite doorway. Gabe immediately threw the first door open and shot into the divider room with Ronnie.

Closing the door behind him, then opening the door in front, Gabe pushed Ronnie out into the western corridor.

"What the fuck is going on?" Ronnie finally managed to ask, not having had the time during their desperate escape.

Gabe never had a chance to answer his friend. As he turned away from the door, there was a blur of movement accompanied by a rush of wind, Ronnie quickly vanishing from where he had just stood.

A scream from several feet down the corridor drew Gabe's attention. He turned to see Ronnie lying on the floor with the winged-monstrosity Lester sitting atop of him. Red spatter already stained the scene, with more flying as Lester mercilessly swiped his bony wings into Ronnie, tearing away chunks of flesh with each swing. Ronnie struggled and screamed for a brief moment, before too much of him stained the surrounding area and he fell forever silent.

"Ronnie!" Gabe rasped, diving at Lester's back. He bowled into the bloodied creature and the two of them rolled along the floor. Gabe got his hands wrapped around Lester's exposed spinal column as they tumbled, using it to keep Lester – as his deadly wing tips - facing away from him. Once they rolled to a stop, Gabe used his writhing fury to power his arms, giving them strength as he torqued the vertebrae. With a pop, Lester's spine snapped in his grip like a No. 2 pencil.

Lester screamed and flapped on the ground like a bird with broken wings. Gabe would have loved nothing more than to stay and stomp the man's head into mush, but stampeding footsteps behind him announced that the rest of the horde were already rounding the corner into his hallway. Gabe settled for a swift kick into Lester's snarling face and took off in a sprint toward the door to *Free Market*.

Gabe rounded the corner to the southern corridor and sprinted to the mid-point where the door awaited. Blake's – now Becca's – horde had already careened around the corner by the time he reached the keypad.

"Work, motherfucker, work!" he shouted as he hurriedly punched the code into the keypad. A beep and a whirring sound from the door told him that his attempt had been successful. As soon as he was able, Gabe threw the door open and, for the first time since the sun had disappeared, he stepped into *Free Market*.

Gabe slammed the door shut behind him, hopefully forever separating himself from *Monarchy*. As he took in his new surroundings, he realized that he had stepped into a completely different world than he had inhabited for the last several hours.

People here were smiling. They were enjoying themselves. Not due to any sick, sadistic pleasures, but due to normal – or at least normal for hipster - things. The music of dueling pianos, the never-ending flow of champagne and wine, and circling trays of something that looked like cat food and crackers. *Pâté*, if Gabe's memory served him correctly.

In the center of the crowd rose the tall, transparent walls of the glass house. People milled about on each floor of the structure, though a majority of the crowd were outside, surrounding it. Through the glass walls, Gabe found the pianos, set up on an elevated platform that served as the house's front porch that was currently serving as a stage. Both pianos had men seated in front of them, joyously tapping at the keys. Microphones were set up around the pianos, their receivers angled down at the piano's music-producing wires.

People were living it up. Drinking, eating; several of the partiers were even fucking. *Everybody* was conversing, laughing, smiling; seemingly having one hell of a time.

Fuck these people and their oblivious mindsets!

Gabe glanced back at the closed door to Monarchy and was surprised to see that it hadn't yet reopened. He took a few stumbling steps forward as he kept a careful eye on the door behind him. Not paying attention to where he was going, he soon bumped into a small, feminine figure. Their legs became intertwined and both went tumbling to the ground. A yelp of surprise and the shattering of a wine glass created a cacophony to Gabe's ears, though only a few people standing near seemed to notice over the loud music of the pianos.

"Hey!" a man shouted at Gabe. "Watch where you're going!" The man helped the woman back to her feet. She was wearing a white dress that now bore a large red stain down the front. Gabe noticed that their stains were nearly matching in color, except Gabe's stains were much more prevalent across his wardrobe.

"Come on, Barbara. This man has had entirely too much to drink," the man concluded, escorting the white-dressed woman away, but not before throwing Gabe a look of privileged disgust.

"Help," Gabe pleaded toward the retreating couple. They never heard him. The rasping of his voice was easily drowned out by the amplified pianos.

From the corner of his eye, Gabe saw the door open. He turned to see Becca step through. She waved behind her and most – if not all - of her staff accompanied her, now in their unthreatening, human forms. Lester brought up the rear, apparently having already recovered from his snapped spine.

Becca scanned the crowd and quickly found Gabe. She smiled darkly at him. Gabe quickly backed away, threading himself into the thick crowd until he could he longer see her.

"Help," Gabe choked out, tugging at a random partier's sleeve. The man scanned Gabe's appearance and pulled his arm away with a look of disgust equaling the one he had recently received from the stained-dress woman's man. Gabe looked down at himself. Red splotches all over his tattered clothes. A hand wrapped in a makeshift bandage. A boot covered in brown muck that reeked of shit.

"Fucking people can't handle their booze," the man spat before walking away.

Gabe turned around to find another gentleman standing behind him, laughing with a circle of fellow partiers. Gabe grabbed the man's arm and spun him around. "Help me," Gabe squeaked out. The man repeated the previous patron's reaction by scanning his eyes along Gabe from head-to-foot. "I'm not drunk!" Gabe tried, hoping to cut off the man's reaction of disgust.

The man laughed. "Well, maybe you should be, mate!" The man had an Aussie accent and a drunken sheen glazing his eyes. He held out his half-empty flute of champagne to Gabe.

Several yards past the champagne-bearing man, Gabe's eyes reacquired Becca through the crowd. She was waving at a couple of her staff members, ushering them to move toward the gallery's front doors.

Gabe took the offered champagne and chugged it down. Fuck it...why not?

"People are trying to kill me," he begged to the Aussie after draining the champagne flute. "I seriously need your help."

"Listen, mate," the man replied, pointing at his ears, "I can barely hear you through all this racket. You'll have to speak up."

Gabe was about to try again when Becca turned and her eyes met Gabe's. "Fuck," Gabe squeaked, then backed away into a thick throng of partiers. The Aussie shrugged and threw an arm up to get the attention of a nearby floor waitress.

Gabe weaved through several of the gathered patrons toward the front doors of the gallery, or – as Gabe remembered it - the black-hole portal to the outside world. As he neared the exit, he saw two of Becca's staff members had already arrived at the darkened doors. They were carefully scanning the crowd, waiting for Gabe to reveal himself.

Fuck...fuck...fuck! Gabe wasn't sure what to do. He couldn't hide in the crowd forever, he knew that. He briefly wondered if Becca would unleash her monsters on the crowd to get to him. He supposed she would, but only as a last resort. The Arte Blanche wouldn't be very useful to her if it became famous for a mass-massacre.

Or maybe it would actually draw more people in? Who the fuck could tell with today's fucked-up society!?

"I suggest you accompany me quietly, Mr. Daniels." Gabe heard from behind his shoulder. He turned to see a familiar – if not welcome – face.

Lurch.

"Fuck you," Gabe responded, extending his middle finger toward the large, gangly man. A woman nearby huffed at seeing Gabe's vulgar display. She turned away and barged her way through the crowd.

Jesus, these people were some stuck up, prissy assholes!

Lurch slid up to Gabe and wound his arm around his shoulders. "Mr. Daniels, we don't want to cause a scene. It's bad for business. I strongly urge you to accompany me back into *Monarchy.*"

"Like I give a fuck about your business," Gabe spat. He was all about creating a scene. Anything to get these fucking peoples' attention. He drove a fist directly into Lurch's balls, then brought it up to go crashing into his jaw. Instantly several nearby crowd members jumped into to aid the tall man.

"Hey, man," one of the responders said, pushing Gabe away from Lurch. "Not cool, bro!" Gabe fell backward, knocking a couple more partiers down with him as he fell. Gabe quickly regained his feet and saw another man reach down to Lurch and help him back to his as well. He also saw that he had created a scene, just not the one he had intended. The partiers weren't rushing around in fear. Instead, Becca had spotted him again and snapped her fingers at a couple nearby staff members. She pointed and the white-tuxedoed men came barreling toward Gabe.

"What's your problem, man?" another onlooker asked, helping one of the women Gabe had knocked over after being pushed.

Gabe thought about pummeling the man to the beat of the pianos behind him. Maybe if he kept attacking the patrons, they would finally fucking respond.

It was the music that sparked an idea in Gabe's mind. He turned to stare at the two pianos. They were back-to-back with the musicians frantically pounding at their keys. Gabe eye the microphones set up to amplify the music throughout the room.

Perfect!

Gabe barraged his way through the thick crowd toward the pianos, risking a glance back at the pursuing staff members. They were urgently forcing their way through the crowd, earning annoyed looks from the patrons. Gabe knew he had to be quick.

He pushed through the gathered crowd until he emerged in a small clearing around the pianos. He could hear his pursuers pushing through the crowd behind him and knew he only had a moment before they arrived. He ran up to one of the microphones and tore it way from its stand.

"Be still, all trapped souls that hear these words," Gabe hurriedly croaked into the microphone. His voice was still gravelly and weak but the mic amplified it so that it boomed throughout the gargantuan room.

The staff members instantly froze, stopping their pursuit. The music ceased. Even the crowd silenced, the dull roar of their conversations ending as all eyes turned toward the strange man on the microphone.

"Death has not given you your desired end," Gabe continued, the first smile in what felt like forever curling his lips. "Instead, only another master." Gabe spotted Becca through the crowd. Her eyes had grown infinitely wide as she realized what Gabe was doing.

I'm going to free all these motherfuckers from your rule, bitch! Gabe thought, though he was careful not to say the words and break from the verse.

"Yet, even another master now beckons. Come unto me. Serve me; your new God"

"Gabe! Stop!" Becca's loud, begging shout flowed over the crowd. She was attempting to fight through the crowd to get at him, but her progress was slowed by the thick volume of bodies.

Too slow.

Fuck you, cunt! Gabe's internal voice mocked as his external said, "Let loose the shackles that bind you. With these final words spoken, you will be mine."

"You don't know what you're doing, Gabe!" she warned.

"I claim your body, your soul, your mind. Now, and forever, until your bonds be broken..."

"Don't set them free! They can't be trusted!"

And you can!?

"Be obedient unto me."

Becca stopped struggling through the crowd to stare pleadingly into Gabe's eyes. "Please, Gabe! You have to trust me on this!"

Not a chance in hell! Still, Gabe felt a twinge of doubt in his soul as he paused before saying the finally word.

"Amen." He finished, leaving the specter of doubt to wither.

Gabe laughed into the microphone, throwing his hands forward with both middle fingers extended toward the stunned Becca. "Fuck you, bitch!" he growled into the mic.

Gabe was feeling damn proud of himself. He wanted to bask in the elation of his victory. And he would have, too...

...except that's when all hell broke loose.

INTERLUDE

13

"*The wheels on the bus go round and round, round and round, round and round,*" the man sang merrily as the large conveyance rattled loudly as it travelled the rough road beneath its tires. "*The wheels on the bus go round and round, all around the town!*"

"Shut the fuck up, Giles!" the guard screamed from his position at the front of the bus.

Not to be dissuaded, Lester sang even louder into the next verse. "*The wipers on the bus go swish, swish, swish...*"

"Fucking hell!" the tall man seated across from Lester shouted over the rhythmic noise. "Stop your fucking wailing!" The man wore bracelets that matched Lester's own – the kind that were connected with a chain that further connected with anklets down below.

"Sure thing, Lansky," Lester replied to Owen's outburst. He sat silent for a moment, watching as the guard up front seemed to relax at the ceasing of Lester's disturbance.

Lester smiled at the guard, then suddenly - and very loudly - he burst back into song. "*The people on the bus go up and down, up and down, up and down…"* The guard shot up to his feet and quickly marched back to Lester's seat.

"I said to shut the fuck up, inmate!" the guard yelled as he took the butt of his shotgun and slammed it into Lester's temple. Lester yelped against the sudden pain. He allowed a moment for his swimming vision to stabilize before he sat back up and began laughing.

"Is that all you got?" Lester mocked, through his laughter. A wet trickle ran down the side of his face. Lester extended his tongue from his mouth and flicked it toward the warm stream. The tip of the muscular organ barely reached, but Lester managed to get a bit of the sticky fluid with the tip, receiving the salty copper taste of his own blood. "Mmm mmm…delicious! Though it would be better if I had access to fresh fruits over these last few months." Lester left his coy smile to burn into the guard,

"Yeah, laugh it up, psychopath," the guard replied, clearly looking disturbed. "Soon, you're either going to be as docile as a goldfish or you're going to be brain-dead. I don't really care which."

Lester's smirk vanished from his face.

Owen shifted in his seat across the aisle. "What do you mean?" he asked, his concern seemingly matching Lester's own.

The guard laughed. "You'll all see soon enough," he promised with a wink toward Lester.

Lester imagined what he'd do to this guard if he was able to get free from his cuffs. Maybe split the man's throat vertically, right down the center? Yeah, that'd be nice. If he'd been home, he would peel the skin away from the guard's throat and pin it to the corkboard wall of his basement. Maybe then he'd extract the guard's teeth with some pliers. Lester's heartbeat pumped a little faster as he pictured taking the liberated teeth and gluing them onto the flaps of throat skin, transforming the guard into a nightmarish creature. Lester would snap some photographs in the hopes that someday he'd sell his creature design to Hollywood. Lester was sure they'd appreciate his eye for creating disgusting, terrifying new monsters for their films.

It's too bad the ones he had already created were most likely no longer in existence. He was sure the police had confiscated his art pieces from his basement and had probably fucked them all up. It was obvious to him by their faces when they first had entered the basement, that they weren't appreciative of his unique eye. They turned green when they saw his creations – literally, they darkened to a shade of green, something that Lester had always thought as hyperbole - many of them vomiting in his dank, subterranean chamber of magnificence.

They had seemed especially dis-appreciative of his corner display depicting a gathering of elves. Not like those elves shown in the cartoons, with their queer-looking, rosy cheeked countenances, but the way elves were really supposed to look. Dark and evil.

The only thing the various cartoons and claymations had gotten right were the fact that elves were short creatures. At first, Lester had tried to find midgets to fill his display, but it turned out that there weren't that many of them running around and he had to improvise. That's when he began taking the children he'd find wandering around the neighborhood. They served nicely in a pinch.

Instead of rosy cheeks, his elves were pale-faced. The only rose-colored anything was the line around their facial skin where the flesh ended. He had left the faces attached to the front of their skulls, but had removed all the flesh from the backs and tops; exactly the way elves should be.

Another fallacy of the television depictions were those stupid, green hats they wore. Instead of pointy hats, the elves were supposed to have pointy heads. That detail had taken a little creativity on Lester's part, but he had eventually came up with an easy enough answer. He just had to make a small incision in his model's abdomens and remove a rib from within. Using a strong adhesive that he had purchased from a homebuilder's store, he'd had been able to glue the broken rib to the top of the elf's exposed skull, leaving it standing aloft like a demented unicorn's horn. It wasn't exactly a pointy head, but Lester thought it made his elves stand out, looking even more awesome than the originals. Besides, if some Hollywood know-it-all decided that he wanted to keep the pointy hats, they'd fit nicely over the elves' horns.

Lester sighed in his seat as he rode the bus down memory lane. He had put a lot of work into his various downstairs displays and his stomach grew queasy whenever he thought about what the authorities had probably done to all of his fine work.

Of course, Lester knew that his wondrous creations would all still be intact if not for his temper. The bodies his temper had left behind were much less carefully hidden than those that his passions had transformed into ghouls and monsters. Most of the time, somebody had simply pissed him off and he had dealt with them appropriately. Though, on a few occasions, a particular beast of his would be taking too long to fashion and he would have to provide a quick-fix to assuage his bloodlust. He had tried his best to dispose of those bodies in a manner that would not tie them back to himself, but he had fucked that up at some point. It's not like he could take them back and store them in his basement. They would just be clutter, getting in the way of his true work. He never had been informed exactly which body had tipped the police off to him, but he formed a few theories on that front.

"You need to stop eye-fucking me, Giles, or I'm going to give you another taste of my shotgun butt," the guard warned Lester, visibly uncomfortable under the prisoner's stare.

"I'm just imagining some fun things I could do with you," Lester replied, not exactly in apology.

"What? You going to carve holes in me and fuck my dead body?" the guard asked.

That accusation – not the first time he had heard it since his arrest – is what led to Lester's theories on how he had been caught. If Lester were forced to admit that he had a vice, there was one that he couldn't deny. The dead turned him on. His crimes of passion would often turn into passion of a different sort. He was convinced that it was his seed, left planted in one of several various bodies that came to mind, that had led the police straight to him. He was also sure that this was the reason most people felt the need to inform him that he was the most fucked up individual that they had ever met...and *that* was coming from his fellow prisoners, some of which were chained up in this very bus with him. All of them murderers in their own right.

It had piqued Lester's interest when he had seen the other prisoners being loaded onto the bus with him. Especially Owen Lansky. He knew Lanksy was a cannibal. One that should have been notorious for his deeds. The police had arrested him on the porch of his suburban home, finding two large freezers filled with carefully butchered human body parts. Somehow, Jeffery Dahmer had gotten all the love for that type of crime and Lansky had flown under the radar. Like himself, Lester felt that Lansky had been robbed of his well-earned spotlight.

Still, gathered on the bus that day was quite the interesting motley crew of individuals. For some reason, the guards had decided to transport them all on the same day. Nobody knew where they were going, or why.

As his thoughts bounced around his head, Lester winked at the guard. The guard shivered and looked away, not delivering the promised blow from the shotgun.

Pussy!

Lester had never flaked when he'd promised somebody pain. It was just plain dishonest.

As everybody seemed to settle back down, Lester began thinking up another song that he could wail. He hadn't yet decided on which, when the bus slowed and turned into a large cobblestone driveway protected by a fancy gate that seemed to open on its own. The bus bumped slowly along as it traveled along the straight and stony path until the driveway curved into a large circle surrounding an ornate fountain.

"Where the fuck are we?" Lester heard somebody behind him mumble. He was similarly curious himself.

The loud screech of air brakes announced their arrival. Lester had to admit to himself that he was rather impressed by the house on the other side of the window. It was a large, sprawling building surrounded by a well-tended lawn. The building itself towered three stories in the air and stretched nearly three football fields in length. It was new – or, at the very least, newly renovated – and lacked the charm of the southern plantations that he had grown up near, but he supposed it had a new-age flair that would be hard to dismiss. Add some creeping vines around its large façade, and fill it with the kind of delightful treats that Lester would gladly craft, and the place would make a most-impressive house of horrors.

Preceded by a hiss of air, the door on the bus squealed as it folded inward. "Get your asses up, inmates!" the guard barked. The men around Lester rose warily, unsure as to what the fuck was happening. Lester briefly considered employing some civil disobedience in the matter, but ended up standing with the rest of them, his sense of curiosity getting the better of him.

They lined up in the center aisle and awaited the guard's signal. He was staring out the open door, waiting for something. When he saw what he was looking for, he finally nodded. "Alright, you twisted fucks, today will either be the luckiest day of your worthless lives, or the unluckiest. I'm not sure which."

Lester peeked through a window in the direction the guard had been staring. He saw four people approaching the bus. Three men and a woman. One of the men was blonde and looked like a pretentious pussy, another one looked like some kid fresh out of college. The third man, who stood at the end, was a chunky fuck. Lester wanted the chunky one. The best sex he had ever had was with some holes he had gouged in a fat man's torso. There was just something about the flabby, greasy makeup of human fatty tissue that made his dick go *pop*!

The woman was a damn fine sight, though. Beautiful; absolutely stunning. Lester thought he'd save her for later and take her the old fashioned way. Some orifices needed no exemplification.

"Listen up," the guard barked. "You're all going to walk out of this bus and line up out front for inspection. I know you don't have a clue what's happening right now, but trust me when I say you don't want to fuck this up. Do your best at trying not to look like complete psychopaths. Got it, Giles?"

Lester wasn't sure why the guard had picked him out of the lineup of his fucked up peers, but he'd play the guard's game. "I got it. I can't help but to hang on every word that comes out of that pretty mouth of yours," Lester teased, followed by a faux-sensual licking of his lips.

Fire briefly burned in the guard's eyes, but he turned and waved his shotgun for the prisoners to follow him out of the vehicle. When his feet hit the ground underneath, he turned out of the doorway and kept a careful eye on the prisoners as they all passed by him to line up on the cobblestoned surface of the circular driveway.

The pretentious-looking man looked the prisoners over before turning to the guard. "Seven, huh? I was only expecting three, maybe four."

The guard shrugged. "I was sure I'd find more. I guess you have more faith in your fellow man than I do."

Mr. Pretentious looked over the lineup one more time and nodded in approval. "Yes, I think you all will do nicely."

Lester considered telling the man that he would *do* him rather un-nicely, but he stayed silent, wanting to see how this was going to play out.

"Hello, gentlemen," the pretentious man addressed them, "and welcome to the Zellers estate 2.0."

******

Blake was pleased to see the men before him. He knew they were some of the worst society had to offer. They were perfect for what he had in mind.

Danner – the ever wary Danner – had tried to convince Blake not to do this, but his pleas had fallen on deaf ears. Since becoming intimate with the histories of Amytis and Elizabeth Bathory, Blake had grown increasingly intrigued by the most depraved souls in history. He couldn't resurrect most of the ones that had come before, but when he found a way to access some of the ones that inhabited the present world, he couldn't resist. Besides, Blake's newest recruit needed some training in his particular method, and this presented a great opportunity.

"Watch carefully what happens to these men, my dear," Blake said to the woman that he had recently christened Becca Larson. "Come to know my process, because soon you will play an important role in what I do."

Professor Cliff Tawney repeated the words in her native language. She was still learning the English language thanks to the painstaking efforts of the professor, but Blake knew from the progress reports that she still had a long way to go before she approached fluency.

He turned back to the lineup of men. "You all have been chosen to receive a very unique offer for men in your situations. I have worked it out with members of the Government to take you on to serve as my personal staff. Instead of facing a life in the dark holes that you have been writhing in, you could choose to come and work for me."

Several of the men looked at each other in confusion, many of them soon breaking into laughter. "You have to be fucking kidding me," one of the men chuckled. Blake recognized his tall façade as the cannibal, Owen Lansky. "You know who we are, right?"

"Yes, Mr. Lansky, I do. I know exactly who *you* are. Some of the others here I am unfamiliar with, but I look forward to growing acquainted with them. I know that you personally have killed over twenty men. You have a burning passion for it, as I understand. You also relish the way certain body parts taste. Am I correct, so far?"

"Yes," Owen admitted, "and I freely admitted to everything. I am not regretful about a single one of the men that I killed. I only regret getting caught. Despite even that, I would consider myself more stable than some of the freaks here." Owen leaned his head toward the man that stood next to him. Another man Blake recognized. Lester Giles.

"I am well aware that you all are the worst of the worst; completely unrepentant of your crimes," Blake revealed. "I am also aware that I have discovered a unique treatment to cure you all of such tendencies, making you hospitable to society again."

Murmurs rang out through the line of prisoners. "You're not going to lobotomize us, are you?" one prisoner asked. "Cause that shit's against our rights!"

"No," Blake assured. "I'm talking about something much more effective. In the meantime, you men will have the privilege of staying with me here in my home. You'll be locked away in your own rooms, of course, as you await the treatment. Soon, though, I am sure that you will all come to appreciate my offer."

More murmuring. A few insults were flung in the billionaire's direction. He simply responded by turning to Danner. "Danner, would you mind escorting these men inside?"

"Of course, sir." Danner turned to the men and motioned for them to follow him into the house.

"Shouldn't he have a gun?" the guard asked as he watched Danner leading the men away.

"You needn't worry. Danner is more than capable of handling himself," Blake assured.

The guard looked unconvinced. He watched the prisoners carefully as they approached the house, ready to act, if necessary.

Becca leaned over to Cliff and rattled off something in her language that Blake couldn't understand. Cliff replied, then relayed the conversation to Blake.

"She was asking about the guard's shotgun. She wasn't sure what it was," the fat man explained.

"What language was that?" the guard asked.

"Hungarian," Blake answered, reasonably certain the guard wasn't versed enough in the language to hear the small differences between the modern day variant and the older one which Becca spoke.

"What is it with you billionaires and your fondness for foreign women?" the guard asked. "You, Donald Trump...am I missing something about overseas women?"

Blake gave a courtesy laugh, but didn't reply any further.

"Doesn't matter, I guess," the guard conceded after a moment. "But I really do want to know how you convinced those congressmen to agree to your scheme here," the guard prodded after the last of the procession disappeared into the house.

This question, Blake answered. "Money, of course. Coupled with the promise that my treatment works, ridding those senators and congressman of these potential public relations powder kegs."

"How so?"

"These are some of the worst men inhabiting our prison system, yet the powers that be have managed to keep them out of the eye of the public. Multiple unsolved murders and a plethora of missing persons reports, of course, but that just stokes the flames of the public's fear, providing more funding for law enforcement; a platform all these men of power have in common toward their re-elections. Granted, it took a lot of money and influence to find out about them myself, but should other members of our illustrious society discover these profane secrets, it'd be awfully embarrassing to certain members of our government, wouldn't you agree?"

"I suppose so," the guard related.

"So, you could say that I'm simply providing our government a service by ridding them of these burdens. With the promise that they will not cause any further harm, of course. Even the vilest of our politicians don't desire unnecessary bloodshed."

"I look forward to seeing your results," the guard said. "If you can truly tame these beasts, that could go a long way toward fixing our prison system."

"What do you mean?" Blake asked, confused.

The guard looked at the billionaire and laughed. "You didn't really think these men of power were simply going to drop off the worst society has to offer at your doorstep and leave them with you unchecked, did you? They want somebody keeping an eye on you to make sure this doesn't all blow up in their faces."

Blake had been expecting this, but had hoped he'd be wrong. He wanted carte blanche when it came to dealing with these men. Still, he had a contingency plan for just such a turn of events.

"I know that you're not a simple prison guard. So, what's your name?" Blake asked.

"Special Agent Fenton," the man answered. "Grady Fenton."

"Well, Special Agent Fenton, come inside and make yourself at home," Blake invited. "It sounds like you may be staying with us for a while."

"Indeed," Grady agreed.

"Perhaps I can come to convince you to quit you current occupation and come to work for me someday," the billionaire offered. "After all of this is concluded, of course."

"Doubtful, Mr. Zellers," Grady replied. "I love my job."

"We'll see," Blake promised. "I have something to show you that may change your mind."

"I have to warn you Mr. Zellers, my job is to support corrupt people, but that doesn't mean that I'm corrupt. Bribes aren't going to work on me."

"No. No bribe," Blake assured. "Have you ever heard of the Judas Cradle?" he asked.

"Can't say that I'm familiar with it," Grady answered. A few hours later, he became *very* familiar with it.

"Amen," the haggard man spoke into the microphone. He was awfully cute for a homeless man, she thought, assuming that he had to be impoverished given the tattered and soiled state of his appearance.

Jill Holland – or "Jawbone Jill", as people had teased for as long as she could remember - was on her fifth glass of champagne for the evening. An imbibed amount far less than most of the crowd around her, while simultaneously being two glasses more than she should have allowed herself. She wasn't much of a drinker and was prone to the worst kind of hangovers, but one didn't often get a chance to attend the makings of history, so she had stayed and indulged more than she knew she should have. To have been at the unveiling of The Louvre would have been one of the most remarkable occurrences that Jill could have imagined, so there had been no way that she would have missed this opportunity. After having arrived, she found the art at Arte Blanche was a little too *modern* for her usual taste, but – if you put faith in the art world's largest publications – you'd think that the place was this generation's Louvre.

Still, she had given serious thought toward leaving early on several occasions throughout the night. The revelers around her were extremely excited by the all-night affair, but she had grown weary many hours before. She certainly wasn't hating the night, with its dueling pianos and ample conversation with individuals of shared passions, but the only reason she had stayed was the exorbitant amount she had paid for her invitation. Leaving the event early would be extremely wasteful on her part, especially with the rumored grand finale that her fellow parishioners kept hinting at. Something Blake Zellers himself was supposedly going to conduct as the sun rose over the horizon.

Blake Zellers.

She paused on her thought of the man. If she were being honest with herself, it was him more than the money that had kept her there. More accurately, the thought of a chance at catching the billionaire's eye. She had ensured that she was at the front of the crowd during his opening introduction to the Arte Blanche, then again as he gave his speech in that dreadful exhibit of his, Suffering For Art. Leave it to a *man* to dream up something so horrid. It wasn't his art that drew her to him, though. She'd heard several speeches of his on art throughout the world and she knew that he shared many of her keen desires on the subject, even if his own interpretations were lacking.

That, and she found him to be adorably cute. She couldn't exactly pinpoint what she found attractive about him — he lacked many of the physical attributes that she found appealing in men — but there was definitely something there. Again, if she were being honest with herself, she would have realized it was the money. Wealth was the great magician that could make the ugliest of men desirable to even the most beautiful of women. Jill certainly wouldn't have said that Blake was an ugly man, but her honest self would agree that he wasn't nearly physically beautiful enough for her to gawk at, as she had been doing.

In her mid-thirties and never having been married, Jill knew that she, herself, wouldn't be considered a looker neither. Sure, she'd felt the passions of men often enough, but that didn't mean anything. Men would put their dicks in anything warm and wet. She had never been seriously courted, though.

Men had often told her that she had beautiful eyes. They had complimented her body; not the tightest thing in the world, but far from obese. Looking in the mirror, she often found lots of wonderful attributes about herself. All but one: her jaw. She had cursed her chin since she had been a child. It reminded her of Jay Leno whenever she'd look at it. It just sat there, imposing on an otherwise average-to-beautiful exterior. One day, she promised herself, she was going to do something about it. An unhealthy fear of surgery – having heard too many horror stories about women being under anesthesia – had prevented her thus far. She certainly had the money for it, thanks to her successful line of clothing that she had designed, but her fear of the procedure kept her from it.

One day, though...one day she would have her bulbous jaw removed, and on that day, she would be beautiful.

"Fuck you, bitch!" the man on stage growled into the microphone, flipping the bird at somebody in the crowd.

My lord! Jawbone Jill thought in disgust. *That was entirely uncalled for.*

Jill was staring at the man on stage when she felt two hands fall on her shoulders and start kneading her muscles. Why did men always think that women were dying to have their hands on them? Jill knew that she would never know the answer to that question. Damn little boys, all of them. She reached up without looking back and slapped the hands away, letting whoever it was behind her know that she was disinterested.

"It's about goddamn time!" a voice lost from the crowd elated. She couldn't see who had spoken it, nor could she understand what had happened to elicit such a statement. It seemed to be aimed at the man onstage, but a lackluster poem, followed by rude vulgarity, hardly seemed worth praising.

Suddenly, from the same direction as the elated voice, the crowd erupted into a loud ruckus. What was happening? What was she missing? Jill rose to her tiptoes and craned her head, trying to see what had prompted the sudden unrest. Had Blake Zellers reappeared for his rumored finale? If so, he was early. Sunrise was still nearly three hours away.

Jill was still straining to see over the crowd when the two hands from behind her fell back onto her shoulders. Annoyed that the mystery man hadn't gotten the message, she spun on her heels, turning her entire body to face whatever pervert lurked behind her.

There was indeed a man back there, staring at her. He was huffing, his eyes widened further than she would have thought eyelids could spread. He was obviously scared out of his damn wits, though Jill wasn't sure why. She didn't consider herself all that intimidating of a woman, but if she had somehow scared the piss out of him, all the better. Maybe he wouldn't be so quick to violate a woman's personal space next time.

That's when she realized that the hands were still kneading away at her shoulder. In fact, as her mind replayed the last couple seconds, she realized that they had never left. She had spun so spontaneously and quickly, she knew there was no way somebody could have reacted quick enough to fling themselves around with her.

Jill twisted her neck until she could see the fingers gently digging into her flesh. She let her eyes travel up a pale, lanky arm until the limb ended. Not at a shoulder, like any arm ought to, but into a bloody red stump.

Now Jawbone Jill knew why the man behind her had seemed frightened within an inch of his life.

Jill screamed.

Before she could run, something heavy crashed into her from behind, knocking Jill to the floor. As she continued screaming, she saw that it was the scared man behind her that had knocked her over. He was lying next to her, the back of his skull now missing.

Jill screamed some more.

She began frantically pawing at the hands on her shoulders, trying to knock them away. At first, she thought she had been successful with the hand on the left as it released her, but then it came shooting forward to wrap its strong grip around her repulsive jaw. The thumb dug into the soft flesh underneath, while the four accompanying fingers wormed their way into her mouth and gripped along her lower teeth.

Jill bit down as hard as she could, feeling a warm wetness flood into her mouth. She was gnashing her teeth at the fingers when the second hand slapped down on her forehead. Its fingers crawled down her face like a sickly spider, until they were able to jam themselves into her mouth, gripping along her upper row of teeth.

Each having secured their own tight grips, the hands began pulling apart from one another.

Jill's screams ratcheted up as she felt her mouth being forced open. She swatted, pawed, scratched...damn near everything her hysterical mind could grasp, in order to rid herself of the two hands. They were strong, though....*too* strong! No matter what she did, they refused to release their grip.

The hands pulled until her mouth couldn't open any further, then they pulled some more. Jill's screams skewed from fearful to agonizing as she felt the corners of her mouth rip apart as if they were nothing more than sheets of paper. Warm blood escaped the newly-opened wounds to go flooding over her ears.

Soon, her lower jawbone started twisting under the hand's intense pressure. A loud snap told Jill that the mandible had broken free of the temporal bone in her skull. Another snap as the other side soon joined the first. With one final tug, the bodiless arm removed the jawbone from the rest of Jill's face, easily pulling apart any stray strands of sinew that remained.

Jill – left wide-eyed and choking on the rush of blood that now poured down her throat – looked on in horror as the second hand joined its partner and they worked together to free her tongue from its resting place in the liberated former half of her mouth. The slug-like muscle freed, one of the hands walked it over to a decapitated head on the floor that she had not yet noticed. The head was propped up on the stump of its neck and seemed to be smiling in anticipation.

The head opened its curved lips to let the hand stuff Jill's tongue into its mouth. It bit down in the center of muscular organ, freeing a geyser of blood to rush down his chin. The disembodied head chewed on the tough meat, its eyes rolling in delight. Once finished, the head looked into Jill's eyes and spoke. "Thank you, my dear. Most delectable."

Of course, Jill couldn't respond.

As the shapes of the panicked room began to fade in her eyes, Jill looked away from the grotesque head, not wanting such a sight to be her last. She only managed to move her gaze away a few inches before her body stopped obeying her commands. She was left looking into the dead eyes of the man that was missing the back of his head.

The last thing that Jill ever saw was her own reflection in the dead man's eye. The only thing that remained of her lower face was a ragged, gaping hole.

As the blackness took her over, Jill realized her bulbous jaw hadn't been so bad after all.

Gabe was caught up in a moment of euphoria. He was proud of himself for outsmarting that fucking bitch he knew as Becca. His eyes scanned over the crowd, feeling like a hero.

That feeling didn't last long.

"It's about goddamn time!" a voice rang out from the crowd. Gabe swerved his eyes to the source and saw that it had been spoken by Lester Giles.

Lester's wings separated from his back, springing forward with a whoosh of leather. He drove the wings' bony tips into the backs of two nearest standers-by, whose eyes had been glued on Gabe's stage. The formerly celebratory men now stood stock-still, spears of bone jutting out from several areas of their bodies.

Lester retracted his wings from the bodies, letting the dead men crumple to the floor. He wasted no time, finding another partier standing nearby and swiping his wings at the unfortunate man, instantly cleaving off large chunks of the front side of his body.

The crowd in Lester's immediate area erupted into a frenzy. The frenzy soon expanded, running through the crowd like a roaring fire as many of the other acolytes followed Lester's lead and started tearing through the gathered crowd.

"You've got to be fucking kidding me," Gabe squeaked. He found Becca, still standing in the place he had last seen her. She was no longer staring at Gabe, though. She was watching her fellow undead, her eyes wide in their own kind of horror. Gabe knew that she didn't care much about the lives being lost, she was more concerned with the loss of her newfound wealth as there was going to be no way to sweep something like this under the carpet.

Geysers of blood erupted from several patches of the crowd. A flash of bright, blue light drew Gabe's attention. Gabe looked over to see a balding man holding a patron at arm's length. No, that wasn't quite right. The man wasn't balding. He had dark hair running around the sides and back of his head, but the hairless top was a bright red patch, mottled with melted flesh. He had only dark, charred sockets where his eyeballs should have been.

The patron shook uncontrollably as a stream of electricity shot from the acolyte's blackened eyeholes. The patron's skin was blackening with a stark sizzle where the ends of the electric stream met his body. Gabe watched as the partier's eyes boiled and exploded out of their sockets, leaving a reddish-white goop dribbling down the man's face.

Blake must have had an electric chair as one of his torture scenes, Gabe realized as his attention was drawn away by another —much closer - scream.

Gabe's eyes fell on a man seemingly made of metal. His entire body gleamed of chrome as he bear-hugged another struggling patron.

"Let him go!" another man screamed at the metal-demon, beating at him to try to free the entrapped patron. The metal-man removed one arm from the ensnared patron and grabbed the protestor. He drew him in and head-butted the guy with his chrome-plated skull. The man instantly went limp, nothing left of his face but a crater of mush. The metal man let the faceless body fall to the floor and resumed his bear hug on the struggling patron. Gabe's jaw dropped as the metal man's face liquefied and blazed a hot orange. The molten metal poured out to coat the trapped man's flesh. White smoke escaped from the sizzling flesh beneath the metal coating.

Gabe had a horrific idea of what had created this creature. Blake must have covered the poor guy in molten metal. Gabe could only imagine the screams such a death would elicit.

A kooky voice from above drew Gabe's attention away from the metal man.

"Oh my...that looks like fun," Ophelia said from a window on the top floor of the glass house. Gabe could see that the floor was crammed tight with bodies, the onlookers from the lower floors having rushed up to escape the maelstrom below.

Gabe tried to scream up to them to get out of there, but his voice was still nothing more than a low hiss. By the time he thought to use the microphone he still had gripped in his hand, it was already too late. Ophelia's exterior morphed into a runny ochre and she exploded in a spray of wet shit. The geyser of feces blanketed the packed crowd, instantly dousing a majority of the people that had crammed into the room. The screams started immediately, drowning out the sizzling of flesh through the open window.

Gabe – disgusted - turned away from the scene. His eyes found the front exit, where much of the remaining crowd was pushing toward in their panic. Orange flames flickered at the door. The flames were in the form of two separate halves of a man that Gabe recognized from earlier as *Split Kindling*. The two halves were blocking the door, trying to keep the crowd at bay. Gabe noticed that the flaming creature wasn't trying to actively harm anybody, merely trying to keep the crowd away from the doors. Nevertheless, several of the patrons burst into flames as they tried to push past him, their frantic brains too panicked to care about the danger the flaming half-bodies posed.

"Daniels!" a voice called out to him. Gabe looked down to see a face he recognized approaching the stage. It was Grady Fenton – or, as Gabe thought of him: the gaping-ass man. Grady was nudging his way against the flow of the crowd as he approached Gabe.

Gabe started backing away when Grady yelled out to him, "Stop. I'm trying to help."

"Kiss my ass!" Gabe mutedly shouted in return, turning to escape.

"Goddamit, Daniels. I said stop!" Something about the way Grady said it caused Gabe to pause. As Grady managed to force his way onto the stage, he said, "We're not all evil assholes. We need to stop this!"

Gabe turned back to Grady, keeping his fists at the ready. "Why the fuck should I believe you!?"

"I'm a former Special Agent, for fuck's sake!" Grady said, as if that would convince Gabe. Seeing that it didn't, he continued. "Many of us were just unlucky, everyday people that got sucked into this shit. Same as you."

Gabe watched Grady carefully as he spoke.

"Some not so much," Grady added, shooting a look over to Lester, who was tossing a young woman into the air and spearing her on her way back down. He was definitely enjoying this shit.

"You going to help me get out of here, then?" Gabe asked. Grady had closed the gap enough to hear Gabe's strained voice.

"Jesus Christ, man. Would you grow a pair!?" Grady chastised. "Like I said, we have to stop this shit. These people are being slaughtered."

"Well, what the fuck do you suggest? I have a hard time seeing how we're going to get past that flaming fuck at the door to get these people out of here."

"Don't worry about Joel," Grady said, pointing toward *Split Kindling*. "He's only trying to keep these sadistic fucks - like Giles - from escaping and killing more people. He's not going to be able to keep them in here forever, though. *We* need to get back to *Suffering For Art*, immediately!"

"We!?" Gabe asked incredulously. "Go back to *Suffering*?" he asked, even more incredulously. "Why the fuck would *we* do that?"

"You need to get the leash back on these beasts!" Grady implored. "Say the incantation by their earthly remains and take back control."

"Fuck that and fuck you!" Gabe replied. "I don't want anything to do with these fuckers other than to send them all back to Hell!"

"You can!" Grady insisted. "Take back control, then use the book to end all of this. The spell is in there. Send us all to the afterlife...forever! God knows I'm ready to move on," Grady's eyes looks saddened during the last part, reminding Gabe of Danner's earlier confession. Gabe couldn't decide if that was a good sign or not.

"Ah, hell!" Grady swore, looking over Gabe's shoulder. "We have to hurry. Zellers' bitch is having similar thoughts."

Gabe turned to follow Grady's line of sight. He found Becca pushing her way through the crowd, heading toward the door to *Monarchy*. "You think she's trying to get back to *Suffering For Art?*" Gabe asked.

"You bet your ass she is. Say what you will, she ain't stupid. She's going to get all of this shit back under her own control, and then we're all fucked!"

Gabe considered his situation. He was responsible – albeit, unwittingly - for the carnage happening around him and he needed to end it somehow. Ceding the power back to Becca, however, wasn't going to do anybody any favors.

"Fuck!" Gabe swore in frustration. It was squeaky, but it was the loudest sound his throat had let pass since Becca's assault. "Fine," Gabe relented, "let's fucking do this then."

Grady smiled and led Gabe into the maddened crowd.

Gabe pushed his way past panicked bodies. People were scurrying in all directions, trying to get away from the charnel house that *Free Market* had become.

"Jesus!" Gabe griped, happy to hear the volume returning to his strained voice. "We're never going to get to Becca in time."

"Just keep pushing," Grady instructed. "She hasn't even made it out of the room yet. We can still catch her in time."

Gabe stretched to see over the bodies surrounding him. Grady was correct, Becca was close to the exit door, but was fighting through a particularly thick bundle of people as they pawed at their nearest exit from this hell.

Gabe shouldered his way through a tight knitting of bodies in front of him. He bent low, ready to employ a football move on the next line of patrons when something barreled into them, knocking them all out of his way. Gabe's hair tickled him and he got a whiff of ozone.

"What the fuck!?" Gabe shouted, startled backward. He looked down at where the cleared bodies had landed and saw that they had been bowled over by another body, this one shaking and sparking. Bright flashes of electricity jumped off the shaking man, coursing into the bodies that lay under him. "That electric guy's victims conduct electricity too?"

"Sparks charges them like a capacitor and uses them like electric grenades," Grady confirmed. "We have to keep moving," he urged, pushing Gabe forward.

"The guy's name is Sparks?" Gabe asked, pushing aside a couple that were holding each other tight in terror as they watched the same horrific scene.

"His actual surname. It's what gave Zellers the electric chair idea," Grady said, confirming Gabe's suspicion as he navigated around the frightened couple.

Gabe stepped over a body he at first thought was dead, until the body rolled under his feet. Gabe looked down and his ears began picking up muffled screams escaping from the body. Looking at the man's face, Gabe nearly wretched. Whoever this man had been, he sure as fuck wasn't going to have an open casket at his funeral. All that was left of his face was a pool of molten flesh in the shape of a handprint. His lips had been melted together, the source of hi muffled screams. His eyelids were similarly fused. There was nothing at all left of the man's nose, other than a gaping hole covered in runny flesh.

Looking at the poor sap rolling on the floor, Gabe pictured Becca's hand melting at Titus Lichtner's touch. Gabe increased his pace, knowing the *Brazen Bull* was near, and he definitely didn't want to run into *that* guy.

Next, Gabe tried pushing by a group of men fighting each other. Neither of them were Arte Blanche staff. Gabe assumed that, in their frenzy, something had provoked one of the already high-strung men, causing the outbreak of violence.

Gabe chose to ignore the scene, attempting to push his way past, when a fist struck his mouth. "Get away from me!" the man attached to the fist screamed.

The man sent a flurry of punches at Gabe, which he narrowly avoided. Seeing as how the man wasn't going to let him pass, Gabe did what he had to do and sent his fist into the man's kidneys, instantly causing his attacker to collapse to his knees. Gabe followed up with an uppercut to the man's chin, and the man fell backward, knocked unconscious to the floor.

Perhaps he'd be safer down there, Gabe hoped.

"Come on," Grady said, emerging from a cluster of bodies, having come back for Gabe after getting too far ahead. Gabe pushed through the next cluster and followed.

Through the turmoil of *Free Market*, Gabe was surprised he was able to single out any source of screaming, but there were some particularly shrill ones escaping the glass house above him. He looked up to see that the third floor was now completely consumed in brown muck, looking like a New York City sewer line had exploded within. Bodies crammed the glass stairwell in a mad attempt to escape the third floor, down to the second. Many of them were already covered in splotches of the brown filth, their faces betraying the agony they felt as Ophelia's acidic shit did its work.

Others had seemingly escaped unscathed. Any relief they may have felt was short-lived, however. A flood of the murky excrement soon rushed through the stairwell, exploding out onto the second floor. All of the third floor refugees disappeared into the immediate surge of the brown river, which tapered off halfway across the room to settle as an ankle high puddle. Those not having been caught in the full wrath of the downpour immediately began screaming as the muck settled around their feet. Several tried hopelessly running away, but the acidic shit performed its nasty magic quickly and they never made it more than a few steps before their feet were too desiccated to carry them any further. One by one, they stumbled and fell into the viscous sea.

Gabe stared in awe at the scene. Ophelia's lake of shit had grown impossibly large, each body consumed adding to its mass. Gabe pictured the title creature from the movie *The Blob*. He turned away from the glass house with heightened dread and pushed through another thick cluster of bodies.

Gabe emerged in a small clearing. He attempted to quickly hop through, into the next tightly packed cluster, when the momentary gap quickly disappeared as a group of nearby bodies swayed backward, knocking him off to the side. Gabe's feet caught on an obstruction on the floor and he went tumbling to the ground.

Gabe looked past his feet to see what had tripped him up. His eyes landed on a body of a dead woman who appeared to have had the entire lower half of her face ripped away. His stomach turned at the sight, but even worse was what lie on top of her. Two disembodied arms held a decapitated head between their hands. They were holding the gore-drenched head face down, allowing it to dig its teeth into the side of the dead woman's neck. As he watched, the hands turned the gnawing head up so its eyes connected with Gabe's own.

"Lurch?" Gabe asked, sickened and confounded.

"Hello, Mr. Daniels," Owen greeted, strips of the woman's flesh dangling from between his teeth. "I must say, Blake Zellers has outdone himself with the Arte Blanche. The menu here is fantastic, wouldn't you say?" Lurch gave Gabe a sickly smile, then the hands wheeled his face downward, his teeth going back to work on the woman's tattered neck.

Gabe felt bile rise in the back of his throat as he scrambled back to his feet. He caught sight of Grady ahead of him, already pushing through the next cluster of bodies. He followed, hurrying to catch up.

"Shit!" Gabe heard Grady curse when he caught up to the man. "She's made it to the door."

Gabe looked up. He couldn't see Becca through the crowd, but he could see the top of the door to *Monarchy* as it inched open. It seemed that she was struggling to open it against the mass of bodies pressing against it.

"Goddammit! We have to hurry!" Grady shouted.

They had arrived at the back corner of the house. Maybe fifteen more feet remained between Becca and themselves. With as much of the crowd that occupied the remaining space, Gabe knew it'd be a hard-fought fifteen feet. He pushed hard to get through the thick crowd. He wasn't being nice about it anymore. Gabe grabbed one man's collar and yanked as mercilessly as he could, dragging him out of the way. He jabbed the next with his right elbow, and the next with his left, easily gaining another foot. He tried the elbow trick again, striking something cold and hard, causing a flashing pain of protest to shoot up his arm.

"What the fuck!?" Gabe shouted, rubbing at this elbow. When he looked up to see what his elbow had hit, he saw the metal man turning around to face him. His chrome hands were clamped together, some kind of goop stuck between them. As Gabe's eyes traveled down from the clasped hands, h saw that there was a human body dangling beneath. That's when Gabe realized the metal man had just squished somebody's head as if his hands were a trash compacter.

"Daniels?" The metal man asked, clearly surprised to see him.

"Fuck me," Gabe groaned as the metal man's hands released the pancaked mass. He quickly snapped his chrome hands around Gabe's head. Gabe struggled but couldn't free himself from the acolyte's grip. He was lifted off his feet, courtesy of the unforgiving vice around his skull.

The metal man was smiling as he increased the pressure, blurring Gabe's entire world out of existence.

48

As his vision swam, Gabe tried fighting back by driving a fist into the metal man's face. The only thing the move accomplished was the feeling of a knuckle shattering in Gabe's hand.

"Get off him, Isaacs!" Gabe heard from somewhere nearby. Grady popped up in between the metal man's arms and pushed them apart. The pressure at Gabe's skull immediately ceased and he fell to the ground. "We're trying to stop Zeller's bitch from taking back control of all of us. Come and help us," Grady tried pleading with the metal man.

The metal man – Isaacs, as Grady had called him – clearly burned with anger when his eyes set on Grady. "You're the one that delivered us to that sick son of a bitch!" Isaacs accused. "I thought the men in that bus were fucked up, but that rich prick had us all beat."

"I'm sorry about that," Grady tried, "but he was supposed to have a cure for you all. I had no idea what that psychotic fuck's idea of a cure was! He killed me, too!"

Isaacs stared silently at Grady for a moment, then, "You may be able to regenerate like the rest of us, but I'm still going to enjoy feeling your skull pulverized between my two hands."

Grady turned back to Gabe, his face having the look of a man who has just come to a tough decision. "Keep going, Daniels. Stop that bitch!" he instructed.

Before Gabe could protest, Grady sprung high into the air, narrowly avoiding the clash of Isaacs' hands as he clapped them together with incredible force. Gabe watched as – in mid-air – Grady backside ripped open into its wide, cavernous form, and arced down onto Isaac's metal-plated skull. The metal man's head was instantly consumed by the gaping maw of Grady's ass.

Jesus Christ! That shit is straight-up, fucking weird, Gabe thought, watching the scene play out.

Unable to see with his head completely consumed by Grady's ass, Isaacs stumbled around, his hands pawing at Grady's legs.

"Move, Daniels!" Grady urged as Isaacs stumbled into the rear wall of the glass house. A sharp crack snapped through the air when the metal body hit the house, leaving behind a spider-webbing of fractured glass on the otherwise transparent wall.

Gabe turned to look toward his destination. He saw the door had finally opened enough to let somebody through. The blockade in front of the door thinned out as several bodies poured through it. It cleared enough to allow Gabe a quick glimpse of Becca as she squirmed her way through the opening. Their eyes met briefly. Becca smiled at him and threw up her middle finger in his direction. She slammed the door behind her, just as another group of panicked patrons crashed into it, trying desperately to escape.

Gabe resumed pushing through the crowd, both of his hands now aching in protest of their various injuries. It took him a couple more minutes, but he finally neared the last group huddled by the exit. As he arrived, a blur of motion streaked into the tightly-packed mass of bodies. A fountain of blood immediately followed.

"What the fuck!?" Gabe asked, reeling back from the sudden blood storm.

Tattered patrons collapsed to the floor, allowing Gabe to see the exit door in its entirety. Unfortunately, it also allowed him to see a blood-soaked avian form standing between him and the door.

Lester's eyes met Gabe's with a smile. "Daniels...I was hoping to run into you."

Gabe had no response other than a play on the old Bugs Bunny cartoons. "Suffering fuck-otash," he mumbled, as he stepped forward to presumptive death.

Lester met Gabe's advance with a furious spin like a freakish Tasmanian devil, his wing tips slicing dangerously through the air.

Gabe knew a direct assault had no chance of succeeding against such a defense, but he had to try if he was going to get through the door. He looked around for anything he could use to aid in an attack. His eyes landed on one of the shredded bodies at his feet.

There was no fucking way this was going to work, Gabe though as he hefted the remains of the body up into his arms. He held the cadaver forward at arm's length and began his charge toward the deadly maelstrom.

The tactic fell miserably short. As soon as the hoisted body entered the arc of Lester's wings, the flesh was quickly sheaved away, turning into flying chunks and splatter as surely as if it had wandered into the blades of a lawnmower. Gabe reeled back as the body disintegrated in front of him, but not before one of Lester's wing tips nicked his wrapped hand, tearing away a good inch of flesh between his ring and middle fingers.

"Goddammit!" Gabe shouted – a loud, hearty sound, even if it did still crackle quite a bit.

A crack of thunder roared over the panicked screams of the crowd, instantly drawing both Gabe's attention. The metal man was still struggling to remove Grady from atop his head. They again came away from the base wall of the glass house, this time leaving behind a large, splintering crack that ran as far up as the third floor. Another crack extended horizontally, travelling half the depth of the house until it eventually ceased upon arriving at the rear corner. Like watching a sped up version of a large river erode the land, several side streams formed, dangerously splitting the entire left pane of the house's first floor wall.

Isaacs spun a couple times, still battering Grady's legs with his arms. The former special agent's legs now hung limply, having had all the bones shattered within by the metal man's reinforced blows. The pair once again crashed into the base of the glass wall. Same as before; a thunder erupted from where they collided, followed by a crack spreading upward and outward.

The whole of the crowd had frozen, now staring at the scene playing out at the glass house. Even Lester had ceased his deadly Tasmanian devil impression and stared on in morbid curiosity.

Isaacs spun a couple more times, then launched himself backward. The duo hit against the front corner of the glass house, barreling right through it in a shower of broken glass. The entire house shifted a fraction of an inch to the left. The edges of the cracked glass turned white as the fractures' rims broke apart under the new pressure forced upon them by the destruction of the supporting corner. A loud groan of protest escaped the house, filling the air of *Free Market*.

At this point, even Ophelia had stopped her rampage within the house. The top two floors were now nothing but lakes of brown shit and she had been working her way down the stairwell to the first floor. The flow of feces in the stairwell suddenly stopped and coalesced into a cylindrical form which rose from the transparent steps, reminding Gabe of the worm-like water shifter in the movie *The Abyss*. The bulbous tip of the worm swayed back and forth, as if examining the damage to the wall.

Gabe disparagingly knew what was about to happen. He only had seconds to act. Keeping his left foot planted, he pirouetted, sweeping his right leg low along the floor. His ankle impacted Lester's own, knocking the distracted abomination off of his feet. Before Lester could react, Gabe propelled himself into the air, leaping over Lester's splayed body. He landed at the exit door and punched in the code. It took less than a second for the lock to disengage, but within that second, the mounting pressure on the lower left well proved too much for the damaged glass pane to handle. The entire wall exploded into a spray of glass. Any person unfortunate enough to be standing nearby was instantly shredded by the sharp shards.

As soon as Gabe heard the lock release, he yanked open the door and dove sideways through the opening. As he passed through, his peripheral vision caught two things. One was Lester regaining his feet. The second was the glass house tilting to its left with a monstrous creaking until it came crashing down to the floor. Gabe's legs cleared the open doorway just as a storm of shattered glass exploded through the hole.

Gabe hit the ground and instantly rolled onto his back. He looked at the thousands of glass shards that had been thrust through the doorway. Some were covered in glistening red, some brown. A large painting on the wall opposite the door had been shredded by the glass into unrecognizable shreds of canvas. Gabe's heart dropped as he realized that all of the people trapped inside had undoubtedly met a similar fate as the house came crashing down.

One positive was that Becca's beasts had probably met a similar fate. Gabe wasn't sure how long he had until they reformed, but he figured the resulting carnage had bought him a few moments, at least, to get to Becca and end this whole thing before she had backup.

The silence in the hall was eerie, especially after the previous maelstrom of screams and whimpers. Gabe picked himself up off the floor, ready to make his way to *Suffering For Art* to cross his last task off the list. As he stood, a woman's whimpers traveled through the doorway from *Free Market*.

Fuck! Somebody was still alive out there!

Gabe stepped to the doorway to see who had survived. He didn't have time to personally help them just yet, but he figured maybe he could give a little advice. He wasn't sure exactly what. Maybe, "Don't move until I get back. Oh, and stay away from all that brown stuff that smells like it just came from the Taco Bell version of that *Super Size Me* guy."

Hey…at least it was something.

Gabe stood in the doorway and found the whimpering woman standing in a doorway to one of *Free Market*'s side exhibits. The door had been broken through, probably in the crowd's frenzy. The woman must have been inside the exhibit, protected by the wall when the house had come crashing down.

Gabe was about to call out for her when a brown tendril whipped out from the muck-covered pile of glass in front her. The tendril reminded Gabe of a cartoon frog's tongue – if the frog's tongue had been made of rotting human feces. The feces-phalange wrapped around the woman's legs several times. The sizzling had already started by the time she was pulled through the glass and into the underlying sea of shit.

"Fuck!" Gabe cursed, feeling helpless. He began to turn away when a flash of pain erupted in his leg. When he looked down to find the source, he saw a spear of bone jutting out from a thick pile of glass just inside the doorway. The bone ended inside his leg, about halfway up the calf.

Gabe twisted away, snapping the bone spear off in his leg. He stumbled and fell backward onto the floor. Shards of glass exploded off the ground as something large burst out from under it and barreled its way through the open doorway.

Gabe looked up in horror to see Lester, rolling around in agony. He was covered int eh brown of Ophelia's shit. Most of his flesh was missing, leaving a snarling skeleton in its place. Sizzling sounds escaped him as his flesh attempted to grow back, only to be once again consumed by the acidic shit.

Lester didn't even seem to notice Gabe. He was rolling along the floor, screaming in agony as he tried to get the brown muck off of him. His wings – which were now nothing more than jagged bone, the fleshy part having been torn up by the glass and further consumed by the shit – scraped along his own body as he desperately tried to flick away all of the chunky slop.

Lester seemed busy with his own issues, so Gabe decided to let him be and go after Becca. Besides, he didn't want to get anywhere near the flesh-eating shit that covered that maniac. First, though, Gabe had to remove the rib from his calf. Thankfully, it hadn't gone all the way through. Gabe knew it wouldn't be pleasant, but he thought he'd still be able to move on the injured leg. He gipped the exposed bone, counted to three in his head, and pulled. The rib came out, but Gabe couldn't hold back the painful groan that the act elicited.

Drawn by the sound, Lester halted his thrashing and looked through his one remaining eye at Gabe. The other socket was now nothing more than a pool of Ophelia's shit. "Daniels!" he squealed.

"Fuck my life," Gabe moaned.

"I'm going to fucking kill you!" Lester screamed, starting after Gabe. He couldn't fly, nor could he walk on his fleshless legs. Instead, he crawled forward on the tips of his wings; a demented, bony spider.

Gabe thrust himself to his feet, but went crashing back down when the foot of his newly-injured leg planted into the tile floor. The impact had been too great and Gabe hadn't been prepared for the pain that followed.

As Gabe fell back to the floor, something fell from his pocket and clanked against the tile. He looked over at the object and saw its polished surface gleaming back at him.

It was the Bic lighter he had found in *Midnight In The Garden Of Good And Evil*.

Gabe snatched the lighter up, flipped open the top, and struck the igniter. He smiled as the orange flame appeared, flickering atop the wick.

With a newfound confidence: "It must really be *shitty* to be you right now," Gabe joked.

Gabe cringed at his own joke, admitting to himself that he would never have made it as a writer, but didn't let that stop him from throwing the lighter at Lester. The winged abomination tried to move out of the lighter's path, but Gabe's quarterback arm proved true, the flame caressing the methane-producing excrement lining Lester's skeleton.

Lester instantly burst into a ball of flame, what remained of his withered form exploding out into thousands of fiery bits.

"Fuck yeah!" Gabe made a fist and pumped his arm in victory. After the self-congratulation, he picked himself up off the floor, careful to not aggravate his injured leg. He bent down and snatched the broken rib off the ground. He had great plans for his newly-acquired weapon.

It was time to finally finish this nightmare, once and for all.

Gabe limped his way around the southwest corner of Monarchy, headed toward *Suffering For Art*. More importantly, headed toward that bitch, Becca.

"I'm going to end that fucking bitch!" Gabe mumbled to himself, wincing with every step of his damaged leg.

As he arrived at the door to A Morsel's Journey, Gabe noticed two things. One, that the light above the door flared a discouraging red. He wasn't going to be cutting through that way.

The second thing he noticed was an unmoving body of a man sitting with his back propped against the door. He was clearly dead, though Gabe wasn't sure from what. The man was sitting near a puddle of bloody vomit. His chin and lips were covered in bits of the same. The man's dead eyes were bloodshot and Gabe could see many of his veins had darkened underneath the skin. The veins had grown damn near black in color.

Gabe didn't recognize the man and assumed it was one of the few that had made it through the exit door from *Free Market* when Becca had made her escape. He passed the body and kept moving. There was nothing Gabe could do for the man anyway. He silently hoped the other people that had escaped were holed up somewhere, having avoided a similar fate. Maybe *A Morsel's*

Journey. That'd possibly explain why the door was locked. Smart move on their part, if that was the case.

Gabe rounded the northwest corner and saw another body splayed out further down the hall, near the direct entrance to *Suffering For Art*. Gabe took a couple more waddling steps toward the door when it struck him that he was likely already too late to stop her from reciting the enchantment. Still, he should have enough time to at least fuck up her pretty face before her demon squad managed to piece themselves back together. That'd at least feel good, if nothing else. Life's little victories. Besides, it wasn't like he could just walk out the front door now. Not with *Free Market*'s man-eating lake of liquid shit.

Gabe let his fingers travel over the form of the lighter in his pocket. Maybe he could just throw the flame into *Free Market* and blow his way out of the building? He considered it for a moment, then pushed the idea to the back of his mind. He figured the more likely outcome would be him blowing the entire building to hell, himself included.

Another idea popped into Gabe's mind. He may be too late to stop Becca from claiming back all the dead souls, but, he remembered, there was one dead body *not* in *Suffering For Art*.

Gabe spun on his good leg and stared at the entrance to *Wanders Never Cease*.

Gabe smiled. "I got you now, bitch." Becca may already own all of the other souls, but if Gabe owned her's, he could still end this entire nightmare the easy way.

Gabe waddled to the door with newfound purpose. He pushed it open, stepped inside, and...

...was stopped as Becca appeared from the other side and wrapped him in a tight embrace. Before he could react, she had planted her lips against his and ground them together with passionate fervor.

Gabe was ashamed to admit that his lips weren't the only parts of his body that stirred at her kiss.

After getting past his initial shock, Gabe grabbed Becca's shoulders – eliciting a stark protest from both his injured hands – and shoved her away from him, holding her out at arm's length. "What the fuck do you think you're doing?" he asked her with ire.

"I wanted a kiss," she answered simply, as if it were the most natural request in the world. "I knew that you'd come here – it really was the best plan, you know - so I waited. After a quick stop in *Suffering For Art*, of course."

In a sudden motion, Gabe clutched her throat with his least injured hand, and squeezed. "I'm not in a making-out kinda mood, you psychotic cunt!" Gabe spat as he constricted her airway.

Becca just smiled at him, her eyes gleaming with satisfaction. She even managed to squeak a small laugh through her tightened throat.

"What's so funny, bitch!" Gabe asked, his arm shaking with the fury he was using to fuel his grip. Then, suddenly, that same arm twitched. In fact, his whole body twitched, his muscles seemingly going into some kind of frenetic spasm. A violent contraction forced his fingers straight, unwillingly letting Becca's throat out of their grasp.

"What the fuck is happening to me?" Gabe asked, feeling his body betraying him. His wrath had been replaced by an equal helping of horror.

"That would be my kiss," Becca beamed. "More specifically, the poison the kiss contained, which now streams through your body."

Gabe remembered Danner's explanation of Amytis' death. She had been poisoned by Daniel. It made a certain fucked-up kind of sense that her afterlife ability would be to spread that poison to others.

"Just be happy that I held back during our first kiss. This toxin is very powerful in its natural state, and I assure you that it hurts like a motherfucker," Becca explained. "The poison that inflicts you, however, is completely controlled by me. I can make it hurt more..."

The agony in Gabe body intensified as proof of her point.

"...or hurt less."

The pain mercifully backed down, becoming just a dull thud in his veins.

"I can keep you alive for weeks, or kill you in seconds," Becca added. "Though, before you ask, I cannot remove it from your body once infected. That is the only limitation I have discovered, in case you are still planning to take control of me and force me to do it."

That had indeed been Gabe's next plan, thought up during her little speech. Well fuck...that didn't leave him a lot of options.

"Now," Becca continued, "let's talk about how you really want to die. The poison is wonderfully effective, but wouldn't play well as a scene in *Suffering For Art*, I'm afraid."

Gabe stared into her eyes for a moment, trying his best to come up with another plan. He was certainly fucked, but maybe he could still accomplish something before he died.

"I know exactly how I want to die," Gabe answered.

Becca looked pleasantly surprised by his admission, obviously expecting him to take longer to come to terms with everything. "Good. Let's hear it," she prodded.

"I want to go out with a bang."

Becca looked confused by his answer.

"The same bang that brings down this entire fucking place!"

Before Becca could respond by amping up his pain again, Gabe brought up the rib he still held and jammed its sharp tip through her jaw, twisting it up into her brain. Her eyes rolled backward and her warm blood poured down the rib, soaking Gabe's hand. He held her like that for a moment, then let her body fall.

Gabe felt his agony increase as the poison in his system amped up to its natural level, no longer being held back by Becca's control. Gabe fought through the pain to walk out into the long passageway. He moved as fast as he possibly could with his bum leg. He needed to get to *Free Market* before Becca recovered. Or before any of those other asshole monsters in there could do the same. Gabe knew he wouldn't win a fight with any of them at this point. He was too weak and broken, fighting against the ravages of his body.

Gabe pulled the lighter from his pocket. He struck the igniter and let the orange flame motivate him on his mission. The last mission he would ever attempt.

"Fuck you, Arte Blanche! Fuck you!" Gabe shouted at the walls as he rounded the southwest corner.

Ahead, Gabe saw that Lester still lay in many pieces, most of which still held their own golden flicker. The flaming pieces were scooting toward one another, but slowly enough that Gabe knew Lester wouldn't pose a threat to his mission.

He arrived at the entrance to *Free Market* and looked through the door. He saw that Ophelia's lake of shit was still spread across the entirety of the floor.

Perfect!

Gabe cocked his lighter-bearing arm back, ready to throw his final pass.

Unfortunately, that pass never happened. Gabe was quarterback-sacked by his own body, his own muscles suddenly and violently seizing on themselves. The lighter fell from Gabe's hand to land harmlessly on the floor. Gabe collapsed to his knees, lost in an agony unlike any he had ever felt before.

Footsteps could be heard rounding the southwest corner. Gabe looked over in their direction and saw Becca, holding the bloody rib in her hand.

Goddamn, she looks pissed! Gabe thought.

Good!

Becca stomped over to where Gabe knelt in pain.

"Nice try!" she said when she arrived. She let the rib drop from her hand and knelt next to Gabe to look directly into his eyes.

"Let's try this again," she said. "You *are* going to die, Gabe Daniels. Either now, from the poison, or later, by some other means. Make your choice."

Gabe's thoughts were hard to discern in his head, the pain was so great. He nodded, anything to cause her to loosen up the poison's deadly grip.

She did. The pain lessened. Not much, but any improvement at all was like angels singing in Gabe's ears.

"Now, how do you want to die? How do you want to be remembered?" Becca asked.

Gabe was beaten. Too tired to fight anymore. So, he told her.

This time, she agreed.

EPILOGUE

Martha Hawkins had been awaiting this day for months. She had scored two tickets to the grand reopening of Arte Blanche on the radio and had given the other to her best friend – and reigning bridge champion at their local Daughters of the American Revolution chapter – Ruth.

Martha's husband had passed away a couple years ago, so she had the extra ticket to give away to whomever she chose. Not that her husband would have gone anyway; he had never been into art. Though, looking around, many of the other patrons there weren't really into art, either. It just so happened that this gallery was the hot place to be right now. Tragedy seemed to always beget equal parts intrigue and fascination. And Martha knew – hell, the entire *country* knew - that Arte Blanche had one helluva tragedy to its name.

It had now been nearly a year since the original grand opening and the terrible accident that had occurred on that horrible night. An entire house made of glass had collapsed inside *Free Market*, killing everybody in attendance. The incident had made national headlines and sparked outrage among the American citizenry. So much so, that Blake Zellers had held a news conference, announcing that he would be leaving his art gallery, and a majority of his wealth, to his new wife, Becca Zellers. After that, he had seemingly disappeared from the public, rumors indicating that he was hiding out in his father's former estate in Rhode Island.

Becca Zellers had become the face of the Arte Blanche and she had kept it shut down for the last year as the gallery underwent repairs, also allowing the lawsuits to play out as well. Martha had heard that the enormous amount of money awarded from those suits was paid out of the funds that Blake Zellers had kept to himself. Martha sure hoped that was the case. Becca seemed like a legitimately nice lady – she had been involved in several charitable events, even having started her own charity for children with cancer - and didn't deserve to have such burdens land on her. Besides, it wasn't her fault that that son of a bitch Blake Zellers hadn't bothered to ensure better construction of his glass house, despite the multiple billions of dollars he had lying around. Martha agreed that he should pay every penny of those lawsuits. It served him right.

As far as the Arte Blanche itself went, Becca Zellers had done a marvelous job rebuilding. The glass house was back, built much more sturdily this time around. If people were concerned about another accident, they sure didn't seem to show it. The house was already rented out until far into the next year.

Martha wouldn't be staying there, though. That was for sure.

Martha had been enjoying the other exhibits Arte Blanche had to offer. She wasn't particularly fond of the one she was in now – the much-hyped *Suffering For Art* – but she begrudgingly understood its fascination to stronger-stomached types.

"Absolutely dreadful," Ruth commented from Martha's side. They were both looking at a model of a man who had his back carved open with his ribs and skin forming grotesque wings.

"Blood Eagle, the placard says," Martha relayed to Ruth. "Who comes up with this crap?" she added in disgust.

"Is there anything I can help you two ladies with?" The voice came from behind Martha and she spun around to respond.

"We're fine. Thank you," Martha said to the nice-looking lady in the white tuxedo. Her name tag read: Ophelia.

"Please let me know if I can be of any assistance," Ophelia said with a bright, beaming smile.

"Oh...Oh!" Ruth suddenly exclaimed, her hand spasmodically slapping against Martha's shoulder. "Is that Becca Zellers?" she asked before Ophelia could turn away. She pointed toward the end of the exhibit scenes where she was sure she had just spotted the billionaire heiress talking with some man in a white tuxedo.

"Indeed it is," Ophelia confirmed.

"Do you think it would be okay if my friend and I met her?" Ruth asked, clearly excited by the prospect.

"Of course, ma'am. I will gladly walk you over to her." Ophelia gestured for the two ladies to move precede her.

Martha and Ruth were both shaking with giddiness as they approached Becca Zellers. Neither of them had ever met a celebrity before.

As they neared, Martha caught part of the conversation Becca was having with the white-tuxedoed man.

"You had me, you know? You could have just uttered the enchantment after stabbing me with the rib."

"Yeah, well...it's no secret that I can be an idiot sometimes," the man admitted, looking extremely depressed by whatever he was talking about.

"Ms. Zellers, these nice ladies wanted to have a word with you," Ophelia interrupted, introducing Martha and Ruth to the illustrious billionaire.

Becca Zellers turned from her conversation and looked at the two new arrivals. "Hello ladies. How are you two enjoying the Arte Blanche?"

Despite not having set foot in a school for over fifty years, Martha felt like a giddy school girl again. "It's fantastic," she blathered in response.

"I love *all* the work you do," Ruth added, in a similar state to Martha.

"Why, thank you!" Becca beamed, looking particularly grateful to the women for their compliments. Becca pointed at the man standing next to her and said, "My colleague and I were actually just admiring the newest addition to this exhibit. Have you ladies seen it?" Becca turned to point at the scene behind her.

Martha looked the scene over. Like the others in *Suffering For Art*, she was not particularly impressed by it, but she wasn't going to let Becca Zellers know that. "It's wonderful," she said instead.

The scene showed a man standing inside of what looked like an old iron sarcophagus, only the inside was lined with spikes. The spikes extended through the model body of the man in a most gruesome fashion.

Martha recognized the man modeled as the same man that Becca Zellers had been talking to. The man noticed her staring at him and spoke up. "Yes, that is me in there. I'm as proud of it as I could hope to be," he admitted, though there was something about his tone that caused Martha to doubt the man's sincerity. "Trust me when I say that there is no more-fitting way for me to be forever preserved in the annals of history."

Martha caught the man's smirk as he said the word *annals*. She was a bit taken back by the inappropriate way that he had mispronounced it, but held her contempt in check due to the presence of their revered hostess.

Instead, she investigated the placard standing in front of this new addition to the exhibit.

It read:

Iron Maiden. Model: Gabe Daniels.

FINIS

AFTERWORD

Oh, what fun! If you are reading this, then I assume that you have finished Arte Blanche and that you cared enough to see what the author had to say about it. If you haven't read it, then I highly suggest that you stop reading at this point and go back to read the novel before continuing on. Spoilers will be present and I would hate to ruin the fun for you.

Arte Blanche started off as a simple idea that formed in my head after my wife dragged me to an art gallery near downtown San Diego. Rest assured, that art gallery was nothing like the Arte Blanche, at least in the horrors that the latter possesses. Walking through that art gallery astounding me, nevertheless. Just the weirdness of some of the exhibits. The kookiness, if you will. One such exhibit was very similar to *Beauty Through Rage*, for instance. I found myself continuously rolling my eyes at what people consider art.

That's not to say that I didn't enjoy the gallery – I actually enjoyed it quite a lot – but that didn't change my fascination with the strangeness of the place. I knew that creating my own art gallery would be incredibly fun. I was in the middle of writing SIXTEEN YEARS AGO – the epic-length novel that has plagued me for the last couple years – but I knew I needed to take a break from that to explore this fascinating new world that came to me as I wandered through that art gallery with my wife.

As soon as we arrived home, I made a bee-line for my computer and instantly knocked out the first chapter. More-or-less, exactly as you read in the previous pages. I showed that first chapter to my wife and we were both instantly hooked. It was then time to create the Arte Blanche.

Originally, seeing as how it was supposed to be a temporary distraction from SIXTEEN YEARS AGO, I had planned on this being another novella, similar in length to CHAPLAIN. However, as I wrote chapter-after-chapter, new ideas constantly bombarding me, I knew that the gallery was growing to the point that a mere novella couldn't contain it. The result was the 441 pages you've read before this.

Early on, I knew this novel was going to be my ode to Eighties Horror; filled with gore, camp, and even the perfect amount (hopefully) of cheesiness. If you enjoyed this book, and haven't seen some of the Eighties classics like: Return of the Living Dead, Re-Animator, Killer Klowns From Outer Space, The Blob, Night of the Creeps, Hellraiser, Society (this one is largely unknown, but highly worth it), and The Nightmare on Elms Streets (1,2,3, & 5; the others are *overly* cheesy), then do yourself a favor and go watch them. You won't be disappointed. And those are just the tip of the iceberg when it comes to Eighties horror. If you're new to the cinematic pleasures of that decade, I envy you.

One last note before I go. In the Babylon chapter later in the novel, much is mentioned about the "powers" Amytis has over men. It wasn't explained much here and ultimately didn't matter, as Gabe's night of horrors went on. That was intentional on my part. To learn more about Amytis' special power, you'll need to read Sixteen Years Ago when it comes out. While she doesn't feature in the upcoming novel herself, the powers she possesses are front and center. Fear not, however; Amytis/Elizabeth/Becca will be back in a later novel. I have great plans for her further down the road.

Anyway, I hope that you enjoyed Arte Blanche and I look forward to entertaining you again. Don't forget to rate Arte Blanche on Amazon and Goodreads!

-DAVE

Read on for the bonus short story:

THE BLACK RING

|

The Black Ring was originally released as an exclusive short story; released in six parts, over six days, on David W Coons Jr's Facebook page.

For information on David W Coons Jr, his upcoming books, author-created grotesque imagery, and even the occasional short story like this, go to Facebook and follow him now.

https:www.facebook.com/davidcoonsauthor
|

Beep

The familiar sound of the barcode scanner rang in Brent's ear.

Beep

"Have you had this brand yet, sir?" the cashier asked, holding up a box of Dragon's Breath cereal.

"Uhh…no," Brent answered, caught off guard by the cashier's break from his mundane scan-slide-scan routine. "They're for my son. He saw a commercial for them and begged me to buy him some the next time I was at the grocery store."

Brent remembered the commercial featuring some sort of small dragon that blew rainbows out its mouth as opposed to searing flame. He had rolled his eyes at the overly-cartoonish advertisement, but apparently it had been enough to entice his son Caleb into a beggar's fit.

"Keep an eye on the little guy," the cashier warned. "I hear there's a new fad out there where kids are using this stuff to make marijuana edibles. You know, what you guys used to call reefer."

Brent sized up the kid behind the register and decided that the young man was most likely speaking autobiographically. He would have wagered a fair sum that this kid had recently made the very treat that he was warning Brent about.

"I'm pretty sure 'reefer' went out of style before even my time. We just called it pot," Brent corrected. "…or maybe Mary Jane," he added, an early-nineties Tom Petty song suddenly springing up in his head.

"Cool," was the kid's simple reply as he scanned the last couple items on the conveyor belt. "That'll be $68.42."

Brent winced at the sum, appalled at how much the cost of groceries had increased in recent years. Still, he shelled out the cash and grabbed the two bags of groceries off the counter.

The walk out to his car was brief. The parking lot – like the grocery store itself – wasn't large. Situated at the end of a comparatively small town, the surrounding woods encroached against the property on two sides; the other two lined by the highway and a skeletal building that once been a video rental store. The foliage had grown so close that he had to squeeze the bumper on his black Ford Mustang convertible into a tight gap lined with stray branches of nearby shrubbery to pull fully into his parking spot.

Brent stopped at the rear of his vehicle and placed the grocery bags on the ground to free up his hands. He dug into his pocket and withdrew a crowded keyring which he used to open his trunk. Brent snatched the two bags off the cracked asphalt and unceremoniously placed them in the trunk. Careful to avoid smashing his fingers, Brent slammed the trunk closed.

I really hate going to the store, Brent thought as he entered the car. He started the engine and backed out of the parking spot. *That's strange...I don't remember parking over a puddle*, Brent thought as he shifted into drive and started the short journey home.

******

The first bag emptied and put neatly away, Brent dug the cereal box out from the second grocery sack. As he withdrew it from the paper bag, a black blur came tumbling from the bag. Whatever the object was, it arced downward to the kitchen floor, taking a bounce on the tile, and then rolled for a moment until it hit the bottom of the counter. It spun in place like a dreidel before eventually falling to its side where it finally laid still.

"What the hell?" Brent asked out loud, though nobody was in the room to hear him. He placed the cereal box on the counter and leaned down to examine the mysterious object.

"I'll be damned," Brent wowed.

It was a ring. A ring of such deep black that it looked as if the tiny thing was sucking the light out of the space in its immediate vicinity. "How'd that get in there?" he wondered as he reached out to retrieve the ring. Brent certainly hadn't purchased such a thing.

"Jiffy" is a word most people use incorrectly. Everybody has heard the term, "I'll be back in a jiffy". Its technical meaning is a measurement of the time that light takes to travel the distance of a nucleon (or a centimeter, depending on who you ask); so basically, an infinitely tiny amount of time. But as Brent picked the ring up off the tile floor, a "jiffy" is exactly how long it took him to realize that he had just made the biggest fucking mistake of his life.

"Please tell me you found those two assholes?" the voice crackled over the radio.

"Not yet," Dwight answered into the mouthpiece. "Though I just heard some screaming toward town. I'm checking it out now."

Dwight silently hoped the scream wasn't from an innocent that the escapees had stumbled upon, though he had a hard time imagining another scenario. He couldn't see the two convicts giving away their position so carelessly.

"Let me know the second *you find those fucks!"* the voice swore through the radio.

"Will do," Dwight confirmed, clipping the mouthpiece back into its spot on his gun belt, right next to the Krueger County Prison badge that he wore.

His hand never strayed far from the belt. Immediately after the mouthpiece was secure, Dwight spotted a prison-issued sneaker sticking out from behind some brush. "Don't move!" Dwight commanded, keeping his hand around the butt of his holstered pistol as he quickened his pace until he was in view of the recently-escaped prisoner.

"What the fuck?" Dwight gasped. The two Flores twins had been hard enough to tell apart given any normal situation, but identifying whichever one of the two was sprawled out on the ground in front of Dwight now, was damn near impossible. "Jesus Christ, Flores...what happened to you?"

Flores - whichever one of the two brothers he happened to be - was unable to answer. He wasn't quite dead yet, though Dwight could tell by looking at him that he would be soon. The blood bubbling between his lips and running down his chin blotted out whatever response the Flores brother was trying to give. That alone wasn't what convinced Dwight that the man was soon to be joining whatever dark angels roamed Hell. No; that had been derived from the large puddle of blood and human offal the man was lying in. It was a miracle the man still had even a glimmer of life left in his eyes.

Dwight nervously scanned his surroundings, searching for the other Flores brother, or any other threat that may be lurking. Seeing nothing, he slowly stepped toward the present twin.

"Where is your brother? Who did this to you?" The questions came pouring out of him as he stepped forward. Dwight's nerves had shot up full throttle and he asked the questions anyway, knowing full well that Flores' answers would not be forthcoming.

As Dwight took another step forward, his kicked something small into the air. Dwight looked down at the object that he had disturbed and saw that it was round and black. "Is that a ring?" Dwight asked, bending over to inspect the item. As he bent down, the gurgling sound coming from the downed Flores brother increased, becoming frantic. Dwight looked up and saw the man staring at him. He was agitated and his dimming eyes had brightened with fear. "Is this your brother's?" Dwight asked the agitated man. Flores responded by wildly shaking his head from side to side. Despite the denial, Dwight reached out to retrieve the ring from the dirt.

More gurgles…the man was trying to tell Dwight something vital.

Dwight was scared. Of what, he had no idea, but something had fucked up Flores badly, and Dwight needed backup to arrive soon.

He fumbled at his radio with one hand as the other reached down to pluck up the ring. He knew that he should leave it for the forensics team, but his hand was acting seemingly of its own accord.

"Fuck!" Dwight's sudden howl broke the calmness of the woods. As soon as his fingertip brushed on the ring's metal surface, his fingers violently snapped closed around it, completely out of his control. The move was so sudden and filled with ferocity that Dwight felt the bones in two of his fingers shatter inside their protective bags of flesh.

Dwight's screams filled the air, the pain unlike anything he had been victim to in his entire life. Unfortunately, it didn't stop there.

The ring-bearing hand snapped and twisted, finishing by cocking over to his other side. The hand jammed the ring onto his left hand's index finger. The ring was a size too small for Dwight's meaty finger, but that didn't matter. It was jammed on with enough force that the skin tore from the tip of his finger and folded back like an accordion, bunching up under the ring's final resting place near the knuckle. Dwight's screams cut sharply into shrilling madness.

As soon as Dwight's right hand was emptied, a searing pain engulfed that arm all the way up to the shoulder. Dwight watched in horror as the pigment of his arm darkened to a blackness that was only matched by the ring itself. Then, as if by some invisible signal, the black arm vanished into a waterfall of black liquid that splashed into the dirt below.

Dwight's mind went into shock at the sight. His bellows stopped as he plodded forward in a daze. Through the haziness of Dwight's world, he knew he needed to seek help. His chest was now flaring with pain and he knew he was going to blackout soon...or worse!

Dwight wasn't sure how much time had passed in his zombie-like progression, but he soon saw a parking lot come into view. He tried calling for help as soon the parking lot came into sight, but the only things that exited his mouth were a wet gurgle and a mist of black. Dwight knew then that hellish feeling in his chest was his insides – including his esophagus – liquefying, as his arm had done.

Dwight had almost made it to the parking lot when the haze in his head finally overtook him and he collapsed to his knees in front of a black Mustang convertible. Thick bushes lined the parking lot on either side of the car's bumper. The only available path forward was to crawl over – which Dwight was in no shape to do – or underneath the vehicle.

Footsteps! Somebody was coming.

Dwight tried speeding up his crawl, but when he planted his right toes into the ground to push forward, his entire leg buckled in on itself and then came pouring out his pant leg. Dwight briefly turned to take in the horrifying scene. Even his pant leg was dissolving into the black liquid.

The approaching feet stopped behind the vehicle that Dwight was underneath. Two grocery bags were placed on the ground next to them. Dwight reached out, his arm hovering over the grocery bags, hoping to grab the man's leg and get his attention. Instead, the last thing that Dwight saw before his eyeballs poured down his cheeks, was his ring-bearing hand disappear into a black rain, freeing the ring to fall into one of the paper bags.

Part Three
<u>**May 28th, 12:33pm**</u>

"Hurry the fuck up, Miguel! They're right on our asses!" Hector shouted to his trailing brother.

"I'm coming…I'm coming!" Miguel huffed as he tried to keep up with his more fitness-oriented brother. "Jesus Christ…can't we take a quick break?" Miguel glanced back along their escape trail and strained to spot the plume of smoke rising into the air. It was a long way's back now, puny against the horizon. "We've had to have gone at least three or four miles by now."

"Not far enough, *puta*! They're not going to chase us for a couple miles and then say 'Fuck it…they're gone!'," Hector challenged. Hector was the older of the two brothers by all of eight minutes, but he had always played the part of caretaker to his younger brother. God knows their parents had never been up to the task.

Hector stopped to let Miguel catch up. As Miguel arrived, through heavy breathing, he pleaded, "Just thirty seconds…Please!"

Hector scanned the woods for any sign that somebody was approaching. Not seeing anything, he reluctantly acquiesced. "Fine. Thirty seconds, but that's it!."

"What the fuck ya think happened to that truck?" Miguel asked through rapid breaths.

"I don't have a fucking clue. Don't care, neither. It worked out for us and that's all I need to know."

"That guy looked scared out of his fucking mind," Miguel related, his breathing starting to come back under control.

"What was that shit he gave you?" Hector asked.

"I'm not sure," Miguel answered. He reached his hand - still clad in the heavy duty work gloves from the prison work detail - under the orange vest and into the pocket of his jumpsuit. "I think it's a ring." Miguel pulled the circular, black object from his pocket and studied it for the first time. "A strange one, though. All black; kinda cool looking actually."

"Is it obsidian?" Hector asked, eyeing the object.

"Nah. Obsidian is shiny. This is dull as fuck. That guy sure seemed scared of it, though; that's for sure."

"Yeah...no shit! What was that he was telling you?" Hector asked.

"He was saying something about burying it, then, right before he died, begged me not to touch it. He was straight-up loony tunes. I think he..."

"Oh shit!" Hector interrupted. "I think we've hit a town." Miguel looked up from the ring and saw that his brother was staring further along their path. Miguel followed Hector's gaze and saw a building. It couldn't have been more than a hundred yards away.

The sight of the building reinvigorated Miguel. They had a real chance to remain undiscovered by the correction officer's if they could find a good hiding spot in the town. "Well, what are we waiting for? Let's get moving," Miguel prodded.

"About fucking time," Hector swore, then tore off towards the town. Readying himself to follow, Miguel hurriedly attempted to stuff the ring back into his pocket. As his gloved hand fumbled to slide its way into the thin opening, he noticed something dripping from his palm. When he opened his glove towards his face, he saw that the palm was filled with a gooey black liquid; the glove itself disintegrating before his eyes.

"What the fuck?" Miguel swore, trying to shake the ring loose from his hand. It didn't come loose. He tried again, thinking the black goo may have been holding it on there like some kind of glue, when the last of the fabric dissolved, allowing the ring to make contact with his skin. The resulting effect was immediate.

Miguel's index finger cocked inward, the knuckle breaking to allow the finger to lay completely flat along his palm. Next, the two joints along the finger's length snapped, the phalanges shattering, leaving the finger as loose skin filled with fragments of bone. Then, doing its best impression of a stubby serpent, the finger slithered its way into the ring's hoop and did a wavy sort of dance until the ring rested at his knuckle. Through the entire event, no more than a frightened whimper escaped Miguel's lips. The pain was intense; the shock that consumed him even more so.

"What the fuck are you standing there for?" Hector had noticed his brother hadn't joined him and had looped back to find out what was happening. In such a hurry as he was, he failed to realize the depth of the horror etched into his brother's face. He grabbed his brother by his jumpsuit's shoulder and began dragging him along.

It was enough to break Miguel from his spell long enough to shout, "Don't!", but it was too late. Miguel's hand shot up to his shoulder and clutched Hector's wrist with a vice-like grip. The hand violently twisted the appendage, snapping the bone within. Hector shrieked and clutched his broken wrist with his good hand.

"What the fuck!" Hector shouted at his little brother. "What the fuck was that f…" That was as far as he got when the possessed hand shot up and snatched Hector's tongue. Hector's eyes filled with terror as the hand squeezed the slimy, pink organ and ripped it from his mouth. A torrential flood of crimson spilled from Hector's lips.

Hector fell backwards, instinct taking over and causing him to scurry backwards, away from the creature causing him harm. Instinct didn't recognize relation.

"I'm sorry," Miguel cried. "It's the ring...it's the ring!" As if his hand was being pulled by some phantom god, Miguel's hand dragged him forward, chasing after the retreating brother.

Hector's frantic escape was cut short when he unwittingly backed into a tree. He attempted to twist to his side to go around the obstacle, but it was too late. The ring-bearing hand had neared enough to whip out and snag his ankle. The hand jerked back, brutally dragging Hector through the dirt, toward his younger brother. As soon as the hand released Hector's ankle, it sprung up to his belt line and ripped the orange jumpsuit open, exposing Hector's ass.

"What the fuck is happening!?" Miguel cried as his arm coiled up and then, with greater power than Miguel could have ever summoned up on his own, the hand plunged deep into Hector's rectum.

Hector screamed!

Miguel could feel the warmth of his brother's insides as his fingers squirmed through a tangle of something coiled and slimy, until it brushed against a firm, bulging blob. The hand gripped the blob tight and pulled, tearing it out of Hector's body, a trail of intestines following the object out. When exposed to the daylight, Miguel recognized the blob as his brother's stomach.

Miguel vomited, the bile mixing with the blood drenching his hand. The hand released the stomach and Hector turned onto his back to look up at his brother. Panic stained his eyes, but his body was too abused to do much more than lie there.

The blood and bile sizzled on Miguel's hand, until it had completely evaporated into the air. Revealed beneath, was his hand, now matching the color of the cursed ring. The blackness peeked from under the orange sleeve of the jumpsuit and quickly consumed his hand.

Miguel wasn't even able to scream as the rest of his body followed suit.

******

Hector knew he was dying before his brother had even vanished into a puddle of black goo. He had already come to accept it. He now knew, without a doubt, that there were things worse than death out there.

It hadn't taken long for his brother to completely turn black, then liquefy. That short amount of time was enough, though. Enough for Hector to find peace in death.

He watched as his brother's orange jumpsuit quickly dissolved in the black liquid, then even the liquid itself vanished, steaming into the air.

"Don't move!" Hector heard the warning.

Too late! All traces of his brother and the black goo that he had become had vanished. The black ring the only sign to suggest anything had ever been there at all.

"Faster! Faster!" Clyde panicked. They hit a bump in the road, causing his head to bang against the roof of the speeding truck. Clyde could have put his hands up to quell the impact, but a bump on the noggin was a small price to pay not to lose the box being held tightly in his lap.

Clyde inspected the box for probably the thousandth time. "I'm getting worried," he told the driver in the seat next to him. "I think it may be eating its way through the box."

"Like it did through the box back in the lab?" Geoff asked from the driver's seat.

"Yeah."

"But that was just a rubber glove that it ate through in the lab. You've got it in pure fucking titanium right now!"

"I know!" Clyde shouted. "I watched as Charles and Hank underestimated this damn thing! I won't be making the same mistake." Clyde flashed back to the laboratory. One miscalculation was all it took for the lab to become a fucking slaughterhouse. They had known the ring had "special" properties, but the scope of which, they could have never imagined.

"How were we supposed to know how powerful that thing is? We don't even know *what* that thing is!"

"Just keep driving!" Clyde instructed. "We need to get to Lawson now! He's already prepping the cannon, but warned me that it'll still take about ten minutes to load this fucker. I don't know if we even have *that* long and we've still got fifteen miles to go."

"I've got this pedal grinding metal. This is as fast as she goes."

Clyde glanced at the speedometer. It showed them going just under a hundred, but it felt more like twenty to Clyde. As they rounded a tight curve in the road, the truck's weight shifted, giving the feeling like it was about to pop up onto two wheels. Despite that, Clyde still prayed for the damn machine to go faster.

"What the fuck!" Geoff suddenly shouted. Through the windshield, Clyde saw what prompted Geoff's sudden outburst. Parked on the side of the street was a large bus, its wheels hugging the pavement. Nearby were a group of orange-vested prisoners, picking up trash under the watchful eyes of armed corrections officers. Clyde processed all of this in a flash, which was apparently not enough time for Geoff to swerve out of the way of the parked bus.

The truck's driver's side collided with the front of the bus, forcing the truck to violently spin out counter-clockwise from the collision. Clyde's head smashed against his window, cracking the thickened automotive glass and splitting the flesh lining his skull. Not even two full rotations in, the truck's spin halted. Its momentum carried the large vehicle on, however; skidding sideways for a moment, before the tires caught against the asphalt and sent the truck flipping into the air.

Geoff – having neglected to buckle himself into his seat – was launched into the roof of the truck as it crumpled against the road during the first flip. Somehow, over the ear-blistering cacophony of destruction, Clyde heard a sickening snap as Geoff's neck cocked at a grotesque angle against the roof.

Clyde didn't have the time to consider the implications of the sound, as the truck immediately flipped back onto its wheels, over again onto the roof, back to the wheels, and finally, back to its roof one last time; Geoff's body doing its best impression of a pinball the entire time.

As the truck came to a rest, Clyde founded himself suspended upside down by the seatbelt that he had fortunately buckled himself into. His ears rang. Everything in his sight was wavy as Clyde scanned his surroundings; everything except for the pounding in his head. It was tough to fight through the haze, but he managed to concentrate long enough to free the seatbelt clasp. As soon as he activated the switch, his body plummeted headfirst onto the roof. From his crumpled position on the roof, Clyde reached up and pulled the door handle, freeing himself to spill out onto the street.

"Jesus Christ," Clyde swore, sitting with his back against the truck's exterior, watching the world spin in front of him. He knew he should be moving away from the volatile mixture of fire and fuel behind him, but he had exhausted his energy for the moment and just wanted to enjoy the dancing landscape.

"Fuck!" Clyde cursed, suddenly sitting up. "The ring!"

Clyde lifted himself to his knees and turned to search the inside of the burning vehicle. He scanned the truck's cab, finding broken glass, dangling wires, and, of course, Geoff's dead body, bloodied beyond recognition. But no titanium box. "Where is it?" After glancing at his hands to ensure his gloves were still whole, Clyde reached in and shifted the wreckage around. At first, nothing; then he saw it.

The box was jammed into the bent remains of the steering wheel, though how it got there, Clyde would never know. The most horrifying part was that the box was now open, the clasp apparently having broken during the wreck. The ring itself was dangling from a jutting piece of the broken clasp, precariously dangling over Geoff's fractured body.

"Don't fall!" Clyde willed the dangling ring. He carefully reached out with his gloved hands. He was reluctant to handle the ring with only the leather barrier between them, but he only needed enough time to place it back securely in the box. He wasn't sure how much more time that would buy him, but it was the only option readily available. He had almost reached it when something in the truck's frame gave, and the whole thing shifted. It was enough to free the ring from its perch and Clyde watched, seemingly in slow motion, as the ring dropped through the air, landing in the muck that had been Geoff's face.

The reaction was instantaneous. Geoff's body jerked upright, emitting a loud, gurgly scream. The ring was currently stuck in the unidentifiable puree of gore, but it wouldn't be enough to keep it attached for long. Clyde watched in horror as one of Geoff's eyeballs emerged through the red sludge. The eye – looking like a bulbous, white worm – squirmed its way towards the ring's hoop, elongating itself into condom-shaped bubble to squeeze through the narrow opening. A mixture of blood and colorless liquid dribbled from the edges of the eyeball as the outer layers were sheaved off by the ring's edge as it squeezed its way through the ring's hoop. Once through, the eyeball inflated back to its normal size, trapping the ring in place on the stalk.

Ring safely held in place, the Geoff creature leapt toward the wide-mouthed Clyde. Clyde reacted just in time, throwing himself sideways to avoid the monster's pounce. Geoff's missed leap sent his broken body arcing into the dirt. He recovered quickly though, the body turning so the lone eyeball could focus on Clyde.

Clyde jumped up and ran.

The ring gave chase.

Clyde was glad to find that he had unwittingly chosen to go in the opposite direction of the stunned group of prisoners and guards. It was better if Geoff's eye didn't catch on any other prey. Clyde ran as fast as his feet would carry him, only looking back to ensure the monster was still on his trail.

Think! Think! Clyde urged himself. He didn't have a plan, but he knew he had to do *something*. He had to get this situation contained. Maybe if he could hide for a moment, he could use his cell to call Lawson for help. Lawson's place was entirely too far to lead the creature all the way there on foot. Maybe Lawson could send somebody to provide support?

The only problem with that plan was that Clyde didn't want to lose sight of the monster, even for a moment. The worst-case scenario would be for the ring to find its way into a populated area. He didn't even want to consider what would happen then.

Clyde turned back again to check on Geoff. His heart jumped into his throat when he saw that the creature was a lot closer than he imagined. Within leaping distance! Clyde knew this because that is exactly what happened. The monster leaped, sending Geoff's broken body colliding into Clyde's own. Clyde hit the ground and the two of them rolled along for several feet.

Once the roll had stopped, Clyde found himself on his stomach at the bottom of the two-man pile. He quickly squirmed onto his back and his got his hand's up just in time to stop the monster's next attack. He wrapped his hands around the remains of Geoff's throat, temporarily holding the creature's mangled head at bay. He squeezed as tight as he could, but it was tough to maintain his grip. His hand kept slipping on the slick gore that coated the creature's neck.

At first, Clyde was unsure of the monster's intentions. It was as if it were trying to head-butt him. No, not it wasn't its head that the creature was trying to bring closer, Clyde quickly realized, it was the dangling eyeball. It was trying to get the ring inside Clyde's mouth.

Clyde used all his strength to keep his arms straight, keeping the ring at a distance. Thank God the creature wasn't stronger! Still, he knew he wouldn't be able to hold it off forever.

His arms were already burning. He knew he had to act quickly. He mustered up the strength for one good push, just enough to free his hand up so he could quickly snatch the eyeball out of Geoff's head.

He missed!

The creature responded with another gurgling scream, blood misting from the oozing cavity that used to be Geoff's mouth. Clyde tried to get his hand back between him and the monster, but Geoff moved too quickly, rearing back and driving himself forward, head-butting Clyde with his mangled forehead. Clyde felt the jagged tatters of Geoff's skull as they penetrated his facial skin from the force of the blow. Clyde screamed at the sudden pain, but was relieved that the ring had somehow not managed to make contact with his skin.

Not having the time to celebrate that fact, Clyde tried the maneuver again. This time he caught the dangling orb and ripped it right out the creature's head. Separated from the ring, Geoff's muscles lost all tension and his body crashed down on Clyde.

"Thank-fucking-Christ!" Clyde shouted into the air, pushing Geoff's motionless remains off of him. He unsteadily tried crawling up to his feet, but stumbled and fell back to the ground. He shot his hands out in front of him to stop his fall. It worked, but through his glove, he could feel the eyeball burst against his palm as his hand smashed into the dirt. Clyde pulled the deflated, slimy husk out of the ring and discarded it to the dirt with a sickening plop.

Clyde started to run, continuously switching the ring from one hand to the other, hoping that switching up the exposure point would keep his gloves whole for at least a while longer.

Not more than thirty feet into his journey, a loud thunder cracked through the air, accompanied by a sharp pain in Clyde's side. When he looked down he could see a crimson stain blooming across his shirt.

Not thunder, it turned out…but a gunshot!

Clyde turned to see one of the prison guards pointing a gun at him with a shaky hand. "F-Freeze!" the officer demanded. The man must have caught part of the battle between Clyde and Geoff. Given what was left of Geoff now, and the uniform that his dead body was clad in, Clyde couldn't blame the officer for freaking out. Unfortunately, Clyde didn't have time to be held up, explaining a situation that nobody would believe anyway. At least not until it was too late.

Clyde ran on. The officer tried giving chase, but his feet became tangled in the dead-again body of Geoff and he tumbled forward, spilling roughly to the ground.

Clyde kept running. He ran on for several moments until his energy waned and the pain in his side grew to an intolerable level. Looking down at himself, Clyde knew he was losing blood too quickly to get much further.

A scuffling from a nearby bush caught his attention. "Is it one of the C.Os?" Clyde heard from behind the same bush.

"Hello?" Clyde asked the bush.

Unsure if the blood loss was playing tricks on his mind, the bush answered. "No…I think it's one of the guys from the truck." A face appeared through the bush. Clyde recognized the orange vest underneath it as the loss of blood finally forced him to his knees. At his new eye-level, Clyde could see the man was wearing thick gloves.

"Take this." Clyde pulled out the ring and extended it toward the man. It wasn't ideal, but it was the only play that Clyde had left. Now being a good distance away from the wreck, Clyde knew that this convict had used the confusion of the wreck's aftermath to make an escape. Clyde doubted that he could convince the man to stop off fifteen miles down the road, so he asked for something that he hoped the man would actually do. "Bury it. Bury it deep and bury it soon! Don't dawdle."

It was better than nothing, Clyde thought.

"And don't touch it!" Clyde warned, hoping that his tone was dire enough to properly scare the man. "For the love of God, don't ever let it touch your skin!" A confused look spread across the man's face. Enough fear was mixed in that Clyde felt his warning would be heeded.

Even with this final assurance, Clyde felt no peace as everything turned black.

Part Five
May 27th, 6:12am

"C'mon baby...just a little bit more...just a little bit more," Charles chanted, his eyes glued on the screens.

"Sir!" an excited Neill suddenly exclaimed. "We've done it! The particles are travelling one meter per second *over* light speed."

"Yes!" Charles shook his fist in victory. "CERN, eat your hearts out." CERN – the scientific entity responsible for the Large Hadron Collider in Europe – were going to shit their pants when they heard about what Charles' team had just accomplished here. Sure, those scientific engineers had pioneered the technology required for the American supercollider that Charles now managed, but it hadn't been especially hard to take what they had created and make improvements. His European counterparts may have discovered the Higgs boson particle, but Charles had even grander hopes for his baby right here in the middle of the good old United States of America.

"Standby for proton collision," Charles instructed. The space grew quiet as all the PhD's in the room dove into their screens, awaiting the vast amount of data that was about to be captured through the numerous sensors placed along the nineteen mile long pipeline. "Initiate!"

One may assume that causing two particles to collide at greater than light speed would be a powerful enough impact to be felt or heard for miles away. Some doomsayers even predicted it'd be calamitous enough to cause destruction on a planetary scale. Those that expected such a thing would have been terribly disappointed by the lackluster reality of the situation. The only sign at all that such an event had occurred was the flow of data running across the lab's multitude of monitors.

"Are we good?" Charles asked the room.

"Good, sir. We did it. Over twenty terabytes of data has been captured." Applause erupted throughout the room.

Charles smiled. "Alright, shut her down."

It took nearly an hour for the accelerator to slow down from such an incredible speed, not that any of the staff were complaining. That first hour had barely been enough to crack open the vast amount of data they'd need to sort through. To a man, they were all buried deep into their screens when the particle accelerator had finally stopped completely.

That's when the sirens began to wail.

"What in the hell is that?" Charles asked, tearing himself away from the post-action report he was writing.

"Sir!" an excited voice sounded from the front of the large room. "Sensors are picking up a foreign object in section 17 of the pipeline."

"What?" Charles asked, astounded. "What kind of object?"

"I don't know, sir," the technician stated. "Something solid, measuring approximately one cubic inch." Not a large object to most, but a behemoth compared to the usual size of object that the scientists were used to studying.

"I've got something, sir," piped up another voice from off to Charles' right. "I'm seeing a flood of unidentified particles materializing in the pipeline immediately after proton collision. I'm going to need time to analyze the readings further, but I can tell you that they weren't in there before the test."

"That's impossible!" argued Charles. "Anything travelling that fast would have torn right through the structure."

"My readings are showing that the foreign particles were microscopic in size when they were formed, sir," the voice informed.

"Perhaps these disparate particles coalesced after the machine was stopped," Hank - Charles' close friend and second-in-charge - theorized.

Charles threw a curious glance at his friend. "That'd be damn strange, don't you think?"

Hank nodded, but didn't add anything to the statement.

"Well, whatever the hell it is, we're going to need to get it out of there," Charles sighed.

"Are you sure that's a good idea, Charles?" Hank asked. "We have no idea what the hell we're dealing with here. Never has a run like this produced anything sustainable."

"Yeah, I'm sure. We'll have to replace an entire section of the pipeline too. That'll be costly, but I don't see that we have any other choice. We can't run the accelerator again until the pipeline is clear."

"Screw the accelerator!" Hank snapped. "We need to know what this damn thing is before we go messing with it."

Charles considered his friend's warning and made a decision. "Listen up!" Charles shouted out to the assembled team. "If you own a sensor near this thing, I want all the data that you can give me on it. Chemical composition, radiology; the whole works. Theo?"

A large man wearing black coveralls rose from where he was sitting off to the side of the room. He was Theo Joplin, Charles' lead engineer, and had been the lead on the pipeline's physical construction, as well as continuing to be in charge of all maintenance of the system. "Sir?"

"Start assembling a team to extract this thing," Charles instructed. "I want them decked out in full protective gear and equipment. We are *not* going to take any chances with this damn thing, understood?"

Theo nodded. "On it, sir!" He signaled three men from his section to follow him and they went running out of the room.

Hank shook his head at Charles' stubbornness. "Once again, I have to ask, are you sure that this is a good idea?" he asked in skepticism.

"No," Charles admitted with a sigh. "But, as long as we take all the necessary precautions, I don't think there should be a problem."

Hank didn't look convinced. "God help us if you're wrong."

******

May 28th, 11:19am

After a full day of sensor readings, the object remained a mystery. Other than trace elements of carbon and magnesium, the chemical composition of the object could not be identified by the lab's computers. The only satisfactory reading they got off the thing was a density reading. Whatever its chemical makeup was, those combined elements were roughly as dense as steel. There were no indications that the object was emitting anything dangerous, however. As far as the sensors could tell, the object wasn't emitting anything at all. Charles had decided that assurance – along with a growing sense of curiosity – were enough for him to give the green light for Theo's team to begin extraction.

It took nearly four hours to cut into the pipeline and safely remove the foreign mass, then another forty-five minutes to transport the thing the seven miles to the lab where it was now contained.

Charles was currently eyeing the object through the thick fiberglass walls of the glovebox it had been placed in. Looking like nothing more than an exceptionally dark lump of coal, the object appeared benign enough.

Hank – who had personally volunteered to be the first to examine the object, not wanting to pawn it off on any of his men – had his hands inside the rubber gloves that gave the glove box its name. Through the gloves, he was holding the object, slowly turning it for a thorough visual inspection.

"It's definitely a hard solid," Hank informed. "Feels smooth. Like obsidian, but lighter somehow."

"Lighter?" Charles questioned, surprised by the revelation. "Didn't the scan reveal it to hold nearly the same density as steel? It should be heavier, not lighter."

"Definitely curious," Hank agreed, still turning the object.

"What the hell?" Charles said suddenly, leaning towards the fiberglass wall. "Is that thing melting?" A black substance had appeared around the unidentified lump. It was some sort of liquid, running down the length of the gloves until it dripped off, pooling on the bottom of the glovebox.

"I don't think it's melting," Hank replied, having stopped the lump's examination to stare at the new curiosity. "The surface area hasn't changed. Maybe it's coming from the inside of the...

"What the fuck!" Hank suddenly screamed, jerking his right hand out of its glove. In his palm sat the black object, looking as if it had fused to Hank's skin. Charles looked from the object to the recently-formed hole in the empty glove – the edges still dissolving into black goo – and instantly understood that the black liquid was not a result of the strange stone melting, but was the remains of the glove itself as the rubber melted away. Especially strange seeing how the rubber gloves were blue – not black – in color.

"Get it off me!" Hank was screaming, shaking his hand to rid it of the terrifying object. The effort was wasted as the object didn't budge.

It didn't remain that way for long, however. The black lump soon disappeared, seemingly melting into the pink layers of Hank's skin. Charles watched in horror as his friend's eyes clouded with darkness, until all that was left in his sockets were two orbs, the same deep blackness as the foreign object itself.

Charles retreated from his friend – keeping his eyes glued on Hank – until he had backed up against the room's door. He blindly fumbled for the door handle while watching Hank's black orbs survey the room as if seeing it for the first time. Charles paused to watch – partly in scientific curiosity and partly in horror – but he kept his hand primed on the handle. Hank lifted his hands in front of his face and studied them. The black eyes traveled down his arm, then over the clothes that covered the rest of his body. His mouth twisted in a look of curiosity at the clothes and Hank reached down to rip off a piece of his shirt, which he quickly discarded after coming to some kind of conclusion about the substance.

The eyes shifted down to Hank's palm. The left came over to pinch the flesh of the right, seemingly studying it. Then, Hank spoke. "Too…" he paused after squeezing out the syllable. He looked as if he was searching his vocabulary for the next correct word. "…deteriorated. No!" Hank shook his head. "Too *old*." The orbs came away from his palm and settled on Charles. "Need new flesh."

That was enough to break Charles from his trance. He hastily twisted the handle and shot out of the room. He stopped only to slam the door shut behind him; but, for that, it was already too late. Hank shot forward at an incredible speed and rammed the door, causing it to crash into Charles and knocking him backwards onto the floor.

Charles tried to scamper away, but Hank was instantly upon him. Charles' gaze shot up to stare into the two black orbs, but instead saw the blackness melting out of them to be replaced by Hank's normal – yet horrified - eyes.

"Charles..." Hank's voice trembled. "What is happening to me?"

A loud crack split the air as Hank's left wrist suddenly snapped backwards. A dark bulge stretched at the base of Hank's index finger, the black emerging from his pores to form a perfect circle around the extremity. Hank removed the newly-formed ring from his finger and slid it onto Charles'. Charles was too mortified to resist. As soon as the ring made contact with his flesh, any control that Charles had left in him was immediately stripped away.

Hank maintained his grip on the ring as his hand darkened. The hand then dissolved into the same black ooze as the glove had earlier. The darkness travelled up from there until it had consumed the entirety of Hank's body. Soon, the only thing left of Hank was the sticky, black puddle that Charles was left lying in.

Not that Charles had any concern for the puddle. He was too consumed with the pain and fear that radiated through his flesh from where the black ring sat on his finger. Strange things were happening to his flesh – both external *and* internal. Things Charles couldn't even begin to comprehend.

By the time Charles felt his body rise on its own, his mind had already completely snapped. What was left of him finally walked through the door of the room, and the search for more flesh commenced.

******

Clyde was breathing heavily as Geoff held the gun steady on the outer door of the facility.

He had been watching the camera feed as the black clump had eaten its way through the rubber glove and attached itself to Hank. He had stared on in horror as Hank attacked Charles and slid the newly-formed ring onto the finger of his former boss. He had even stayed long enough to see Charles attack the next team member he had come across, then that team member attack the next; so on and so forth. Some people were simply butchered by the current wearer of the ring, while others would come to possess it and begin butchering others themselves. There was no rhyme or reason that Clyde could see for why one person would be slaughtered, while another would become the terrified new owner of the disturbing piece of jewelry. He just knew that it was happening, and it was happening like wildfire.

Clyde had only watched a few moments of the video feed before leaving his post and running out of the building – locking the doors behind him - to where Geoff stood his security watch at the compound's gate.

Was Clyde a coward? Maybe, but he doubted anybody else would do anything different, given what he had seen on the video feeds.

He had hurriedly explained all that he had seen to the security guard and had convinced him to train the gun on the building's exit, ready to shoot anything that was foolish enough to come through. "We can't let anybody out, wearing the ring or not!" Clyde had explained. "I saw this thing disappear into Hank's body. We can't trust that it won't do the same to somebody else in order to make its escape."

"Why aren't we just making a run for it?" Geoff asked, his own gun trained on the door.

"We can't let that thing make it out of there. It tore through the lab in mere minutes. How long do you think it would take to tear through a town? The entire state? Or even worse?"

It didn't take long for Clyde's nightmare to come true. Something slammed against the opposite side of the glass doors, causing the glass to web into opacity. Another thump, and the glass exploded outward. A large body emerged through the newly-created opening and Geoff immediately fired two rounds, center mass, into the figure's stomach.

Clyde watched as Theo Joplin's midsection crumpled inwards and the large man fell to his knees. A quick scan revealed Theo's black coveralls gleaming wetly, but no black mass around his finger. Instead, his hands held a titanium box, which he gripped tightly, despite the pain that had to be raging through his body from the bullet wounds.

Geoff looked like he was ready to administer another volley of rounds into Theo, but Clyde held him off. Together, they carefully stepped toward the hunched man.

"What the fuck did you shoot me for?" Theo huffed as they neared.

Clyde ignored the question – and his sudden guilt – and asked the only question that really mattered: "Where's the ring?"

"In here." Theo raised the titanium box. "And you don't want to know what I had to do to get it, either."

"Is there anybody else alive in there?" Clyde asked, nodding towards the lab.

"No...I don't think so." Theo's breaths were ragged, the large man clearly struggling to breathe.

Undaunted, Clyde continued on. "What were you bringing that thing out here for?"

"I was going to take it to Donald Lawson up at Lawson Industries, about forty miles north of here. He's a friend of mine."

"What was he going to do with it?"

"Shoot the fucker into space." Theo finished with a sharp wheeze and a coughing fit.

"What?" Clyde asked, confused. "How the hell would he do that?"

"Lawson Industries has developed a space cannon to cheaply deliver supplies to the space stations. It's expected to save NASA billions of dollars."

"Bullshit!" Clyde interjected. "I would have heard about something like that."

Theo shook his head. "It's not finished yet. He has figured out enough to get the payload out of the atmosphere, though he hasn't gotten the damn aiming problem figured out yet. Of course, we don't need to aim it. We just need to get this fucking thing off of our planet."

Clyde looked to Geoff for support. Geoff simply shrugged. "Fuck it. I don't have a better plan."

"Yeah, neither do I," Clyde reluctantly agreed.

"Take it," Theo said, holding the box out towards Clyde. "Get it up to Lawson."

"Come on," Clyde replied, grabbing onto Theo's shoulder to help the man to his feet. "You're coming with us, big man."

Theo slapped Clyde's hand away. "No! I'll never make it. Take this thing and go!"

Clyde looked at the blood pooling around Theo's knees and knew the man was right. He took the box from Theo's weakening grip and looked the man in the eyes. "I'm sorry."

"Don't be...just get..." Theo erupted into another coughing fit and collapsed from his kneeling position. "Just go!" he shouted.

Clyde stared at the dying man until Geoff shook him out of it. "Come on. Let's get to my truck and get the fuck out of here."

Clyde nodded silently, then turned to begin the journey up to Lawson Industries.

Part Six
<u>**MAY 28th, 1:03pm**</u>

Brent's fingers snapped closed around the ring.

"What the hell!?"

The hand moved on its own to grab the other, which Brent instinctively jerked away. The ring hand responded with another swipe to grab Brent's free hand. This time it snapped out lightning-quick, tearing several of Brent's muscles with the unnaturally-fast movement. The ring hand seized Brent's free wrist and twisted, snapping his radius and ulna as easily as a couple of twigs.

Brent's arm hung limply, allowing easy access to his index finger. The ring slid on smoothly and the other hand dropped away.

"What is happening to me?" Brent squeaked. He felt as if he were suddenly living in a nightmare. One that couldn't possibly be worse.

A sharp intake of breath came from across the kitchen, drawing Brent's attention. "You got the Dragon's Breath cereal!" young Caleb exclaimed.

Brent knew that he'd been mistaken…the nightmare had just gotten considerably worse.

"Stay back, Caleb," Brent tried saying, but the only thing that came out was a wheeze and some flecks of black liquid.

Caleb failed to notice his father's predicament, his attention solely on the box with the smiling rainbow dragon. He darted across the tile floor to snatch up the box and look it over with his six-year old eyes.

Brent could do nothing but watch on in horror as his ring-bearing hand grabbed a kitchen knife off the counter and swung it into his beloved son's throat.

Tears streamed down Brent's face as his son finally noticed him, his eyes wide and filled with shock. The colorful box of sugar dragons fell to the kitchen floor. Caleb soon followed, his throat slowly sliding off the long blade of the kitchen knife, leaving a red stain on the gleaming blade.

Brent's hand was already turning black as his fingers made their way into the newly-formed hole of his son's throat. He could feel as his digits wrapped around the segmented hose of Caleb's esophagus and held on tightly as the pressure of the ring's circumference vanished from around his index finger.

The last thing Brent ever saw before his body became a puddle of black sludge, was Caleb's wide-open eyes flood with perfect blackness and his lips curling into a sinister smile before speaking the words, "New flesh!"

******

The entity was pleased.

It had no way of knowing how long it had been trapped in its prison between the dimensions…just that it had been eons. Nor did it have a clue on what freed it from its eternal damnation.

But finally it had found a proper host. A host whose flesh had not decayed from age. Flesh that was strong enough to hold him.

The destroyer of worlds smiled as its new body rose from the strangely smooth floor. It was time to add another planet to his list of conquests.

READ ALL BOOKS BY
DAVID W COONS JR

Available on Amazon at:
http://amazon.com/author/davidcoons
-and-
Booksellers Everywhere

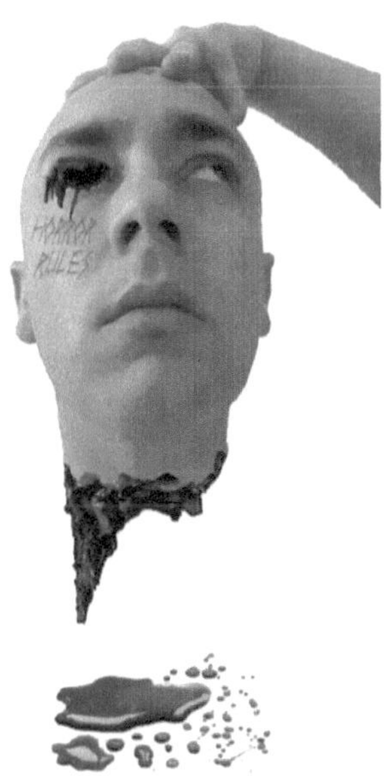

DAVID W COONS JR is not only a horror writer, but an all-around horror enthusiast. His books include Arte Blanche, Chaplain, and the horrific novelette By The Hour.
He is originally from the small town of Jerome, Idaho, but currently resides with his wife and two cats in San Diego, California.
You can follow him at the following websites:

https://www.facebook.com/davidcoonsauthor
https://www.goodreads.com/DavidWCoonsJr
https://www.amazon.com/author/davidcoons